"Tanya, are you okay?" he asked again.

Her breath shuddered out in a ragged sigh. She must have been holding it, and she murmured, "I think so…"

But he heard the doubt in her voice and eased up so she could roll over and face him. "Were you hit?" he asked. He ran his hands down her sides, checking for wounds. Just for wounds…

But he found soft curves and lean muscles instead. Heat tingled in his hands and in other parts of his body. A few minutes ago he'd thought she was going to kiss him. Their mouths had been only a breath apart, but maybe that was because he'd leaned down—because he'd wanted to kiss her so badly his gut had twisted.

The woman got to him as no one else ever had. And that made her dangerous—almost as dangerous as the shooter.

GROOM UNDER FIRE

BY
LISA CHILDS

Published in Great Britain 2014
by Mills & Boon, an imprint of Harlequin (UK) Limited,
Eton House, 18-24 Paradise Road, Richmond, Surrey, TW9 1SR

© 2014 Lisa Childs

ISBN: 978-0-263-91361-3

46-0614

Harlequin (UK) Limited's policy is to use papers that are natural, renewable and recyclable products and made from wood grown in sustainable forests. The logging and manufacturing processes conform to the legal environmental regulations of the country of origin.

Printed and bound in Spain
by Blackprint CPI, Barcelona

Bestselling, award-winning author **Lisa Childs** writes paranormal and contemporary romance for Mills & Boon. She lives on thirty acres in Michigan with her two daughters, a talkative Siamese and a long-haired Chihuahua who thinks she's a rottweiler. Lisa loves hearing from readers, who can contact her through her website, www.lisachilds.com, or snail-mail address, PO Box 139, Marne, MI 49435, USA.

To my wonderful groom—Philip Tyson— thanks for an amazing first year of marriage. And to the woman who raised him to be the wonderful man he is, Shirley Tyson—thank you for being such a loving and supportive mother. You are a phenomenal woman, and I am so lucky to have you as a mother-in-law.

Prologue

Their petals dried and brittle and as black as tar, the roses arrived the day after the announcement was printed in the paper. There were a dozen of them in the box, the thorny stems twisted around each other like barbed wire.

Tanya Chesterfield's finger bled from the one she had been foolish enough to touch. Crimson droplets fell onto the white envelope of the card that had come with the *gift*.

Her hand trembled as she fumbled to open the envelope. Maybe she should have just tossed it and the flowers into the trash. But she had to see if it was as threatening as the other notes she'd received anytime she had seriously dated anyone the past ten years.

She wasn't just dating now, though. She was engaged. And it was that engagement announcement that she pulled from the envelope.

The picture of her and her intended groom had been desecrated with a big black *X*. But that wasn't all the marker had scratched out on the announcement. The date of the wedding had been changed to date of: *DEATH*.

Chapter One

"You're messing with me," Cooper Payne accused his older brother. He hadn't been gone so long that he'd forgotten how they all handled any emotional and uncomfortable situation—with humor and teasing.

"I'm giving you an assignment," Logan said, but he was focused on the papers on his desk as if unwilling to meet Cooper's stare. "Isn't that what you wanted?"

After his honorable discharge from the Marines, he had come home to River City, Michigan, in order to join the family business. The business his brother had started: private security protection. Not his mother's business: weddings.

"I want a *real* assignment," Cooper clarified as he paced the small confines of Logan's dark-paneled office. "Not some trick our mother put you up to."

"Trick?" Logan asked, his usually deep voice rising with fake innocence. "Why would you think it's a trick?"

Frustration clutched at his stomach, knotting his guts. "Because Mom's been trying to get me to go to this damn wedding before I even got on a plane to head back…"

"Home," Logan finished for him. "You're home. And Tanya Chesterfield and Stephen Wochholz are your friends. Why wouldn't you want to attend their wedding?"

Because the thought of Tanya marrying *any* man—let

alone Stephen—made him physically sick. He shook his head. "We were friends in high school," Cooper reminded his brother and himself. "That was a dozen years ago."

And as beautiful as Tanya was, it was a miracle that she wasn't already married with a couple of kids. It wasn't as if she would have been pining over him. They hadn't shared more than a couple of kisses in high school before agreeing that they were better as friends just as she and Stephen were. But now she was marrying Stephen...

They made sense, though. More sense than he and Tanya ever would have. She was a damned heiress to billions and he was an ex-marine working for his big brother.

Maybe...

Logan was focused on him now, studying him through narrowed blue eyes. Cooper looked so much like Logan and his twin, with the same blue eyes and black hair, that people had often questioned if they were actually triplets. But Cooper was eighteen months younger than Parker and Logan. And they never let him forget it.

Finally Logan spoke, "Stephen still considers you a friend. He requested you be his best man."

"How do you know that?" he asked. Before his brother could reply, he answered his own question, "Mom..." As much as he loved her, the woman was infuriating. "She's obsessed with this damn wedding!"

"Weddings are her business," Logan replied with pride.

For years their mother had put all her energy and love into her family—taking on the roles of both mother and father after her police-officer husband had been killed in the line of duty fifteen years ago. But when her youngest—and only girl—had gone off to college, she had found a new vocation—saving the church where she and Cooper's father had been married from demolition and turning it into a wedding venue with her as planner.

"And *security* is our business," Cooper said. His brother had promised him a job with Payne Protection the minute his enlistment ended. He had even brought him directly to the office from the airport, but that had been a couple of days ago and he had yet to give him a job. Until tonight…

"That's why you need to get over to the church," Logan told him.

"For security? At a wedding?" He snorted his derision.

"Tanya is the granddaughter of a billionaire," Logan needlessly reminded him.

As if Cooper hadn't been brutally aware of the differences between her lifestyle and his, her grandfather had pointed out that a fatherless kid like him with no prospects for the future had nothing to offer an heiress like Tanya. Benedict Bradford had wanted a doctor or lawyer for his eldest granddaughter—a man worthy of her. He hadn't considered a soldier who might not make it through his deployments worthy of Tanya. Neither had Cooper. The old man had been dead for years now, but Benedict Bradford would have approved of Stephen, who had become a corporate attorney.

"Being a billionaire's granddaughter never put her in danger before," Cooper said. Or his mother definitely would have told him about it. And if that had been the case, he wouldn't have waited until his enlistment ended before coming home.

Logan lifted up his cell phone and turned it toward Cooper. "This might say otherwise…"

Coop peered at a dark, indiscernible image on the small screen. "What the hell is that?"

"Black roses," Logan replied with a shudder of revulsion. "They were delivered to the church today."

"That doesn't say danger," Cooper insisted. "That says mix-up at the florist's."

Logan shook his head. "The wedding's tomorrow, so the real flowers aren't being delivered until morning."

Cooper arched an eyebrow now, questioning how his brother was so knowledgeable of wedding policy and procedure.

"It's *Mom*," Logan said. "Of course we help her out from time to time. Like now. You need to get to the church."

"You just said the wedding's tomorrow."

"So that means the rehearsal's tonight," Logan said with a snort of disgust at Cooper's ignorance.

But he'd already been gone—first to boot camp and then a base in Okinawa—when their mother had bought the old church. He had no knowledge of weddings and absolutely no desire to learn about them.

"So if someone wants to stop the wedding from happening," Logan continued, "they'll make their move tonight."

Someone wanted to stop the wedding. But Cooper had no intention of making a move. Nothing had changed since high school. There had been nothing between Tanya and him then but friendship. And there was less than nothing between them now. He hadn't talked to her in years.

But if she was in danger…

HER HAND SHOOK as Tanya lifted the zippered garment bag containing her wedding gown toward the hook hanging on the wall of the bride's dressing room. It wasn't the weight of the yards of satin and lace that strained her muscles but the weight of the guilt bearing down on her shoulders. *I can't do this! It's not right...*

But neither was her grandfather's manipulation. Even a decade after his death, the old man hadn't given up trying to control his family. A couple of decades ago, he had bought off Tanya's father, so that he had left her mother and her and her sister, forcing them to move in with her grandfather.

That place had been the exact opposite of the bright room in which Tanya stood now. The bride's dressing room was all white wainscoting and soft pink paint. That house had been cold and dark. She shuddered at just the thought of the mausoleum. But then she smiled as she remembered who had called the drafty mansion that first. Cooper Payne.

He had kissed her there—after he'd pushed her up against one of the pillars of the front porch. That kiss had happened more than a dozen years ago, but her heart beat erratically at the memory. It had never pounded that hard over any other kiss. Her very first kiss...

Maybe that was why it had meant so much. Maybe that was why, even though it had been years since she'd seen him, she thought so often of Cooper Payne. It was probably good that he'd turned down Stephen's request to be his best man. Good that he wasn't going to be standing there when she followed through with this charade.

She wouldn't be able to utter her vows—to *lie*—with him looking at her. Not that he'd ever been able to tell when she was lying...

He had believed her when she'd agreed with him that the kiss—and the few that had followed it—had been a mistake, that they were only meant to be friends. She had nodded and smiled even while her teenage heart had been breaking.

Maybe it was the memory of that pain that had kept her from ever falling in love again. But then there had also been those threats. Stephen was convinced they were empty. But what if they weren't?

Should she risk it, as Stephen had advised? Or should she forfeit her inheritance?

She glanced into the antique mirror that stood next to where the garment bag hung, but she quickly turned away from the image of blond hair and haunted green eyes. She couldn't even look at herself right now. If she followed through with this farce, she would never be able to look at herself again.

She breathed a ragged sigh. She wouldn't miss the money; it had never been hers anyway. But she'd had plans for it—good plans, charitable plans…

Her grandfather had never practiced any charity—not even at home. Benedict Bradford had really been a mean old miser. So giving away his money would have been the perfect revenge for how he'd treated her mother and her and her sister.

But a wedding shouldn't be about revenge. Or money. Or even charity. It should be about love. And while Tanya loved her groom, she wasn't *in* love with him.

"I—I can't do this…"

Not the wedding. Not even the damn rehearsal. She crossed the room and jerked open the door to the vestibule and nearly ran into Cooper Payne's mother. Petite and slender with coppery-red hair and warm brown eyes, Mrs. Payne was exactly the opposite of her tall, dark, muscular sons. Only the youngest—her daughter— looked like her.

"What's the matter, honey?" the older woman asked as she gripped Tanya's trembling arms. "Are you all right?"

Tanya shook her head. "No, nothing's right…"

"I know the rest of the wedding party hasn't shown up yet, but there's no rush," Mrs. Payne assured her, her voice as full of warmth and comfort as her eyes. "Reverend James and I—"

She didn't care about the rest of the wedding party. "Stephen—is Stephen here?"

Mrs. Payne nodded. "I showed him to the groom's quarters a while ago, so that he could stow his tux there for tomorrow, like you've stowed your dress. Then you'll have less to worry about for the ceremony."

There was not going to be a ceremony. But Tanya couldn't tell anyone that until she'd told Stephen. He'd concocted this crazy scheme in the first place because he was her friend, because he'd always been there for her. But she couldn't take advantage of that friendship, of him.

"Where are the groom's quarters?" she asked.

"You need to wait until the others show," Mrs. Payne said. "So that the rehearsal can proceed just as the ceremony will tomorrow."

"No, I—I need to talk to Stephen," she insisted. "Now." Before the farce went any further.

Mrs. Payne's brown eyes widened. But after having worked with so many happy couples over the years, she must have realized something was off with them—that Tanya was hardly an ecstatic bride. "The groom's quarters are behind the altar."

Tanya crossed the vestibule and opened the heavy oak doors to the church. Since night had already fallen, the stained-glass windows were dark. The only light came from the sconces on the walls, casting shadows from the pews into the aisle. So she didn't notice that the red velvet runner was tangled. She tripped over it, catching herself before she dropped to her knees. That was weird—usually Mrs. Payne never missed a thing. No detail escaped her attention.

The wedding planner had worked so hard that guilt tugged at Tanya. She hated to disappoint the woman. But she couldn't go through with a lie.

Stephen would understand that. It wasn't as if he thought of her as anything other than a friend either, so he wouldn't be hurt.

The door to the room behind the altar stood ajar. She pushed it open to darkness. "Stephen?"

Had he changed his mind, too? She didn't blame him, but she doubted that he would have just left without talking to her first. She fumbled along the wall, feeling for the switch, when her fingers smeared across something wet. That wasn't something Mrs. Payne would have missed either. The chapel was spotless.

Tanya flipped on the switch, bathing the room in light—and discovered it had already been bathed in blood. It was spattered across the floor, the couch and the wall. Panic and fear rose up at the horror, choking her, so that she could barely utter the scream burning her throat.

COOPER HEARD IT. Even though the scream wasn't loud, the sheer terror of it pierced his heart. He ran past his mother, who was already halfway down the aisle of the church—and toward the danger. Years had passed since he'd heard it, but he had instinctively recognized Tanya's voice.

"Stay here," he ordered his mother as he reached beneath his leather jacket and pulled his weapon from the arm holster.

She pointed behind the altar, to the room from which light spilled. And Tanya. She backed out of the doorway, her hand pressed across her mouth as if to hold in another scream. As he rushed up behind her, she collided with Cooper. Then she pulled her hand away and screamed again.

He spun her around to face him. "It's okay," he assured her. "It's me."

Her green eyes, damp with tears, widened, and then she clutched at him, pressing against his chest. "Cooper! Thank God it's you!"

Her slight body trembled in his arms that automatically closed around her, pulling her even closer. She fit perfectly against him. But he was just comforting her, just making sure she was all right.

"What's wrong?" he asked. "Are you hurt?"

She shook her head, and her silky blond hair brushed against his throat. "No, no…"

He peered over her head into the room, and then he saw it. All the blood…

So much blood.

Despite his order to stay put, his mother joined them. "What's wrong—" she started to ask but gasped when she saw it, too.

"Call 911," Cooper said, thrusting his phone at her.

Then he stepped inside the room to look for the body. With that much blood, there had to be a body…

A dead one.

Chapter Two

"There is no body…"

Cooper's words drifted to Tanya through a thick haze of shock. He wasn't speaking to her, though; he hadn't since he'd asked if she was hurt. Of course he had been busy—searching the church and the surrounding grounds as well as talking to his family and the police officers who had arrived to investigate the scene of the crime.

The police had spoken to her. A somber-faced male officer had asked countless questions and not one of them had been if she was okay. Mrs. Payne had shooed off the man a while ago when she'd brought Tanya the cup of tea that was cooling in her hands. What the older woman had told the officer was right—Tanya had no idea what had happened. She'd only turned on the light to find the blood. All that blood…

The smear she'd found on the wall stained her hands. That was why she hadn't lifted the cup. It was why the heat of the tea would never warm her. She had blood on her hands…

"So we don't know," Cooper continued, his dark head bent close to his brother's, "if we're looking at a homicide or abduction."

Was it Logan or Parker to whom he spoke? They were

identical twins. Whichever one it was asked, "*Why* would it be either?"

Cooper shrugged shoulders so broad that they tested the seams of his black leather jacket. Despite the blood and the fear, during that moment she'd clung to him, she'd felt safe—with his arms around her. Just as he hadn't talked to her, he hadn't touched her since then either. Maybe that was why she felt so cold that she trembled.

"This is Stephen we're talking about," Cooper's brother persisted. "He was everyone's friend in high school. Did he change that much?"

"No," Tanya replied. "He's still everyone's friend." Her best friend. Where was he? And what had happened to him?

"Then maybe this isn't what it looks like," the twin replied.

"It looks like a crime scene," Cooper said. Yellow tape cordoned off the groom's quarters that police techs had photographed and processed for prints and whatever other evidence they'd found. "There's a lot of blood. The signs of a struggle. It's obvious somebody was dragged down the aisle."

That was why the runner had been bunched. Like the walls of the groom's quarters, it had also been stained with blood. While she'd been in the bride's room, someone had attacked her groom and dragged him from the church. How hadn't she or Mrs. Payne heard any of the struggle?

Tanya had been in the bride's room, deciding that she did not want to be a bride. Mrs. Payne had been downstairs in her office talking with the reverend. Unable to have a rehearsal without a groom, the minister had left after talking to the police.

"What the hell did you do?" the maid of honor, Tanya's

sister, shouted. She ran down the aisle toward the front of the church where Tanya sat in the pew near where the Payne brothers stood. But Rochelle didn't make it very far before she tripped over the rumpled runner.

Tanya's only other bridesmaid, who was also Cooper's sister, rushed up behind her and helped her to her unsteady feet. "Rochelle, let me get you some more coffee…"

"I don't need coffee!" Tanya's little sister shouted, her words only slightly slurred. "I need to know what she did with Stephen!"

"What *I* did with him?" Tanya asked. She set the teacup on the pew and rose up to meet her sister as Rochelle finally made it down the aisle.

"You don't care about him at all," Rochelle accused. "You've just been using him to get Grandfather's money. That's all you care about!" She vaulted herself at Tanya, knocking her to the ground.

The shock finally wore off—leaving Tanya able to register the pain. She felt the hardness of the floor beneath her back and the weight of her sister, who, despite the fact she was younger, was quite a bit taller and heavier. She could barely breathe with her on top of her. And she felt the sharp sting of her sister's slap. She had no right to fight back—not when everything Rochelle said was probably true.

But this was not the time or the place for Rochelle to throw one of her temper tantrums. Tanya had been trying to hold herself together for so long that she finally snapped under the emotional and physical pressure. "Grow up, you brat," she yelled. Using probably more strength than necessary, she shoved her sister back.

Rochelle didn't stay off. As Tanya stood up, her sister launched herself at her again. But this time strong hands caught Tanya before she hit the ground. With an arm wrapped around her waist, Cooper lifted her nearly off her feet.

The other bridesmaid, Nikki Payne, caught Rochelle, and tried to control her swinging hands and flailing feet. For her efforts, she took a hit to her face.

"Whatever happened to Stephen is your fault," Rochelle accused. "It's all your fault!"

Another stinging blow connected, bringing tears to Tanya's eyes. But the tears weren't from physical pain. Rochelle's verbal assault had hit her harder than her slap. Because she was right.

Whatever had happened to Stephen was all Tanya's fault. She literally had his blood on her hands.

"Aren't you glad you had brothers?" Cooper asked his sister as she rubbed her fingertips along the scratch on her cheek and winced. Nikki had somehow subdued her friend while Cooper had carried Tanya out of her reach. When Rochelle had been swinging, Tanya had barely defended herself from her younger sister's attack. Maybe she was in shock over having found Stephen's blood in the groom's quarters.

"Yeah," Nikki agreed. "You guys just punched each other. It was more civilized."

"We never punched you," he said.

"No," she agreed with a heavy sigh, almost as if she was disappointed that they hadn't. As the youngest and the only girl with three older brothers, she had often been left out of their roughhousing because they hadn't wanted to hurt her.

Tanya and her sister didn't have that relationship. Rochelle had definitely wanted to hurt her. How badly, though?

He could understand Rochelle being resentful of her

sister. Tanya was far more beautiful—with more delicate features and blonder hair and a thinner figure than her sister. But how deep was that resentment?

"Why'd you bring her here?" Cooper asked. At least he hoped Nikki had been the driver.

"She's Tanya's maid of honor," she replied. "I've been looking for her all night to make sure she got to the rehearsal."

"Mom put you to work, too?"

She sighed. "Enlisted me as part of the wedding party. I think she suspected there'd be a problem with Rochelle, and she and I have known each other since high school."

"You did subdue her." So much so that the woman sat quietly in a pew now, tears streaming down her flushed face. She seemed more distraught over the groom's disappearance than the bride was.

"Please point that out to Logan," Nikki beseeched him. Their eldest brother was on the other side of the heavy oak doors, talking on his cell phone in the vestibule. She shot him a glare through the windows at the back of the chapel. "He keeps me tied to a desk. He refuses to let me do an actual physical protection assignment."

Cooper bit his tongue before he verbally agreed with Logan. Nikki was so petite and fragile looking—just like their mother with her copper-colored hair and big brown eyes. But she had handled herself remarkably well with the taller and heavier Chesterfield sister. He touched her scratched cheek, making her wince again.

"Hey, I didn't want to hurt her," Nikki explained. "Or I would have taken her down faster. She's a friend, though…" Then she reached out and squeezed his arm. "I'm sorry about Stephen. Do you have any idea what happened?"

"We don't know anything for certain. There's a hell

of a lot of blood in the groom's quarters. But until the crime lab does a DNA test, we don't even know for certain that it's his." Except if it wasn't, where the hell was he, then? If there wasn't all that blood, Cooper might have believed his friend had just gotten a case of cold feet. He might have believed that if Stephen was marrying any woman but Tanya.

"Mom confirmed he was the only one in the room," Nikki said.

"Where was his best man?" Cooper asked.

Nikki lifted a reddish brow. "Where was *he?*" she asked, obviously referring to him.

"I told him I couldn't do it," Cooper reminded his little sister.

"Why not?"

"Why?" Cooper asked. "Why did he even ask me? We haven't seen each other in years."

"He showed up at the house to see you every time you were home on leave," Nikki said. "He stayed in touch."

But they'd both been busy. The letters few and far between and Cooper's visits home even more infrequent. He shrugged. "I just thought it was weird that he didn't have a closer friend he wanted to stand up there with him."

And weirder that he wanted Cooper. They had been good friends in high school—so good that Stephen must have realized how Cooper had really felt about Tanya. Had he wanted to rub his face in the fact he'd gotten the girl Cooper had wanted? And if so, then they hadn't really been that good of friends.

But Cooper still cared about him—still wanted him safe—which he probably would have been had Cooper actually been his best man. Then Stephen wouldn't have been alone in the groom's quarters.

"There are a couple of guys who were planning on

standing up there with him," Nikki said. "A friend from his office and a cousin, but I recruited them to help me find Rochelle. We'd been searching all the bars in River City."

"How'd you know that's where she was?" Maybe Logan was underestimating their sister's potential as a security expert.

"She left me a drunk voice mail."

Cooper glanced over at the crying woman and sighed. "So interrogating her would probably be a waste of time until Mom gets more coffee in her."

"You don't need to interrogate her," Tanya said as she rejoined them with an ice pack pressed against the cheek her sister had viciously slapped.

Apparently his mother was prepared for every wedding emergency—even catfights between the bride and maid of honor. What was her plan to handle a missing groom?

"I can tell you whatever Rochelle can," Tanya said.

But would she be truthful with him? "You'll tell me why she thinks you're just using Stephen to get your inheritance?"

Nikki nudged his arm. "Easy. She's not a suspect."

Maybe she should have been. As he'd already noted, she wasn't nearly as upset as a madly in love bride should have been when her groom mysteriously and apparently violently disappeared. When Cooper had quietly, so she wouldn't overhear him, questioned her reaction earlier, his mother and brother had insisted she was in shock.

But her green eyes were clear now and direct as she replied, "I'm not using Stephen."

"What about the inheritance? Your grandfather died a decade ago—don't you already have your money?" But if she did, why pick his mom's place for her wedding?

The chapel was small and the reception hall in the basement was hardly elegant enough for a billionaire bride.

She shook her head.

"Not yet," another voice chimed in to answer for her. A burly gray-haired man joined them inside the church. With his muscular build and military haircut, he looked more like a cop, but Cooper recognized the lawyer, Arthur Gregory, who'd made countless house calls to the mausoleum. "Neither she nor Rochelle will inherit until they marry."

If Rochelle was right and her sister was just after her inheritance, wouldn't she have gotten married ten years ago? Wouldn't Rochelle have?

"He's trying to control us even after his death," Rochelle murmured. "Mean son of a—"

"Miss Chesterfield," the lawyer admonished her. "Your grandfather had only your best interests at heart."

"He had no heart," Rochelle retorted. "The only reason he wanted us married was because he didn't think a female had enough brains to handle the kind of money he was leaving to us." She uttered a derisive snort. "Like our father did such a great job. He blew through all that money Grandfather gave him to divorce Mom and take off."

Cooper had never known what had happened to Tanya's father. She had always avoided talking about him. He'd been sensitive to that since he'd never wanted to talk about how he had lost his dad either.

"Mr. Gregory, is there a way around the will?" Tanya asked the lawyer.

Her sister gasped. "We don't even know what's happened to Stephen and all you care about is the money?"

"I care about him," Tanya said. "That's why I need the

money. In case this is a kidnapping, I'll need it to pay the ransom to get him back."

Arthur Gregory sighed. "There is no way to inherit that money unless you're married, Miss Chesterfield. And as you know, you only have a few more days…"

Tanya flinched as if the lawyer had slapped her, too.

"Why only a few more days?" Cooper asked.

"If she doesn't marry before she turns thirty, she forfeits her half of the inheritance," Rochelle replied. "Then I'll get it all when I marry."

The young woman must have been too drunk yet to realize that she'd just announced her motive for getting rid of her sister's groom. But if she was behind Stephen's disappearance, why was she so distraught over it?

"I need that money," Tanya repeated, "in case there's a ransom demand…"

If Stephen was alive…

But if he wasn't, why wouldn't his body have been left in the room? Someone had taken him for a reason. And what better reason than money?

"The only way you can access your funds is to marry," the lawyer insisted.

"Then she'll have to marry," Cooper's mother said as she joined them inside the church. She carried a tray with cups on it—probably filled with coffee, judging by the rich aroma wafting from the tray.

Rochelle seemed to have already sobered up. But Cooper was tempted to reach for a cup. He suspected it was going to be a long night.

"But if Stephen's been kidnapped, we won't get him back until I've paid for his return," Tanya pointed out.

"So you'll marry someone else," the wedding planner matter-of-factly replied as if it were easy to exchange one groom for another.

"Who?" Cooper asked.

His mother turned to him, her eyes wide with surprise that he hadn't already figured it out. "You, of course."

Cooper had had no intention of attending this wedding, let alone participating in it. He hadn't wanted to be the best man…and he sure as hell wasn't going to be the groom.

Chapter Three

Tanya's heart stung with rejection. She hadn't had to hear his words to know that Cooper had no intention of becoming her husband—for any reason. When his mother had suggested it, he had looked more horrified than he had when he'd seen the blood in the groom's quarters.

But she could hear his words now. He didn't know that, though. His family had gone into the bride's room for a private discussion. Tanya hadn't intended to invade their privacy, but she'd left her purse in that room along with her dress. And she really wanted to leave.

She couldn't stay here any longer—not with that crime scene tape draped across the entrance to the groom's quarters. Not with Stephen's blood on her hands...

And not with Cooper's words ringing in her ears.

"There is no way in hell that I am marrying Tanya Chesterfield!"

"Cooper!" his mother admonished him as if he were a little boy who'd cussed in church.

"Mom!" he retorted. "You've been pushing me to attend this wedding since you first talked to Tanya about planning it—either as a guest or the best man. You are not pushing me to the altar as her groom."

She could have opened the door; it was the bride's room, after all. But she was no longer going to be a bride.

Her groom was missing and the only other man she would want to take his place had flat-out refused. Not that she really wanted Cooper as her groom or anything else…

She turned away from the door. Instead of revealing that she'd been eavesdropping, she would leave her purse and just walk home. Her apartment was on the third floor of a home in the same area of town as Mrs. Payne's Little White Wedding Chapel, so it wasn't far. And her landlord on the ground floor had a spare key to her place.

But as soon as she stepped outside the heavy oak doors, the night air chilled her blood and she shivered. Stephen was out here somewhere. With whoever had hurt him.

Why hurt Stephen? Why not just hurt her as the threats she'd been receiving for the past ten years had promised?

As she descended the steep stairs to the sidewalk, she shivered again and wished she would have agreed to ride along with Nikki and Rochelle. But she hadn't wanted to be in the same room—let alone the same car—with her sister. Since Rochelle was six years younger than she was, they had never been particularly close, but they had gotten along well enough. Until Tanya had become officially engaged…

She should have asked someone else to be her maid of honor. But she'd thought that maybe including Rochelle would bring her around, would bring them closer.

Instead, they were more at odds than they had ever been. At least the cold air felt good on Tanya's still-stinging cheek. She lifted her face to the breeze and let it caress her skin. Maybe walking home wouldn't be so bad after all.

It was dark. But streetlamps, the ones not covered with overhanging branches, illuminated the sidewalk. Despite the light, she tripped over a crack and remembered the velvet runner. Stephen had been dragged down the aisle so that he couldn't become her groom.

Cooper Payne would have to be dragged down the aisle in order to become her groom. It wasn't going to happen. She was going to lose her inheritance, but far worse, she was going to lose her friend.

A car drove slowly past her, its windows tinted so she couldn't see inside it. Whoever the driver was, he or she was traveling well below the speed limit—nearly at the speed with which Tanya was walking. She shivered again—this time with a sense of foreboding instead of from the cold.

And she remembered those threats—all those promises that she would lose her life before she would ever inherit her money. Had Stephen's disappearance just been a diversion, a way to distract her from protecting herself?

Not only had she left her keys in her purse, but she'd left her cell phone, rape whistle, inhaler, EpiPen and pepper spray, too.

"COME ON," COOPER urged his brother. "Tell her it's a crazy idea."

But Logan didn't even glance at their mother. He just continued to stare at him, as if considering.

"It's crazy," Coop insisted.

His mother glared at him. "I thought the Marines would teach you some respect."

"I didn't call *you* crazy," he pointed out. "Just your idea…" It was ridiculous. Tanya had obviously thought it so ridiculous that she hadn't said a thing, as if she'd gone back into shock. So they'd just left her sitting there in the church—alone—as Stephen had been in that now-blood-spattered room. A frisson of unease trickled down his spine like a drop of ice water.

Tanya had been alone in this room earlier, but she'd been left unharmed. Probably so she could pay the ransom to recover her groom. She would be safe out there—especially as there had been an officer or two hanging around yet to finish processing the crime scene.

"But it's not crazy," Logan said. "It's brilliant."

"Br-brilliant?" Cooper choked on the word and coughed.

And his mother slapped his shoulder. "Of course it is." But she seemed surprised, too, that her oldest would agree with her. She had always said that although Logan was a twin, he definitely had a mind of his own.

"Can't you see that?" Logan asked with concern, as if Cooper was more dim-witted than he'd remembered.

So Cooper mentally stepped back, as he often had had to during his deployments, and he assessed the situation. "Stephen's missing. Maybe he just got cold feet." Even as he said it, he doubted his words. The Stephen he'd known had been an honorable guy; he wouldn't have just run away—especially not from Tanya.

Cooper had been the only man he knew of who had run from her—back when they'd been kids and his new feelings for his friend had overwhelmed him and also because her grandfather had made him see that it would never work out between them. It didn't matter that the old man was dead now; Benedict Bradford was still right.

"Then why all the blood?" Logan persisted.

Cooper visualized the crime scene that may not have been a crime scene at all. There was a small hammered-copper sink in the room with a mirror above it. He could have been shaving his neck and slipped with the blade, nicking his artery. "Maybe he accidentally hurt himself."

But there had been no razor or anything else sharp left at the scene...

"If that was the case, he would have gotten help," Logan pointed out. "Mom and Tanya and even Reverend James were all in the building, too."

"But we didn't hear anything," his mother reminded him.

Desperate to believe that Stephen would return, Cooper persisted in his argument, "Maybe, when you guys didn't hear him calling, he left and got help somewhere else."

"His car is still in the lot," his mother pointed out.

"He could have called a damn cab," Cooper remarked.

"But then he would have showed up at an E.R. by now," Logan argued. "Parker and a team of Payne employees are checking every emergency room and med station, and Stephen hasn't shown up anywhere yet."

Cooper begrudgingly admitted, "Maybe he has been abducted."

"Why?" Logan fired the question at him even though the answer was obvious.

Conceding his loss of this argument, he groaned before replying, "For Tanya's money."

"Which she can't access until she's married," his mother chimed in again. "She won't be able to pay the ransom when the demands are made."

His mother was right. Unfortunately.

But there was another possibility, one he hated to even voice, but he forced out the words, "He could be dead."

Cooper's guts tightened with guilt at the horrific thought. If only he'd agreed to be the damn best man, he would have been in that room with him, he could have protected him. Hell, if he hadn't dragged his feet getting to the church…

As if he'd read his mind, Logan reassuringly gripped his shoulder. "You don't know that…"

No, he didn't know if Stephen was dead, but he knew that he could have helped—had he been at the church in time.

"Neither do you," Cooper said, which probably infuriated Logan since his eldest brother thought he knew everything.

"Then where's his body?" Logan asked. "Why would his killer take it with him? Why wouldn't he have just left it in the room?"

Cooper wasn't the one with the law enforcement background. "You were the cop." A detective actually and a greatly decorated one, just as their father had been a police officer. "You know it's harder to press murder charges, let alone convict, without a body."

"The crime scene techs said that it looked like a lot of blood because of the spray, but there wasn't enough for someone to have bled to death," Logan reminded him.

"Yet." But if he was injured and didn't get help… "We should be out there looking for him, not wasting our time with this crazy discussion."

"Parker and his team aren't just checking hospitals and med centers. They're looking for him everywhere," Logan reminded him. "They've checked his place, his work—all of his usual hangouts."

"And they haven't found him," Cooper said. "We need to search harder and even then we may not find him alive." Or at all.

How many people had gone missing to never be seen again? He'd personally known a few—in Afghanistan.

"There's still time to help him," his mother insisted. Despite all she'd lost when her husband had died, she still remained an optimist. "But in case there is a ransom demand, Tanya will need her inheritance to pay it."

"So *someone* needs to marry her," Logan said.

His mother patted Cooper's arm again but more gently this time. "It's all right," she said as if he were a child she was reassuring about going to the dentist. "If you don't want to do it, Parker can."

Parker, the playboy, marrying Tanya? His gut churned at the thought—it was even crazier than *him* marrying her. In fact, him marrying her actually made the most sense since they knew each other, since he had actually kissed the bride before. Besides, it was his fault that Stephen had disappeared. If only he'd been in the groom's quarters before Stephen had been taken…

Rejecting his mother's suggestion, he shook his head. "I'll do it."

His mother clapped her hands together. "Great. I will call a certain judge I know to rush a new marriage certificate, and we'll proceed with the wedding tomorrow, just as we'd planned."

He was getting married *tomorrow?* Panic gripped him, squeezing his chest so tightly that he couldn't draw a deep breath.

"Maybe someone should tell the bride that," Logan suggested with a slight grin.

His mother gestured toward a leather purse sitting on the floor beneath a hanging garment bag. "She wouldn't have left without that, so she must still be here."

But she wasn't. As they had for Stephen, they searched the entire church. But they didn't find her.

Only the blood…

It was dried. It was old. It wasn't hers.

There was no fresh blood. No signs of a new struggle. No Tanya.

"Where could she have gone?" Cooper asked, and now he was panicking for another reason than getting married tomorrow. He was panicking that he might not be able to get married because the bride had disappeared like the original groom.

"Maybe she decided to walk home," his mother suggested.

The police officer who had been watching the parking lot in case Stephen returned for his car had mentioned seeing her leave the church.

"You actually think she could walk to the estate?" Cooper asked, shaking his head. "No way."

The mausoleum was on the other side of the very sprawling city. The distance between the church and the estate was more of a marathon than an evening stroll. But the officer hadn't seen a cab.

"She lives just a couple of blocks over," his mother said. "She rents a third-floor apartment."

"An *apartment?*" he asked, even more confused. She was a billionaire's granddaughter and she *rented?*

"She hasn't inherited yet," his mother reminded him, "and on her salary as a social worker, she can't afford to buy her own house."

So why hadn't she married sooner? Why wait until within days of forfeiting her inheritance? Despite having known Tanya for years, he really had no idea who she was. Of course, he had been gone for most of those years.

Now he had no idea where she was…

He grabbed her purse from his mom and opened it up. Her cell phone was inside—along with an inhaler, an EpiPen, a can of pepper spray and a shiny whistle. Given some of the danger social workers confronted, she should have carried a gun, too. He flipped open her wallet to read the address on her driver's license. The picture distracted him for a minute. Even on the tiny snapshot, she was beautiful—her blond hair shining like gold and her green eyes sparkling as she smiled brightly.

That was what had been so different about her to-night. The fear. The anxiety. She wasn't the Tanya he remembered because she was a woman now, not a care-free teenager.

"Look at that," Logan said with a slight grin. "Not even married yet and already carrying her purse." That was the way their family had always handled strife and loss—with wisecracking.

But Cooper didn't have time for it now, not with Tanya missing. He was going to follow her route from the church to her apartment and find her—hopefully alive.

"Shut up," he said. "And keep an eye on Mom."

She shouldn't be alone in a building where someone had already been abducted, just as Tanya should have never been left alone. Once he was her husband, Cooper would make damn sure that she stayed safe. But now he wondered if she would even make it to the altar.

THE CAR WITH the darkly tinted windows circled the block again like a cat stalking a bird. Was the driver waiting for Tanya to step off the sidewalk? She needed to cross the street if she intended to head home.

But if she headed home, wouldn't she be leading the driver right to her door? But given the threats she'd received through the mail, her stalker already knew where she lived. So if the driver was her stalker, he already knew where she was going.

She needed to turn back to the church. But if the others had left...

Mrs. Payne would have locked up, locking Tanya's purse and phone inside the bride's room. But she hadn't been gone that long, surely someone might have stayed behind.

Cooper?

She wasn't certain she wanted to see him, knowing how he felt about the thought of becoming her husband for just a few days—until she inherited. Once the money was hers, she could divorce him. Maybe he didn't know that; maybe she should have explained. But she hadn't wanted to force him to do something he clearly did not want to do.

They had once been friends. Good friends. Along with Stephen, they had been like the Three Musketeers—studying and hanging out together. But now Cooper acted like a stranger. Had his deployments overseas changed him that much?

Or was she the one who had changed? She used to want to have nothing to do with her grandfather's money, but then she had nearly married to inherit it. Had gone so far as to plan a wedding to a man she loved but wasn't in love with…

Tanya shivered at the cold wind and the eerie sensation that someone was hiding in the darkness, watching her. Coming for her. But then it wasn't just a sensation. It was a certainty.

She blew out a ragged breath as the car circled again, driving even more slowly along the street. As long as she stayed on the sidewalk, maybe she would stay safe. But then the car tires squealed as the driver jerked the steering wheel. Sparks flew from beneath the front bumper as it scraped over concrete as the car jumped the curb and headed right for her.

She screamed, her legs burning as she ran.

But it didn't matter how fast she ran or how loud she yelled, she couldn't outrun a motor vehicle. She hadn't been able to save Stephen, and now she wouldn't be able to save herself.

Chapter Four

For the second time that night, Tanya's scream pierced the air and Cooper's heart. The car's lights illuminated her. Her eyes were wide and her face pale with terror. He hurried to catch up but she was ahead of him, the car between them.

"Run!" he yelled, urging her to move as the car barreled down on her where she ran across the front yards of a row of houses. As a kid she hadn't been able to run very far or very fast because her asthma would act up. Hopefully, she'd outgrown that.

Cooper had already drawn his weapon. But if he shot at the driver, the bullet might pass through the windshield and hit Tanya before the front bumper of the car could. So he aimed at the tires and quickly squeezed the trigger.

One back tire popped, deflating fast so that it shredded and slapped against the rim. But despite the flat, the car continued forward—straight toward Tanya.

Still running, Tanya veered between two houses. But the houses weren't so far apart that the car couldn't follow her.

Cooper shot out the other back tire and the car swerved, careening across a lawn. It scraped against a tree and proceeded to the street, cutting off another vehicle that blared its horn. Sparks flew from the rims riding the asphalt, but the car didn't stop. Yet. Eventually it would have to, though, so Cooper figured he might be able to catch up to it on foot.

But he had a greater concern. "Tanya!"

He ran across the yards, stumbling over the deep ruts that the car had torn in the muddy spring lawn. Then he veered between the two houses as she had. Lights flickered on inside those houses, brightening a couple of the dark windows. They must have heard either the car or his yelling. His throat burned from the force of his shouts. "Tanya!"

He nearly stumbled over her where she lay sprawled across the ground. The light from the houses cast only a faint glow into the backyards, so he could barely see her. He holstered his gun and then dropped to his knees beside her. His hands shook as he reached for her.

Despite his efforts to stop it, had the car struck her anyway? Had it run over her once it had knocked her down? He couldn't tell if she was conscious or not, if she was alive or dead. Her hair had fallen across her face, the strands tangled. He brushed it back as he slid his hand down her throat, checking for a pulse. Thankfully, she started breathing, but laboriously, the breaths rattling in her chest.

Obviously she hadn't outgrown her asthma and all the running had brought on an attack. She opened her eyes, the light glinting in them.

"Are you okay?" he asked. "Do you need your inhaler?" He'd left it in her purse back at the church, though.

She sucked in a shuddery breath and then choked and gasped.

Cooper wanted to pick her up and cradle her in his arms, but he didn't dare move her if she was hurt. "Did the car hit you?"

Bracing her palms on the ground, she began pushing herself up. But Cooper caught her shoulders, steadying her. "Don't move. If you're hurt—"

"I'm not hurt," she said as she tried to control her breathing. "I just fell."

Maybe she'd only been out of breath from running as fast as she'd had to so the car wouldn't have run her over. "Are you sure?"

"I'm not hurt," she repeated. "Because of you…" Then she threw her arms around his neck and clung to him as she had when he'd first arrived at the church. "Thank you!"

But Cooper couldn't accept her gratitude—not with the guilt plaguing him. It wasn't just guilt that had his heart racing, though. It was fear. And probably her closeness. With every breath he took, he breathed her in; she smelled like flowers and grass. And the grass reminded him that she could have been killed. He grabbed her shoulders and pulled her away from him. "What were you thinking to leave the church on your own?"

She tensed. "I was thinking I wanted to get the hell out of there."

Was that his fault for not immediately agreeing to his mother's suggestion that he marry her? Had he hurt her pride?

"Then why didn't you leave with Nikki when she took your sister home?" he asked.

She uttered a mirthless chuckle. "Do you really think I would have been any safer with my sister?"

"She wouldn't have tried to run you over with a car," he pointed out as he helped her to her feet.

She stumbled as if her legs were still shaky. But instead of leaning on him again, she steadied herself. "No," she agreed, "but she might have tried to shove me out of one."

He couldn't argue that, not after the way Rochelle had attacked her in the church.

"Cooper!" Logan called out to him as he ran between the houses and joined them in the backyard. "I couldn't catch the car."

He had forgotten that his brother had been right behind him when he'd left the church. His order for Logan to stay with their mom had been overruled—by their mother. She'd reminded them that the police officer was still in the parking lot and even if he wasn't, she could take care of herself. She was armed, and their father had taught her how to shoot very well.

Logan was huffing and puffing for breath. "I could barely keep up with you."

When Cooper had heard Tanya scream, he had taken off running. He reached for his cell phone now. "Did you call the police?"

"Called 'em," Logan said, which was confirmed with sirens whining in the distance. "Did you get a better look at the car than I did?"

"Long and dark," Cooper replied. "With the windows too darkly tinted to see inside."

"What about the plate?"

"There wasn't one."

This hadn't been some drunk driver whose car jumped the curb and veered into a yard. This near-miss hit-and-run had been planned.

Just to scare her or to kill her?

TANYA HELD HER breath, pressing down the fear that threatened to choke her. She stared up at the dark windows of her apartment, wishing she could see inside, but she stood on the sidewalk three floors below. Light flashed behind the arched window in the peak of the attic where she lived.

Was it the beam of a flashlight or the flash of gun-fire? She gasped, and the breath she'd held escaped in a rush of fear.

"You shouldn't have let him go inside alone," she admonished his brother. "The driver of that car could be in there, waiting…" For her. And Cooper would step into the trap her stalker might have laid for her.

She should have had one of the police officers who'd taken the report for the near hit-and-run bring her home. They had offered a ride and protection. But the Payne brothers had assured the officers that they would make sure she stayed safe.

How? By putting themselves at risk?

Logan chuckled. "Cooper can handle himself and whoever he might encounter." His slight grin slipped into a frown that furrowed his brow. "He wouldn't have survived three deployments in Afghanistan if he couldn't."

But how many soldiers had survived war only to come home and die in an auto accident? Or some other freak crime—like a shooting? She kept her gaze trained on those third-floor windows and saw another flash of light.

Reaching out, she clutched Logan's arm. "I see something! Something's happening up there!"

Logan's gaze rose toward the third floor, too. "I don't see anything…"

But he must have been concerned, too, because he pulled out his cell phone. He pressed a button for what must have been a two-way feature and then he called out, "Cooper?"

Not even a crackle of static emanated from his phone, it remained dead.

She shuddered as the horrible thought occurred to her that Cooper might have been dead, too. She hadn't heard any shots, but some guns had silencers. She knew that from watching TV. The person who might have been waiting in her apartment could have had one.

She tugged on the sleeve of Logan's wool overcoat. "You need to go upstairs and check on him!"

"He needs to stay with you," a deep voice coming out of the darkness corrected her. "Like someone should have stayed with you at the church so you didn't go running off on your own."

She hadn't started running until the car had jumped the curb to chase her down. But she didn't bother pointing that out since the sharpness of his voice showed he was already angry with her.

And Logan was already asking, "Did you clear the apartment, Cooper?"

"No."

Logan snorted derisively. "Why not? It doesn't look that big."

The studio apartment had formerly been a ballroom, so it was bigger than it looked—with a bathroom tucked into a wide dormer. If the attic space didn't have issues with being too hot in the summer and too cold in the winter, the rent wouldn't have been affordable enough for her.

"I cleared it for intruders, but there were other threats," Cooper explained.

Logan tensed and held up his phone, his fingers ready to press buttons. "What do we need? Bomb squad?"

"If it was a bomb, I would have taken care of it," he assured his brother. "No, it was *literally* other threats." He passed his brother the desecrated engagement announcement.

While Tanya sucked in a breath of indignation that

Cooper had gone through her things, his brother released a ragged breath of relief.

But Cooper wasn't relaxed. His jaw was clenched so tightly that a muscle twitched in his cheek. He was obviously mad as hell, his dark gaze intense as he stared at Tanya.

She glared back at him. He was only supposed to make sure her place was safe. The thought of him going through her boxes and drawers and closets reminded her of all the things he might have found, like her weakness for silk and lace underwear.

"There are more of those," he told his brother. "Did you know about the threats?"

"No," Logan replied.

"Now you know," Cooper said. "Get on it. Check out her ex-boyfriends, her cases at work—"

Logan grinned. "Are you forgetting which one of us is the boss, little brother? I've been doing this for a while. I need to talk to the client first to get the names of those ex-boyfriends and difficult cases."

Cooper shook his head. "I'll do that."

If she were actually a client, she would rather talk to Logan. She could be more honest with him because she suspected he would be less judgmental. But she wasn't actually a client and needed to remind the protective Payne brothers of that. "I haven't hired—"

Cooper interrupted her as he spoke to his brother. "Tanya and I need to talk."

As if Logan, too, had forgotten he was the boss, he nodded his agreement. "I need to touch base with Parker..."

Probably to see if he had found Stephen. But if he had, he would have called. Even if he'd found him dead, he would have called. She shuddered now, so forcefully that she couldn't stop trembling.

"If you completely cleared her place, get her inside," Logan, as the boss again, ordered. "She's freezing. Or in shock…"

"Or getting pissed off that she's being ignored," Tanya suggested. "Yes," she continued, ignoring them as they had been ignoring her, "she's definitely pissed off."

Logan patted his brother's shoulder before heading toward his car parked at the curb. "Good luck. You may be the one needing protection now."

As if Tanya could take out a Marine, no matter how angry she was. And she actually wasn't as angry as she was scared. For Stephen. For herself. For Cooper…

"I won't hurt you," she assured him.

He uttered one of his brother's derisive snorts as if he didn't believe her. "Did you tell Stephen that, too?"

Her palm itched to slap him as her sister had slapped her. Her cheek throbbed at just the memory of that blow—or maybe because she'd hit it again when she'd done the nosedive running away from the car. Bristling with anger and with guilt over Stephen's disappearance, she said nothing as they climbed the stairs to her apartment.

Since he had the keys he'd gotten from her landlord, he unlocked the door and stepped inside first, as if checking again for an intruder. Then he flipped on the lights.

A banker's box had been knocked over, the contents spilled across the library table that also served as her dining table and desk. She gasped. "Someone was in here?"

He shook his head. "Not that I could tell."

"You did this?" He must have gone through her things in a hurry. Maybe he hadn't had time to look through her closet and drawers. She glanced around, but it appeared nothing else had been disturbed. So she focused again on the contents of the box. All those threats...

She had packed them away—hoping to forget them but not foolish enough to throw them all out.

"You haven't exactly been forthcoming with information," he bitterly reminded her. "If we're going to find Stephen, we need to know everything."

If...

She wasn't naive. She knew it was very likely that they would never find Stephen...either alive or dead. But she wasn't ready to face that possibility. She would have preferred Cooper offer assurances and promises. But she knew him better than that. He would never give her what she wanted from him—at least he hadn't when they were teenagers.

"There isn't much to tell you," she said, especially when it came to exes. "I haven't really dated much." Because of the threats. And maybe because of him, but she didn't want him to suspect that she'd hung on to an old crush. "I've been too busy with work."

"How long have you been a social worker?" he asked. "Since you graduated college? You must have handled a lot of cases."

She sighed as faces jumbled in her mind. "A lot," she agreed, "but none recently. At least not personally. I became a supervisor four years ago. I delegate now." Which meant giving too much work to too few employees.

"Now," he said. "But four years ago there must have been cases you handled that hadn't gone well."

She flinched, remembering the losses. The people she hadn't been able to help. If she had Grandfather's money, she could do so much more than she was able to do now. "Of course there were cases that went badly. Children I had to remove from neglectful or abusive parents." She shuddered at the painful memories. "But that was years ago…"

"Some people have a hard time forgiving the person they perceive tore their family apart," he said with a glance out toward the street. "Mom says Logan has never missed a parole hearing for the man who shot my father. He's determined to make sure that the guy never gets out of prison—at least not alive."

"What about you?" she asked. He had never talked about his father's death before, but back then it had been too recent and probably too painful for a teenage boy to process let alone express.

"What about me?" he asked as if his feelings didn't matter. "I haven't been here for any of the parole hearings." And maybe that was why he thought his feelings didn't matter—because he had been gone so long. He had left his family.

And her. But they'd only just been friends, high school friends who often drifted apart after graduation. She hadn't really meant anything to him. But she knew that his family had meant everything to him.

"If you had been here, would you have gone to those hearings?"

He shrugged. "I think it's best to leave the past in the past."

She and Stephen were his past.

"But most people don't feel that way," he continued. He passed her a legal pad and a pen. "Write down the names of the guys you've dated. And write down any cases you remember where someone might be holding a grudge against you."

"I really can't," she protested. "There are privacy laws I have to obey."

"What about Stephen?"

He was her best friend. And he was missing. If there was any chance of getting him back, her pride and her job could be damned. So she wrote down some names.

"He knew," she said, finally defending herself from his earlier comment. "Stephen knew about the threats."

Cooper sucked in a breath. "And he wanted to marry you anyway? He must love you a lot."

As a friend. But if she told Cooper that, he would think the same thing her sister did—that she was just using Stephen to get her inheritance.

"I love him a lot, too," she said. *But only as a friend.*

Cooper's jaw went rigid again, as if he was clenching it. He nodded. "Stephen's a good man. And a lawyer. Your grandfather would have approved."

Probably, but only until she'd given away all his ruthlessly earned money.

"We have to find him," she said. And she couldn't rely on an overworked police department. "I really can't afford Payne Protection—not until I get my inheritance. But I want to hire your family." They specialized in security, working mainly as bodyguards, but Logan and Parker were both former police officers. And Cooper was...Cooper. The kind of man who stopped a speeding car from barreling over a woman.

Had she even thanked him? She couldn't remember now; it had all been such a blur of terror and disbelief and then relief.

His brow furrowed with confusion. "We're already on the job. Why do you think I showed up at the church in the first place?"

She had been so upset over finding the blood in the empty groom's quarters that she hadn't given it much thought then. "I don't know...maybe you had changed your mind about being Stephen's best man."

But that wasn't the case. She already knew that from when she'd eavesdropped outside the bride's room. He had been pretty clear that he'd wanted no part of his mother's manipulations. Why had the wedding planner been so intent on getting Cooper to attend the ceremony? It wasn't as if he would have stood up and protested their union—at least not to claim her as his bride. Definitely not to claim her as his bride...

"I wish I had agreed to be his best man," Cooper admitted. "Then I would have been there..."

Her heart lurched. "And you could have been hurt, too." Or worse...

Just as his brother had said while they'd waited for him to make sure her apartment was safe, he reminded her, "I can take care of myself."

Cooper wouldn't have gone anywhere willingly. Not that Stephen had. *Poor Stephen*...

"And I can take care of you, too," he said. "I'll keep you safe."

He had already proven that—when he'd stopped a speeding car.

"That's why I showed up at the church," he said. He scooped up some of the shriveled petals that had fallen from the black roses. "Mom took the delivery of these and knew something was wrong."

"I'm sorry I brought your mother into this," she said, suspecting that could have been the reason for some of his anger earlier. "I thought those threats were empty. I didn't believe anyone would actually act on them." Or she would have never agreed to marry her best friend. "I've been getting them for years..."

"How many years?" he asked.

She sighed and replied, "Ten years."

"Around the time your grandfather died?"

Cooper remembered when Grandfather had died? He had been deployed at the time; he must have had greater concerns on his mind than her loss—such as it had been. Benedict Bradford had never been a very warm or loving man.

"Yes," she replied. "I didn't get them all that often—only when I started seriously seeing someone."

"Someone sure didn't want you collecting your inheritance," he mused, staring down at the box of threats.

She sighed again. "They got what they wanted." And they'd gotten Stephen, too. Would they give him back… without the money?

Her stomach churned with dread and worry that they wouldn't, that she might never see her dear friend again. And the tears she'd been fighting back for so long rushed up with such force that they burst out. She couldn't hold back the sobs while tears streamed from her eyes.

Strong arms wrapped around her, pulling her close. And a big hand gently patted her hair. "No, they haven't gotten what they wanted."

She shook her head, and his fingers slipped through her hair and skimmed down her neck. A rush of heat stemmed her tears. "There're only a few days before my thirtieth birthday. I hope we find Stephen before then." She doubted that they would, though. "But even if we do, I can't put him at risk again. I can't marry Stephen."

"You're not going to marry Stephen," he agreed.

Because her groom was missing…

What if he was already dead? Her heart beat heavily with anguish. And more tears trickled out, sliding down her cheeks.

Cooper wiped them away with his thumbs. "You're going to marry me."

Her heart rate quickened to a frantic pace. She gazed up at him in disbelief. "What? You didn't agree to that."

"I changed my mind," he said. "I'm going to be your groom. You're still getting married tomorrow."

Maybe Rochelle's slaps had hit her hard enough to addle her brain. She couldn't understand what he was saying. What he meant…

Maybe it was because he was too close, his arms around her—his heart pounding hard against hers. And he was leaning down, his head so close that she could see tiny black flecks in the bright blue of his eyes. She could see the shadow of his lashes on his cheeks and the stubble that was already darkening his jaw.

She wanted to reach up and run her fingers over that stubble, up his chin to his lips. All these years later she still remembered how they felt—silky but firm. But she didn't want to just touch his lips; she wanted to kiss them. The urge was so great that she rose on tiptoe.

But before she could close the slight distance between their mouths, she jerked out of his arms. She couldn't be having these thoughts—these desires for Cooper. She needed air to clear her head, so she moved toward the big arched window that looked out onto the street below. But before she could lift the bottom pane, the glass shattered.

Gunshots echoed.

And she was falling to the ground, pushed down as more gunshots rang out. Pain radiated throughout her body and she wondered if it was already too late.

Would she live to see her wedding day?

Chapter Five

Glass showered down over them, nicking Cooper's face and the back of his neck. Too bad he still had his military brush cut. Blood trickled from his nape over his throat.

He needed to jump up and return gunfire. But that would mean leaving Tanya unprotected. And he couldn't do that. Again. He covered her body with his, pressing her into the hardwood floor.

Since the shooter on the street wouldn't be able to hear them, he leaned his face close to her ear and whispered, "Are you okay?"

She shivered, trembling beneath him. But she didn't speak. Maybe *she* was worried that the shooter could hear them.

But the gunfire had stopped. Maybe the assailant was just reloading. Or maybe he had gone.

"Tanya, are you okay?" he asked again.

Her breath shuddered out in a ragged sigh. She must have been holding it, and she murmured, "I think so…"

But he heard the doubt in her voice and eased up so she could roll over and face him. "Were you hit?" he asked. He ran his hands down her sides, checking for wounds. Just for wounds…

But he found soft curves and lean muscles instead. Heat tingled in his hands and in other parts of his body. A

few minutes ago, he'd thought she was going to kiss him.
Their mouths had been only a breath apart, but maybe
that was because he'd leaned down—because he'd wanted
to kiss her so badly his gut had clenched.

The woman got to him as no one else ever had. And
that made her dangerous—almost as dangerous as the
shooter.

She squirmed beneath him. Apparently she was still
as ticklish as when they'd been kids. He used to tickle
her then—just as an excuse to touch her.

But he'd had a reason to touch her this time. "Are you
hurt?" he asked again.

When his hand skimmed over her rib cage, she sucked
in a breath. "Just sore," she murmured, "from my fall."

She'd fallen twice. Once in the church when her sister
had attacked her and again when the car had nearly run
her down. Actually, three times since he'd shoved her to
the floor—which was unyielding hardwood.

He wasn't doing the greatest job protecting her. Maybe
Logan had been right and he wasn't ready yet for a field
job. But he couldn't imagine anyone else protecting her.
Or marrying her.

She lifted her hand and skimmed her fingers over his
throat, making his pulse leap even more wildly. And her
eyes widened with shock and horror. "You're bleeding!
You've been hit! We need to call an ambulance!"

He brushed away the trickle of blood. "It's just a
scratch from the flying glass."

He brushed some of those glass fragments from her
silky blond hair and his fingertips tingled. He didn't even
notice the bite of the glass. All he noticed was the fresh
flowery scent of her and the soft feel of her. She was so
close. He only needed to lean down a few inches to close
the distance between them and press his lips to hers.

"I'm fine," he assured her. But he wasn't. He was tempted to kiss his best friend's bride while the man was missing. But hell, Cooper was the one who was going to marry her. Tomorrow. He drew in a deep breath to steady his racing pulse. "We should call the police."

"He's gone?" she asked hopefully.

He wasn't certain about that…even though he had heard the squeal of tires as a car sped away.

"We still need to call to report the shooting." There could be shell casings recovered. Witnesses questioned that might be able to identify the shooter. He reached for his cell phone.

And then he heard the footsteps, the stairs creaking beneath the weight of the person stealthily climbing up to Tanya's apartment. Maybe the shooter hadn't sped off in the car with the squealing tires. Maybe he had come upstairs to make sure he'd killed his intended victim.

Cooper drew his weapon from the holster on his belt. He pointed the barrel at the door as he scrambled to his feet and helped up Tanya. He shoved her toward the only other room in the studio apartment. The bathroom.

"Get in the tub," he ordered her in an urgent whisper. Where he'd been, grenades were routinely tossed in houses. Or machine-gun fire that cut through walls like scissors through paper. "And stay down."

He didn't know if she did as he told her because she closed that door. And another opened, slowly, the old hinges creaking in protest. His finger twitched on the trigger as he prepared to pull it, especially as the first thing that entered the apartment was the barrel of a gun.

He waited to get a target before he took his shot. But just as he was about to squeeze the trigger, the intruder stepped from the shadows and revealed himself.

"Damn it, Logan!" he cursed his brother. "I almost shot you!"

Logan holstered his gun and gestured toward the broken window. "Looks like you got a little trigger-happy already."

Cooper begrudgingly admitted, "I didn't fire my weapon." Then he pointed toward the holes in the drywall ceiling. "The shooter was down on the street."

Which had probably saved Tanya's life and his, because the trajectory of the bullets had sent them tunneling into the ceiling instead of into their bodies.

Sirens blared and blue and red lights flashed, refracting off all the broken glass. "And now the police are down there," Logan pointed out with a slight sigh of relief.

Either the landlord or a neighbor must have called them. Cooper hadn't had the chance to dial yet. He'd been too distracted. Tanya had distracted him.

"Why are *you* here?" he asked his older brother, who was also now his boss. "You checking up on me?" He couldn't blame him if he was. His first assignment with Payne Protection and he was already blowing it. First, he'd lost Stephen, and he'd nearly lost Tanya more than once.

"You said you were going to get some information for me," Logan reminded him. "Tanya's list of difficult cases and exes."

"What? Were you waiting in the car for it?" Cooper asked—almost hopefully. Because if his brother had been just outside, he would have seen something.

Logan shook his head. "No. I went back to the church to check on Mom and she ordered me back here."

"She ordered you?" Cooper teased. "I thought you were the boss."

Logan chuckled. "Doesn't matter who's listed as CEO, Mom will always be the *boss*."

"She sent you back for the list?" Maybe their mother was running Payne Protection, too.

"She sent me back for Tanya."

More footsteps sounded on the staircase. "That's probably the police."

"Once you two give your report, I need to take Tanya with me," Logan said.

"So Mom doesn't trust me to protect her?" He flinched at the pang of regret. She had always had more faith in her oldest son than her youngest.

Logan chuckled again. "No. It's all about tradition or superstition…"

"What is?" Cooper asked as his head began to pound with confusion and exhaustion. He'd endured tours of duty that had been less dangerous and stressful than this night. "What are you talking about?"

"Mom doesn't want you to spend the night before your wedding with your bride."

Usually Tanya sank into her claw-foot tub with a sigh of relief as the hot water eased the tension from her body. Her tub would never again relieve her stress because she had never been as scared as she was crouched down beneath the rim.

Someone was obviously determined that Tanya wouldn't live to see her wedding day. With Cooper agreeing to take Stephen's place as her groom, the wedding could take place as scheduled—the next day. So Tanya would have to die tonight.

Would Cooper die with her? Had he already? She'd heard no shots.

But then the bathroom door opened to men with guns.

But they were uniformed police officers. Cooper hadn't come for her. She had heard no shots—only the rumble of male voices. Had he been hurt worse than he'd claimed? Had he really been bleeding from just a scratch?

The heat flushed her face; she was embarrassed that strangers had found her hiding in her bathtub. At least she was fully clothed, though.

"Are you okay, ma'am?" a young officer asked as he helped her step over the porcelain rim.

Her legs trembled slightly, in reaction from all she'd endured that day and in exhaustion. "I'm fine," she said. "Is Mr. Payne all right?"

"Which Mr. Payne?" he asked.

When she stepped out of the bathroom, she found the brothers talking to another officer.

"This is the third report we've had to file for you guys tonight," the older policeman said with a grunt of disgust. "What on earth is going on?"

"We wish we knew," Logan replied.

"You've got a missing groom and someone trying to kill the bride," the police officer replied as if the head of Payne Protection had asked him the question. "And my wife thinks my daughter's wedding was a disaster…"

Tanya wasn't going to have a wedding. She opened her mouth to call it off, but then she remembered Stephen and that blood in the groom's quarters. His blood…

What if he was being held for ransom? And she couldn't meet that ransom?

Those thoughts kept running through her head—even as she answered that officer's questions:

No, she hadn't seen anything. She hadn't gotten close enough to the window to look out before the glass shattered. No, she had no idea who might have been behind this attempt or the other one on her life.

She lifted her gaze and caught Cooper staring at her, as if he doubted her. His eyes were narrowed, speculative. Did he have some idea who'd taken Stephen? Who had just tried to kill her?

She waited for him to share his suspicions with the police. But he said nothing to add to the report before they left. He didn't even say anything when his brother told her to pack a bag because *he* was taking her someplace safe.

"But what if someone tries to contact me about Stephen?" she asked.

"Then you'd better be alive to take the call," Logan said. "The purse you left at the church is in my car. Is your cell in there?"

Her face flushed with embarrassment again. "Yes, and the cell is the only phone I have." So she didn't have to worry about a call coming into a landline. She had no reason to stay in her apartment, especially as damaged as it was from the gunfire—the window shattered and drywall dust sprinkling down from the holes in the ceiling, covering the furniture and the hardwood floor.

"Then grab your charger," Logan advised, "and whatever else you need."

"I already have a bag packed." She grabbed a suitcase out of her closet. She'd already had it packed for her honeymoon, which was nothing more exotic than a hotel suite—with separate bedrooms—at an inn on the Lake Michigan shore just outside the city. She had left more lingerie in her drawers than she'd packed, and she was the only one she'd figured would see it. That wasn't going to change just because her groom had.

"I'll take that," Logan offered, reaching for her suitcase.

Cooper finally spoke, asking, "Where are you taking her?"

"Safe house," his brother replied.

He arched a dark brow. "Are you going to tell me where?"

"Doesn't matter," Logan said. "You're not staying there. Parker's taking you to another safe house."

He groaned in protest. "Why can't I just go home?"

"Because Mom gave me orders to make sure both the bride and the groom stay alive to make it to the church tomorrow."

"I don't need Parker to keep me alive," Cooper said, his male pride obviously wounded.

Tanya remembered how hard he had struggled to be his own man growing up—instead of the shadow of his older brothers. She suspected it was why he'd joined the Marines instead of going into the police academy.

Logan snorted. "I know that. I need Parker to keep you away from Tanya."

Her pulse quickened with excitement. Did his brother think that Cooper was attracted to her? Maybe she hadn't been the only one who'd wanted that kiss—that kiss that never happened...

"Mom gave me all kinds of orders based on wedding superstitions," Logan said, "that the bride and groom need to spend the night before the wedding apart or they'll have bad luck."

Tanya laughed now and then flinched at the brittle sound of her own laughter. She probably was on the verge of hysteria brought on by the events of this horrible, horrible day, and by exhaustion. "Bad luck? Mrs. Payne is worried we'll have bad luck?" Another hysterical laugh slipped out. "Like we haven't already? My groom has been...abducted! I've nearly been run down and I've been shot at," she reminded them as if the shattered glass and the holes in her ceiling weren't reminder enough. "What else could go wrong?"

Logan pointed out the obvious. "You or Cooper could get killed."

Her stalker obviously wanted to stop her wedding. So Tanya had no doubt that there would be more attempts on her life and—if the stalker had figured out that Cooper was her new groom—on his, too, before the night was over.

She suspected the night would seem endless, unless it ended—forever.

"You were not supposed to come here," Parker protested as Cooper unlocked the door and stepped inside the condo unit. "This is not the safe house."

Cooper flipped on a switch before stepping inside. "I don't need a safe house."

"Those shots could have been meant for you," Parker pointed out.

He shook his head. "After the car tried running over Tanya? No, the shots were meant for her." Had they been fired high just to scare her? Or had they actually been meant to kill her? His guts clenched with dread and fear. "Are you sure she's safe with Logan?"

Parker laughed. "Have you been gone so long that you've forgotten who Logan is? Logan Payne always keeps his word. If he promised he would keep her safe, he will keep her safe. It's you I'm worried about…"

"Me?" Cooper asked, confused by his brother's concern. "I told you the shots weren't meant for me."

"If someone's figured out you're standing in for the groom, they could have been. Look what happened to Stephen."

"We don't know what happened to Stephen," Cooper reminded him. "That's why we're here." At Stephen's condo.

"I've already been here," Parker said.

The unit was in a high-security high-rise complex. The condo's living room was enormous and its kitchen gourmet with dark cabinets, granite countertops and industrial appliances. Even if she didn't inherit her grandfather's money, Stephen could offer Tanya a much better life than Cooper could. If he could be found...

"But when you were here, you were looking for Stephen."

"And anything that might lead us to him," Parker added. "We didn't find anything."

Cooper picked up a laptop from the coffee table. "Did you look at this?"

Parker shook his head. "It's password protected." He took the computer. "Nikki might be able to crack it, though. But what's she going to find? His kidnapper wouldn't send an email to Stephen. He'd send it to Tanya."

"We don't know that this is a kidnapping." He was beginning to think it less likely with every minute that passed without a ransom call being made.

"We don't know what the hell this is..."

And looking around Stephen's place didn't reveal any more clues. There was no blood here. No signs of a scuffle at all.

There was a suitcase open on Stephen's bed. But he hadn't packed it as Tanya had hers—for their honeymoon. Had he changed his mind? Had he gotten cold feet?

There were no pictures of his fiancée in Stephen's bedroom. The only photo of her anywhere was in the second bedroom that he must have used as an office. It wasn't even the engagement photo of the two of them. It was a photo of the three of them—Stephen, Tanya and him—at their high school graduation, clad in their caps and gowns. He and Stephen had worn maroon and Tanya was in white, standing in the middle of the men, like a candle in the dark.

Had she come between them literally? Maybe it was simple jealousy that had brought on Cooper's doubts…

"Nice picture," Parker said. "I noticed it earlier."

"It's old." And staring at it made Cooper feel old. "Where are the recent photos of them? Of Tanya?"

"Maybe on his phone?" Parker mused. "I take them with mine and never bother printing them off."

Cooper nodded. He did the same when he cared enough about something to take photos, like of his squad. Or some of the Afghani children. Or the countryside that had actually been quite beautiful…

"Nobody found his phone," Cooper recalled.

"It must be with him."

Or with his body.

"Nikki's been trying to track the GPS on it. But she hasn't been able to pick up anything. Maybe the battery's been removed."

"Or the phone destroyed…"

"You don't think he's been kidnapped," Parker said.

He shrugged. "I don't know what to think." Or maybe he was afraid to think it. But a lot of years had passed since that graduation picture. He wasn't the same person he'd been back then. Probably neither was Tanya or Stephen…

"You're not going to find any answers here," Parker said, tucking the laptop under his arm. "We need to get you to that safe house before Logan loses it." His cell phone started to play music. "Speak of the devil…"

Cooper laughed since Parker's ringtone for his twin was "Sympathy for the Devil." He pulled the door closed and followed Parker down the hall to the elevator.

"We'll be there in a little while," he assured his twin.

"We stopped back at Stephen's. No, we didn't really think he'd show up there…" He rolled his eyes at Cooper as the argument continued.

Apparently, the years hadn't changed Logan or Parker, they still fought like the teenage girls Cooper had once accused them of being. He was still grinning over that memory when they stepped off the elevator and crossed the foyer to the outside doors.

A strange sensation chased up and down Cooper's spine and he hesitated before pushing open the doors. But Parker, perhaps distracted with his call, didn't notice Cooper's hesitation, and he continued through them into the dimly lit parking lot.

Cooper had learned long ago to heed his instincts, so he reached for his gun. But before he could draw it from its holster, shots rang out.

Chapter Six

Tanya jerked awake to darkness. But she was not alone. She heard a voice—a deep voice murmuring quietly as the speaker was probably trying not to wake her.

But then the voice rose to a panicked shout. "What the hell's happening? Parker? Cooper?"

She jumped up from the bed and scrambled toward the voice. But she couldn't find the door. She slid her palms along the wall until finally she found the door-knob and turned it.

"What's going on?" she asked as she burst into the hotel suite's sitting room where Logan Payne paced and shouted his brothers' names into his cell phone.

He turned to her in surprise, as if he'd forgotten she had been sleeping in one of the bedrooms of the suite. His eyes were wild with fear and frustration. His brothers needed him, but he had been stuck protecting her. She saw all that on his face—his handsome face that was so like Cooper's.

"What's going on!" she demanded.

He lifted his broad shoulders in a tense shrug. "I don't know." And it was obviously killing him.

"Why are you so worried about them?"

He hesitated, his jaw clenched the way Cooper so

often clenched his, before he finally answered her, "I heard gunshots."

Again. Someone had been shooting at Cooper again. "I thought you sent them to a safe house, too." Apparently that house hadn't been as safe as the one to which Logan had brought her.

"They didn't make it there yet," Logan said. "They stopped at Stephen's condo."

If Stephen had gone back home, he would have called her before now. Even if he had changed his mind about marrying her, he would have called her. Wherever Stephen was, he didn't have access to a phone.

"Why did they go there?" she asked.

"Cooper wanted to search it himself for clues..." Anger flashed in Logan's eyes. "On the job one day and thinks he's a detective..."

"We need to make sure they're all right," she said. And she was grateful now that she'd slept in her clothes instead of changing into something from her suitcase. She actually hadn't meant to, but she'd been too exhausted to change when Logan had brought her to this strange "safe house," which was actually a very small hotel suite in a very obscure hotel.

Logan shook his head. "Not *we*. You're staying here."

"Cooper's getting shot at because of me," she reminded his eldest brother.

"You don't know that."

"He's only been home a couple of days after years of being gone," she said. "There's no reason for anyone else to be shooting at him."

"We don't know that the shots I overheard were being fired at them."

"Stephen's condo isn't exactly in the bad part of town,"

she argued. "It's safe there." Safer than where she lived and definitely more affluent.

"We don't know what happened," Logan said. "So you're going to stay here while I find out."

"You're leaving me alone?" she asked, doubting that either his mother or Cooper would approve of that.

"I know you're afraid," Logan said.

She was afraid. For Cooper and Parker—far more than herself.

"So take me with you," she said, desperate to find out if Cooper was okay. She wasn't about to lose another prospective groom.

"No." Logan shook his head. "You're staying here. And you're staying safe." He lifted his gun from the holster under his arm and held it out to her.

She stared at the weapon and shook her head. "You're going to need that."

"I have another one in the car," he said. "But by the time I get to Stephen's complex, I'm sure the shooting will be all over."

Cooper could be all over. After more than a decade away from his family, he could have been killed days after returning home. Pain clutched her heart at the loss— *the tragic loss*—that would be. And now she wished she had kissed him…if only just to see if it still felt as magical and sensual as she'd remembered all these years.

"So hang on to this," he said as he pressed the gun into her hands.

The metal was cold and heavy and uncomfortable to grasp. She hadn't been deployed like Cooper, but as a social worker she'd seen more than her share of tragedies— many of them caused by guns. She wanted to shove it back onto Logan. But she didn't want to keep him from checking on Cooper and Parker. So she held on to it despite her revulsion.

"And lock yourself in the bedroom," Logan ordered her. "If anyone tries coming through the door without identifying himself, squeeze the trigger and keep shooting until you run out of bullets."

What then?

She would have asked if she hadn't already known the answer. If she used all the bullets and not a single one struck her target, even though she'd tried hard not to break Mrs. Payne's superstitions, she was still out of luck.

"WHAT THE HELL was that?" Parker griped as he lay sprawled across the asphalt of the complex parking lot. "You knocked my phone out of my hand and probably destroyed Stephen's computer."

"You're welcome," Cooper replied.

Parker cursed him as he stretched his arm under a car, grappling for his phone. He cursed again as his fingertips brushed against it and pushed it farther from his reach.

"What's a phone when I just saved your life?"

Parker scoffed, "Sure, you saved my life."

"Someone was firing real bullets at us," Cooper reminded him. And might fire some more if they lifted their heads above the car they crouched behind for cover. "If you think they were blanks, maybe I should have let one hit you."

"You really expect me to thank you?" Parker asked in astonishment.

"That's the usual custom when someone saves another person's life," Cooper said. Maybe he hadn't been gone that long, since he was easily falling back into the old pattern of bantering with his family. "In some countries, that would make you my indentured servant. You would have to wait on me hand and foot in reward for my heroism."

But even as he teased Parker, he listened for more gunshots, for the sound of a car's engine or tires, or a person's footsteps…

"All those damn medals and commendations went straight to your head," Parker griped. "You wouldn't have had to save me if you hadn't put me in danger in the first place."

Cooper sputtered, "How is any of this my fault?"

Parker jammed his shoulder against the rocker panel of the car and stretched his arm farther toward the phone. "You wanted to come here—"

"You came here earlier tonight," he reminded his brother, "and nobody shot at you."

"Yeah, because I'm not getting married tomorrow." He shuddered as if the mere thought of marriage horrified him, and inadvertently pushed the phone farther to the other side of the car.

If they were certain that the shooter was gone, they could have gotten up and walked around to the other side. But maybe that was what the assailant was waiting for…a clear shot.

Cooper had knocked Parker down so quickly and dropped to the ground himself that the shooter had only managed a couple of shots.

Had no one else heard them? No sirens wailed—not even in the distance. Parker needed that phone to call 911 since Cooper had left his in the car with the battery pulled out of it so that nobody could track it. Their car was parked on the other side of the lot.

Struggling to keep his face straight as he uttered the lie, he said, "I thought those shots were meant for you."

"Me?" Parker was all astonished sounding again.

"You're the playboy." He had been in high school, and according to the letters he received from Nikki while he was overseas, that hadn't changed. "You must have pissed off a husband or boyfriend lately."

Parker shuddered again as if in remembrance. "Not lately." He hesitated as if considering. "No, not lately." He nudged Cooper's shoulder. "Those shots were meant for you, little brother. You're the one marrying the Grim Reaper bride."

"Hey!" He smacked his brother upside the head, like Logan so often had his twin and Cooper. "Don't call her that!"

Parker smacked him back. "I know she's hot and you've always had this crush on her, but you need to remember that you're not marrying her for real. And if that shooter has his way, you're not going to marry her at all."

They paused in their scuffle to listen. Had a door opened and shut? Was someone here?

"I was supposed to take you right to that safe house," Parker said in a low grumble. "If that shooter doesn't kill us, Logan will…"

Something scraped against the asphalt, and Cooper peered under the car to see a pair of dark shoes advancing toward them. The man stopped on the other side of the car, then leaned down and picked up Parker's phone.

"Hey, Paula, Cathy—quit your bickering and stop cowering behind that car," Logan said with a chuckle of amusement and relief.

"We are not cowering," Cooper informed his eldest brother. But his pride stung over how Logan had found them arguing behind a vehicle. He must have secured the scene first, though, so Cooper jumped up from the pavement. "We took cover."

"While I was on the phone with Parker, I heard the shots," Logan said. "I take it you're both okay." He narrowed his eyes and studied Cooper then glanced down at his twin. "Neither of you got hit?"

Parker stood up and rubbed his ear. "I wouldn't say that. I took quite a hit from our little brother."

"Where's Tanya?" Cooper asked. He didn't have time for their teasing. He peered around the parking lot, looking for Logan's vehicle. "You didn't bring her along, did you?"

Logan shook his head. "She's at the safe house."

His pulse quickening with anxiety, he asked, "Alone? Did you leave her alone?"

"There's another guard on perimeter duty."

"Someone sitting in a car out front?" he asked. "Like he couldn't be compromised…" His stomach lurched as a horrible realization dawned on him. "What if these shots were a diversion? A way to lure you away from her?"

Logan shook his head. "Like the shooter would know I would be on the phone with Parker. Hell, he probably doesn't even know Tanya was with me."

"He could have been watching back at her place." From the threats Cooper had found packed away in that box, it looked like this person had been stalking her for years. "He could have seen who she left with and followed you."

Logan's pride was obviously stung now. He lifted his chin. "I was *not* followed."

"Even you can't be sure of that," Cooper challenged him.

Just the tiniest flicker of doubt flashed in Logan's eyes. "Damn it. Damn you…"

"Tell me where she is!" he demanded. The first light of dawn streaked across the dark sky. It was now his wedding day. His mother's superstitions be damned, he had to check on his bride—to make sure that he hadn't already lost her.

THE HOTEL SUITE had been eerily silent for so long that Tanya had become aware of noises she had never heard before—like the sound of her own blood rushing through her veins. The soft thump of her racing pulse. The whispery *whoosh* of her breaths coming in and out of her nose.

How long had Logan been gone? Too long for Parker and Cooper to be all right. If they hadn't been hurt, he would have come back by now.

Unless the shots had been a trap to lure Logan away from her...

She had known there would be another attempt on her life—another attempt to stop her from marrying and inheriting. She should have known that no place would be safe enough for her.

Or Cooper...

She never should have agreed with his becoming her groom. But she'd worried that she might need that money to pay a ransom for Stephen's safe return. But there had been no call, no demand. She glanced at her phone and noticed that the screen had gone dark. Was it just in sleep mode?

She tapped the screen, but it remained black. She had plugged the phone into the charger, but maybe the charger wasn't plugged into a live outlet. Was it one of those that was connected to the wall switch?

What if she'd missed the ransom call because her phone was dead?

She wanted to flip on the switch by the door, but then the lights would come on, too. And she preferred sitting in the dark. That way, if someone got inside the suite, they might not check her room since there would be no light streaking beneath the door. They might think that she had left with Logan.

She should have left with Logan. Then she wouldn't be helplessly waiting for news about Cooper. She couldn't lose Stephen and him in one night.

Her heart was beating harder now, so loudly that it deafened her to the other noises she should have heard. The noises, like the door to the hall opening, like the footsteps that might have warned her that she was no longer alone in the safe house.

But she had no clue she wasn't alone anymore until the doorknob rattled. She'd locked it, but the lock was flimsy. Heck, so was the door. It wouldn't take much for someone to force his way inside. Or shoot his way inside…

But she had a gun now, too. She clasped it in hands that had gone clammy and numb from holding the heavy weapon. Could she uncurl her fingers enough to pull the trigger?

Could she pull the trigger at all? And fire bullets into another human being?

Suddenly, the door opened. And she squeezed…

Chapter Seven

"Damn it," was the least offensive of Cooper's curses as he ducked. The bullet tunneled into the woodwork near his shoulder.

And Tanya screamed and dropped the gun.

Instead of ducking again, Cooper launched himself at her—knocking her back onto the bed in case the gun fired another round when it hit the ground. But it only spun across the threadbare carpet like a bottle at a game of spin the bottle. It stopped with the barrel pointing at them.

Cooper cursed again because he was tempted to kiss her—especially when she cupped his face in her hands and stared up at him as if she wanted his kiss, too.

"You're alive," she murmured.

"No thanks to you," he reminded them both. "I guess Logan was right when he said I needed protecting from you." He'd known she was lying when she said she wouldn't hurt him. He'd had no doubt she would hurt him—just as she had when they were kids and she'd so readily agreed with him that they were just friends. "I didn't think *you* would shoot me, though."

Tears sprang to her eyes, brightening the already vivid green. Her hands dropped from his face to the bed where she grasped the sheets. "I'm sorry! I'm so sorry! I thought you were someone else…"

"My brother? I was tempted to shoot him myself when I realized he'd left you alone." Since the guard Logan had stationed outside had fallen asleep in a car parked in the lot, he had essentially left her all alone.

"I shouldn't have fired the gun until I saw who it was," she said. "But your brother told me to shoot anyone who came through the door without announcing himself."

"And announcing myself in Afghanistan would have gotten me killed for sure," Cooper mused. "But I'm beginning to think I was safer there—I actually may have gotten shot at less."

She shuddered. "Logan was right? He heard shots on the phone?"

Cooper nodded.

"Outside Stephen's condo?"

Cooper nodded again. "Just as we were leaving the complex, someone started shooting. Neither of us got hit. They may have only been firing to scare us."

"To scare *you*," she said, "so you won't marry me."

"Don't worry," he assured her. "I don't scare easily."

"That's not good," she said. "Because if he can't scare you off, he'll try to kill you."

The way *he* had her.

"That's why I have to call off the wedding—to keep you alive," she said.

"What about a ransom demand on Stephen? You won't be able to meet it if you don't marry."

Her hips arching into his, she wriggled beneath him until she slid out from under him. Then she grabbed up the phone and charger and plugged it into another outlet. "No missed calls," she said with a sigh of relief. Then her brow furrowed. "No ransom call…"

"We don't know that there won't be one," Cooper pointed out.

"Wouldn't it have been made already?" she asked anxiously. "Why would they wait?"

He shrugged. "To see if you actually can get the money together."

"But if they don't want money to give Stephen back, we'll have gotten married for nothing."

His pride stung—at least that was all he hoped it was—that she obviously did not want to marry him. But then, Cooper hadn't wanted to marry her either. "We can fix that then."

"An annulment," she said with a sigh of relief. "I was going to tell you that you don't have to worry that I'll think this is permanent. As soon as I get my inheritance, we'll get divorced. But an annulment is better..."

Because with an annulment, it would be as if they had never been married. But the only way an annulment could be granted quickly was if the marriage was never consummated. He ignored the flash of disappointment he felt; he'd known this wasn't going to be a real marriage.

He wasn't the real groom. Stephen was. Cooper was just the stand-in groom. Stephen was the man she loved; she'd told him herself. Cooper was...just the man she'd nearly shot.

"Fine," he agreed just as readily as she had agreed that they were just friends all those years ago. "We'll get an annulment. But first we have to get married."

She shivered as if the prospect terrified her. "I don't want to put you in danger, though."

And he realized she was terrified for *him*. He reached out for her hand and then tugged her back down onto the bed next to him. "You're not putting me in danger."

She shook her head. "By marrying you, I am."

"You're not the one trying to shoot me," he said. "Well, at least not until just now."

"I'm really, really sorry," she apologized again, her beautiful face tense with regret and fear. "I never should have taken the gun from your brother."

Anger surged through Cooper again. "He never should have left you alone."

Logan was the boss, but Cooper wouldn't let bad decisions like that go unchallenged—professionally or personally.

"He was worried about you and Parker when he heard the shots," she defended. "I was worried, too." She entwined her fingers with his. "I don't want anything to happen to you."

She probably only said that because of their past friendship—because they had once been so close. But they hadn't been for years. She'd written letters after he left, but he hadn't replied to hers. He hadn't wanted to think about her moving on with her life when he had just moved.

"I survived three deployments," he reminded her. "I'll be fine." And he intended to make sure that she would be, too.

She lifted her other hand to his face and skimmed her fingers along his jaw. Her fingers trembled. "I don't want anything to happen to you…"

His heart lurched. Could she actually care about him?

"Your family worried so much when you were gone," she said. "If something happened to you now…"

"It won't." Because he wasn't going to risk his heart on her again. She was more concerned about his family than she was him.

She nodded. "Okay, then, if you're certain you'll be safe, I'll marry you."

He wouldn't be safe—not even with his resolve to not risk his heart on her. She was so damn beautiful that he doubted he would be able to control his attraction to her. Even now he was so tempted to lean forward, to close the distance between them and press his lips to hers.

But then she was the one arching up and forward and closing the distance between them. "Thank you," she murmured.

Maybe she meant to kiss his cheek.

She probably meant to kiss his cheek.

But Cooper turned his head, and her mouth met his. It should have been just a quick peck then. But she gasped and the kiss deepened. Cooper couldn't help himself—he dipped his tongue between her parted lips and tasted her.

She was even sweeter than he remembered.

Her fingers clasped his face and she kissed him back, her tongue flicking across his. Touching. Teasing…

They weren't teenagers anymore. A kiss wasn't just a kiss. They knew where it could lead, and they were sitting on a bed. Cooper fought for control and pulled back, just as Tanya did the same.

Her face flushed and eyes widened, she panted for breath. She moved her lips, but no words formed. Obviously she didn't have any idea what to say either.

Cooper glanced down to where the gun barrel pointed at them like that spin-the-bottle. But that wasn't why she'd kissed him. She had obviously only meant to kiss his cheek—probably out of gratitude.

But Cooper was less concerned about why she'd kissed him than he was about why he'd kissed her. He knew she loved another man—a man who had always been a good friend to him, even when Cooper had physically and emotionally let distance grow between them. Kissing the man's fiancée was an act of betrayal.

Unless…

No, he had no proof. Not yet. He had no reason for his suspicions. Except maybe he wanted to think the worst so that he wouldn't feel so damn guilty.

Shaking his head, he murmured, "That didn't happen."

Her eyes still wide, she nodded in agreement.

"I wasn't even here," he said.

"What?"

"If my mother asks, you didn't see me last night or this morning…"

Her lips curved into a slight smile. "Her wedding traditions?"

"Superstitions," he corrected her. "We are not to see each other until…"

Light streaked through the blinds at the hotel room window. It was his wedding day.

"Until we meet again at the church," she finished for him.

"Try to get some sleep," he suggested.

"What about you?"

He shrugged. After that kiss? He doubted he would be able to close his eyes without imagining where that kiss could have led, without anticipating a honeymoon that would never happen, thanks to her wanting an annulment. "I don't need much sleep anymore."

"Even after today?" she asked, her thick lashes blinking as she struggled against exhaustion to keep her eyes open.

He'd had longer, more dangerous days. He gently pushed her back until she lay down on the bed. Then he pulled the blanket over her, as exhaustion overwhelmed her and she fell asleep. He needed to stand up, needed to step away from the bed before he was tempted to crawl into it with her and hold her. But he couldn't stop staring at her beautiful face. It had been so long since he'd seen her. And tonight he'd nearly lost her—twice.

But then he sighed as he remembered that she wasn't his to lose. A shadow fell across the floor, and he reached for his weapon.

"I thought you didn't want to come to their wedding because you didn't care anymore," Logan remarked from the doorway. "But that's not the case at all. You didn't want to come because you care too much."

He pulled his hand away from his holster and replied to his brother, "She and Stephen were my best friends in high school. They helped me through losing Dad."

"She's more than a friend to you."

He shook his head in denial, but still he couldn't stop staring at her. "No."

"Maybe I'm wrong," Logan said, but his tone indicated he thought otherwise. "But she was right. You should get some sleep."

"I need to make sure she stays safe."

"I'll do that," Logan said.

When Cooper turned toward him, his older brother lifted his hands as if to ward off an attack. "I won't leave her again even if you're begging me for help."

"I won't…" If he wound up begging, it wouldn't be for Logan.

"Take my help tonight," Logan said, "because you're going to be primary protection for her at the wedding and after…"

On that honeymoon. But they wouldn't get to that if they didn't survive the wedding. Someone was so determined to stop that, judging from the recent shooting attempts, he or she didn't seem to care who died—the bride or the groom.

HOURS HAD PASSED, but Tanya's lips still tingled from that kiss. What had she been thinking to kiss Cooper Payne?

He wasn't the teenage boy with whom she had once been friends. He was a man now, and his kiss had proven that. But then, even as a boy, he'd kissed like a man.

She released a shaky breath.

"It's going to be okay," Mrs. Payne promised as she opened the bride's dressing room door and ushered Tanya inside. Sunshine bathed the room, setting its soft pink walls and white wainscoting aglow.

And Tanya nearly believed her. She had always had so much admiration for Mrs. Payne. Tanya's mother had wallowed in self-pity after her husband chose money over a life with her and her daughters. But Cooper's mother had lost the love of her life through a horrible tragedy and yet she had put aside her own anguish and heartbreak to be the rock her children had needed her to be.

Tanya had leaned on her all those years ago herself. And she leaned on her now, giving her a big hug. "Thank you for everything you've done."

Mrs. Payne patted her back. "You're like one of my own, sweetheart. I would do anything for you."

That was the kind of mother Tanya hoped to be some-day. But when would that day be? She had to live through this wedding and subsequent annulment to have hope of ever having another wedding—a real one.

"I'm so sorry that I'm putting your family in danger," Tanya continued. The Paynes had already been through too much tragedy. She hoped she wouldn't bring another one upon them.

"You are not responsible for any of this, Tanya." Mrs. Payne chuckled. "And, honey, my boys have been put-ting themselves in danger since the day they were each born. Climbing trees too high. Riding bikes too fast. Then joining the police force and the Marines." She shook her head and sighed.

When Cooper had joined the service after high school, Tanya had been almost relieved that they had never taken their relationship beyond friendship. She would have been so worried about him, so devastated if anything happened to him…

"Isn't that hard on you?" Tanya asked. "After what happened…"

"To their father?" Mrs. Payne uttered another sigh, a wistful one, and her face softened—the faint lines she had entirely disappearing so that she looked like the young girl she must have been when she fell in love with Mr. Payne. "Having them act so much like their father has kept him alive for me—and probably for them."

"But they put their lives at risk…"

Mrs. Payne let out an indelicate snort. "Living puts our lives at risk—driving a car, taking a bus, going to the mall or a movie…bad things happen everywhere. Not just Afghanistan. Cooper survived that—he can survive anything."

Tanya wasn't as confident of that as his mother.

The older woman gave her a slight nudge toward the garment bag hanging from the hook on the wall. "Start getting dressed, honey. Your sister and Nikki are on their way."

"Rochelle?" She tensed with shock and concern. "She's still going to stand up there with me?"

"She's your sister. Family sticks together."

The Payne family definitely did, but not the Chesterfield family. Money had always divided them and probably always would.

Knuckles wrapped against the door. "That better not

be Cooper. I told him to stay away from you until the wedding." She opened the door to Tanya's grandfather's lawyer.

"I'm sorry to interrupt," Mr. Gregory said. "But I really need a word with Ms. Chesterfield."

"Tanya," she corrected him as she so often had had to over the years. Her grandfather may have demanded formality but it made her uncomfortable.

Mrs. Payne studied the handsome gray-haired man intently before nodding. "You'll do…"

The lawyer's face reddened and he uttered, "Excuse me, ma'am?"

Mrs. Payne had been single a long time. Perhaps she was finally ready to envision a future for herself instead of just helping brides and grooms get ready for theirs.

"Tanya needs someone to walk her down the aisle," Mrs. Payne explained. "I was going to enlist my eldest boy, but it would be better to have someone who's been part of Tanya's life."

Arthur Gregory had been a part of her life for a long time—since before his hair had gone gray and he'd developed lines around his dark eyes and his tightly lipped mouth.

"I'm sure Ms. Chesterfield would rather—"

"No," Tanya interrupted him. "I would be happy to have you walk me down…" To her stand-in groom. If not for Stephen's disappearance, Cooper probably wouldn't have even attended the wedding.

"I'll leave you two to discuss it," Mrs. Payne said as she bustled from the room and closed the door behind herself.

The lawyer stared after the petite woman. "She's something else…"

If Tanya remembered correctly, Mr. Gregory had never married. "Mrs. Payne is wonderful."

"But misguided," the lawyer said.

"I'm sorry she enlisted you in the wedding," Tanya apologized. "If it makes you uncomfortable, you don't have to participate."

"The whole wedding makes me uncomfortable," he admitted.

She had a million reasons of her own, but she asked, "Why?"

"I'm worried that these people may be taking advantage of you."

If anything, it was the reverse, she was taking advantage of them. "They are helping me."

"But you wouldn't need help if Stephen hadn't disappeared," he said.

"Exactly."

"He disappeared from *here*." The lawyer stared at her as if that meant something.

She arched a brow in question.

"And immediately after that, *she* suggested that her son take his place."

Tanya wasn't exactly certain why Mrs. Payne had pushed Cooper into that—unless she wanted them together. Had she been aware all those years ago that Tanya had had a crush on her son?

"That was very sweet of her to help me out. I only have a couple of days until I turn thirty." And Stephen hadn't been found yet. She didn't dare wait until the last day—in case that ransom demand was made.

"It was perhaps too convenient," Mr. Gregory suggested.

"What are you saying?"

"Your grandfather always worried that you and your sister would be taken advantage of because of your inheritance."

Like their father had taken advantage of their mother. What little money her father had left her, their mother had used to track down their father. She'd obviously intended to use it to buy back the man's love that her father had bought off. Tanya and Rochelle hadn't seen or heard from her since she'd left.

Her voice sharp in defense of her friends, she replied, "That is not the case with the Paynes."

"Your grandfather did not trust Cooper Payne," Mr. Gregory said. "He warned the boy years ago—"

"He what?" she gasped, both shocked and horrified. "Did he try to buy off Cooper, too?"

The lawyer shook his head. "He just pointed out to him that you were out of his league."

She would like to believe that her grandfather wouldn't have done such a humiliating thing to her and Cooper, but she knew better. The old man had enjoyed humiliating and manipulating people, especially his own family.

"You *still* are out of his league, Tanya," Mr. Gregory continued. "The only reason you're marrying him is because your real groom conveniently disappeared."

Remembering all that spattered blood, she flinched. "There was nothing convenient about Stephen's disappearance." Terrifying? Yes. Convenient? No.

"It is convenient for Cooper Payne since he's stepping in as your groom. I can't believe that his mother managed to obtain a marriage license at such short notice."

Neither could Tanya, but Mrs. Payne was definitely a full-service wedding planner. There was nothing she wouldn't do for a bride.

It wasn't awe in the lawyer's voice, though. It was suspicion. Tanya narrowed her eyes and glared at Mr. Gregory. "If you're implying that the Paynes are responsible for what happened to Stephen, you're dead wrong."

"This is why your grandfather put the stipulation on your inheritance," the lawyer said cynically, "because you tend to be too naive and trusting."

She laughed. No one had *ever* accused her of being either of those things. "Grandfather didn't know me." Because he'd never made the effort. "And neither do you. Moreover, you don't know the Paynes at all. They are known for their honor and protectiveness. They would never harm anyone."

"You think that is still true of Cooper?" he asked her. "He's been to war. You don't know how that can change a man. He isn't the boy you remember."

Tanya had thought so, too, but then she had seen glimpses of that boy—in his camaraderie with his family and his concern for her and Stephen. And in his kiss…

"Why would Cooper hurt Stephen?" she asked.

"Jealousy," he suggested. "Over you…"

"We were never anything but friends." Because that was the way he'd wanted to keep it.

Mr. Gregory chuckled. "The kid mooned around after you. He had a major crush on you. That was why your grandfather told him to stay away from you."

She'd thought he'd stopped coming to her house because he'd considered it a mausoleum. She hadn't minded. She and Stephen had both liked it at his house better. The Payne household was warm and noisy and full of love.

"That was a long time ago," Tanya reminded him.

The lawyer shrugged. "So maybe it's about money now. He's probably not making much working for his family. But marrying you…"

"You think Cooper is marrying me for my money?" She nearly laughed again since it was really the reverse. *She* was marrying *him* for her money. "That's ridiculous."

She'd overheard his argument with his family. The last thing he'd wanted to do was marry her.

"Then have him sign a prenup," he suggested, and he patted his ever-present dark leather briefcase, "and prove that he has no interest in your inheritance."

She shook her head. "I can't ask him to do that…" Not when he was already making a sacrifice for her. Or, actually, for Stephen. He had only agreed to marry her in case someone demanded a ransom for his return.

He hadn't been missing a whole day yet. There was time. Time to bring him back safely from wherever he'd been taken.

"If you can't ask him, I will," Mr. Gregory offered as he turned for the door.

Tanya grabbed his briefcase to stop him. "No!"

The last thing she needed was her grandfather's lawyer insulting Cooper as her grandfather must have all those years ago. Was that why he'd said they should just be friends? What would he have done if she'd disagreed with him?

Too many years had passed. The past was the past. She had to accept that she would never know now.

"You don't trust him either," the lawyer remarked. "You think he's only marrying you for the money. Tanya, it's not too late. You need to stop this wedding."

She shook her head.

"Take a little time," he urged her. "Think about it. You'll realize you can't marry a man that you can't trust."

It wasn't Cooper that she wasn't trusting at the moment. She opened the door for the lawyer to show him out. "I'd prefer to have Logan Payne walk me down the aisle," she said, dismissing him.

"I wouldn't walk you down the aisle to Cooper Payne anyway," he told her. "Your grandfather would haunt me for certain."

Maybe that was who was causing Tanya all her grief— her grandfather's ghost. She wouldn't put it past the old man to haunt her, especially if he had any idea what she'd intended to do with her inheritance.

But first she had to marry to inherit. She drew in a deep breath to brace herself before reaching for the zipper on the garment bag. As she pulled down the tab, bits of lace and satin fell onto the floor like those black petals from the dead roses.

Someone had hacked the heavy material into small pieces. How much hate did it take for someone to be so vindictive? So malicious?

Tears stung her eyes and she shuddered in dread.

The doorknob rattled. Maybe whoever had cut up her dress had returned to do the same to her.

Chapter Eight

His exit blocked, Cooper was trapped inside the blood-spattered groom's quarters. The police had only just released the crime scene that morning. Cooper hoped they'd found something when they'd processed the room that would lead to whoever had taken Stephen. He wanted his friend safe and unharmed. But Stephen wasn't his only concern...

"Get the hell out of my way," he threatened, "or I'll show you what I learned in the Marines—all the ways I learned how to hurt someone."

"You wouldn't hurt me," Parker said, but a tiny flicker of doubt passed through his bright blue eyes. "I kept you safe last night."

"I saved your life," Cooper reminded him.

Parker shook his head. "I was talking about later." A furrow formed in his brow. "Or was it earlier this morning? I stood watch so you could get some sleep."

"You stood watch? On your back?" Cooper chuckled. "You kept me awake with your snoring."

"It wasn't my snoring that kept you awake," Parker said.

And he was right. It hadn't been concern for Tanya's safety either—he'd trusted that Logan wouldn't leave her again, that he would definitely make sure she arrived safely at the church. It had been concern for his own sanity—after that kiss—that had kept Cooper from getting any sleep.

"Wedding jitters kept you awake," Parker said. He tugged at his bow tie as his neck reddened. "I don't blame you. This damn thing feels like a noose."

"It's going to feel more like one if you don't let me pass you," Cooper threatened.

Parker chuckled. "I understand wanting to make a break for it, but I promised Mom that I wouldn't just get you to the church but I'd get you to the altar, too."

"I have to go to the bride's room," Cooper said.

Parker shook his head. "You're not backing out now."

"Don't worry," Cooper said. "It's too late for Mom to get your name on the marriage license instead of mine."

"It's too late for you to back out, too," Parker said, "because if this is about the ransom and she doesn't get the money…"

Stephen would be killed. "Has anyone called with a ransom demand?" The last he'd heard nobody had yet, but that had been hours ago…in Tanya's hotel room right before they'd kissed.

"According to Logan," his twin relayed, "no."

"This isn't about ransom," Cooper said, "but it is about the money."

"You think you've figured it out," Parker realized.

He shrugged since he had no proof. His biggest concern was that his suspicions were correct. And that the bride was alone with the person who wanted her dead.

Instead of reasoning with Parker, he just shoved him aside and hurried out into the empty church. No guests had arrived yet. Hell, it was his wedding, and he wasn't even sure who had been invited. Only the wedding party had arrived. Him as the groom and Parker as his best man.

According to Logan, the bride had arrived safely, too. But had she stayed that way?

He rushed down the aisle to the vestibule and knocked on the door next to the restrooms. No one responded, so he pounded harder. "Open up!"

The lock clicked and the door creaked open only a couple of inches. A chocolate-brown eye narrowed and glared at him. "What are you doing here?"

He lifted a brow and then made a show of glancing down at his tux. "I don't know. What am I doing here—in a monkey suit?"

"You're a monkey?" his sister teased.

His heart lurched at her laughter. God, he'd missed his family. He'd missed his siblings' relentless teasing and his mother's relentless bossing. He had missed someone else, too.

Her voice called out to his sister. "Nikki, is that Cooper? Has he changed his mind?"

"He has if he's as smart as you've always said he was," a bitter voice chimed in. Despite her hysterical outburst the night before, Rochelle had showed up to support her sister. Or sabotage her?

"You can't see her," Nikki told him. "Mom would have a fit over the bad luck you'd have if the groom saw the bride before the wedding."

Mom and her damn superstitions...

He assured her, "I don't want to see the bride." Again. He'd already seen her on the morning of their wedding day; he had already kissed the bride.

"Well, if you're here about that other thing—" she lowered her voice so only he could hear her "—Stephen's computer..."

"Have you made any progress?"

"I might have if it hadn't gotten smashed up..."

He flinched with regret. He needed to know what was on that computer. "Is it beyond repair?"

"No," she assured him. "It's just going to take me a little while longer. And we're kind of busy at the moment." She lowered her voice again. "Someone cut up Tanya's wedding dress."

His heart clenched. "Is she all right?"

"Yeah, Mom fixed it."

"The dress?"

"No, there was no fixing that dress," she said with a shudder. "It was completely destroyed."

And his suspicions increased. Cutting up a dress was an act of incredible jealousy and pettiness.

"Mom found her another dress." Nikki uttered a wistful sigh. "Wait until you see her…"

He stepped forward, but his sister shoved on his chest and pushed him back. "You're going to have to wait," she told him. "Mom's gone above and beyond for this wedding and you're not going to ruin it. You are not seeing the bride."

"I actually want to see the maid of honor."

Nikki opened the door a little farther. She wore a dress in some bronze color that complemented her reddish hair. She narrowed her brown eyes and glared at him. "I know what you're thinking, and you're wrong."

He nodded and acknowledged, "I might be. Let me talk to her."

Rochelle pushed past her friend and stepped into the vestibule with Cooper. She wore the same bronze dress as his sister but it wasn't nearly as flattering. Maybe that was because of the resentful look on her face. She hadn't bothered doing anything with her hair either; it hung in lank strings around her bare shoulders. "Have you come to your senses yet?" she asked.

"Maybe…" he murmured as he studied her face. Her eyes, a grayer shade of green than Tanya's, were red-rimmed and swollen as if she'd cried all night. That could just be what she did every time she got drunk. He had met his share of sloppy drunks over the years. Or maybe she had been that upset over Stephen's disappearance.

How upset had she been over his engagement to her sister?

She expelled a shaky breath of relief. "That's good. You shouldn't marry my sister."

"Why not?" he asked. "Do you want your grandfather's inheritance all to yourself?"

She sucked in a breath. "I—I don't care about his money."

"What do you care about?" he asked. "Stephen?"

Tears shimmered in her eyes and she nodded again. "She didn't care about him at all."

"Then why would she marry him?"

"For the money, that's all she cares about," Rochelle said. "No, that's not true."

"No," he agreed. Tanya had become a social worker, she wouldn't have done that if she didn't care about other people. And she wouldn't have been promoted to supervisor if she didn't care enough about her job to be good at it.

"You," Rochelle said, her resentment now turning on him. "She always had a crush on you."

He would have told her how wrong she was, that Tanya had only wanted to be his friend, but he didn't want to interrupt Rochelle. The more upset she got, the more she might reveal.

"So your marrying her is exactly what she wants," she said, bitterness making her voice sharp and her face ugly. "And Tanya always gets what she wants."

And Cooper suspected that Rochelle always wanted what Tanya had.

"Have you talked to Stephen?" he asked.

She gasped. "Of course not."

"Why 'of course not'?"

"He's missing."

"Yes," he said. "Do you know where he is?"

She gasped again. "You think I have something to do with his disappearance?"

"I think you're jealous that he was going to marry your sister," he said, and he had no doubt that he was right about that. He just wasn't sure about the rest of his suspicions. "And jealous women can be quite dangerous..."

She stepped closer to him, her eyes bright and her nostrils flaring. "You have no idea how dangerous I can be."

He was afraid that he might have a pretty accurate idea.

She stepped back and shook her head. "You know, marry my sister with my blessing. I think the two of you deserve each other." She stepped back inside the bride's room and slammed the door behind her.

"You don't have Parker's way with the ladies," Logan remarked as he joined Cooper in the vestibule.

"Neither do you." Which was more ironic since they looked almost exactly alike. Logan wore his hair shorter than Parker's but not as short as Cooper's military cut.

"That's fine with me," Logan remarked. "I would rather stay single than do what you're about to do." He pointed toward the church. "Parker and the reverend are waiting for you."

"Did Mom send you to get me?"

He shook his head. "No, to get Tanya."

"Déjà vu."

"I'm walking her down the aisle."

She had no one else to do it. Her father had abandoned his family. Her original groom had disappeared. That left only Cooper and his family. He hoped they would be enough to keep her safe.

His mom stepped out of the church and crooked her finger, beckoning him inside. Unlike his siblings, he didn't always blindly obey his mother. She hadn't wanted him to enlist but he had. He had even fought her plan the night before…until he had realized that she was right.

The best way to keep Tanya safe was to marry her. But who was going to keep *him* safe? Because the minute he saw her looking both ethereal and sexy in white lace, he realized that he was in the most danger in which he had ever been. He was in danger of falling irrevocably in love with the woman about to become his wife.

IN HIS BLACK TUXEDO and white pleated shirt, Cooper Payne looked so handsome that he completely stole Tanya's breath. He wouldn't have fit in Stephen's tuxedo. Mrs. Payne must have extra suits available the way she had dresses.

Actually, she'd had only one extra dress on hand. A very special dress…

Cooper's gaze met hers and his eyes widened. Was that because he recognized his mother's dress?

Tanya had the moment Mrs. Payne had brought it to her to replace the destroyed dress. She had seen that dress in the wedding portrait that hung over the mantel in the Payne living room. And she had refused to wear it. The woman that Cooper was going to marry for real—*for a happily-ever-after not just until we get an annulment*—deserved to wear that dress.

Not Tanya.

But Mrs. Payne had insisted in that gracious, indomitable manner of hers that tolerated no refusal or argument. And as she'd also pointed out, Tanya had no other options. Unless she wanted to get married in jeans and a sweater, she had to wear Mrs. Payne's wedding dress.

Maybe she should have gone with the jeans—then she wouldn't feel like such a fraud. Actually, she felt like a bride. A real one. Especially with how intently her groom was staring at her.

The strapless gown was all vintage lace and sparkling beads with a formfitting silhouette. Much more formfitting on Tanya than it had been on the petite bride who'd originally worn it. Mrs. Payne must have worn high heels so that the hem hadn't dragged on the floor. Tanya had forgone shoes. She felt the runner under her bare feet, the red velvet soft against her skin. Each step brought her closer to the altar.

To her groom.

As it had the night before, her heart pounded so loudly that she heard it as well as her blood rushing in her ears. The organ was drowned out. She never heard what Logan said to her as he leaned down and kissed her cheek. Even the first words the minister spoke were lost to her.

Then Cooper took her hands in both of his and her heart stopped beating entirely for a moment. She felt like that teenage girl she'd once been—the one who'd dreamed every night of Cooper Payne declaring his love for her. But then she reminded herself that all that Cooper had ever declared for her was friendship.

She would like to believe that he'd only done that because her grandfather had warned him off. But if Cooper really wanted something, like joining the Marines, he hadn't let anyone scare him off or talk him out of it. Just as he hadn't let getting shot at—twice—the night before scare him away from marrying her. But he wasn't marrying her for her.

He hadn't really wanted her. Then. Or now.

He was marrying her for Stephen—for his safe return. If Stephen was safe...

Was it already too late to save him?

Tears burned her eyes, blurring her vision even more than the veil that Mrs. Payne had also loaned her. It was a thin, delicate lace through which Tanya had had no problem seeing earlier.

"Do you take this man to be your husband, Tanya?" the minister prodded her as if he'd asked the question before.

A couple coughs disrupted the eerie silence of the church. But there weren't many guests. Even when she was going to marry Stephen, she had insisted on keeping the guest list to a minimum. And now Stephen's family and friends weren't present—thanks to the calls Mrs. Payne had made.

It would have been more than just awkward to marry another man in front of them. They wouldn't have understood that she was doing this for him—for Stephen.

Cooper squeezed her hands and nodded as if in encouragement.

And Tanya found herself opening her mouth and whispering the words, "I do."

But was she doing this for Stephen or for herself? Because she was fulfilling that childhood fantasy she'd had of one day marrying Cooper Payne. But in her fantasy, Cooper loved her and wanted to become her husband.

And as he'd had to with her, the minister had to repeat his question to Cooper, "Do you take this woman to be your wife?"

She stared up into Cooper's vivid blue eyes. Like the

minister and those few guests, most of which were his family, she waited for his reply. She wouldn't blame him if he changed his mind—if he refused to marry her.

She held her breath. And the church grew eerily quiet again.

Cooper cleared his throat and finally spoke, "I do."

For a moment Tanya let herself believe it was real—that Cooper Payne was so in love with her that he wanted to become her husband. That he wanted a happily-ever-after with her—and not just until the annulment.

Tears of happiness burned her eyes and she furiously blinked as she tried to clear her vision. But the tears kept burning her eyes and the back of her throat.

She coughed and choked, struggling to breathe. Finally she realized that it wasn't tears of emotion but smoke that was blurring her vision.

The church was on fire.

Tanya knew it couldn't be an accident, not after everything that had happened last night. It was arson. Someone had purposely set the church on fire. The only question was, had the exits been blocked or would they be able to escape the building before flames engulfed the guests and the groom?

She would be dead long before the flames claimed her. Tanya's lungs burned and her airway swelled as she struggled for breath. The asthma that had haunted her childhood flared again, choking her. Usually her asthma only acted up in the spring with seasonal allergies or in the winter if she was unfortunate enough to catch a cold.

But smoke had always been her biggest trigger. Cigarette smoke and bonfires had brought on embarrassing and life-threatening attacks during her teenage years. Back then, her inhaler had saved her. But she didn't have it with her now. It was in her purse, which she had left in the bride's dressing room.

She would never make it that far before passing out— before dying. Mrs. Payne had definitely been right to be superstitious. Seeing the groom before her wedding had brought Tanya terrible, fatal luck…

Chapter Nine

Cooper caught the man's arm, holding him in place before he could run as the others had toward the vestibule. "Do it!" he ordered the minister. "Pronounce us man and wife!"

The man choked and sputtered, the words whispered and hoarse, "I now pronounce you man and wife."

It was official. Tanya Chesterfield was not just his bride—she was now his wife. But she was coughing harder than the others, her shoulders shaking and body trembling as she struggled for breath.

Would he soon become her widower?

He caught her up in his arms and followed the others toward those doors at the back of the church. Logan carried their mother. With an arm around each of them, Parker helped both Rochelle and Nikki while the lawyer and the minister hurried out ahead of Cooper and his bride.

The air was thick in the church, burning Cooper's eyes and nose. He recognized this kind of smoke too well—it brought horrible old memories crashing over him. Parker held open the doors so Cooper could carry Tanya over the threshold and through the vestibule. Logan held open the doors to the outside while also trying to hold his mother from rushing back inside the church.

"We have to find the source of the fire," she said, tears streaming from her eyes. It probably wasn't just the smoke making her cry but fear for the chapel she had already fought so hard to save once. "We have to put it out—it'll take too long for the fire engines to arrive."

Cooper shook his head. "There is no fire."

Mom stared hopefully up at him. "But all the smoke…"

"There're no flames," he pointed out. "No heat."

"So what is it?" Logan asked as he coughed and his eyes streamed tears. This wasn't the kind of man who cried. He hadn't even cried as a kid—not even when their dad died. He had stayed strong for all of them.

"Tear gas," Cooper said. His eyes stung but stayed dry. He was used to this stuff—to chemical attacks used to flush soldiers out into an ambush. He peered outside and ordered his family, "Get back in here. The shooter could be out there."

But right now gunfire was the least of his concerns. He glanced down at his bride lying in his arms. She hadn't just passed out from fear. She was too still for that—too lifeless. "She's not breathing!" he realized, his heart slamming into his ribs.

"The gas must have aggravated her asthma," her sister said.

And he remembered the attacks she'd had in their youth, like at the site of the bonfire when she'd struggled for breath. "Get her inhaler!"

"She always has one in her purse," Rochelle replied. Finally showing some concern for her sister, she ran toward the bride's dressing room. But she returned moments later clutching Tanya's open bag. "It's not here."

Someone had set off the smoke bomb and stolen Tanya's inhaler. This person knew her well—too well. He put aside his suspicions for the moment to focus on his bride, though. He dropped to knees in the vestibule and began CPR. Pressing his lips to hers, he tried breathing for her—tried to give her his breath to bring her back.

"I'm calling 911," Logan said as he pulled his cell phone from his pocket.

But Cooper knew it would be too late. By the time the ambulance arrived, Tanya would have been deprived of oxygen for too long.

"Unless someone took it, too, I have something," his mother murmured. She pushed past her eldest son and hurried back into the church, disappearing down the stairwell to the basement banquet area, kitchen and offices.

"I hear sirens," Nikki said. "Someone must have reported the smoke."

Rochelle began to cry. "She's not breathing. She's not breathing…"

Footsteps pounded on the steps as his mother ran back up the stairs. "I have her extra inhaler," she said. "When we were planning the wedding, I made sure she brought a spare in case she forgot to bring hers on her wedding day."

Cooper grabbed it from her and pressed it to Tanya's open lips. She wouldn't be able to breathe it in—would it get through her compromised airway? Would it reduce the swelling?

He pushed it down so that it produced a puff of medicine. But most of it escaped her open mouth. He did it again. But there was no response. Her eyelids didn't so much as flicker, and she didn't breathe.

Had he already lost his wife?

EVERYTHING WAS DARK, as if Tanya had dropped into a black hole. But then awareness crept in—first with sound.

She could hear the beeping and buzzing of machines. The squeak of wheels on linoleum. And voices…

"She should have not been exposed to that gas," a man said, his tone chastising, "You're lucky her inhaler worked."

"I wasn't sure that it would. She was already unconscious." This voice she recognized as her husband's. But was Cooper actually her husband? She dimly remembered the minister pronouncing them man and wife. Then Cooper had swept her up in his arms.

Or had that all just been part of her fantasy?

Was any of it real?

"And she's still unconscious," Cooper continued.

"But she's breathing."

"Was the inhaler enough?" Cooper asked, his voice gruff with obvious concern. "Is she going to be all right?"

If not for the beeps and buzzes, Tanya would have thought she'd slipped into unconsciousness again. Because the man paused that long before replying, "We'll know when she awakens…"

"When?" Cooper asked hopefully. "Or *if…?"*

She was already awake. Her eyes were just too heavy to open, and her throat too dry and achy to speak. She struggled to move her fingers, but she was so weak, her muscles so leaden and appendages so heavy.

"I'm sorry," the man said. "I don't know…"

Since she hadn't recognized his voice, she'd just assumed he was a doctor. But maybe not…or he would realize that she was going to be fine.

She had to be fine.

A big hand closed over the fingers she struggled to move. And as he had in the church, he squeezed as if prodding her again. "Come on, Tanya, wake up…"

She tried again to raise her lids, but they were so

heavy. The effort exhausted her, but she gained a small space, enough that some light filtered between her lashes. She was fighting back the blackness.

But she wasn't fighting alone. Cooper held tightly to her hand as if pulling her back to him. "Come on, you're too tough to let this damn coward beat you…"

She had to be strong—not just for herself but for Stephen. She couldn't take a ransom call if she wasn't conscious. Then Cooper marrying her would have been for naught. She had to assure him that wasn't the case, so she concentrated on her fingers and managed to move them within his tight grasp.

He gasped. "Tanya? Can you hear me?"

She bent her fingers again, wriggling them. Then she managed, finally, to open her eyes.

"You're awake!"

She nodded weakly. And then, after licking her dry and cracked lips, she tried to speak. "Is—is…"

"Don't hurt your throat," he advised. "Just rest."

She shook her head now, which caused a wave of dizziness that threatened a return of unconsciousness. "Is everyone…okay?"

If his mother's Little White Wedding Chapel had been destroyed, she would never forgive herself. "Did the fire…"

"There was no fire," he said.

"But the smoke…" She coughed, just remembering it, as her airway and lungs ached.

"It wasn't a fire," he assured her with another squeeze of her fingers. "Someone opened a tear-gas canister in the church."

She coughed again. "Was anyone else…"

He shook his head. "No one else was hurt. Only you…"

"My asthma…" It didn't often flare up. But when it

did… Remembering his conversation with the man who must have been the doctor, she asked, "You found my inhaler in my purse?"

"There wasn't one in your purse, but Mom had gotten a spare from you earlier."

She'd seen the inhaler and the EpiPen for her peanut allergy when she'd taken her makeup bag out of her purse. "But it was there earlier…"

"Not when you needed it."

Someone hadn't opened the tear-gas canister just to stop the wedding. He or she had been trying to kill her. Her eyes stung and not from that smoke. She blinked hard, but the moisture leaked out.

The thin mattress depressed as Cooper joined her on the bed. Sitting down beside her, he pulled her into his arms, lifting her away from the pillows and the bed. "It's okay. You're safe now."

"You found out who's been doing this?"

He uttered a heavy sigh. "No, but we will. We'll find out."

She shivered as cool air blew in the back of her gown. And she touched the rough cotton. "Your mom's dress— is it okay?"

If they'd cut her out of it—if they'd destroyed it, it would have been as big a tragedy as the church burning down.

"It's fine," he assured her. "You need to stop worrying about everything and get some rest."

"I need to get out of here." She was definitely in a hospital, and not just in a curtained-off area of the emergency room. She had been admitted.

"You're too weak," he said.

"You said I was tough," she reminded him.

"You are—it's a miracle you survived at all. You

weren't breathing for so long." He shuddered now. "For too long…"

She managed to lift her hand to her head, which still felt too light—too hazy—as if she were still trying to see through the veil. She was tired. Weak…

Tears burned again, but she managed to blink them back this time. She had to be strong…enough to leave. "But if they call…"

"Logan has your phone," Cooper said. "He'll take the call."

"They might hang up…if they don't hear me…" And then what would happen to Stephen? He had already been hurt—that blood had to have been his. There'd been no one else in the groom's dressing room. "I need my…"

"Real groom," Cooper finished for her.

Incorrectly. She just needed her phone. And Cooper. But he was pulling back and standing up.

"We'll find him," he assured her. "We're all working on finding him."

Just then a knocking sounded and the door creaked open. "Is she awake? Is she all right?" a woman asked, her voice soft with concern.

"Yes," Tanya answered Cooper's sister. She was touched by the younger woman's concern but also disappointed that her own sister hadn't come to check on her. How had their relationship fallen apart so badly? "I'm fine."

Nikki's brown eyes, so like her mother's, warmed with affection and relief. "I'm so glad. You gave us quite the scare—some of us more than others, though." She glanced at her brother, as if checking to see if he'd recovered from that scare.

But Tanya doubted he had been very shaken. After surviving a war zone and returning home, the man had been shot at—twice—and hadn't lost his composure or his temper. He was unflappable.

"Is your mother okay?" Tanya asked.

"Worried about you," Nikki said. "But she's fine. Mom's the toughest woman I know."

Tanya suspected her daughter was tougher than she knew. "Your mom isn't the only one."

"She's not," Nikki agreed. "You're pretty tough, yourself. None of us thought you were going to make it."

If that was the truth, where was Rochelle? Didn't she care about her older sister at all? Tanya sighed, too, and shook off the self-pity. A relationship took two people to make it work. Maybe she had never tried hard enough with Rochelle. She'd been so busy with work and with trying not to think about Cooper. With trying not to worry about Cooper being deployed. With trying not to miss Cooper...

"She has no clue how close she came to not making it," Cooper said. "Even now she's more worried about Mom and Stephen and everyone else than she is herself. She needs to get some rest."

"She needs you to stop talking about her like she's not here," Tanya said, annoyed that he thought her so weak and more annoyed that she was so weak right now. At least physically...

Nikki laughed. "I forgot how long you two have been friends."

So had Tanya. But in her mind, they had never been just friends, even though she'd agreed with Cooper that that was all they'd been.

"You both act like an old married couple already," Nikki continued, "and it's only been a few hours since the wedding from hell—" She squeaked, as if wishing back her words, and her eyes widened in shock. "I'm sorry—"

Tanya had spent too much time around the Paynes not to know that this was how they dealt with every situation—with humor. And she was touched that she'd been included in that teasing.

"No, it definitely was the wedding from hell," Tanya agreed. The smoke had made her think she was in hell. Even now her throat still burned—her lungs still ached.

"I—I shouldn't have called it that," Nikki said, clearly embarrassed. "Mom would kill me."

At least Nikki would know who was trying. Tanya had no idea who wanted her dead. But she had to ask, "Have you found out anything about what happened at the church?"

Nikki opened her mouth, but Cooper shook his head. "You nearly died at the church," he said. "You need to rest if you're going to fully recover."

Tanya shook her head in denial. But her vision blurred with black spots as oblivion threatened to claim her again. She wouldn't admit it, but he was right. Exhaustion was overwhelming her, making her lids so heavy that she couldn't keep her eyes open any longer. Maybe if she closed them for just a moment…

His deep voice dropping to a whisper, Cooper said, "Let's let her sleep." The door creaked open as he ushered his sister into the hall.

Was that why he wanted to leave—so she could rest? Or because he didn't want her to hear whatever he was about to discuss with his sister? She tried to swing her legs over the bed, tried to sit up, but her legs were too heavy to move. And she couldn't lift her head from the pillow, let alone her torso, from the bed. The effort exhausted her completely so that she settled more heavily against the pillows. And sleep claimed her.

She had no idea how long she'd been out before the

door creaked open again. It couldn't have been that long, though, because she was still exhausted.

"That was fast…" she murmured sleepily. Nikki must not have had much to tell him. "I hope you didn't hurry on my account…"

He hadn't had to rush back to her bedside. It wasn't as if he were really her husband. Well, maybe he was really her husband—legally—but not emotionally. He wasn't in love with her. He hadn't actually wanted to marry her at all.

If not for Stephen…

"Did you find Stephen?" she asked.

Still he said nothing…

She fought to drag her eyes open again, but she only managed a little crack—just enough that she could peer between her lashes. And see the pillow coming toward her face.

She couldn't see who held the pillow—it blocked his or her face as it headed toward Tanya's. But she could see that the person wore scrubs. A member of the hospital staff? Or just someone posing as an employee?

Tanya lifted her arms to fend off the pillow. And she opened her mouth to scream. But she was still too weak—too weak to fight off her attacker—too weak to scream before the pillow covered her face and cut off her breath as effectively as the tear gas had.

She couldn't count on her new husband to save her again. She had to find the strength to save herself. Or die trying…

Chapter Ten

Wedding from hell.

Tanya had agreed with Nikki's assessment. Why? Because of the tear gas? Or because she hadn't married the groom she'd wanted—the one she loved?

"Has anyone found Stephen?" Cooper impatiently asked Nikki before they'd even walked far enough from Tanya's room so she wouldn't overhear them. Not that she would…

She was completely exhausted. He shuddered again as he remembered how close he had come to losing her.

Nikki shook her head.

"What about his computer?" he asked. "Did you find anything on it?"

Nikki's gaze dropped from his and she stared at the floor. She still wore her bridesmaid dress—that long bronze satin that made her look taller and older than he'd realized she was. Maybe it was the dress, but Cooper finally realized that his little sister had grown up. He'd been gone so long that he'd kept thinking of her as the child she'd been when he'd left. But she was a woman now.

Men in the hallway stared at her as they passed—until Cooper glared at them. Then they hurried along. Nikki didn't notice their interest though as she continued to ignore his question.

"What did you find?" he prodded her.

"She drunk emails like she drunk dials," Nikki spoke tentatively as if trying to purposely be vague. "I'm sure it didn't mean anything."

Because this was Nikki and not Logan or Parker, he held on to his patience and calmly asked, "What didn't mean anything—an email? You got into Stephen's email?"

Nikki bit her lip and nodded.

Not only had his little sister grown up but she'd acquired some serious skills, too. That computer had hit the asphalt hard the night before.

"What did you find?" he asked again. His patience had slipped away. He didn't want to leave Tanya alone for very long. But then, she wasn't alone as he had noticed someone in scrubs slip inside her room. Probably the nurse checking on her again...

Or the doctor...

He needed to check on her again himself—to make certain she was all right. Because he had that niggling feeling in the pit of his stomach as he had right before Parker had stepped into the line of fire at Stephen's condo complex.

"C'mon, Nikki!" he prodded her again—more forcefully.

"Rochelle sent Stephen some emails."

"Some?"

She nodded.

"I know she's your friend." Though he couldn't fathom why. "But you need to be straight with me."

"She was begging him not to marry Tanya."

He wasn't surprised. It was obvious that Rochelle was

against her sister's marrying Stephen even though she had showed up at the church for the wedding. Of course, Tanya hadn't married Stephen, though. She had married him. His heart slammed into his ribs as the truth fully sank in—he was married.

To Tanya…

But he wasn't the groom she'd wanted. That man was missing.

"She'd written more than that in those emails," he surmised.

Nikki grimaced and replied, "She said that if he left Tanya at the altar and married her instead, he would get all the inheritance instead of just half."

That niggling feeling intensified until Cooper grimaced from the force of it.

"Rochelle would probably be so embarrassed that I saw those," Nikki said. "And especially that I told you. She must have been drinking when she sent those emails…"

"Was she drunk or greedy?" Cooper asked. "Does she want the money all for herself?"

"I didn't think she wanted her grandfather's money at all," Nikki said. "She hated the old man so much."

"Maybe it's not the money she wants," Cooper said. "Maybe it's the man."

"So you think she's using the money to lure Stephen away from Tanya?" Nikki asked. Then, shaking her head, she added, "Never thought I would be happy I had brothers instead of sisters…"

"She's your friend," Cooper reminded her.

Nikki sighed. "I always felt sorry for her growing up in Tanya's shadow."

"What do you mean?"

"You don't know?" Nikki asked in astonishment. "And she's your wife."

"Only because Stephen disappeared." Or had he really?

"But you always had a crush on her," Nikki said. "All the guys did. She's beautiful and sweet and smart. It must have been hell having her for an older sister."

"So how much does Rochelle resent her?" he asked. "Enough to try to kill her?"

Nikki gasped. "Rochelle can be a brat sometimes, but she's not a killer."

"What about Stephen?"

"She would *never* hurt him," Nikki said. "Like you had the crush on Tanya, she's always had a crush on Stephen."

"She has the two greatest motives," Cooper pointed out. "Love and money."

Her lips curved into a teasing smile. "Well, I know which one motivated you…"

"Motivated me for what?" Did she think him responsible for Stephen's disappearance?

"To marry Tanya Chesterfield."

"I work for Payne Protection now," Cooper reminded her. "I only want to keep her safe." But that niggling sensation told him something was wrong. He turned back toward Tanya's room. Why hadn't the person in scrubs come back out?

"What's wrong?" Nikki asked.

But he was already heading back down the hall. As he approached the room, he heard a clang as something fell over and then that all-too-familiar sound of Tanya's scream. Fear for her safety overwhelmed him. "Call security!" he yelled at Nikki. He was reaching for the door when it banged open and that figure in scrubs came running out.

The person wore a surgical cap and face mask. Cooper would have reached for him, but the person also carried a gun, the barrel pointed at his chest. But he didn't fire. Instead, he kept running.

Nikki turned as if to follow, but Cooper caught her arm and tugged her inside the room with him. "Call security," he repeated. "Call Logan…"

Even as he barked those orders, his attention was on the woman in the bed. Or half out of the bed. The sheets had tangled around her, trapping her legs so that she hadn't been able to free herself.

She had been at the mercy of a madman while he'd been talking in the hall. He had failed to protect her. Again. Some husband he was proving to be; no wonder he had never intended to marry.

"Are you all right?" he asked.

Her face was flushed, but she was breathing—in pants and gasps.

"Call the doctor!" he yelled that order at his sister now.

Nikki, her eyes wide with shock and concern, hurried from the room to do his bidding.

Tanya clutched at his arms. "I—I fought him off."

"Yes, you did," he said, his chest swelling with pride that she had rallied her strength after having come so close to death just hours before. But then, she'd been fighting for her life, and he knew the fear of death could bring on a miraculous surge of strength.

"He—he tried to smother me…"

That explained the pillow on the floor. "He had a gun," he told her—no doubt the gun that had already fired so many shots at them.

She shuddered. "Why didn't he just shoot me?"

"Maybe he wanted it to look like you just stopped breathing again," he said. "And he didn't want anyone to hear the gunshot and catch him." He should have chased after him. But when Tanya screamed, he had to make certain she was all right. His heart hadn't stopped furiously pounding with his concern for her.

Tears glinted in her eyes. "Will he ever get caught?" she asked. "Will this ever be over?"

He silently cursed himself for not reaching for that mask. But with the gun pointed at his chest, he may have not lived to identify his killer. "Did you get a look at his face?"

The tears brimmed on her bottom lashes before spilling over onto her face. "No..."

Would she have let herself recognize her attacker if it was the person Cooper had begun to suspect? Would she be able to face the reality that someone she loved wanted her dead?

He wasn't sure he could accept it.

"That's fine," he assured her. "We'll catch him." Or die trying...

"I did something else, though," she said, and she lifted her hands from the sleeves of Cooper's tux to hold them up.

Blood smeared her fingers.

"You scratched him?" He hadn't seen any marks around the mask, but that had covered nearly all of the attacker's face.

She nodded. "I only got his arms..."

He whistled in appreciation of her strength and ingenuity. "You also got his DNA." And a definite conviction once Payne Protection tracked down the would-be killer. "That's my girl..."

THAT'S MY GIRL...

He had said that, but Cooper had yet to act as if Tanya was his girl. He wasn't even acting as if she was his wife, and they were on their honeymoon. They had spent the first night of that in the hospital. Cooper had stayed with her, but she didn't mistake his vigilance for love.

He wasn't acting like a husband; he was acting like a bodyguard. Instead of carrying her over the threshold of their hotel suite, he carried a gun and peered around him. "You'll be safe here," he assured her. "Nobody followed *us* from the hospital."

"What if they followed the others?" she asked.

"Then the plan worked."

The plan had consisted of Logan leaving the hospital with one of his female employees, who had worn a blond wig. And Parker had left with Nikki, who had also been wearing a blond wig. Since each of the men had worn the same ball cap, they had looked nearly identical except to her. Cooper was the most muscular and handsome. But someone else might have been fooled.

"Will they be safe?" She didn't want anyone else getting hurt because of her.

"They're all bodyguards," Cooper reminded her. "Since it's our job to protect others, we should certainly be able to protect ourselves."

He could. But, as a Marine, he had training that the others didn't have.

"You're not worried about them?" she asked.

A muscle twitched along his tightly clenched jaw. "It's not my job to worry about them."

But he clearly was.

"It's my job to worry about you," he said.

That was what she really was to him. Not his girl. Not his bride or wife. Not even his friend. She was just a job.

Maybe she wasn't as recovered from her asthma attack as she'd convinced the doctor, because she was suddenly so weary she dropped heavily onto the couch.

"You just told me I was safe here," she reminded him.

He had driven such a circuitous route to the hotel that *she* wasn't even certain where they were. But when they'd driven up, she had seen sunlight glinting off water and realized they were close to Lake Michigan. She would have stood up now and looked out the window to see if they had a lake view, but after what had happened last time, she didn't dare risk it.

"You're safe." He dropped onto the couch beside her and skimmed his knuckles across her cheek. "But I'm still worried about you. You've been through a lot the past couple of days."

She would have brought up that his mother might have been right about her wedding superstitions, but then she would have been bringing up the kiss that had happened when they'd been alone in a hotel room, like now.

"The doctor signed my release," she said. "I'm fine."

He studied her face as if he doubted the doctor's opinion. Did she look that bad? Nikki had brought her makeup, which Tanya had used to cover the dark circles beneath her eyes. But maybe she should have left the circles since they had been the only color in her very pale face.

Nikki had also brought the suitcase she'd packed for the honeymoon. But given that she and Stephen were only friends, her honeymoon clothes were more comfortable than sexy. She wore dark jeans with a green sweater.

Cooper also wore jeans, ones so faded and worn that

they clung to his muscular thighs, and a black sweater that clung to his muscular chest. He had ditched the cap and his black jacket before joining her on the couch.

"You're fine," he finally agreed. "Physically…"

She nodded, and his hand fell away from her face. But she could still feel his touch. Her skin tingled and her pulse raced with his closeness.

He continued, "But emotionally…"

Had he realized that she was falling for him? Was he about to give her the just-friends speech again?

"I am emotional," she admitted, embarrassed when she remembered how often she had cried in front of him just over the past couple of days. "But it's because I'm worried. About Stephen. About your family."

And, most especially, you…

But if she admitted that, he would know for certain that she'd fallen for him. And he would probably not only be appalled but offended that she didn't think him capable of protecting himself and her.

"And I'm worried about how naive you are," he said. "And how badly you're going to be disillusioned because of that…"

"Naive?" She laughed in amazement that she had been accused of that twice in as many days. "You think I'm naive? I'm a supervisor at the Department of Social Services for the second-biggest city in Michigan. I wouldn't have lasted a week on the job if I was naive or easily disillusioned." Her laughter turned into a heavy sigh. "In fact, I'm realistic enough to believe that somebody from one of those cases I've handled may be stalking me."

"It's gone beyond stalking," he bitterly reminded her.

She flinched. "Yes, Stephen was abducted."

"Someone's trying to kill *you*," he said. "And that person very nearly succeeded."

And he seemed more worried about her than Stephen.

"It could be someone who got angry over how I do my job," she said. She'd had to make some very unpopular decisions over the past several years.

He shook his head.

"You don't believe that." She studied his face now as intently as he had studied hers moments ago. "You've been acting strangely, like you have some idea who the culprit is. Do you?"

He just held her stare, his gaze locked on hers. Despite the brightness of the blue, there was also darkness in his eyes—as if the tragedy he'd witnessed was still there, haunting him. "I have my suspicions."

"Why won't you share them with me?" They were husband and wife—weren't they supposed to share everything? But they hadn't even shared a kiss yet to seal their union.

"I'm not sure you can handle it," he admitted as if she was some fragile female needing his protection.

While she did need his protection, she wasn't fragile. "I've been through a lot in the past couple of days." She smiled ruefully. "Certainly nothing like you've been through when you were deployed, but—"

He pressed a finger over her lips as if to block her from putting her foot any further into her mouth. But he was smiling ruefully, too. "You're tough," he said. "You've handled getting almost run down and shot at, smoked out and smothered…"

She shivered as he trailed off because she realized he considered this worse than all those things. Then she drew in a deep breath and asked, "Who?"

"You think this is about revenge for something you did or didn't do on your job."

Against her better judgment, she'd given him a list

of names. But she suspected he had not pursued any of those leads. "And you don't think so?"

He shook his head. "I think it's about the money."

"That's why I needed it to pay the ransom."

"What ransom?" he asked. "There's been no ransom demand."

Once she'd gotten her phone back from Logan, she'd kept it in her pocket. It hadn't rung. Her stomach churned. "That's not good for Stephen…"

"No, it's not," Cooper agreed.

"You think he's dead?" If he was, she might as well have murdered him herself—since she was the reason he'd died. "That's why they haven't called?"

He said nothing, just stared at her as if debating the wisdom of sharing his suspicions.

Pain clutched her heart. She needed to know if Stephen was dead. "Cooper?"

"I think they haven't called because Stephen can't make his own ransom call."

Maybe she wasn't as recovered as she'd thought, but she couldn't fathom what he was telling her. "What?"

"I think it's Stephen," he explained himself. "I think Stephen's trying to kill you."

The best friend she'd ever had? She laughed at the ludicrous thought of Stephen betraying her. Because if Cooper was right, Stephen didn't have to shoot or smother her. The betrayal alone would kill her.

Chapter Eleven

Did her laughter have an edge of hysteria to it? Had his admission struck her too hard?

Cooper studied her face for signs of distress. But he saw only the beauty of her flushed skin and sparkling green eyes. She had always distracted him. Maybe he wouldn't have had so much trouble in school if she hadn't been in so many of his classes.

"You don't believe Stephen could do this." Did she love him that much that she couldn't see him for the man he must have become?

"I would sooner believe *you* were trying to kill me."

He sucked in a breath, as stung as if she'd physically slapped him. "You could actually believe that I would try to kill you?"

"You've been gone a long time," she reminded him. "I don't know you anymore. I know Stephen. We've stayed friends all these years."

"Obviously you've been more than friends," Cooper said, trying to keep any bitterness from slipping into his voice. He had chosen to leave; what they'd done in his absence was none of his business. And it wouldn't have been even if he'd stayed.

But now Tanya was *his* wife. So she was his business.

Tanya's face flushed an even brighter shade of red. But all she said was, "Stephen has always been there for me."

"Until the wedding."

"That wasn't his fault."

"I'm not so sure about that," Cooper said.

Her brow furrowed with confusion. "How can you think that? You saw the blood. The signs of a struggle."

"If there was really a struggle, why didn't you or Mom hear it?"

She jumped up from the couch as if unable to sit still for his accusations. While she paced the small space in the living room of the suite, she kept her distance from the window. She obviously didn't feel safe.

And she wouldn't until they'd caught whoever was trying to kill her. But in order to do that they had to consider all the viable suspects.

"Your mom was in the basement," she reminded him, "talking to the minister. And I was in the bride's dressing room, way on the other side of the church. Someone must have hit him in the head while he was distracted and knocked him out in the groom's dressing room. That's why we didn't hear anything."

"We don't even know yet if the blood that was found is his," Cooper reminded her. DNA results didn't come back as quickly as they did on television shows.

"Now you're saying he hurt someone else?"

If Cooper was right, Stephen had hurt *her*—physically— a few times. And now emotionally...

"It might be his blood," Cooper amended. "But he could have drawn some earlier and sprayed it around the room."

She shuddered at the gruesome idea. "Why would he do that?"

"So you would think he was dead or hurt..." And

then she wouldn't marry, forfeiting her inheritance to her sister.

Obviously still in denial, she shook her head. "He wouldn't do that. It wouldn't even occur to Stephen to do something like that."

"He might not have been acting alone," Cooper pointed out.

She stopped in her tracks and stared at him. "Do you think he hired someone?"

"I don't think he had to hire someone."

"Someone was willing to help him?" She stared at Cooper for a few moments and sighed. "You already have someone in mind? Who?"

"Your sister."

"Rochelle?" She didn't laugh the way she had when he'd suggested Stephen might be behind the attempts on her life. But her brow furrowed again, this time in consideration, and she asked, "Do you think she hates me that much?"

He shrugged. "I don't know Rochelle. Like you said, I've been gone a long time. I feel as if I barely know Nikki—she was so young when I left."

"Nikki adores you," Tanya assured him. "Rochelle doesn't adore me. She can't stand me." Her voice heavy with resignation, she admitted, "She just might hate me enough to try to ruin my wedding. But Stephen would never work with her to hurt me."

Cooper had worried about telling her what he'd learned. He hadn't wanted to hurt her, too. So he hesitated.

But, of course, she noticed. She stared at him through narrowed eyes. "You found something that made you suspicious of them."

He shrugged. "Maybe I'm just suspicious of everyone."

She nodded. "Yes, you've changed. You're not the boy I used to know. You're cynical now."

He had reason to be. As a teenager who'd lost his dad, he'd had reason to be. "Everybody grows up and changes."

"I'm not so sure about Rochelle," she ruefully admitted. "But if you're trying to tell me that Stephen's changed…" She shook her head. "I know him too well."

"Did he tell you about all the emails Rochelle sent him?"

She tensed, as if his words had struck her.

"So he didn't tell you…"

She shrugged. "That doesn't mean he was hiding them," she defended Stephen. "Maybe he didn't want to cause any more trouble between me and Rochelle. I can't imagine those emails were telling him how lucky he was to be marrying me."

"No," he replied. "She didn't want him to marry you at all. She wanted him to marry her—for *all* the money."

She laughed. "And that's why you think they're working together?"

"All is more than half," he pointed out. "It's powerful motivation."

"Not for Stephen. He doesn't care about the money."

"Everybody cares about money—especially *that* amount of money." Given how wealthy her grandfather had been, her inheritance had to be millions—maybe even billions.

"Grandfather's lawyer told me that you care about the money, so much that you may have gotten Stephen out of the way so you could marry me yourself."

He flinched with a little twinge of guilt. He had been jealous of Stephen marrying her but not so petty that he would have wished harm come to him. He had considered Stephen his friend before he'd begun to consider him a suspect.

She laughed. "But I assured Mr. Gregory that you really didn't want to marry me at all—that's why I didn't let him bring that prenup to you."

"You should have let him," he said. "I would have signed it." And he really wished he had. He didn't want her doubting him. It wouldn't be easy to keep her safe if she didn't trust him.

"I was worried that you might be offended."

"That he thinks I want your money? Or that he thought I got rid of Stephen to get it?" Apparently, Arthur Gregory thought even less of Cooper than his employer had. He shrugged off the man's accusation; he didn't care what anyone—except Tanya—thought of him.

She laughed again but nervously this time. "He didn't think the money was your only reason."

"What other reason would I have?" Stephen had always been a good friend to him. He'd even tried to stay in touch after Cooper had gone away. But Cooper had been determined to put his past behind him and move on from his loss—of his dad and of Tanya. But by doing that he'd almost lost more—his family and his life.

"Me." She laughed again with self-deprecation. "He thinks you always had a crush on me."

If he wanted her to trust him, he had to be straight with her. "I did."

But if he was being completely honest, he shouldn't have used the past tense. Because he definitely still had a crush on her—one so big that he maybe should have even called it *love*.

GIDDINESS RUSHED OVER Tanya, so that her breath quickened and her pulse raced and her head grew light. Maybe she wasn't completely recovered from the asthma attack. Or maybe she was still that teenage girl who had been madly in love with Cooper Payne.

But that love had been crushed years ago—when Cooper had insisted they were just friends. "If he was right about that," she said, "was he right about my grandfather warning you to stay away from me?"

He sighed and nodded.

And hope flared that maybe he had shared all those feelings she'd had for him.

But then he spoke. "He was right, though. We had nothing in common then. You were going off to college and I was going off to the Marines. Maybe it was smarter to never get involved than to get involved and break up."

"Why would we have broken up?" she asked. She never would have broken up with him. She would have written him letters daily. She would have waited for him to come home to her. Maybe she had waited anyway—since she'd never fallen for another man the way she'd fallen for the boy he'd been.

"We had nothing in common then," he repeated. "And we have even less in common now."

"Are you sure about that?" she asked. "You want to protect people—as a Marine and now as a bodyguard. I want to protect people, too." That was why she'd wanted her inheritance—to help more families than the state's limited budget allowed her to help.

"As a social worker, you do protect them," he said. "I'm actually surprised your grandfather didn't talk you into pursuing a different career."

"He tried," she admitted. "But I wasn't as easy to manipulate as you must have been."

He scowled as if she'd insulted him. And then he laughed. "Your grandfather didn't manipulate me."

"He got his way," she said. "Just like he's getting his way now—getting me to marry for his money."

Cooper laughed again. "I was the last person he wanted you to marry, so he's definitely not getting his way."

"Mr. Gregory said that Grandfather would haunt him if he'd walked me down the aisle to you." She sighed. "I sometimes wonder if he's haunting me now, with all that's happened—the threats, Stephen's disappearance…"

His mouth curved into a small grin. "You think a ghost is responsible for all this?"

"I'd rather blame a ghost than myself."

"None of this is your fault," he assured her.

"You want me to believe its Stephen's."

"And maybe Rochelle's, working together."

She shuddered. "I don't want to believe it's either of them."

"What about me?" he asked. "Do you want to believe it's me?"

She shook her head. "No."

Yet goose bumps lifted on her skin. What if it was him? What if Mr. Gregory had been right? And she was alone with the man who'd gotten rid of Stephen?

"I see your fear," he said. "You may not want to believe it, but you're worried that your grandfather's lawyer could be right about me." He reached inside his jacket where he kept his gun holstered. But he pulled out his phone instead. "I'll call one of my brothers to take my place."

"Don't," she said.

But he'd already pressed a button on his cell—probably the two-way feature. Instead of a voice emanating from the speaker, gunshots rang out. And he cursed. "Logan! Logan, damn it! Are you all right?"

"Go to him," she urged. "Make sure he's safe!"

Cooper shook his head. "I can't."

"You can leave me," she said. "I'll be safe. Or do what Logan did and leave me a gun."

"I can't go to Logan." Cooper brushed his hand over the top of his head before clenching his fingers into a fist of frustration. "Because he didn't tell me where he was going. Neither did Parker."

She was shocked. "You didn't trust each other?"

"We didn't want anyone to be coerced into revealing the other's location."

Like any of his family would have given up any of the others. They weren't like her and her sister. Rochelle had tried to talk her groom out of marrying her. Out of spite or greed?

"Logan!" he shouted into the phone.

The shots reverberated and then tires squealed. And Logan finally replied with a string of curses. "The weasel got away again."

"Did you see him?"

"Not his face," Logan griped. "Had a hat pulled low, sunglasses and his collar pulled up."

"Could it have been Stephen?"

"Same height and build," Logan replied. "Could've been…"

And for the first time Tanya realized it was a possibility that Stephen had turned on her—that he'd decided he wanted all the money. She was dimly aware of the rest of Cooper's conversation.

"Are you all right?" he asked his brother.

"Yeah, but the hotel will be pissed over the windows of our suite getting shot up."

"Seems to be this guy's M.O."

"Coward," Logan cursed him. "The police are coming. They probably won't be surprised to see *me* again…"

"Good luck," Cooper murmured before clicking off. "I'll call Parker."

"Wait!" she implored him. "It doesn't make sense that Stephen would do this. He has money."

"People with money never seem to think they have enough," Cooper replied. "Your grandfather was certainly never satisfied."

Not just with the size of his bank accounts but with his family either.

"But Stephen…" She shuddered. "It makes no sense, especially now. We're already married. Why keep trying to kill me?"

"If you listened to your lawyer, I'm probably doing it so I can collect your inheritance myself."

"But Rochelle could challenge you," she said, "since our marriage hasn't been consummated." Heat flushed her face that she'd brought up that idea—and an image in her head of Cooper. Naked.

"What?" he asked, his eyes dilating as if he had conjured an image of his own.

"She doesn't even have to kill me to collect her inheritance," Tanya realized. "All she has to do is wait until tomorrow and challenge our marriage."

"What do you mean?"

"If we don't consummate our wedding before my birthday, she could challenge its validity." Knowing Rochelle, she probably would anyway—just to be spiteful.

Cooper nodded as realization dawned on him. "And then she and Stephen can marry and collect it all?"

She hesitated, unwilling to believe that her best friend could have agreed to betray her. Then she sighed in resignation and replied, "Yes."

"We can lie," he said. "We can say that we consummated our marriage. How is she going to prove we're lying? Aren't you a good liar?"

She had never been until that day she'd agreed with him that they could have only ever been friends. He was the only one who had ever believed her lie. "According to my sister, no."

Because Rochelle hadn't believed that Tanya was in love with Stephen. She'd realized that she'd only intended to marry him to collect her inheritance.

"I would lie to Rochelle," she said. "But I couldn't lie to a judge if my sister challenges us in court. For my job I've had to testify a lot, and if it was ever proven that I committed perjury…" All those other cases could be called into question. It wasn't a risk she was willing to take.

"Then what do you intend to do?" he asked. "If I'm right about Stephen, you don't need to inherit to pay his ransom."

"There has been no demand…" Her groom had not been kidnapped. He could still be hurt, though. Or he could be out there shooting out windows and running down people with cars and tossing tear-gas canisters.

"So you don't need the money," he said.

But she did need the money. For all those people she wanted to help and for an even better reason now. "Then if you're right, Rochelle and Stephen will get it all."

"Not if we can prove what they've done."

"Can we prove it?" she asked. "Are those emails enough to bring any charges against them?"

"No," he admitted. "We would need more evidence."

"Evidence that we might never find," she said. "I work cases where I know there's neglect or abuse, but so many times I haven't been able to prove it." Until it was too late…

She blinked against the sting of tears.

And Cooper squeezed her shoulder. "You really care about your job, about those people…"

Too much to let Rochelle collect money that could help them.

"I care," she said. "Do you?"

"I want to protect you, Tanya."

She drew in a deep breath to gather her courage. "Then make love to me. Consummate our marriage."

Chapter Twelve

Make love to me.

He couldn't have heard her correctly. He must have been daydreaming. And his heart was only pounding as wildly as it was because of the shots he'd heard being fired at his eldest brother. It wasn't because he was hoping like hell that he had heard her *correctly*.

Desire rushed up, choking him, so that he had to clear his throat before asking, "What did you say?"

Her face flushed a bright shade of pink. Clearly too embarrassed to speak, she just shook her head.

Nobody had ever accused him of being too sensitive. Maybe he would have to learn some sensitivity—now that he was a married man and all. But he wasn't a really married man unless...

"You heard me," she challenged him.

"I heard you," he admitted. "But I don't understand you." If she was so in love with Stephen...

"I thought I'd made it clear," she said.

He shook his head now—trying to clear the passion from it, so he could think clearly.

"If Rochelle challenges this marriage in court," she said, "I won't perjure myself."

He wanted her. But he wanted her to want him, too,

as more than a means to an end. "So you want to sleep with me to spite your sister?"

"To stop her from getting what she wants," Tanya replied. "The money."

"And what about Stephen?" What were Tanya's feelings for her missing fiancé? She had been so loyal in her defense of him. Where was that loyalty now?

"If you're right and they're on this together, she can have him!"

"*I* don't know what's right or wrong," Cooper admitted. "I was just saying it was a possibility that they could be in on it together."

"Because of the emails," she said with a nod.

She was as hurt as he had worried she would be if he shared his suspicions. But he'd had to be honest with her then. And now.

"But maybe they're not," he said. "We didn't find any reply to her email from Stephen. So maybe he has nothing to do with any of this." He actually hoped that was the case or he had lost a friend, too. But if Stephen wasn't in on it and had been seriously injured, Cooper may have already lost a friend. And then he'd married that friend's bride.

That made him the biggest betrayer.

Tears glistened in her eyes. "I don't know what I want to believe anymore. If he's working with Rochelle, at least he's alive. He's a snake," she cursed him, "but he's alive. If he's not working with her, where is he?"

"We're still looking for him," Cooper assured her. "Parker's in touch with all his old contacts from when he worked Vice." While Logan had quickly moved from patrol to detective, Parker had preferred working undercover. Or, if his reputation was to be believed, under *covers*.

Cooper would like to get under covers with his bride. But for the right reasons...

Like mutual desire. Need. Love...

"Vice?" she asked. "What would that have to do with Stephen?"

"Parker's informants are on the streets," he said. "They hear things. They see things." And hopefully one of their tips would lead them to Stephen. "And everyone on the Payne Protection payroll is working on finding him and whoever has been shooting at you."

"At you and your brothers, too," she reminded him. "I'm sorry—sorry for all the trouble I've been. I shouldn't have asked you to..."

"Make love to you?"

She flushed again. "I know it wouldn't have been making love. I know we're not really married."

"The minister pronounced us man and wife," he said. Had she been aware of that or had she already passed out?

"You made him do that before we left the church," she said, her head tilted as if she searched for the memories. "Everybody thought the building was on fire, but you made him finish the ceremony..."

"I recognized the kind of smoke," he said. "I didn't think we were really in danger. But then you stopped breathing..." He shuddered at his own memories of their ceremony and of holding her lifeless body in his arms.

"You saved me," she said. "Did I thank you for that?"

"I don't want your gratitude," he said.

He wanted *her*. Body, soul and heart. But no matter what the minister had pronounced them, she was not really his wife.

"I know you're just doing your job," she said. "But it's *my* life you keep saving..."

It was more than his job. She was more than his job.

And in saving her life, he was saving his own. Because without her...

"I can't ask you for anything else," she said, her face still flushed but downturned—as if she was unable to meet his gaze. "Forget what I said..."

It would be easier to forget his name than to forget what she'd suggested, what she'd asked him to do—with her.

Make love...

Tanya looked for a hole to crawl into, but despite her pacing, she hadn't worn one into the floor. So she glanced toward the door that led to the bedroom. But her face got even hotter with the embarrassment coursing through her. "I—I should probably..."

Unpack? She had so few things in her bag. Rest? She'd already slept more in the hospital than she had the past few months as she'd wrestled with the idea of marrying Stephen only for her money.

What wouldn't she do for that money?

She had asked Cooper to sleep with her. But had that been for the inheritance? Or was that just because she really, really wanted to sleep with her husband?

From the way her pulse raced and skin tingled, she suspected it was the latter, and she'd just used the money as an excuse.

"I—I just need to be alone for a little while," she admitted. Like maybe the rest of her life...

But when she headed toward that open bedroom door, he caught her wrist and stopped her in her tracks. "You can't leave yet."

"I'm just going into the other room..." The bedroom.

"You can't leave me yet," he said.

She turned back and chanced a glance at his face—his very handsome, very serious face. "It's not like I'm divorcing you," she teased, or attempted to, "I'm just leaving this room."

"You won't have to divorce me," he reminded her.

Because they hadn't consummated their marriage.

"The minister pronounced us man and wife," he continued, "but we never sealed it with a kiss."

"You want to kiss me?" she asked. But even as she turned up her face to ask the question, he was lowering his head. His lips brushed across hers in a nothing kiss—a mere whisper of breath and warmth.

Was that it? Was it over?

She wanted more. So she reached up, closed her hands around the nape of his neck and pulled his head down again. And she kissed him back.

The passion she'd had for him over a decade ago had been a young girl's passion. What she felt now was a woman's passion—hot and deep and overwhelming in its intensity.

She kissed him with all the heat burning inside her. First he was tense against her, but then he groaned. And his arms closed around her, pulling her up against him. Her breasts pushed against his chest.

And his tongue pushed against her lips before sliding between them, sliding over her tongue. Did he taste her desire? Did he know how much she wanted him?

She moaned as need overwhelmed her. But this was just a kiss…

The kiss that they should have had on their wedding day. But she had nearly died.

She had nearly lost this opportunity to kiss Cooper again. But she wanted so much more than his kiss…

So she moved her fingers from his nape down to his broad shoulders. Then she moved her hands lower, to press her palms against his chest. He tensed again, as if he expected her to push him back. But instead, she slid her hands over the impressive, rippling muscles of his chest. But his sweater separated her hands from his skin. So she reached for the waist of it and tugged it up, her knuckles skimming across the washboard muscles of his abs. He finished the job for her, first taking off his holster and gun and setting them onto the table next to the couch. Then he dragged the sweater over his head and dropped it onto the floor.

Damn. The man was hot. Figuratively and literally... so damn hot.

She burned up just from touching him.

Then he was touching her, too. His hands slid down her back to her waist. But he locked his hands around it and lifted her, swinging her up in his arms. He carried her into that room she'd wanted to go into—to be alone.

But when he dropped her onto the bed, she clung to him, unwilling to let him go. "Stay with me," she pleaded. She arched up and pressed a kiss to his lips, and another to his shoulder, and another to his chest, where his heart pounded furiously.

"Are you sure?" he asked.

In reply, she pulled off her sweater and shimmied out of her jeans. Maybe he'd already noticed when he'd gone through her apartment earlier that week that she had a thing for fancy underwear. She wore some now: a lacy red bra that barely contained her breasts and a matching thong.

He groaned again. "I hope to hell you're sure..."

"Very sure." And it wasn't about the money. Or the spite...

She wanted Cooper Payne because she had always wanted Cooper Payne. She opened her mouth to tell him, but he kissed her.

He kissed her passionately, his tongue sliding in and out of her mouth. And he touched her, sliding his hands over her stomach.

She sucked in a breath at the heat of his touch. And her skin tingled everywhere. She waited for his hands to move, to slide up, and finally they moved toward her breasts, tracing the underwire of her bra before undoing the delicate gold clasp between the cups. Her breath escaped in a gasp when he touched her breasts.

And her heart pounded madly.

She grabbed his arms to tug him onto the bed with her. But he pulled back.

She tensed, worried that he'd changed his mind, that he was about to say that he didn't want her. But he unsnapped his jeans and pushed them down and his underwear. And he proved he wanted her very much.

His erection jutted toward her. She reached for it. But he caught her hand and lifted it over her head. "Not yet," he said, "or this'll be over all too soon."

It must have been a while for him since he'd been deployed.

But instead of rushing, he took his time. He lifted both arms over her head, which had her breasts arching up as if begging for his touch.

He touched. First with his hands, caressing her skin. Then with his fingers, he teased her nipples.

Pressure built inside her, unbearable in its intensity. She squirmed on the bed, pushing her hips against his. That thin strip of lace separated her from his flesh. But it was already dampening with her desire for him.

Then he touched with his lips, skimming them over her skin before closing them around a nipple while he plucked at the other. She arched off the bed and moaned.

It had been a long time for her, too. She'd blamed her

lack of relationships on the threats. But now she knew…
she'd been disappointed with every man she'd ever dated
because he hadn't been Cooper.

She wasn't disappointed now.

He kissed her mouth while he moved his hand over her
stomach. He pushed aside that scrap of lace and teased
her with his fingers.

"Cooper…" She nearly sobbed his name as the pressure built to a new intensity. "Please…"

He kept kissing her, moving his mouth from her lips
to her breasts. He teased her before moving his mouth
even lower on her body. Finally he pulled off that thin
strip of lace and tossed it onto the floor with the rest of
their clothes.

She clutched at the sheets as he made love to her with
his lips and tongue. And she screamed as sensations raced
through her, releasing that intensity.

She was trembling. But she wasn't the only one, his
arms shook a little as he braced them on the bed and covered her body with his. She reached between them and
closed her hands around his erection. It was so smooth
but hard and pulsing as if it had a life of its own. She
parted her legs and guided him inside her, arching up
as he thrust.

He was big—so big—that he stretched and filled her.
But somehow they fit. Perfectly. She locked her arms and
legs around him and matched his rhythm. They moved
as one. The pressure building inside her she could feel
in the tension in his body, the tightness of his muscles.

Cords extended in his neck. A vein in his forehead.
And that muscle twitched along his jaw, as if his teeth
were gritted. Still, a groan slipped out.

He reached between them and pressed his thumb to
the most sensitive part of her. An orgasm shuddered

through her body with such force that she screamed. She screamed and sobbed his name.

He joined her, pulsing and pumping inside her. And another groan tore from his throat with such force it would probably leave his voice hoarse. He collapsed on top of her.

She welcomed his weight and heat. She'd felt so alone and cold for so long. But then he rolled off her, taking away his warmth. And his body filled with tension again.

Was he already regretting what they'd done?

She had no regrets—except that it was already over. She wanted to do it again. She reached out a hand and touched his shoulder. "Cooper—"

He turned and pressed a hand over her mouth. "Listen…"

And then she heard it, too. Footsteps in the hall outside the hotel room door. First they passed. Then they stopped and turned back. And stopped again. Through the open bedroom door, she could see that a shadow fell from beneath the door to the hotel hallway.

And the knob of that outside door rattled.

His hand had slid away so she could speak, but she only risked a whisper. "You said nobody knows where we are…"

"Nobody does."

Obviously someone did. And they had come for them. For her…

The knob rattled again and they watched as the tumbler turned and the lock—unlocked.

Tanya wanted to scream again, but it was caught in her throat on the fear that was overwhelming her.

Chapter Thirteen

His gun was in the other room and his pants were on the floor. Some bodyguard Cooper had proved to be. But he let none of that distract him as he had let Tanya distract him. He vaulted out of the bed and grabbed for his gun in the living room of the suite. He managed to unholster and aim the barrel at the door as it opened.

He could have waited for the suspect to step inside, but if the shooter started firing wildly again, he might hit Tanya. Cooper hadn't shut the door between the bedroom and living area. But he couldn't see her. She had scrambled out of bed, hopefully to put on some clothes.

He hadn't had time.

"Come any closer and I'll blow your head off!" he threatened.

A laugh rang out; it was loud and grating and obnoxiously familiar. "Don't shoot your favorite brother!" Parker poked his head around the door and then he laughed again, more loudly, as he spied Cooper's nakedness.

"Get out!" he yelled at him.

"Okay, okay, I'll be waiting outside." Parker stepped back out and pulled the door closed.

"You told me they didn't know where you are," Tanya

said, her voice full of accusation and embarrassment. She was fully dressed now, while he stood naked before her.

"I didn't think they did…"

Had one of them followed him? Didn't they trust him? Then, given how badly he had just lost his objectivity, they were right not to trust him.

Cursing beneath his breath, he hurriedly grabbed up his clothes and pulled them on. Even though he knew it was Parker who'd broken in, he strapped on his holster and weapon, too, before stepping outside the hotel room.

Parker leaned against the wall opposite the door. He was still chuckling. "And they say *I'm* the playboy…"

Forcing the words out between gritted teeth, Cooper said, "I am not a playboy."

"That's right," Parker said. "You're a married man now."

Officially married now that they had consummated it.

"And you're a damn fool," he retorted. He wasn't just teasing now.

"A damn fool that tracked you down," Parker taunted him.

Guilt overwhelmed Cooper. He had failed to protect Tanya in every way. "How?"

"I have my sources."

"Have they turned up Stephen yet?" That would explain Parker's reason for tracking him down.

He shook his head. "No."

"Then why are you here? Did you just get bored?"

He laughed again. "Yeah, I didn't get sent undercover with a girl."

"Nikki's a girl."

"She's my sister," he said with great disgust.

"You two didn't get shot at?"

"*We* didn't get followed," he said with a huge grin. Logan wasn't about to live this one down.

"Neither did I," Cooper said. "So why'd you track me down and blow our hiding place? And a better question yet, why on earth did you pick the lock and open the door?" He had very nearly shot him.

"I heard the screaming," Parker said.

Heat climbed from Cooper's neck into his face. *He* was never going to live this one down. "Maybe you're not the playboy everyone thinks you are if you've never heard that kind of scream before…"

Parker punched his shoulder. "I've never had any complaints."

"At least you've dated polite women…"

Parker laughed again. "You're funny. I've forgotten how funny you can be."

So had Cooper. He'd left his family because they'd reminded him of his father—and his loss and the tragedy and grief. He'd forgotten the teasing and laughter. The fun. He'd lost that when he'd left.

But if he didn't find out who kept shooting at all of them, he risked losing that again. "Why are you here?" he asked. "Is Logan really all right? He didn't get hit?"

"Of course not. If it had been at all close, Candace would have jumped in front and taken the bullet for him."

It was no secret to anyone but Logan that one of his employees was hopelessly in love with him. Cooper had had to be back only a few days to figure it out.

"If Logan's fine, why are you here?"

Parker groaned. "Mom."

"Logan's letting her interfere in his business again?"

"She's Mom," he said as if that explained it all, and it actually did. "He was only appeasing her by saying that if I could find you, he'd have me bring you back."

"Why?"

"Because he thinks if I could find you, someone else could, too. However, he is completely underestimating my skills." But instead of being resentful like Nikki, Parker simply shrugged—unconcerned.

Logan wasn't the only one guilty of underestimating Parker; Cooper had, too. "He may be right…" Had he been gone so long that he didn't know the city as well as he once had? "How did you find me?"

"Figured you'd pick a nice place—it being your honeymoon and all." He smirked.

"And you have contacts here?"

"Higher-class contacts, but yeah."

"Where are we supposed to go now that you've blown this spot?"

"Back to the church."

"Like that place is safe…"

"Mom thinks it is—not because of the place but because we'll all be together. She thinks we're stronger that way than split up."

Given that Logan had just been shot at, Cooper couldn't argue her logic. If they had been together, someone would have been able to chase down the shooter while the one getting shot at took cover. "We can all be together, but we don't have to be at the church."

"Since the little tear-gas bomb changed her plans for yesterday, she wants to have your reception today," Parker explained.

"It's a little late for that."

"It's not too late for Tanya's birthday party."

"That's tomorrow," Cooper reminded them. She'd had to be married by that time in order to collect her inheritance. But not only did she have to be married, she'd had to consummate that marriage. Cooper had to remind himself that was the only reason they'd made love—for money.

Love had had nothing to do with it—at least not on her side.

"Mom doesn't think the food will last another day."

And given that Logan had just been shot at again, maybe he and Tanya wouldn't either.

SMOKE ROSE FROM the tiny flickering flames. Tanya closed her eyes to block out the fire. Then she expelled the breath she held and hoped that she'd blown them all out. All thirty of them. There had been enough room for all of the candles since it was her wedding cake Mrs. Payne had put out for her wedding reception/birthday party.

"Did you make a wish, dear?" the older woman asked.

Tanya opened her eyes and her gaze fell upon her husband. And she wished it was real.

Sure, they had consummated their marriage. But they hadn't made love. At least he hadn't.

She was in love. But she was in that alone.

She wasn't alone now. All of the Payne family and some of their employees had gathered in the high-ceilinged lower level of the Little White Wedding Chapel. It was a beautiful room with brocade wallpaper that looked like lace on the walls, and the coffered ceiling had built-in lights. Lights twinkled everywhere, making the space look like Wonderland. Even the floor had a sparkle to it—as if it had been sprinkled with fairy dust.

And she thought again, as she had when Mrs. Payne had produced that dress, that the older woman could be a fairy godmother. But Tanya was no Cinderella; she was unlikely to wind up with the prince.

"I wished that your dress is really okay," she replied.

Mrs. Payne shook her head in disappointment. "You're not supposed to tell what you wished for."

"Or it won't come true…"

"In this case, it's already true," Mrs. Payne said. "The dress is fine."

"They didn't cut it off?"

Mrs. Payne shook her head. "The paramedic was female. She understood the importance of your wedding dress."

"*Your* wedding dress." Tanya had only borrowed it because someone had maliciously destroyed hers. She glanced around the room until she located Rochelle. Why had she come to the party? To try to kill her again?

With all the Paynes and their associates in the room, she would be a fool to try anything here. But then, she'd been a fool to try anything at all. Had Tanya ever really known her younger sister?

Not like the Paynes knew each other.

She had overheard Cooper's conversation with Parker—their male ribbing. And she had worried that she would never be able to face the older Payne brother after what he had overheard. But when she'd stepped into the hall, he had acted as charming and friendly as he always had.

It was Cooper who acted differently. Or maybe it was that he acted the same, too, and she wanted him to be different with her. He still acted as if they were only old acquaintances. He didn't even act as if he was her friend, let alone her husband.

Her lover.

Disappointment tugged at the smile she'd pasted on when she'd stepped inside the reception hall.

"Now it's time to cut the cake," Mrs. Payne announced. "Cooper, get over here."

He'd had his head bent close to his brothers', as they huddled together in one corner of the room. They were all such beautiful men with that black hair and those eyes so bright a blue they glittered, like all those twinkling lights, even from across the room. Cooper's gaze met hers as he lifted his head.

And her heart clutched inside her chest, stealing her breath for a moment.

"No," she protested her unreciprocated feelings and Mrs. Payne's suggestion. "You can cut the cake. It's not like this is a real reception."

"Maybe it's more real than you're willing to admit," Mrs. Payne said with a little smile and a twinkle in her brown eyes.

Had Parker told her what he'd overheard?

Or had Tanya given herself away with how she couldn't stop looking at Cooper? But she didn't see him as he was now, dressed in his sweater and jeans; she saw him as he'd been in bed with her, gloriously naked and aroused. Wanting *her*...

Or after his last deployment, would any woman have done?

Mrs. Payne squeezed her shoulder. "It will all work out, honey."

How could she believe that—after how tragically she had lost her husband? She had to know that not all endings were happy.

Sometimes things just ended. Like her marriage to Cooper was destined to end—in divorce now since they would not be able to get an annulment after what they'd done that afternoon.

"What will all work out?" Cooper asked as he joined them, his blue eyes narrowed with suspicion.

Did he suspect, as she had come to suspect, that his mother was playing matchmaker for the two of them?

Mrs. Payne smiled and patted his cheek. "Don't worry so much, sweetheart."

"Easier said than done with a shooter on the loose…" He glanced in her sister's direction, too.

Tanya had never seen Rochelle with a gun. She doubted she would be able to fire one at all, let alone with any accuracy. And the night of the rehearsal, she'd been so drunk that Nikki had driven her home and stayed to make sure she was all right. She wouldn't have been able to try to run down Tanya with the car or to shoot out the window of her apartment. So, if she was behind the attempts, she was working with someone else.

Stephen?

The pain of betrayal struck her with a jolt. She didn't want to believe he would hurt her or anyone else. But who else could it be?

Someone from her job wouldn't have known about her inheritance. She had been very careful that no one had learned she was Benedict Bradford's granddaughter. So they would have had no reason to try to stop her wedding.

"You and your brothers will find out who's done all these horrible things," Mrs. Payne said to Cooper. "It's such a shame that the wedding was ruined. You should be in your tux and gown right now."

"But we're not, Mom," he pointed out. "So there's no reason to cut the cake or whatever other nonsense you have planned."

She gasped and pressed a hand to her heart as if her son had driven the knife she held into it. "Weddings are not nonsense. They are tradition. They are the foundation that needs to be laid for a long and happy marriage."

"Mom, you know I'm not the man Tanya was supposed to marry." And just as she'd said, he added, "This isn't real."

His mother, probably wisely, didn't share her cryptic comment with her son. Instead, she handed him the knife. "But it needs to look real." She glanced toward Rochelle, too, who had been joined by the lawyer. "People need to believe this is real…"

Would that bring Stephen back safely? Or was he the threat?

Once Cooper's hand closed around the handle of the knife, Mrs. Payne lifted Tanya's hand and placed it over his. And she squeezed, as if offering her blessing.

Her blessing wasn't what Tanya needed. It was Cooper's love. But his hand tensed beneath hers, as if he couldn't bear her touch.

Now.

He hadn't protested when she'd touched him back at the hotel. Or actually, he had protested—because he hadn't wanted her to rush their lovemaking. He had taken his time with her—kissing and caressing every inch of her.

Her skin flushed and tingled as she remembered how thoroughly he'd made love to her. He gazed down at her, and that glint in his eyes ignited to a hot spark, as if he was sharing those memories with her.

Her lips parted, and her breath escaped in a soft gasp. She wanted him to lean down and press his mouth to hers. She wanted his kiss.

She wanted him.

His hand tensed beneath hers, as if he felt the heat of her desire. Then he pushed the knife through the bottom layer of cake.

Desire heated her skin and blood, sending it racing fast and heavy through her veins. Would she ever not want him? Even here, in front of his family and what was left of hers, she couldn't control her passion for him.

He turned the blade of the knife to lift the cake. It was red velvet with cream-cheese frosting. She couldn't wait for a taste. With his fingers he broke off a smaller piece of the slice they'd cut together and held it to her lips. She opened her mouth and took a bite—carefully—so that her tongue managed to flick across his fingers. She preferred his taste to the cake's.

His pupils dilated and his nostrils flared as he dragged in a deep breath. "Tanya…"

She licked her lips slowly, sensually.

And Cooper groaned.

But then she realized what she tasted wasn't his fingers. Or red velvet cake and cream-cheese frosting. It was peanuts. Or peanut oil.

Didn't matter which one. Either one was dangerous enough to kill her. She didn't carry just an inhaler. She carried an EpiPen, too. But it hadn't been in her purse when Nikki brought it to her.

Now she knew why. Whoever was after her had not wanted her to have access to it after she was poisoned with peanuts. Her tongue felt thick and dry. And her throat was beginning to swell. She lifted her hands to her neck and gasped for breath.

Cooper had brought her back to life once. But she couldn't count on him doing it again. She couldn't count on anything. That was why she was glad they'd made love. Now she wished she'd told him that she loved him.

But she couldn't form the words with her thick tongue and she didn't have the breath to utter them anyway. Her vision darkened as unconsciousness—or maybe it was death—threatened.

Chapter Fourteen

Cooper's skin tingled from the swipe of Tanya's hot tongue. His heart pounded in his chest and his body was tense with desire. Then he heard her gasp—faint, as it was. A few moments ago her face had been flushed, her eyes twinkling as she'd teased him.

Now her face was deathly pale and her eyes were rolling back in her head. He reached out, catching her just as she crumpled, her legs giving way beneath her slight weight. Cursing, he swung her up in his arms.

"Mom! Did you put peanuts in the cake?" He remembered other kids hating Tanya because they hadn't been able to have peanut snacks or PB and J sandwiches in school—because of her allergy.

She had been resented and ostracized for her childhood allergy. Just like the asthma, she must not have outgrown it.

"Of course I wouldn't use peanuts," she replied as she rushed over to them. "I know she's allergic."

Her sister and Stephen would know that, too. He peered around the room, searching for Rochelle. She stood next to Nikki, who had been assigned to keep an eye on her. Of course, Logan had backup for their baby sister. He wouldn't have trusted her alone.

"She got peanuts somehow."

His mother swiped a finger over the knife and tasted. "Someone must have put peanut oil in the frosting."

"Do you have an EpiPen?" he asked hopefully. "Did she give you a spare one of those?"

She shook her head. "No, I didn't think she'd need it. I made sure that nothing had peanuts or peanut oil in it."

Someone else had made sure that something had peanut oil in it. Tanya's throat was probably completely closed. He felt the breath leaving her body as it had just a couple of days ago. "Call 911."

"Use this," a female voice said, and Rochelle held out a pen.

Cooper stared at it, trying to determine if this was another trick of hers. A way to finish off her sister right in front of all of them.

"Why do you have it?" he asked, wondering if she'd taken it from Tanya's purse along with the inhaler.

"I have the same allergy," she explained. "I can't have peanuts."

Mrs. Payne grasped her shoulders. "I'm so glad you haven't had a piece of cake."

Yeah, that was convenient. And so was Rochelle offering a pen for the sister she despised. He didn't trust anyone easily, but Rochelle's attitude and actions had given him plenty of reasons to mistrust her.

"Take it!" she yelled at him. "She can't breathe."

"Isn't that what you want?" he asked. "Your sister out of your way?"

She gasped. "I don't want her dead!" She pushed the pen into his hand. "Do you?"

That was the last thing he wanted. If they'd waited for the ambulance for the asthma attack, Tanya would have died. He couldn't wait now either. So he laid her on the floor. And he injected the pen, right through her jeans, into the outside of her thigh. Years ago she had told him how to do it—in case she needed help. And he had never forgotten.

Just as he'd never forgotten anything concerning Tanya Chesterfield.

She gasped again but then she dragged in a deep breath. Her eyes opened and she stared up at all of them. "I'm okay," she assured them.

Sirens blared as first responders pulled up outside the church.

"I don't need to go to the hospital."

"You're going," he insisted as he lifted her again to carry her upstairs to the ambulance. He wasn't entirely convinced that the medication Rochelle offered wouldn't have some horrible side effect. He had to make sure that Tanya would really be okay.

Because he didn't know what he would do if he lost his wife...

"You're lucky you're not really married to me," Tanya told Cooper, whose long, muscular body was awkwardly sprawled in a chair beside her bed. "You've already spent enough time in the hospital with me."

"Too much," he readily agreed.

She blinked against the sting of tears. "I'm sorry. Usually my allergy and my asthma aren't issues..."

"But someone's using your illnesses to try to kill you," he said. "Someone who knows you well."

"It can't be someone from one of my cases, then," she said. She'd really wished it was—some bad person holding a grudge against her would be so much easier to accept.

Cooper sighed. "It actually could be. Or at least that's what Nikki is trying to convince me."

Because Nikki and Rochelle were friends. It was probably harder for Nikki to doubt her friend than it was for Tanya to doubt her sister. Tanya had found it harder to doubt Stephen.

"Nikki informs me that stalkers are very thorough." He leaned back in his chair and reached out an arm to open the door.

"Nik," he called to the auburn-haired woman who then came into the room. She must have been waiting in the hall. And she hadn't been alone. Rochelle walked inside with her. But she hesitated near the door, as if uncertain of her welcome.

Since Cooper was glaring at her, she had reason to feel unwelcome. But at least this time she had come to check on Tanya.

Last time, she hadn't seemed to care that her sister had nearly died. That was why Tanya had found it so easy to doubt her...because she had never understood her.

"You're really all right?" Nikki anxiously asked.

Tanya nodded. "I'm more embarrassed that this keeps happening." It made her feel like a child again—that demons she hadn't fought since childhood had come back to haunt her and had nearly made her a ghost, as well.

"It's not your fault," Nikki said. "Someone's after you. I told Cooper that it could be the stalker."

"That's why I called you in here," he said. "To explain your theory to Tanya." He stood up. "I need to check in with Parker and Logan." He stared at his sister. "You got this?"

Nikki apparently knew he was talking about more than the theory. He was talking about keeping Tanya safe from Rochelle. She nodded her assurance.

He stepped into the hall without even a glance back

at Tanya. Was he sick of her? Sick of all the drama she'd brought to his life?

"I don't understand how someone could know so much about me," she said. Unless that person had been close to her, had grown up with her.

"Stalkers are relentless," Nikki said. "I've studied them in my psych and criminology classes. A stalker will usually go through their obsession's trash. Some savvy ones hack into their obsession's email."

She shuddered at the thought of someone invading her privacy—reading her private correspondence, seeing what she ate, drank and used and then discarded.

"You'd rather think it's me than a stalker?" Rochelle finally spoke—with her usual hostility.

"Of course not," Tanya said, but she felt a twinge of guilt. "Giving Cooper that EpiPen, you saved me."

"I had to force that pen on Cooper," Rochelle said. "He thinks I want you dead."

Tanya was sick of not knowing who wanted her dead. So she asked, "Don't you?"

Rochelle cursed and shook her head. "You really hate me."

"No," Tanya said. "You're the one who hates me. And I don't know why. What did I do?"

"It's more like what you didn't do," Rochelle replied.

"I don't understand."

"No. And you never bothered to try. You were just like Mom," Rochelle accused her.

"What do you mean?"

"She was obsessed with Dad no matter how big a louse he was. And you were obsessed with a boy."

"What are you talking about?"

"Cooper Payne. You were obsessed with him then. You're obsessed with him now. I saw how you were looking at him back at the *party.* You wanted to eat him instead of the cake."

She couldn't deny that, and heat rushed to her face with embarrassment.

"She would have been safer if she had," Nikki remarked. "Jeez, Rochelle, someone's trying to kill her. Someone's trying to kill your sister. Can't you get over her not paying enough attention to you when you were young?"

"You were so much younger," Tanya reminded her.

Rochelle crossed her arms over her chest and stubbornly held on to her resentment. "Not that much."

"Six years."

"It is a lot," Nikki said. "My brothers still treat me like a little kid."

"I'm sorry," Tanya said. "I should have made more time for you." She should have made her sister feel important since their mother never had; Andrea Chesterfield was nothing like Penny Payne, who had always put her children first, even over her own grief.

Rochelle shook her head and blinked hard as if fighting back tears. "It's just not fair, you know..."

"What's not?"

"You're so beautiful." Rochelle said it with such bitterness it sounded more like a condemnation than a compliment. "You get all the guys."

She only wanted one. "That's not true."

"You had Stephen." Her breath caught as if she was about the cry. "And now you have Cooper. He's the one you really want. What did you do to Stephen to get him out of your way?"

Tanya gasped in shock now. "You think I would hurt Stephen?"

"Absolutely," Rochelle said, "because you've never felt

about him like you do about Cooper Payne. You probably agreed to marry him to get the money because your birthday was coming up and Cooper wasn't back. But then when he got back, Stephen conveniently—*for you*—went missing."

Her sister was in love with Stephen. It was so obvious to her now—because of how she loved Cooper.

"Are you drunk?" Nikki asked her friend.

"No!" Rochelle snapped at her.

"Were you drunk when you sent Stephen that email?" Tanya asked.

Embarrassment flooded Rochelle's face, turning her skin a bright pink. "Which email?"

She had obviously sent him more than one.

Nikki grimaced. She must not have told her friend that her brothers or probably she, since she was the computer expert, had found those emails. And Tanya probably wasn't supposed to share that information. But she didn't care. She wanted answers.

"I'm talking about the email where you beg him to dump me and marry you and you'll give him all your inheritance," she replied.

Tears shimmered in Rochelle's eyes. "It didn't work. You took Stephen for granted all these years, but he stayed loyal to you. He stayed true to you." She blinked back the tears, and anger hardened her gaze. "Too bad you can't stay the same."

"Wh-what do you mean?" Tanya stammered as embarrassment rushed over her now, her face heating with it.

"It's obvious you're sleeping with Cooper," Rochelle replied.

And Nikki gasped. She knew the marriage was only supposed to be one of convenience.

But Tanya's feelings for her reluctant stand-in groom were anything but convenient.

"So I can't give Stephen all the money anymore," Rochelle continued. "You've consummated your marriage before your birthday, so you'll be able to claim your half of Grandfather's money now. Hell, you'll probably wind up with all of it."

Because Stephen was the man Rochelle had wanted to marry, and he was gone.

"You really don't know where he is?" she asked.

"Cooper just stepped into the hall," Rochelle replied. "Can't you stand being away from him for more than a couple of minutes?"

Truthfully, she couldn't. She missed him already. She'd gotten so used to him sticking close to her. But that was because he was her bodyguard—not because he was her loving husband.

"I'm talking about Stephen," she clarified. "Where is he?"

"Why do you think I would know?"

Tanya opened her mouth to reply, but Nikki interrupted, "You've obviously been in contact with him."

"Not since he disappeared," Rochelle said. "I sent him those emails before that."

"That last one was the night he disappeared," Nikki pointed out.

"*You* were the one who found the emails!" Rochelle realized. "And instead of coming to me with them, you went to *her?* I thought you were *my* friend."

Nikki sighed. "Of course I am. I told my brothers."

"*Why?*"

"Because I'm working a case," Nikki unapologetically explained. "Someone's been trying to kill your sister."

"And you all think it's me?" Rochelle looked ready

to burst into tears. But instead she burst out of the room and nearly ran down Cooper in the process.

"You missed all the fun," Nikki accused him.

"What happened?"

"What usually happens when I try to talk to my sister," Tanya replied. "She winds up hating me more." But did she hate her enough to try to kill her?

"You're so lucky you have a fabulous sister like me," Nikki said as she slid her arm around her brother's waist.

Cooper leaned down and kissed her forehead. "I am very lucky."

Tanya envied their relationship. Even though Cooper had been gone for years, he had remained close to his family. Maybe she and Rochelle needed more distance. As offended as Rochelle was, Tanya doubted she would be seeing her again anytime soon.

Tanya found it hard to believe Rochelle had anything to do with the attempts on her life. "I gave Rochelle a reason to hate me this time," she admitted, "when I accused her of trying to kill me."

"You accused her?"

"Not in so many words," Nikki said. "But she picked up on the suspicion—your suspicion."

He nodded. "I am suspicious of her."

"I'm not," Tanya said. "Not anymore anyways. She was too hurt." She had hurt her sister for no reason.

"Sometimes the best defense is a strong offense," Cooper said.

Nikki elbowed him. "You're always so suspicious."

"You need to be, too, if you're going to watch Tanya for me while I check something out."

Pride stinging, Tanya replied, "I am about to turn thirty years old. I don't need a babysitter."

"No," Cooper agreed. "You need a bodyguard."

Tanya wished she could claim that she could defend herself, but if he gave her another gun, she would probably shoot off her own foot.

"You're letting me work as a bodyguard?" Nikki asked, her eyes wide with surprise and hope.

Cooper glanced away from his sister. "I would, kid. I would. But Logan insists that Candace—"

"That jerk," Nikki cursed her oldest brother. "Is he in the hall?"

Cooper nodded slowly—almost reluctantly.

Nikki pushed past him to run out of the room.

"Lot of people running out of here today," he remarked with a wry grin.

"Yes," Tanya agreed with a pointed stare.

"Hey, I need to check this out," he said.

"The doctor's releasing me. I just have to wait for his final orders," she reminded him. "Then I can go with you."

"Absolutely not," he said.

"I'm sure your brothers can handle it." And some sick feeling in the pit of her stomach had her wishing that he would let them because she was afraid that something was going to happen to him. "*You* don't have to go."

"Parker and Logan will be there, too," he assured her, "but *I* still need to go."

"Where?" she asked as her own suspicions overwhelmed her. "What are you so determined to check out?"

"Parker got a lead from one of his informants."

"To Stephen's whereabouts?"

He nodded.

"Are you sure it's a real lead?"

"Not yet."

"But what if it's not?" she asked as that sick feeling grew in intensity. "What if it's a trap?"

"That's why you can't go along. I want you safe."

"I want you safe, too," she said. She just wanted him...

He must have seen the longing in her face because he stepped closer to the bed. "I told you before—this is what I do, what I've been doing, what I'm always going to do."

Maybe it was good that their marriage wasn't real then because she wasn't certain she could handle worrying about him every day when he left for work. But her job wasn't exactly safe either. As Nikki had pointed out, the person after her could have been someone who'd felt she'd wronged them as their caseworker.

"I know," she said. "But I'm worried..."

He leaned down and maybe he'd intended to kiss her forehead, but she lifted her face so that his mouth met hers. And she kissed him with all the need burning inside her.

He pulled back, panting for breath, his pupils dilated with passion. "Tanya..."

That sick feeling persisted, warning her that something horrible could happen to him. Like maybe this time the shooter wouldn't miss.

"Please don't go..."

He kissed her again, just a quick brushing of his lips across hers. She tried to cling, but he pulled back and assured her, "I'll be fine."

She watched him walk away, worrying that this might be the last time. That she might lose him again. Forever...

COOPER USUALLY LISTENED to his gut, but he didn't let the warning twisting his stomach into knots stop him from moving toward the warehouse. It was probably just

Tanya's nerves that he'd picked up on. Or it was his nerves over leaving her alone.

Sure, she wasn't exactly alone. She had Nikki protecting her and Candace protecting both of them. Nikki was green. But Candace had already saved Logan earlier that day; she was an experienced, expert bodyguard.

Tanya was safe. He wasn't so sure about him and his brothers. All the lights were burned out in the parking lot of the warehouse. The building had been abandoned a long time. The metal siding was more rust than whatever color it might have been at one time. And boards covered the windows.

If Stephen had been brought here, Cooper hoped he hadn't been hurt. The place sure as hell didn't look very sanitary or safe.

"You see anything?" the whisper emanated from his cell phone.

Parker was covering the front of the building while Cooper sneaked around a side to the loading docks in the back. With only the flashlight attached to the barrel of his gun to guide him, Cooper found steps leading up to the docks. Like the building, the metal stairs were rusted and protested his weight with creaks and screeches as he climbed them.

"Nothing yet," he whispered back. He shone his light below the docks and noticed that a ramp had been pushed up to the garage door on the end. He headed across the concrete, which seemed to crumble beneath his feet, to that last door.

"Nothing over here," Logan reported from the other side of the building. "Not even a door..." The phone rustled and the other man cursed. He'd gotten to the side of the building that had been overgrown with weeds and thorny shrubs.

Cooper had passed a few doors, rusted ones with equally rusted locks holding them down. Except for the last one. A smashed lock lay on the ground below, next to the rusted ramp, and the door was so rusted that although it had gone up, it hadn't gone all the way back down.

"I found a way in," he reported.

"Wait for us," Logan advised.

But Cooper had already shone his light beneath the door. It glinted off something shiny and black. He crouched down to crawl beneath the door. The rusted metal caught at the back of his jacket, holding him up until he tugged free with a rip of leather.

"What was that?" Parker asked. He'd heard the tear of fabric.

"Nothing." But he'd found more than nothing. He had found a familiar black vehicle. The back tires were both flat. It was *the* black vehicle—the one that had nearly run down Tanya. "But the car…"

"The car?" Logan asked. "I'm on my way around the side. Stay put."

But Cooper focused on the trunk. What if…

What if Stephen had really been abducted?

He glanced around the warehouse, the beam of his flashlight bouncing off old crates, before turning his attention back to the trunk. He grabbed a small tool kit from his pocket and slid a pick into the lock. A couple twists and pulls and the lock clicked. The lid popped up.

He drew in a deep breath before lifting the lid the rest of the way. The trunk was empty. No body. But when he flashed his light inside, the beam illuminated a dark stain. He reached inside the trunk and touched the carpet. The stain was sticky yet…

He lifted his hand and shone the beam onto his skin. The smear was dark red: blood.

Stephen's? Had Cooper been wrong to doubt him? Was he alive? Or had his body been dumped?

He shuddered with regret.

With a rumble that shook the entire warehouse, an engine started. It wasn't the car's, but the car began to move. Cooper slammed down the trunk lid and squinted as bright lights from a forklift blinded him. It was pushing against the front bumper and lifting the car up—driving it into him. He stumbled back as he lifted his gun and fired at the forklift.

But then there was nothing beneath his feet as the edge of the concrete dock crumbled and gave way. He dropped to the ground below and hit the asphalt with such force that all the breath left his body.

But the forklift kept çoming, pushing the car ahead of it. He stared up at the undercarriage of the big black sedan as it fell—on top of him.

Chapter Fifteen

Fear clutched Tanya's heart so fiercely that she was physically in pain. She gasped from the force of it.

"Are you all right?" Nikki asked.

She shook her head. "Not until we know if they're okay."

Candace paced across the kitchen of the safe house where she and Nikki had brought Tanya. This particular safe *house* was Candace's own apartment. And it wasn't in the safest area of town, but then she doubted anyone would dare mess with the female bodyguard.

She must have worn a wig to pass herself off as Tanya because her hair was short and brown. And she was taller and more muscular.

Nobody would mess with Candace. Tanya felt safe with her; it was Cooper she was worried about. "Have you heard anything?" she asked the woman.

Candace shook her head as she lowered the cell phone. "Logan's not picking up." Her facial muscles were tense with concern. "He always picks up..."

Nikki's head jerked in a sharp nod. "He always does..."

"Even when he's being shot at," Tanya remembered Cooper's call to his oldest brother.

"I should have gone with him," Candace said.

Nikki patted the bodyguard's shoulder. "I'm sure he's fine. I'm sure they're all fine."

Candace gripped the cell phone tightly, as if she were somehow reaching out to Logan through it.

Tanya didn't even know Cooper's cell-phone number, and he was her husband.

Was?

Had she already lost him as that gut-wrenching premonition had warned her?

"Logan shouldn't have gone out right now," Candace said. "He shouldn't have risked it..."

Tanya was confused. "Cooper's the one the shooter is after. He just mistook Logan for Cooper." Which was a mistake that Stephen wouldn't have made; he knew the Payne family as well as she did.

"I'm not so sure about that," Candace admitted.

Of course. Logan might have made enemies of his own—while he was a detective with River City Police Department or even through Payne Protection.

"What are you saying?" Nikki asked, her usually smooth brow furrowed with concern.

"He didn't tell you?" Candace asked with a flash of surprise.

"Tell me what?" Nikki asked. "Has *he* been getting threats?"

"Just the usual ones."

Nikki sighed.

And Tanya grasped that apparently she wasn't the only one with a stalker. "What ones?"

"From the daughter of the man who shot his father," Candace explained. "She's furious that Logan keeps showing up to every parole hearing."

Tanya nodded in understanding. "Cooper told me that Logan is determined to keep Mr. Payne's killer in prison."

"He succeeded," Candace shared. "The man died a couple of days ago."

Nikki cursed.

"He didn't tell you," Candace answered her own question. Her lips curved into a slight smile as if she was pleased that her boss had confided in her.

Tanya wondered if he'd told Cooper, because if he had, her husband hadn't shared that news with her. Of course, he'd been a little preoccupied trying to keep her alive—and making love with her.

Nikki grabbed her own cell phone and punched the screen. "Damn it! Answer!"

"I just tried Logan," Candace reminded her.

"I'm trying Parker."

"He's not picking up either?"

Nikki punched her screen again and then cursed again. "Neither is Cooper."

Tanya's knees weakened as fear overwhelmed her.

Candace blinked quickly as if fighting tears. She obviously felt more than employee devotion for her boss; she was in love with him. And Nikki was so scared her eyes were wide and dark in her pale face.

Tanya wanted to offer them comfort. But she needed comfort herself. She needed Cooper, his strong arms wrapped around her—keeping her safe as he had the past few days. She needed her husband.

"Are you okay?" Nikki asked. "You don't look so good."

"I'm tired," she said.

Candace gestured down the hall. "Make use of the guest room I showed you earlier. The bed is comfortable."

Tanya wasn't likely to succumb to sleep—not when she was shaking with nerves. She just needed to be alone, to shed the tears stinging her eyes. She couldn't cry in front of the other women—not when they were both trying so hard to be strong.

She went down the hall, located the guest room then closed the door behind her but didn't turn on the light. She fumbled around in the dark until she found the bed. She dropped onto it and curled into a ball, wrapping her arms around herself—holding herself together since Cooper wasn't there.

She shouldn't have let him go. She was his wife now. Wasn't he supposed to listen to her? Wasn't that how marriage worked? But their marriage wasn't real—even though they'd consummated it. It wasn't real because Cooper didn't love her the way she loved him.

Why hadn't she buried her pride and told him? Maybe if she had, he wouldn't have left her.

But he was Cooper Payne. He didn't fear anything. He never had or he wouldn't have joined the Marines after high school graduation. And he was right; he could take care of himself. And his brothers, as he had taken care of her.

He had to be okay…

She squeezed her eyes shut, but tears leaked out of the corners and streaked down the sides of her face into the pillow beneath her head. Maybe she had fallen asleep, because she awoke disoriented, unsure of what had startled her.

Then she heard the noise. A rattling. She glanced to the door. But the knob wasn't moving. She turned toward the window and found that she was too late. It was already open and a dark figure was sliding over the sill. She opened her mouth to scream, but a big hand closed over her mouth.

Had the person killed Cooper to get him out of the

way? And now he intended to kill her? She couldn't count on Cooper to save her. She had to save herself.

She struggled in his arms, thrashing around so that her elbow jammed into his aching ribs and her knee nearly struck a more sensitive part of his body. Pain overwhelmed him, and he cursed. Then he shushed her. "It's okay. It's me."

She tensed so abruptly that he worried he'd hurt her. He'd wrapped his arms tightly around her while clamping one hand to her mouth. He didn't want the others to know he was in the room with her.

He was supposed to be in the hospital, but he'd checked himself out against doctor's orders. It wasn't as if he would be any safer in the hospital. Tanya hadn't been; he grimaced as he remembered how the killer had tried to smother her.

Was the kidnapper a killer yet? Was Stephen dead?

He moved his hand from her mouth, his palm ablaze from the contact with her silky-soft lips.

"It's you," she murmured as if unable to believe he was real. "It's really you?"

"I'm glad you didn't shoot me this time," Cooper said with a chuckle. But that chuckle shook his ribs, and he groaned.

"Are you okay?" she asked. "What happened tonight? None of you were answering your phones!"

He suddenly noticed the tears on her face. And concern was in her voice. She'd worried about him.

"I'm fine," he said. But even he shuddered as he remembered how close that car had come to falling on top of him. If he hadn't gathered the strength to roll out of the way, it might have crushed him.

His brothers had been so worried about him that they'd

both let the damn suspect slip away again. Who exactly was after him? And her?

He kept his arms clenched tightly around her, needing to feel her warmth and softness—her heart beating in unison with his—the same frantic rhythm. Like when they'd made love, they were perfectly in sync.

"What happened?" she asked. "Why didn't you answer your phones?"

"We were a little preoccupied."

"Did you find Stephen?"

He grimaced as if she'd elbowed him again. Of course she was worried about Stephen. "No," he said. "But we found the car that nearly ran you over."

"So it was a real lead—not a setup?"

He hesitated. He had never liked hearing "I told you so." But she was entitled to say it. "You were right."

"It was a setup? But the car was there."

"The police have it now." Or what was left of it. "They'll process it for evidence." Especially the bloodstain in the trunk.

"Why was it a setup?"

"There was a forklift…" He shrugged and then grimaced again.

Her eyes must have adjusted to the dark because she saw it and ran her fingers over his face. "You're hurt."

"Just a little bruised." Like all his ribs and his back. "I've been hurt worse before."

She gasped in alarm. "Don't tell me that."

"Why not?"

"I didn't let myself think of you over there—in danger. I didn't let myself think that you might never come back." She shuddered. "But every once in a while the thoughts crept in…like you did through the window." She stared up at him. "Why did you come through the window?"

That had been extreme—especially since he'd had to straddle the ledge between the fire escape and her window. "I don't want the others to know I'm here."

"Why not? Don't they want you here?"

"Not tonight," he admitted.

"Because you're hurt."

"I'm fine." And he was, now that he knew she was safe, now that he was with her. Or maybe the painkillers had just finally kicked in, because he didn't feel it now. He felt too many others things with her soft body pressed against his.

Her fingers lingered on his face, stroking along his cheekbones and then his jaw. "I'm sorry…"

"It's not your fault," he said.

"I'm sorry about your father."

"That happened years ago," he reminded her. But sometimes it felt like just days or hours—the pain and loss would hit him so hard. Leaving home hadn't lessened that pain as he'd thought it would.

"But your father's killer just died," she said, "and that must bring that all back."

He tensed in shock. "What?"

"Didn't Logan tell you either? Nikki didn't know."

He suspected Parker didn't know either. Damn Logan. Damn him for trying so hard to take their father's place as the patriarch and the protector.

"Candace thinks that the man's daughter might have been the one who shot at Logan earlier today."

"When he was posing as me?" He shrugged. "I don't know…"

"You don't think so? Whatever happened with the forklift—could it have been meant for Logan?" she asked.

He sighed. "No. It was definitely meant for me. And

it involved the car that nearly killed you. What happened in that warehouse had nothing to do with Logan."

"And everything to do with me…" Her voice cracked with emotion. Guilt?

"It's not your fault."

"I just want it to be over…"

The attacks or their marriage? When one ended, so would the other. Cooper had to keep that in mind so he didn't think it was real. So he didn't think she was actually his wife.

He eased his arms from around her and dropped them back to his sides. "I should let you sleep…"

"I can't," she said. "Not without you…" She wrapped her arms around him and tugged him down beside her.

He felt a twinge, but the painkillers must have kicked in because it wasn't that bad. Or maybe her holding him just felt so good…

"Tanya…"

"I was so worried about you," she said. Her lips touched his cheek, then slid across until she found his mouth. She pressed whisper-soft kisses to his lips, as if afraid that she might hurt him.

He gripped the back of her head, tangling his fingers in her hair, and pulled her closer. Then he deepened the kiss, pressing his lips tightly to hers.

She gasped against his mouth, and he took advantage of her open lips, sliding his tongue between them. In and out. He tasted her—the sweetness that was only Tanya. Her arms tightened around him.

But he pulled back. Not because he was in pain but because he was overdressed. He quickly stripped off his clothes, careful this time to keep the gun within reach of the bed. While he stripped, she'd done the same—tossing aside her shirt and pants and those little strips of lace and satin that had driven him nearly out of his mind.

But he preferred this—skin sliding over skin—as he joined her on the bed again. Her thigh slid between his, her hip rubbing against his erection. It throbbed with arousal. He had never wanted anyone the way he wanted—the way he *needed*—his *wife*.

If the way she was touching him, kissing him, was any indication, she wanted him, too. Or she'd been really worried about him.

If that was the case, he loved the way she expressed her relief. Her lips closed around him, taking him into her mouth, while her fingers teased his nipples. He groaned.

"Am I hurting you?" she asked, all concern.

"You're killing me," he said. "But in a good way."

"Let me make it all better," she offered.

But he stopped her, tangling his hand in her hair again, before she could lower her head back down. He kissed her passionately—their tongues swirling, and their breath coming in quick pants.

Just her kiss nearly had him at his breaking point. He felt as if he was going to burst. He wanted her as crazy for him as he was for her, so he teased her nipples with his fingers, tugging gently at them.

She moaned into his mouth. Then he moved one hand lower, between her legs. And now she whimpered and squirmed against him. Then she bit her lip, holding in a scream while she came—her body shuddering against his.

He shuddered, too, with need. She pushed him back on the bed, and he didn't even feel the pain of his bruised back. He felt only her as she guided him inside her. She rode him, sliding up and down, rocking back and forth. She drove him out of his mind.

She shuddered again as she reached her peak. Instead of biting her lip this time, she bit his. And he welcomed the bite.

It snapped the last of his control, and he joined her in the madness, his body jerking as he thrust deep and filled her. She dropped onto his chest, her heart beating frantically—her breath a hot pant against his throat. Their bodies were still joined, so he didn't move her. He just wrapped his arms around her and held her close.

The pain pills must have really kicked in because he felt sleep coming. And he couldn't fight it off as he had so many times before. The others were in the apartment; if someone else sneaked through her window and she screamed, they would help her. She was safe. So he slept…

SHE HATED TO leave him. But it was only for a moment to answer the call of nature. Carefully, so she wouldn't wake him, Tanya slid out from his embrace and rose from the bed. Immediately she felt empty and cold.

She reached for the robe Candace had left on the back of the bedroom door and wrapped it around herself. Then she slipped quietly out of the room and into the hall.

"Is he in there?" Candace asked.

Tanya jumped and clutched a hand to her throat at the surprise of finding the female bodyguard waiting in the hall. "What?"

"Logan called," she uttered those words with great relief, "and said that Cooper checked himself out against doctor's orders."

Her hand trembled. "How badly is he hurt?"

"Bruised ribs. He hit the asphalt hard when the forklift nearly pushed that car on top of him."

Tanya shuddered.

"The doctor said the fall alone could have broken his back. They wanted to keep him overnight for observation."

The darkness in her room and now in the hall had already grown thinner as night slipped away. Daylight would break soon. So maybe he hadn't left too soon.

"Logan figured he'd broken out to come here," Candace continued, "to come to you."

Tanya nodded. "He's here. He came through the window."

The other woman shook her head. "The fire escape is a couple of windows over. He must have edged along the window ledges."

"Tell Logan he's okay," Tanya said. "Really. He's sleeping now."

"I'll tell him," Candace said as she rushed down the hall—probably to wherever she'd left her cell phone.

Tanya made quick use of the bathroom and returned to the bed where Cooper slept. His breathing was too irregular, as if dreams—or more likely, nightmares—disrupted him. She slipped off the robe and crawled back into bed with him. He had turned toward the wall, so she wrapped her arms around his side and pressed herself to his back.

He grunted and jerked, as if in pain. So she pulled away, giving him room. And giving herself enough room to study his body in the gathering light of dawn.

His back was blue and purple in some spots, dark red in others where the skin was raw. And the usually defined and sculpted muscles were swollen. She understood the doctor's concern now, his reasons for wanting to keep him overnight.

Cooper should have stayed in the hospital. Instead, he'd come to her. Why? It was all her fault.

The car that had nearly crushed him had almost run

her over. That wasn't an accident or coincidence. The killer was sending her a message—that Cooper would meet the same gruesome fate she would.

She shouldn't have married him. If anyone was holding Stephen for ransom, they would have asked for it before now. She didn't need the money. She needed Cooper.

But she couldn't have both.

She really couldn't have either—not without risking Cooper's life. He had been risking his life for years, but that was his choice. She didn't want him risking it for her.

She pressed a gentle kiss to his shoulder. He shifted against the mattress and murmured as if even that soft brush of her lips hurt him. But he didn't awaken. Maybe they had given him pain medication at the hospital that had finally gotten him to sleep.

Or knocked him out.

She was counting on the latter. She edged farther away from him and then rolled off the side of the mattress. The light of dawn wasn't bright enough yet for her to find her clothes without feeling around in the dark. So she felt around on the floor, and her fingers fumbled over something cold and hard. Revulsion had her stomach pitching over finding the gun.

She had nearly shot Cooper. Fortunately, she hadn't known how to aim the thing. She kept her hand on the weapon and considered taking it. But with what she was about to do, hopefully she wouldn't need it anymore.

If the money was what had put her in danger, she didn't want it. She wanted nothing to do with it. Or with Cooper's gun.

Until everyone learned what she'd done, he might need it to protect himself. She passed over the gun and grabbed up her clothes. As quickly and quietly as she could, she dressed.

Cooper was going to be angry over what she was about to do. But she would rather go out alone and risk her life than put him in danger again.

She leaned back over the bed, but this time she pressed her lips to his cheek. He was out, so he probably would not hear her. But she needed to tell him what she'd been too cowardly to declare when he was awake. She needed to know that she had at last said the words. So she whispered them into his ear.

"I love you."

She waited to see if he murmured anything back—not that she expected him to return her feelings. He'd pointed out over and over again that he was only doing his job. She wasn't paying him, but she was definitely going to fire him.

She glanced to the door but remembered how Candace had appeared in the hall the minute Tanya had stepped out of the room. She couldn't go out the door.

So she would have to go out the way Cooper had come in—through the window. He'd left it unlatched, so all she had to do was press her hands against the glass and push up the sash. Cool air blew through the opening, lifting the rumpled sheet that barely covered Cooper's naked body.

She held her breath, afraid that he would wake up and stop her. But he didn't move—not even to cover himself. Was he really all right? He'd left the hospital against doctor's orders. Maybe she shouldn't leave him…

But then her leaving him was exactly what she needed to do in order to keep him safe. She lifted one leg over the windowsill, but her foot met only empty space. Candace had said there was a ledge. She drew her foot closer to the brick wall of the apartment building, and she found it—six or so skinny inches of concrete. She turned her foot sideways and set it firmly on the ledge before crawling out through the window.

She clutched at the brick wall as dizziness overwhelmed her. She shouldn't have looked down—because now she could look nowhere else. Her knees trembled and her heart raced.

The apartment was on the third floor of the building. Until then—staring down into the abyss of the alley—Tanya hadn't realized how far up three stories was. Nor had she considered how far she would fall if she slipped.

Hitting the asphalt from the height of a loading dock could have broken Cooper's back. Hitting it from this height would probably break every bone in her body.

Already bruised and wounded, Cooper had sidled across this ledge to get to her. Why? Only to protect her?

Just how seriously did the man take his job?

Too seriously—when it was likely to get him killed. She had to do this, had to save him from saving her. Because she didn't want to wake him with the cool breeze, she maneuvered around on the ledge enough to push down the window. She couldn't lower it completely—not without bending all the way over, and if she did that, she would fall for certain. But crouching down strained the muscles in her already shaking legs and her feet began to slip.

Clutching at the wall again, she regained her tenuous position on the ledge. And inch by inch she sidled across it toward the fire escape. It was exactly three dark windows over—probably twelve feet. But to Tanya, who was freezing with cold and fright, it may as well have been a mile. She panted and shook as if she'd run twenty.

Her hands were cold and nearly numb from scraping across the brick wall when she reached out for the railing of the fire escape. Her fingers slipped, knocking her off balance so much that her foot began to slide off the ledge.

Had she made it all those feet only to fall now—when she was so close to the fire escape? The killer would be thrilled—he wouldn't have to try to shoot her or poison her anymore. Tanya was going to kill herself with her probably misguided attempt to save the man she loved.

Chapter Sixteen

Cooper hated sleeping because usually his dreams
haunted him with memories of things he had seen or
done, things that he was almost able to forget when he
was awake. But now he awakened with a smile and a
good memory.

Of making love with Tanya.

And of her saying, "I love you."

He must have dreamed that—must have imagined her
whispering those words into his ear. Until a few days ago,
she had been engaged to marry another man. It didn't
matter that Cooper was the one she had actually wed;
he was only a substitute for the man she really loved.

The smile slid away from his face, and he forced open
eyes that felt gritty with sleep and probably the afteref-
fects of the painkillers.

The meds had worn off, because his back ached like
hell. And his ribs protested every breath he drew into
his lungs. And he sucked in a deep breath as he scanned
the empty room.

She was gone. Had someone grabbed her while he
slept? The window was open a few inches—more than
he'd left it when he'd come inside that way. And the gun
was still inside its holster next to the bed. He reached
for it.

If someone had broken in while he slept, wouldn't she have used it just as she'd tried using it the night she'd almost shot him? Tanya was tough; she wouldn't have survived all the attempts on her life if she wasn't.

Maybe she had opened the window for air. Or because he'd gotten too hot sharing the only full-size bed with her. He wasn't hot now, with the cool wind blowing over his bare skin. He hurriedly dressed, ignoring the twinges in his back and ribs, as he pulled on the clothes he'd discarded so quickly the night before.

Her clothes were gone—just as she was. But with the sun only just streaking between the buildings and shining across that open windowsill, it was early yet. Not much past dawn.

He hadn't given her much choice last night before jumping into bed with her. But she had seemed willing then. His skin flushed with heat and desire as he remembered how thoroughly she had made love to him. She had definitely been willing.

So where was she? He opened the door and stepped into the hall. Voices drew him toward the kitchen, where he hoped to find her with the others, sitting around the small round table or leaning against the cabinets. Nikki sat at the table staring at the screen of the laptop in front of her, while Parker leaned back, the chair on two legs, against the wall, with his cell phone pressed to his ear.

Logan reclined against the cabinets, his arms crossed over his chest, like a teacher surveying his class. As the oldest, he'd always thought he knew more than the rest of them. But that was probably just because he kept what he knew secret—like the death of their father's killer.

Cooper would deal with that later, though. He was more concerned with who wasn't in the kitchen than who was. Candace was missing, which was odd since this was her place. But she could have been in the bathroom or her bedroom.

Tanya was gone. And he knew it because of how empty and alone he felt even with his family present. They glanced at him in the doorway, but there was no surprise on their faces. They'd known where he'd gone after checking himself out of the hospital.

What about Tanya? "Where is she?"

And a better question, why were they all there when the person they were supposed to be protecting wasn't? What kind of bodyguards were Payne Protection?

"Did somebody—" his voice cracked with emotion "—take her?" While he'd slept peacefully in the same bed with her? What the hell kind of bodyguard was he?

"Nobody grabbed her," Logan assured him. "Candace saw her leave of her own accord."

"Maybe she got sick of everybody babysitting her," Nikki suggested. "I know how frustrating it is when nobody trusts you to take care of yourself."

"You didn't see her leave," Logan pointed out. "You're not ready to be a bodyguard on your own yet."

Cooper couldn't defend her any more than he could defend himself for having let Tanya slip away.

"She didn't come out of the door," Nikki said in an attempt to defend herself. "She went out the window."

He cursed under his breath since he'd given her the idea. And because he could envision her precariously balancing on that narrow ledge. "She could have fallen..."

And that fall would have killed her. His heart lurched with pain and loss. Was that why they were all here and not out protecting her? Because she was really gone?

"She didn't fall," Logan assured him.

The pain in his chest eased slightly. She wasn't dead. She was just gone.

"You could have fallen, too, when you sneaked in that way," Nikki said, her eyes wide with fear. "You could have fallen *again*." Obviously their brothers had filled her in on what had happened at the warehouse.

"I'm fine," he said.

"You should let the doctor determine that," Nikki said. "You should go back to the hospital."

"Hell, no," he replied. "The only place I'm going is to find Tanya—which all of you should be doing instead of standing around *here*."

"Candace is following her," Logan explained. "She'll make sure Tanya stays safe."

He wasn't so sure about that. "She's not as good as you think she is. She let me slip into Tanya's room—"

"She knew it was you," Logan replied. "I warned her you were coming when I'd discovered you'd snuck out of the hospital."

"But she let Tanya sneak out…" So had he. His gut churned with guilt over having fallen asleep when he should have been protecting her.

Logan nodded. "She saw her on the ledge, but she didn't dare risk startling her and causing her to fall."

It was a risk she'd been wise not to take. But Cooper suspected there'd been another reason—like her boss's orders. "You wanted to see where she'd go, didn't you?"

Logan nodded again.

"You can't suspect her of being involved in this," he said.

"Why not?"

"Because she's nearly been killed time and again."

"Nearly," Logan pointed out.

"You suspect Rochelle," Nikki reminded him with a trace of resentment. "And even Stephen…"

A pang of guilt struck him. The blood he'd found in

the trunk of that car proved a body had been moved in it. Stephen's? He may have even been inside it when Cooper had fired those shots at the car to stop it from running down Tanya.

"Not Tanya," he insisted. "She has no motive..."

"She has the same motive everyone else has," Logan said. "The money..."

He shook his head. "She couldn't have acted alone. She wasn't driving the car that chased her down. She wasn't firing the shots into her apartment."

Logan nodded. "She didn't act alone."

"That's why you let her go, to see not only where she'd go but who she would meet."

Logan nodded again.

"It's not Stephen," he said. "They would have just gotten married..."

"But maybe he got cold feet," Nikki said.

Over marrying Tanya? Cooper doubted it.

"And she got mad at him," Nikki continued.

Mad enough to hurt him? He doubted that even more. "You're wrong about this."

"Probably," Logan agreed.

"Where is she?" By now his brother, who thought he knew everything, probably knew.

"She took a cab to her grandfather's house."

She'd hated that place nearly as much as Cooper had. "Why?"

"It's hers now," Nikki reminded him.

He shook his head. "It doesn't matter to her. That house—the money..."

"Then why did she marry you?" Logan asked.

"In case there was a ransom demand made for Stephen," he reminded them. "This was all about Stephen." It hurt remembering that the woman he loved—the woman he'd married—was in love with another man.

"There was no ransom demand," Nikki said quietly, as if she knew how badly he was already hurting.

His head throbbed along with his back, pain pounding at his temples, as he tried to process what his family was telling him. To doubt Tanya? And now he knew how she'd felt when he'd tried to make her do the same with Stephen. He knew exactly how she'd felt because he loved her.

"How long have you been thinking this?" he asked Logan. He wasn't above lashing out at him when he was in pain. He'd done it when their dad had died. "And keeping it to yourself—like you keep everything!"

Parker clicked off his cell phone and slid it into his pocket. "What are you talking about? What's he keeping to himself?"

Cooper turned on his other brother. "You know that Dad's killer died in prison."

Parker shrugged as if it didn't matter to him, and it didn't matter to any of them as much as it did to Logan. "Not because he told me."

"Candace just told me," Nikki chimed in.

That must have been how Tanya had learned about it. He asked his brothers, "Why didn't either of you tell me?"

"You've been a little preoccupied getting married and all," Logan reminded him. "And truthfully, I didn't know if it would matter to any of you."

Like it mattered to him. They had all been content with the man being sent to prison. Logan was the one who hadn't been able to let go of his anger. Maybe he could now...

Cooper shrugged off the slight much easier than he

could shrug off his brother's doubts about the woman he loved.

"Doesn't anyone want to know why I was on the phone?" Parker asked. With a grin he announced, "We got a real lead this time."

"You thought that last one was a real lead," Cooper reminded him, flinching as his ribs ached.

"We found the car," Parker reminded him.

He'd nearly wound up with it on top of him, but they had found it. "Have the crime scene techs processed it yet? Have they found any prints?"

Logan nodded. "The blood in the trunk matches the blood from the church—same type, at least. DNA is still backlogged."

"What about prints?"

"The steering wheel was wiped clean on the car and the forklift, too," Logan replied. "Stephen's never been fingerprinted, so we don't know if the ones inside the trunk lid are his."

Someone had been alive inside that trunk—had been banging and trying to get out. Cooper's stomach tightened with dread. "We gotta find him."

"We may have," Parker reminded him. "One of my informants spotted that car at another warehouse before it wound up where we found it."

Another warehouse. Cooper's ribs throbbed as if in protest and he groaned.

"You stay here with Nikki," Logan ordered.

"Of course I don't get to go," Nikki resentfully grumbled.

Logan ignored her and continued, "Parker and I will check it out alone—like we should have last time."

Cooper shook his head. "I'm going, too."

"You're already hurt. Want to finish yourself off?" his oldest brother challenged him.

"I want to finish this," he said. "I want to nail the bastard who's responsible for all the shooting and stuff."

"What if that bastard's Tanya?" Logan asked.

God, the man was more paranoid than Cooper was. "It's not." And he had a feeling it wasn't Stephen either—that he had misjudged his friend. He just hoped he had a chance to make it up to him. "Let's stop wasting time and follow up this lead."

He just hoped it didn't lead them to a body.

TANYA SHIVERED WITH cold and dread. The house—or mausoleum as Cooper had called it—had been closed up for years. So it was freezing inside, with no heat or electricity, and it was musty smelling—exactly like a mausoleum.

Her lungs strained for breath, and she wished she'd thought to bring along her purse with the newly prescribed inhaler inside. But the extra weight of her bag might have been enough to make her lose her balance off the ledge entirely.

She'd barely caught the fire escape in time as it was. Her palms still stung from how hard she'd gripped the cold and rusted metal. She'd had to hang on tightly while she'd swung herself over the railing. Her legs had been shaking so badly it was a wonder she'd made it down all the steps to the alley below.

Her legs still shook a little now. But all the furniture was covered with heavy plastic, leaving her no place to sit down. The floor was hard marble and probably like ice now; she couldn't sit on it either. Only faint light filtered through the thick drapes pulled across the windows. It was so cold and dark and creepy.

It was truly like a mausoleum, just minus the wall of drawers containing urns of ashes. Her grandfather's urn was here, though, sitting on the mantel with a fine coating of dust covering the brass. Was he really in there? Or was he behind all the horrible things that had been happening to her?

She wouldn't put it past him to try to kill Cooper. It was bad enough that he'd spoken to him the way he had all those years ago, telling him that he wasn't good enough for her.

She was the one who wasn't good enough for him. He was a fearless hero and she had been a coward, hiding behind his protection.

A door creaked and she jumped—every bit that coward yet. Should she hide until she was sure it was who she'd called to meet her? Should she grab that urn to use as a weapon? She shuddered at the thought of touching it.

"Tanya?" a male voice called out. "Ms. Chesterfield?"

She wasn't Ms. Chesterfield anymore. She was Mrs. Payne. But she hadn't had time to legally change her name, which was good since she wasn't going to keep it anyway. "I'm in here, Mr. Gregory."

Footsteps pounded on the marble as he headed down the hall toward her. "It's quite early, Ms. Chesterfield," he protested. He looked tired with dark circles rimming his eyes, and his gray hair was mussed as if he hadn't bothered to comb it. "We could have scheduled a meeting later in the day."

"Thank you for meeting me now," she said. And for meeting her here, so she knew exactly what she was giving up: nothing. "It really couldn't wait."

"If you want to collect your inheritance today, that's not possible," he said. "It's too big an amount to be easily liquidated. And of course it needs to be divided, with half being held in trust for your sister in the event that she marries before she turns thirty."

"She can have it all," Tanya said. Then and only then did Tanya suspect that the attempts on her life and Cooper's life would stop.

Mr. Gregory shook his head. "She is unmarried. Your grandfather's will stipulates that she, too, must be married before she inherits."

"Then put it all in trust for her." She suspected Rochelle would soon be planning her wedding—if the money was really what she wanted.

Or was it Stephen?

The lawyer tensed. "What are you saying exactly?"

"I'm saying that I don't want my grandfather's money," she said, and guilt and regret overwhelmed her. "I never should have married to get it in the first place."

"I thought that was why you were marrying that Stephen fellow," Mr. Gregory, "just to inherit the money. But the Payne kid…"

"That's why I'm giving it back," she said. Although technically she'd never really had it and may not have had access to it for a while. Maybe it was a good thing that she had never received that ransom demand. Because how would she have paid it?

"You really want to give it back?" he asked. And his shoulders and back relaxed, the tension apparently leaving his body.

Why was he so relieved?

"Is that possible?" she asked. "Technically I had satisfied the stipulations of Grandfather's will before my thirtieth birthday." Today was her birthday.

He waved his hand, dismissing what his employer had wanted. "You can sign a paper claiming that the marriage was never consummated and get it annulled."

Heat flushed her face. "But what if it was?"

"It won't be a problem," he said, and there was a tone to his voice now—an edge she had never noticed before.

To have worked with her grandfather for as many years as he had, he had to have few principles or morals. But could he be...

Was he a killer?

Maybe Cooper's suspicious nature had rubbed off on her; maybe when they'd made love...

Because it made no sense to doubt a man she had known most of her life—especially since he had nothing to gain. But she had goose bumps rising on her skin. It wasn't the cold that had gotten to her. It was this horrible sense of foreboding. Her instincts warned her to get out of the mausoleum before she wound up in an urn like her grandfather.

"Well, if it's no problem, I should be going," she said. But he stood between her and the door. And she was reluctant to walk any closer to him.

"You'll need to sign those papers," he said.

"I'm sure you don't have them with you," she said. "You can draw them up and get them to me another day."

He patted his suitcase. "Actually, I do have them with me."

That seemed too convenient.

She shivered as her unease turned into fright. She was alone with a killer. And her first thought wasn't for her own safety but for Cooper's.

He would never forgive himself if she died when he was supposed to be protecting her. He would blame himself for letting her slip out while he slept. She hoped that he had at least heard her whispered words of love. Because she doubted she would have the chance to tell him again how she felt.

She wasn't certain if Mr. Gregory carried contracts in his briefcase or a gun.

But she wasn't going to wait to find out. She couldn't run for the door, so she turned and ran deeper into the shadows of the mausoleum. But even if she found a place to hide, she couldn't stay there forever.

Eventually Mr. Gregory would find her.

Chapter Seventeen

Cooper's head pounded with pain while his heart pounded with fear. Even though this warehouse looked more deserted and dangerous than the one the night before had, he wasn't concerned for his safety. He was worried about Tanya's.

Sure, Candace was a good bodyguard. But the body she was guarding was too important for Cooper to trust to anyone else. He never should have fallen asleep. But because he had, maybe she was safer with Candace.

"This place has been completely abandoned," Logan said, his voice emanating from the cell clutched in Cooper's hand.

He silently agreed, but Parker chimed in through the two-way, "This is it—the place where my informant saw the black car with the flats."

"Let's go in, then," he said. He didn't have the loading docks this time. Logan had taken that side of the building. He did have a service door—one that was so rusted, he doubted the hinges would hold it in the frame despite the lock. So he kicked it on that side and knocked it loose.

His gun drawn in front of him, he stepped inside the dark building. But after a few minutes his eyes adjusted to the faint light coming through holes rotted through the metal roof.

"Do you see anything?" Logan asked. Something rattled in the phone; he was obviously struggling hard with his doors.

A faint pounding echoed the rattling. Parker must have been struggling, too.

Cooper moved through the maze of stuff left in the building. "Just crates."

And twisted hunks of metal and other debris.

But the light illuminated a strange patch of concrete where the dust had been cleared away. He stepped closer to the crate and the pounding grew louder.

It emanated from the box. The nails on the end of it were fresh, not rusted like the others. What the hell was in the box?

He'd seen too many IEDs in Afghanistan to haphazardly bust open the crate. It could have been a trick—a setup like the forklift. If he opened that newly nailed shut side, it might explode—like so many other explosions he'd seen.

He hesitated and leaned his head against the splintered wood. The pounding in the box echoed the pounding in his head. But then he heard something else—a weak voice calling out, "Help…"

"What did you find?" Parker asked as he joined him beside the box.

Cooper holstered his gun and concentrated on the crate. "Find a crowbar—a screwdriver, something. We've gotta get this open." He clawed at the wood with his hands, driving slivers of that wood into his fingers.

"I got a crowbar," Logan said. He must have had to use one to open the loading dock doors. "What do you need it for?"

Cooper grabbed the bar and wedged it between the

wood, pulling up those newly hammered nails until the side cracked open. His brothers grabbed it and tore it off.

A man was curled up in that crate—his face crusted with blood like his matted hair. It had once been blond but now it was dark with blood. So much blood…

He peered up at Cooper through swollen eyes. "Coop?"

"Call an ambulance," he yelled at his brothers.

Parker already had his cell pressed to his ear. "It could be a while before they make it to this side of town. Should we drive him in?"

Cooper wasn't sure he should move him. But the man moved himself and crawled out of the box onto the concrete floor.

He dropped to his knees beside his old friend. "Stephen, take it easy. Don't move."

But Stephen clutched at Cooper's hand. And guilt clutched at Cooper's heart. How had he thought his friend at all responsible for the attempts on his life and Tanya's? How had he married the man's fiancé while Stephen had been locked up in this crate?

Because believing the worst of Stephen had made it easier for Cooper to act on his feelings for Tanya.

"Do you have some water in the car?" he asked Logan.

His oldest brother nodded. "I'll get it and the first-aid kit."

"And I'll wave down the ambulance," Parker said, before following his twin out of the warehouse—leaving Cooper alone with his old best friend.

"You're going to be okay," he assured him. The wound on Stephen's head still oozed blood. He must have been hit hard—hard enough to spray his blood across the wall of the groom's quarters. "Did you see who hit you?"

It wasn't Tanya, as his brothers had suspected. He was done doubting his friends.

"No…" Stephen moaned as if the sound of his own voice reverberated inside his injured head. How had he handled the sound of his own pounding echoing inside the crate?

"You don't know who did this to you?"

"I know…"

Hope quickened Cooper's pulse. "You know? But you said you didn't see him…" Nobody could press charges on suspicions and doubts; the police and prosecutors needed evidence, like eyewitness testimony.

Stephen tried to speak again, but his voice cracked. His throat was probably as dry as his peeling lips. Cooper's heart wrenched with emotion over how badly Stephen had been hurt. And then he'd been nailed up in a box and left to die.

Footsteps pounded on the concrete as someone hurriedly approached. Cooper glanced up, hoping it was the medics. But it was Logan, carrying a bottle of water. "They're only a few minutes out."

He hoped Stephen had those minutes left…after days of his wound being untreated and being dehydrated. Cooper took the water bottle from Logan, uncapped it and held it to Stephen's lips. He trickled only a little bit into his mouth.

Stephen coughed and sputtered.

Cooper cursed and hoped he hadn't done more damage to his battered friend. What if he aspirated?

But Stephen caught his breath and his voice was clearer when he spoke, "More…"

Cooper trickled more water into his open mouth.

He coughed again but not as violently.

"The ambulance will be here soon," Cooper assured him. "The docs will make you well again."

"Safe…" Stephen murmured.

"You're safe," he promised. "Nobody's going to get to you again." If Cooper would have agreed to be his best man, nobody would have gotten to Stephen the first time. Guilt gnawed at him more than the pain in his ribs and back.

Logan, ever the detective, asked, "Do you know who did this to you?"

Wanting Stephen to save his strength, Cooper answered for him, "He didn't see him."

"At the church," Stephen murmured. "I didn't see him at the church…"

Logan cursed in frustration.

"But I saw him," Stephen said, "when he opened the trunk. I saw him…"

"Who?" Cooper asked. "Who did this to you?"

"Arthur Gregory…"

"Tanya's grandfather's lawyer?" Cooper asked.

Logan cursed again.

"What?" Cooper asked his brother. "I thought you barely knew the guy."

"That's not it." A muscle twitched along Logan's tightly clenched jaw.

And Cooper's heart lurched in his chest as the horrible realization dawned on him. "Tanya's with him?"

"Candace just reported in that the lawyer showed up at the mausoleum."

"Did she stop him from going inside with Tanya?"

Logan shook her head. "I—I advised her not to."

Cooper cursed him.

"I didn't think the man was a threat," Logan said. "What's his motive?"

"Money," Stephen murmured. "I think he took the money…"

And his embezzlement would have gone undetected

if neither Chesterfield heir married before she turned thirty. "Tell Candace to get inside—to protect Tanya!"

His cell already in his hand, Logan nodded. But the phone rang and rang. "She's not picking up…"

"Go," Stephen told him. "You go…to her."

Parker wove through the crates, shoving some aside to make room for the stretcher the EMTs carried. "They're here!"

"Go," Stephen urged him again. "Go to Tanya…"

His heart was already pulling him away—toward the door, toward Tanya. But he told his brothers, "Make sure they take care of him."

"I'm going with you," Logan said. "Parker will ride along to the hospital with Stephen."

Cooper didn't care who did what as long as Mr. Gregory wasn't hurting Tanya. But the mausoleum was on the other side of town. His odds of getting there in time to protect her were pretty damn slim.

He'd been a fool to let her out of his sight—because he might never see her again. Alive.

DUST FILLED HER lungs, making it hard to draw air into them. Her nose tickled and throat burned, but she couldn't sneeze. She couldn't cough. She couldn't even breathe hard for fear that he might find where she was hiding.

She had crawled into a tall cabinet in the butler's pantry. With her knees pressed against her chest and the back of her head pressed against the top of the cabinet, the hard wood was unrelenting against her skull.

The cabinet's door wasn't that thick, so she could hear through it. A door creaked open—maybe the kitchen door—since it was loud enough to reach her ears. And a female voice—maybe Candace—called out her name. "Tanya?"

Something hard and metallic dropped, and it clanged

against the kitchen tiles. Then something heavier struck the ground, too, with a dull thump.

She wanted to call back. But she doubted Candace could hear her now. Had Mr. Gregory killed her?

Tears stung her eyes and burned the back of her throat. But she struggled to contain them. She couldn't give away her hiding place.

"It's useless to try to hide from me," he yelled, his voice alarmingly close.

She sucked in her breath and held it—until her lungs ached.

"I will find you."

He knew she had figured it out because she'd run. She shouldn't have run from him. But she'd only ever been able to hide her feelings from one person—Cooper. Everyone else was able to tell what she was thinking; they could see through her lies.

But what was the point of killing her? Then Cooper, as her husband, would gain her inheritance. Unless he intended to kill Cooper, too.

If only she could get to a weapon...

Maybe the metallic thing that had fallen was Candace's gun. If she could sneak past Mr. Gregory...

"Where the hell are you?" the man shouted, but his voice was fainter as he moved farther away from her. Then she heard footsteps pounding across that marble foyer and then up the marble stairs. Those footsteps moved overhead.

She drew in a breath and pushed open that cupboard door. Her leg muscles twinged as she unfolded them and crawled out of the small space. They nearly gave as she dropped onto the counter and then the floor below that.

She moved on tiptoe across the butler's pantry toward the kitchen, not wanting her own footsteps echoing throughout the empty mansion. Candace had crumpled onto the kitchen floor, a wound on her head oozing blood onto the dingy white tiles. Tanya pressed her fingers to the woman's neck, feeling for a pulse. When she felt the telltale flutter, she breathed a sigh of relief.

But then she glanced around her. If Candace had had a gun, it was gone. Mr. Gregory must have taken it.

Candace was too statuesque for Tanya to move her; she couldn't carry the woman outside and she couldn't leave her here—at Mr. Gregory's mercy.

"Candace?" she whispered. "Wake up…"

The woman shifted, but she didn't regain consciousness. She had moved enough that her pant leg slid up. Metal glinted off a gun strapped to her ankle.

Her fingers trembling, Tanya reached for it but fumbled with the holster clasp.

Footsteps echoed off the marble again. He was coming.

She grabbed at the gun and whirled around with it clutched in her hands.

"At least this time you have the safety on," Cooper remarked. "So you won't blow my head off."

"She won't, but I will," Mr. Gregory said.

Cooper turned toward the man who'd sneaked up behind him. His back was to Tanya now, but for that split second before he'd turned, she'd seen his face. He hadn't seemed very surprised that Mr. Gregory had just threatened to kill him.

He'd figured out what she had.

"Nobody needs to get shot here," he said. He glanced down at the floor. "You didn't shoot Candace?"

"He must have hit her over the head," Tanya said. If only she had warned Candace…

"Like he did Stephen."

"You found Stephen?" she asked. "Is he…?"

"He's still alive," Cooper replied, but he spoke to Mr. Gregory now. "And soon he'll be well enough to testify against you."

The lawyer shrugged. "I will be long gone before I'll be arrested."

"Then just leave," Cooper suggested. "Just walk away right now."

"You'd like that," Mr. Gregory said. "You've been messing up my plans since you got back in the country."

"Your plan was to kill Tanya?"

"That only became necessary when you decided to become her white knight," Mr. Gregory said.

Cooper was acting as her white knight now because he had positioned his body between her and the deranged lawyer and his gun. The barrel was pointed at Cooper's chest now.

"All I wanted to do was stop her from marrying," Mr. Gregory explained, "Stephen Wochholz or anyone else."

Tanya shuddered.

"You didn't want her to inherit the money," Cooper said.

"What money?" Mr. Gregory asked with a chuckle. "The money's gone."

Tanya gasped in surprise. He had embezzled all of it.

"Then it's over," Cooper said. "Just leave. Take whatever you've got left and leave the country."

"I will leave," Mr. Gregory assured them, "as soon as I get rid of you."

Fear overwhelming her, she gasped again. "No!"

"Why are you acting like you care now?" Mr. Gregory taunted her. "You were so desperate a little while ago to get your annulment that you were willing to give up your inheritance to end your marriage."

Cooper tensed. Was he offended? Hurt?

"You hurt Stephen and you kept trying to hurt Cooper," she said, trying to explain why she'd done what she had. To keep him safe…

"Kept trying?" the lawyer scoffed. "I tried to push a car on him."

"But all the gunshots," she said, "at Stephen's condo and at his brother, who you must have mistaken for Cooper…"

"I fired into your apartment but that was to hit you— after he stopped me from running you over." The lawyer snarled. "He kept stopping me…when he saved you from the asthma attack and the peanut allergy. Your sister helped with that. Maybe I should take care of her, too, before I leave the country.

"Nobody else needs to get hurt," Cooper said. "Stephen's going to make it. You haven't killed anyone. So there'll be no murder charges."

"Just attempted murder," the lawyer said. "And embezzlement. I might as well commit murder, too. And for all the times you've messed up my plan, I really, really want to kill you, Cooper Payne."

"No!" Tanya shouted.

But the gun was already raised. Mr. Gregory squeezed the trigger. And a shot rang out.

Chapter Eighteen

Tanya's scream rang in Cooper's ears. The terror in it chilled his blood. But it wasn't his blood that was spilled across the white tile floor. Mr. Gregory lay lifelessly in front of him—a bullet in his head.

"Everybody okay?" Logan asked from behind him. Cooper had distracted the man so his brother could get in place to take the shot—if he needed to. Since the lawyer had been squeezing the trigger, Cooper was fortunate that Logan was a damn good shot. Or he might have an actual hole in his heart instead of just a figurative one.

"Yeah, thanks," Cooper said.

"You could sound a little more grateful," Logan teased as he dropped to his knees and took Candace's pulse. Their family usually handled every emotion with humor; otherwise they would have never survived the loss of their father. Maybe Logan had gotten so good at coping that he didn't betray any other emotions. Or he kept everything inside. "Her pulse is strong."

"I'm strong," Candace murmured as she regained consciousness. "I can beat you arm wrestling."

He chuckled. "Good thing he hit you in the head—since it's so hard."

Cooper hoped her heart was hard, too. Because it was obvious that Logan didn't return the feelings she had for her boss. His big brother couldn't have gotten that good at hiding his emotions. Because if Cooper had found Tanya lying on the floor like that, he wouldn't have been able to tease. His hands would have been shaking too badly to take the shot that Logan had. His heart clutched with sympathy for Candace because he knew how badly it hurt when someone didn't love you the way you loved them.

Tanya wanted a divorce so desperately that she'd been willing to give up her inheritance.

Her hands clutched his shoulder. "Cooper, are you all right?" she asked.

He shrugged off her touch. "Fine." And because he cared so much, he turned and reached out to her. But he didn't pull her into his arms as he longed to do. Instead, he just touched her hair, brushing cobwebs and dust from the silken strands. "Are you okay?"

"Yeah..." She expelled a shaky sigh. "When I realized everything...I ran and hid."

"What were you thinking to meet him here?" he asked. "Alone?" But he knew. She was thinking she wanted to get rid of her husband. And she hadn't cared how much it would cost her. Even her life?

"I didn't know he was the one...behind everything..."

"But you shouldn't have gone off alone," he reminded her. His guts clenched with dread. He hated to think of what could have happened to her—of how she could have been the one lying on the floor—either with a wound on her head or a bullet in it. "It's hard to protect someone who won't let you."

"It's over now," she said. "I don't need your protection anymore."

"No," he agreed. She obviously didn't need him anymore.

"Is it over?" Logan asked the question now. "Gregory

said he only fired those shots at your apartment. He admitted to everything else, so why would he lie about those other times? Parker got shot at outside Stephen's place."

"And you got shot at, too," Cooper remarked as his head began to pound again.

"But I was posing as you," Logan said.

Despite the pounding, Cooper shook his head. "You and Parker can pass as each other. I'm not so sure anyone would have really been fooled into thinking you were me." Then maybe those shots outside Stephen's had really been meant for Parker and hadn't been just because he'd gone out the door first.

"Do you think there's someone else?" Tanya asked with a shudder. "That Mr. Gregory was working with someone else?"

Candace had managed to sit up and lean against the wall behind her. "It's more likely that the someone else has nothing to do with you."

Tanya turned to Cooper, her eyes wide with concern. "Someone else is trying to kill you?"

"Not me," he assured her. "I just got back into the country." And his enemies wouldn't have been able to follow him here. "This is about something else…" Logan. "It doesn't concern you."

A twinge of disappointment squeezed her heart. He had just reminded her that she wasn't really part of his family. They'd only been married a couple of days before she'd decided to end it.

Sirens wailed outside the mausoleum. "As soon as the police are done taking our report, I'll bring you to the hospital to see Stephen."

"Uh, Stephen, of course." She lifted trembling fingers to her face and brushed away another cobweb. "Is he really going to be all right?"

"He's strong to have survived the head wound and all those days of being nailed inside a crate," he said.

She moved her hand to her mouth, as if to hold in another scream.

"And I'm sure he'll be even better once we get our divorce and you can marry him."

She loved Stephen, but she didn't want to marry him. She wanted to stay married to her husband because she was in love with him. Cooper obviously didn't return those feelings. He hadn't even come with her to the hospital. He'd sent her in the ambulance with Candace.

After Candace had been taken for a CT scan, Tanya had found Stephen's hospital room. The minute she stepped inside, she reached out and clutched his hand.

"Don't!" Rochelle yelled at her from where she sat on the other side of Stephen's bed.

He cried out, and Tanya pulled back. Seeing how raw his fingers were, he must have been digging at something. The crate Cooper said he'd found him nailed inside...

She shuddered over the horrors her dear friend had been forced to endure—because of her. "I'm sorry. I'm *so* sorry..."

"You should be sorry," Rochelle snapped at her. "You did all this for nothing—for money that was already gone."

Nikki must have called and filled in her friend about Mr. Gregory. It had been him acting alone in the attempts on her life and Stephen's. Cooper had lifted the lawyer's sleeves to reveal her scratches on his arms. And they'd found evidence that the tear-gas container had been inside his briefcase.

Tears of regret stung Tanya's eyes.

"It's not your fault," Stephen said. "It was my plan that we get married."

Rochelle gasped. "It was?"

"Your sister didn't want the money, but I pointed out everything she could do with it—all the people she could help."

Rochelle's lips curved into the first genuine smile Tanya had seen on her face since she was a child. "Of course it was your plan. You are such a sweet man."

Stephen reached his injured hand out to Tanya's little sister, and he patted her cheek. "You're pretty sweet yourself."

Rochelle? What kind of painkillers had they given him?

Rochelle giggled like the child she'd once been before she'd become a bitter, angry adult. "I'm anything but sweet—Tanya will tell you that. I've been a complete witch to her."

"You didn't know," Stephen said. "I should have told you…"

"Did you know?" Rochelle asked.

Tanya furrowed her brow with confusion. Was her sister drunk? "It was *his* plan."

"Not the plan," Rochelle said with another delighted giggle. "His feelings…"

"Do you mind if I tell her alone?" Stephen asked.

Rochelle nodded and walked out of the room as if she were floating a few feet above the ground.

"Tell me what?" Tanya asked.

"I love your sister."

"You what?" She had never noticed anything romantic between the two.

"I love Rochelle," he said.

She was stunned. "When you disappeared, I realized she had feelings for you, but…"

"I didn't realize it either until I was locked up in that

crate," he said. "Hers was the face I most wanted to see again. Hers the voice I most wanted to hear."

Tanya uttered a wistful sigh, longing for someone to love her like that. And for that someone to be Cooper.

"I'm sorry," he said.

"You have no reason to be sorry," she assured him. "You and I were never anything more than friends."

"You, me and Cooper—the three amigos," he said with a chuckle. "But you and him were never just friends. He married you."

She nodded. "Just so I would be able to inherit and pay a ransom in case one was made for your return."

"I heard he had some doubts about my part in all of this," Stephen said. Obviously Rochelle had told him everything that had happened in his absence. "So maybe he had another reason to marry you."

"For my protection," she said. "Mr. Gregory was trying to kill me."

"You wished it was real, though," he said. "You love Cooper. You always have."

But it was even more hopeless than it had been when they were teenagers. "It doesn't matter," she said, her voice cracking with emotion, "because he doesn't love me. He'll never love…" She dropped into the chair beside his bed and her shoulders shook as she wept.

With his injured hand, Stephen patted her hair.

She should have been the one comforting him after everything he'd endured. But, as usual, he was the one offering her comfort.

"I really love you," she told him.

A noise drew her attention to the door—where Cooper stood. Before she could call out to him, he turned and left, the door swinging shut behind him. He obviously thought she was in love with Stephen. But what did that matter to Cooper since he didn't love her?

"So you wouldn't stand up as my best man, but you want a favor from me!" Stephen exclaimed as he slammed the door to Cooper's office and strode up to his desk.

Coop was officially part of the Payne Protection team and as a family member as well as an employee he'd been given an office—a dark-paneled room that was smaller than Logan's and Parker's but bigger than the cubby they'd given Nikki.

"I thought it was a favor you'd want, too." Given what Cooper had seen and heard a couple of days ago in Stephen's hospital room.

The man had healed quickly—probably because he had someone waiting for him. But he still had a bandage on his head to protect the stitches that had finally stopped the bleeding. And he had dark circles rimming his eyes that were now wide in shock. "You think I want to draw up your divorce papers?"

"I think you want me to divorce Tanya," Cooper admitted with a trace of bitterness. Maybe he was more petty than he'd thought since he couldn't bring himself to be happy for his friends.

"Why?" Stephen asked.

"So you can marry her." Nikki had gone running out minutes ago to meet Tanya and Rochelle at the church to make wedding arrangements with his mother. Apparently Tanya was so anxious to marry Stephen that she'd forgotten that she was still married to Cooper.

He hadn't forgotten. He hadn't forgotten anything about her. The smell of her hair. The taste of her lips. The way she felt when he buried himself deep inside her— the heat and closeness of her body holding him tightly.

He'd felt as if they had become one, just as the minister had said when he'd married them. But Cooper hadn't seen his wife since he'd heard her declaring her love for another man.

Stephen chuckled. "Everybody said that you would change so much once you became a Marine. And after you got deployed…"

He had changed, but for the most part he thought he did a pretty good job of holding back the memories and the nightmares. Even though Stephen was about to marry the woman Cooper loved, he was his friend. So Coop admitted, "I have changed."

Stephen shook his head. "No, you haven't. You're the same fool you've always been…"

"You're the fool," Cooper said, "to come to my office and insult me."

"You called me here with that stupid voice mail you left, asking me to draw up divorce papers for you and Tanya."

He shrugged. "Annulment papers, then. I'll sign whatever Tanya wants."

"Do you know what Tanya wants?"

"You."

Stephen chuckled again. "She told you that?"

He thought back, trying to remember their conversations. "She told the lawyer she wanted to divorce me."

"Did she tell you why?"

"Because she doesn't want to be married to me," Cooper said.

"Did she tell you that?"

His ribs and back hurt less, but now the pain was throbbing in his head. "Why do you keep asking me all these questions?"

"Because I want to make sure you really know what's in Tanya's heart and you're not just assuming."

I love you...

But he had only dreamed that she'd whispered those words in his ear. He had been completely awake when he'd heard her declare her feelings for Stephen.

"I'm not just assuming," he insisted. "I know..."

"Do you know what's in *your* heart?" Stephen asked.

Cooper snorted. He was not going to have this conversation with the man who was about marry the woman he loved.

"I didn't know what was in mine," Stephen admitted. "I didn't know until I had all those days in the box to think about it."

"Are you suggesting I nail myself inside a box?"

Stephen grimaced.

"Too soon?" he teased.

"Just a little bit." But Stephen grinned. "I've missed you, my friend."

And because they were friends, Cooper had to do this. "Draw up the papers for me."

Stephen reluctantly nodded. "If that's what you really want, I will."

Cooper sucked in a breath over the pain of the jab in his heart. "Okay..."

"But I won't do it until you talk to Tanya."

"That's not necessary."

"It is if you want me to do this favor for you," Stephen said. "You have to do this favor for me."

"Talking to Tanya is doing a favor for *you?*"

Stephen grinned. "Yes, and it's a favor that can't wait. You need to talk to her now."

"But she's at the church." Planning his wedding.

"Exactly. You've wasted enough time," Stephen

admonished him. "Talk to her and then tell me if you want these papers drawn up…"

He didn't want them at all. He didn't want to divorce Tanya. But he couldn't stay married to a woman who loved another man. It was time to end his marriage.

Chapter Nineteen

Tanya found it hard to focus on the wedding plans the others were discussing in Mrs. Payne's sunbathed sunshine-yellow office. She could only hear Cooper's voice ringing in her head from the message he'd left on Stephen's phone. She'd been with her friend when he'd played his voice mail. "I need you to draw up my divorce papers…"

He'd promised that he would end their marriage. And Cooper Payne was a man of his word. She felt like a hypocrite—planning a wedding while her own marriage was ending.

Rochelle nudged her shoulder. "I need your opinion," she said. "You're my maid of honor."

"Matron," Mrs. Payne corrected her. "Your sister is married, so she's a matron."

She wasn't going to be married much longer if Cooper had his way.

Rochelle giggled. She did that so often now, since she was giddy with happiness. "If only she were a little more matronly, I would look better."

"You're going to look beautiful," Tanya assured her. "You are beautiful. Radiant even."

Rochelle blushed. "You're a good matron of honor."

Tanya had been so touched that her sister had asked

her, that she was making an effort to end their resentment and misunderstandings and finally form a real sisterly bond. To ensure Rochelle's happiness, she had to put aside her own pain and loss.

"I'm so happy for you both," she said.

Rochelle leaned over and squeezed Tanya's hand. "You could be this happy, too."

"I just told you, I'm happy."

"For me and Stephen. I want you to be happy for yourself," Rochelle said. "Tell Cooper how you feel about him."

She had. But she'd just cowardly whispered the words in his ear. "It doesn't matter…"

"Why not?"

"Because he doesn't feel the same."

"How do you feel about my son?" Mrs. Payne asked with a big smile that suggested that she knew exactly how Tanya felt about Cooper and that she had probably always known.

"How do you?" a deep voice asked. And his tone suggested that he did not know.

He must not have heard those words she'd whispered in his ear that night. "I told you," she said.

"When I was sleeping…"

So he had heard her.

"But I still told you," she insisted. "What about you?" She gathered the courage to finally ask what she'd been dying for years to know. "How do you feel about me?"

And she held her breath, waiting for his answer.

And waiting…

HEAT CLIMBED INTO Cooper's neck as he realized all these women were staring at him. His mother. His sister. Her sister. And Tanya…

She had really said those words; he hadn't just imagined them. She loved him.

"I heard you tell Stephen the same thing," he said.

"I do love Stephen. But like a friend," she clarified. "Not like Rochelle loves him. Not like he loves Rochelle."

And then he got it. "It's their wedding you're here planning."

Rochelle grinned. "You thought she was planning a wedding to Stephen. She's not a bigamist."

"He called Stephen to draw up divorce papers," she shared with her sister.

"He wouldn't do it until I came here and talked to you," he admitted.

"So you're only here because of Stephen."

He was losing her. He felt it, felt her slipping away. "When you said those words to me, did you mean them the same way you said them to Stephen?"

She made him wait. Her body tense, lips pursed as she considered whether or not to answer him. He didn't blame her if she didn't. He'd just told her that he only came here to get divorce papers drawn up. It would take a lot of courage for her to put herself out there first. But Tanya was much stronger than she looked.

"I have never felt about you like I do Stephen," she said. "You and I have never been just friends. At least not on my end."

"Not on my end either," he admitted.

She waited again.

And he hesitated. He had never been a coward before. He hadn't hesitated to join the Marines. He hadn't hesitated to engage in combat. But he hesitated now because Tanya could hurt him more than any bullet or bomb. She'd said the words, but that didn't mean they had a future together. "Your grandfather was right all those years ago. I had nothing to offer you. I have nothing to offer you now either."

"Yes, you do," she said. "You're just not willing to offer it."

"I have no money."

"I don't either," she reminded him. "I've been fine without money."

"Then why were you going to marry Stephen to collect it?"

"She had plans for the money," Rochelle answered for her. "She was going to help people."

Of course she was. No wonder he loved her so much.

"She doesn't need the money to help people," he said.

Rochelle nodded in agreement. "But there actually is some left. Stephen found Mr. Gregory's offshore accounts. And there's already been an offer on Grandfather's house."

Tanya turned toward her sister, her brow furrowing with confusion. "Who would want that thing?"

"A funeral home."

She laughed in delight.

She would inherit some money now since she'd married before her birthday. Would it be enough to put her out of his league again?

"I don't need money," she said as if she could read his mind.

He actually had more than she or his family probably realized. Because he'd needed very little to live on, he'd invested what he'd been paid, and given the bonuses for every time he'd re-upped, it had mounted.

"What about love?" he asked her. "Do you need love?"

Her breath audibly caught and her green eyes widened with surprise and hope. "Do you…?"

"Love you?" He nodded. "Only with all my heart and soul."

"Well, if that's all…" She jumped up from her chair and threw her arms around his neck. She pressed a kiss to his cheek and his chin and his nose. "I love you! I love you!"

"Yeah, yeah," Nikki said, feigning disinterest despite her sparkling eyes. "Tell us something we haven't all known for years and years…"

Cooper laughed. "I want to do it again."

"What?"

"I want to marry you again," he said.

"Another wedding?" his little sister asked. "It's like you know someone who owns a wedding chapel or something…"

"Yeah, it's like…"

His mother chuckled as she always had at the teasing bickering of her children. That was why they'd started doing it so much—to make her laugh.

Tanya pulled out of his arms. "We can't!"

And panic clutched his heart. Had she changed her mind? Did she not feel strongly enough about him to marry him again?

"We can't infringe on Rochelle's day," she said. "This is her time."

"Finally," Rochelle murmured. "We've both taken our time getting here. How about we walk down that aisle together?" she asked Tanya. "We'll give each other away to the men we love."

Two brides and two grooms stood at the altar. There were two best men—so identical in their black tuxes that it was impossible for Tanya to tell one from the other. Until Parker winked at her.

She and Rochelle shared a maid of honor. Nikki juggled both their bouquets. Tanya's was simple and small—just a bunch of yellow roses—while Rochelle's was a trailing mass of colors and textures.

Rochelle's dress was also nontraditional—short and ruffled and the same blush as the color on her smiling cheeks. Since Rochelle had had time to find that dress, Tanya might have been able to find a new one, too.

But there was only one dress she'd wanted to wear on her wedding day. And thankfully the paramedics hadn't damaged it. She wore Mrs. Payne's—Mom's, as Penny now insisted she call her—beautiful beaded lace gown.

Tanya had worried during the few shorts days it had taken Mrs. Payne—*Mom*—to pull together the weddings that she was infringing on Rochelle's day. But her little sister was happier than Tanya had ever seen her. And so was Stephen as he slid his ring on her finger.

Then it was Cooper's turn. He took her hand in his. Her skin tingled from his touch—and from the intensity of his blue eyes as he gazed down at her.

"With this ring, I thee wed," he repeated as he slid a gold and sparkling diamond band onto her finger.

She marveled at the beauty of it. She had known Cooper since they were both kids, but the man could still surprise her. Like when he added his own vows: "I will love and protect you for the rest of my life, Tanya Payne."

Tanya Payne.

"I love the sound of that," she murmured. "I love you. Always have and always will. You are my best friend. My soul mate. My everything…"

Cooper blinked his thick lashes as if he, too, was battling tears. Of emotion. Of love.

"I now pronounce both couples men and wives," Reverend James said with a chuckle.

Stephen kissed his bride. And Cooper lowered his head to Tanya's, his lips pressing tenderly against hers in such a sweet and gentle kiss that tears sprung to her eyes.

"There'll be more kissing later," he promised her in a whisper for her ears only.

She couldn't wait for later. The reception passed in a blur of eating and dancing and laughing. This was the wedding she had always wanted. And it was all the sweeter that she was able to share it with her sister, her friends and her new family.

Parker twirled her around the dance floor. "This wedding's been kind of boring," he complained with a teasing grin. "Nobody's gotten kidnapped, shot at or poisoned."

Tanya blew out a breath of relief that none of those things had happened. Because usually those things happened to her or Cooper. "I don't know what you're talking about," she teased back as the Payne family—*her* family—loved to tease. "It's been the most exciting day of my life."

Cooper tugged her out of his brother's arms and swung her up in his own. "It's about to get more exciting," he said, "we're heading off for our honeymoon now."

Stephen and Rochelle had already left—eager to start the life together that had nearly been denied them. She forced back the guilt and regret. The past was over. Everyone was safe and happy.

"I hope you packed some of that sexy lingerie," Cooper said.

"Oh, I have something special for you," she promised.

"You're the something special," he said.

She clasped her arms around her husband's neck as he carried her up the steps from the lower-level reception hall. He passed through the vestibule and headed down the outside church staircase to the street.

Logan and Nikki stood on the steps, leaning against the railing. Laughing, they flung handfuls of birdseed at them as Cooper and Tanya passed. Parker followed behind, tossing it down on them like rain. An SUV waited at the curb. Across its back window someone had scrawled *Just Married* in chalk. And strings of pop cans had been tied to the back bumper.

"Damn you all!" Cooper playfully yelled at his family.

Tanya laughed, happier than she had ever been.

Until the shots rang out…

Cooper ducked low over Tanya, protecting her with his body and the SUV that he shielded them both behind. But his family—their family—stood on the front steps yet, exposed.

Tires squealed as the car from which the shots must have been fired sped around the corner. She wriggled out of Cooper's arms and turned back.

Logan covered Nikki on the stairs. But Parker was gone.

"Parker!" Cooper yelled his name as he hurried over to the stairs. A hand rose from the thick shrubs on the sides of the stairwell. He clasped it and pulled his brother from the foliage. "You okay?"

"Yeah, yeah," he said, brushing off his tux and their concern. "Logan knocked me over after pushing down Nikki." He turned toward his twin, as if waiting for the smart-alecky comments they continually threw at each other.

But Logan said nothing but sorry. He said it to his brother and sister and then he turned to Tanya and Cooper. "I'm sorry…"

Tanya shook her head. "I thought it was over. Mr. Gregory is dead." But maybe he hadn't been working alone.

"This isn't about you," Logan assured them all. "This is about me. And revenge…"

"You know who it is," Cooper said.

He nodded. "And I'll take care of it. You two leave for your honeymoon." He hugged them both then pushed them toward the SUV. "Leave before the police get here. You've given enough reports during the past week to last a lifetime."

Cooper obeyed his brother and helped Tanya into the passenger's seat before sliding behind the wheel himself. She clutched his arm. "Are you sure?" she asked. "If you want to stay and help him, our honeymoon can wait."

"Our honeymoon waited too long," he said, "because of my stubbornness and pride." He glanced back at his family. "They trusted me to take care of myself while I was in the Marines. I trust Logan to protect himself and the others."

His brother waved them off as Cooper pulled away from the curb. Tanya stared back at them and she couldn't help worrying that it might be the last time she saw them.

Cooper took her hand in his and entwined their fingers. "They'll be okay," he promised her. "They're Paynes."

She smiled.

"And so are you," he said. "You are my wife."

"It's real," she said with a sweet sigh of relief.

"We're still going to consummate it," he teased. "Over and over again…"

She laughed. He was right. His family could take care of themselves—they'd been doing it for years. And now she and Cooper would spend the rest of their lives taking care of each other. "I love you."

"I'm not sure I heard you," he teased, probably in reference to that first time she had uttered those words to him in a whisper.

So she shouted, "I love you!"

"Married a few hours and she's already yelling at me," Cooper remarked to himself.

Tanya laughed again as she envisioned their future together, as she had so many times when she'd been a teenager. But now it wasn't just a fantasy; it was real. They probably would yell at each other from time to time. But they would have laughter, too. And given her job and his, they would probably have danger, as well. But as he'd promised, he would keep her safe. And she would make certain that he always knew how much she loved him— even if she had to shout it.

* * * * *

"I'll do my best to keep this killer away from you, Lindsey. I promise."

"I believe you. Still, you hardly know me." She tilted her face to look at him.

"Then that's something we'll have to change."

Brian delivered a trail of hot kisses down the side of her face and continued a path back up to her forehead. Lindsey turned her mouth into his path, and the fireworks were as explosive as the kiss earlier that morning.

Their tongues danced and explored. His fingers barely grazed her waist and then she felt a tug on both sides of her shirt. Brian backed away, leaving her lips cold and desperate for more of him.

"As much as I'd like to keep on with this—" he dropped another kiss on her cheek "—our first time is not going to be when we could be interrupted at any moment."

She stood there with her mouth open at the audacity of his words. *Our first time?*

THE RENEGADE
RANCHER

BY
ANGI MORGAN

Published in Great Britain 2014
by Mills & Boon, an imprint of Harlequin (UK) Limited,
Eton House, 18-24 Paradise Road, Richmond, Surrey, TW9 1SR

© 2014 Angela Platt

ISBN: 978-0-263-91361-3

46-0614

Harlequin (UK) Limited's policy is to use papers that are natural, renewable and recyclable products and made from wood grown in sustainable forests. The logging and manufacturing processes conform to the legal environmental regulations of the country of origin.

Printed and bound in Spain
by Blackprint CPI, Barcelona

Angi Morgan writes Mills & Boon® Intrigue novels "where honor and danger collide with love." She combines actual Texas settings with characters who are in realistic and dangerous situations. Angi has been a finalist for the Booksellers' Best Award, *RT Book Reviews* Best First Series, Gayle Wilson Award of Excellence and the Daphne du Maurier Award.

Angi and her husband live in north Texas, with only the four-legged "kids" left in the house to interrupt her writing. They recently began volunteering for a local Labrador foster program. Visit her website, www.angimorgan.com, or hang out with her on Facebook.

Many moons ago, I graduated from high school with a small group of kids. Brian & Johnny are fictional characters, but named after two men who won't be returning at our next reunion. I have used the names of people in my hometown, but not their personalities. The characters are fictional, but not my friendships or the respect I have for the namesakes.

Chapter One

Tall, blond and deadly gorgeous.

Brian Sloane knew that Lindsey Cook was a looker. One glance would let any male with eyes know that fact. Platinum blond hair that hung to her waist, classic blue eyes that would disappear next to a clear summer sky and a body that should be gracing covers of magazines. A looker, all right.

This was the longest he'd ever been with a woman and he hadn't met her yet.

He knew how old she was, where she'd graduated from college, that her best friend's name was Beth. All that information was on her internet site. He knew she lived in Arlington, drove a sports car, kept two goldfish and was allergic to cats. She'd had five jobs in the past three years and did freelance web design. He also knew why she'd migrated to Texas after burying her cousin. Jeremy had drowned while they'd been on vacation together about six months ago and she'd stayed after settling his affairs. Her cousin's *female* lawyer had been extrachatty during happy hour.

Unfortunately, accidents happened everywhere, leaving one question he couldn't answer. How long she would live.

Brian entered the sandwich shop and tried not to zoom

all his attention on her. Searching the remaining tables, he noticed no one else was alone, so it was probably safe to assume she was his appointment. "Lindsey?"

"You're Brian?" she asked, extending her hand. Her smile could mesmerize him. He'd watched her work that magic on several customers—male and female—over the past couple of weeks.

"That'd be me." He took a slender palm in his own, gave a quick squeeze and sat at the table. A well-chosen table in the middle of the very empty sandwich shop. The red silky blouse clung everywhere and plunged just enough to make his imagination go a little wild.

"So, you said that Jeremy's lawyer recommended me for a job. Your email said something about a ranch website?"

"Yeah, about that. This might sound strange, but I've been doing some research and—" Was that sudden look in her eyes one of surprise? An alert? How had he messed up?

"No website?"

He stared, thinking hard on what his answer should be. It was important she listen to him. Her life depended on it. He couldn't just say that. Could he? He'd avoided the truth long enough. "To be honest—"

"Excuse me just a sec." She looked into her purse. She brought her keys to the tabletop. Hooked to the ring—now pointed at his face—was a small can of pepper spray. "Who are you and why have you been following me? I saw you in front of the store yesterday and you were in line behind me when I got coffee last week."

"Whoa there." He raised his hands, trying not to jump away from that can. "I really am Brian Sloane. I'm a Fort Worth paramedic, just like I said on the phone. I've got ID."

She shook her head slowly from side to side. Was she thinking about believing him or shooting that pepper spray into his eyes? Okay, so he'd slipped up and not only let her see him a couple of times, but he'd made eye contact at the coffee shop. Who could have resisted? She was smoking hot.

"I'm going to leave," she said, "and you'd better stop following me. Just so you know, I took your picture when you walked in and if I see you again—even by accident— I'll report you to the police as a stalker."

He leaned forward, and she jerked to attention. *Skittish as a newborn colt.* "I know this is a weird way to meet."

"To say the least." She kept the nozzle pointed at his eyes. Extremely close to his eyes.

"But I do have information regarding your family."

"I don't have any family."

"What I mean is…I've been doing research and I think Jeremy was murdered."

"I thought you were an EMT. You sound like a reporter." She brought her finely shaped eyebrows into a straight line, showing her scrutiny and distrust. Not knowing she'd just delivered an insult to highly trained paramedics everywhere by calling him an entry-level EMT.

With a new sister-in-law around his house, he was picking up on a lot of subtle feminine looks that he'd had no clue about before. This look? Well, it didn't leave any room for interpretation.

He shifted. She jerked.

"Just getting my wallet. Okay?"

"Is there a problem, Lindsey?" The guy behind the sandwich counter stopped wiping the display cases.

"I'm fine. Just dealing with another jerk reporter."

"I'm not a reporter." He shook his head, looked at the

big fellow who was very defensive of the woman in front of him and repeated, "I'm *not* a reporter."

"Then why are you following me?"

"It's a long story and I'd rather not have pepper spray aimed at me while I tell it."

Lindsey's long, straight hair gently framed a delicate, expressive, beautiful face that he'd been attracted to since the first picture he'd seen of her online. It sort of took him by surprise when she leaned back in her chair, dropped her hands to her lap and waited, the key ring in plain sight. Her protector returned to cleaning. The shop's patrons went back to business as usual.

"I'd like the short version, please," she said, pushing her hair behind her ear. "You've got five minutes and then I'm leaving."

Short? How did he explain such a complicated story?

"All right. Twelve years ago I thought my brother caused the accidental fire that took the life of one of our former teachers, your second cousin, Gillian Cook. But I was wrong. She was murdered."

"Take it to the police." She pushed back her chair and scooped her keys into her purse, clearly taking off.

"You said I had five minutes."

She stood. Her long hair swayed at her waist, drawing his attention to the fraction of flat belly he could see above her jeans when her shirt rose up as she took a deep breath.

"You have five seconds to remove your hand from my arm or I'll let Craig—" she tipped her head to the sandwich guy, who threw down his bar towel "—deal with you. Four. Three."

Craig dashed to the end of the counter. Brian dropped his hold. Lindsey stared at him as her friend reached for his shirt. He'd been so caught up in her leaving that he hadn't realized he'd grabbed her arm to stop her.

"Sorry. I didn't mean to scare you."

"Wait. Craig, wait." She waved off the man's attempt to lift Brian from the chair—*through* the table. "Look, I'm very tired of people hounding me about my accident-prone family. There have been terrible emails from someone thinking I'm a jinx." She hid her eyes behind slender fingers, then shoved her hair behind her ear again and straightened her back. "I know what happened to my family. I live with it every day, and to have it in the paper or on a blog is disrespectful. It's mean and I've had enough. Just leave me alone."

She tilted her face toward her chest, hiding behind her hair.

"Your family didn't do anything wrong." Brilliant blue eyes opened wide to search him. Why was she ashamed? "Besides, I don't think they were accidents. And I'm fairly certain you're next."

"Seriously? You think someone's out to kill me?" Her long nails were the exact color of one of the flowers on her shirt. It was easy to see with her hand nervously rubbing her collarbone.

"I haven't been stalking you, Miss Cook. Our paths crossed while I was looking into your cousin's life," he explained. It was true enough. He had been looking into Jeremy Cook.

Craig stood guard at her shoulder, ready to do battle, his arms crossed over a massive chest. It was plain why Lindsey had chosen this location to meet a stranger. "Take it to the cops," Craig said. "You ready for me to throw this jerk out?"

One cross look would have Brian's face pulverized before he could defend himself. Well, Craig could try.

Brian had fought with the best around his hometown for a long time. So he shrugged. He'd never convince her while including muscleman in the conversation. She didn't believe him. Hell, he hardly believed himself. His theory was so far out there he hadn't even shared it with his family.

He'd tried, right? That was all he could do. He pressed on the table to push his chair back and long, bright nails tapped quickly near his hand, gaining his attention.

"It's okay, Craig. I'm okay." She looked up at her protector and winked at him, immediately relaxing the big guy and getting her way.

Brian waited until they were alone and lowered his voice, leaning closer across the table. "Look, I'm not a cop or a detective or a reporter. I really am just a horse rancher who pays the bills by working as a paramedic."

"You're wowing me with so many reasons to believe you." She laughed. Her eyes sparkled and were sad at the same time.

He understood that. How an enjoyable moment could catch you off guard and you forget—just for an instant. Then the reason you don't laugh comes rushing back to blur the happy. Yeah, he understood.

"You have every right to wonder about my motives. You should be careful. I should have left this info with your lawyer and never bothered you in person. I'll be on my way."

"Why did you? Come here, that is."

The tap on the tabletop drew his eyes back to her hands, then up her tanned arms, to her shoulders and neck. The slow tap and arch of her eyebrow showed him she knew he'd been taking a long look. He expected a wink any second, and would probably do whatever she asked. He was *that* attracted.

He pushed himself straighter in the chair and caught her doing a little looking of her own.

"I can't convince you to trust me. I'll drop everything off at your lawyer's office after I get out of your hair."

"Wait. I, um… If you're really not a reporter, can you begin again? Take five more minutes?" She brought part of her hair in front of her shoulder and began twisting strands into a tiny braid. "Start with what the police said."

"That I was crazy."

"I can't imagine why." She smiled, sliding back into the chair next to him. "I'm sorry and really trying to understand why you think someone's trying to kill me. You have to admit, it's not news you get every day."

He'd give her that point. He also liked her sassiness. "When you look at each family, the deaths seem to be open-and-shut accidents. But a friend of mine who's big on genealogy did a search. And then there's the regular intervals of the accidents. My brother caught that when—"

"Why do you think I'm next?" she interrupted, eyes worried, her breathing rapid.

"You're the only one left."

Chapter Two

Lindsey wanted to run from the shop and the memories. But the man leaning across the table looking so concerned on her behalf intrigued her. She still had doubts and couldn't possibly believe his theory. It didn't hurt to hear him out. She glanced at the clock behind him. She had plenty of time before she needed to be at work.

His hand covered hers. "I'm really sorry. I shouldn't have said it like that. I'm not used to this kind of conversation."

She could feel the calluses, the warmth, the strength. He looked genuinely worried. A shiver crept up her back. The eerie kind that could make you look under your bed after watching a shark movie. But that was nonsense, just like thinking all her family had been murdered.

"When Jeremy died, I made the mistake of mentioning to one of his friends that he was my last close relative. He didn't wait until Jeremy had been buried before he blogged about the accidents of those close to me. He ranted about how *lucky* I seemed to escape death while those close to me didn't and insinuated there may be foul play."

"That's why you thought I was a reporter. I don't blame you for grabbing your pepper spray."

Brian Sloane wasn't anything like she'd expected.

Honestly, she'd thought the man following her would be a psychopath. Someone following her for a really weird reason like they loved her nails or something. So if this tall cowboy wasn't following her and hadn't been the one asking Craig questions earlier this week, then who was the mystery man and how would she find him?

"Why do *you* think someone wants to kill me, Mr. Sloane?"

"Brian, please. My daddy's still Mr. Sloane and is the only one who deserves that title."

A good-looking cowboy who could charm his way anywhere, she'd bet. It was easy to see the solid, chiseled body just under his T-shirt. Hard not to imagine the strength that came with the square jaw and high cheekbones. *Not so fast, Mr. Sloane.*

"We haven't found a reason."

"We? I thought the police didn't believe you."

"A neighbor and my sister-in-law have been helping me." He leaned his chiseled jaw on his elbow. "Discovering the truth is important to my family. Everybody's chipped in some research time."

"Maybe you should start at the beginning?" And maybe she shouldn't look too much at that million-dollar smile.

"Four months ago, I began trying to find the family of a neighbor and teacher in Aubrey—the town where I live. She died just after my high school graduation in an accident I was blamed for."

"A second cousin who I never met."

He nodded. "I started looking just after Jeremy drowned in Cozumel. His death made the news in Fort Worth, so I recognized his name."

"He was snorkeling. His body had lots of small cuts and scratches. They think he got caught in the coral." She relived Jeremy's drowning almost every night and hoped to forgive herself one day. "Over forty people were in the water and no one saw anything."

His grip on her hand tightened and he nodded as if he understood.

"Mabel, my dad's friend, researched your family tree. Every name she gave me passed from an accident." He paused and removed a piece of paper from his back pocket. "Here. Fourteen names. They're all related to you and all died in the past twenty years. Most out of state."

He pushed the paper over to her with a long finger, then leaned back in his chair, lacing those fingers together behind his neck. His brows arched high, waiting for her to acknowledge his assumptions.

"The police are right. A list doesn't prove anything."

"Don't you see?" He jumped forward, his hand landing a little too loudly on the tabletop.

Lindsey automatically reached for the mace again, stopping herself when she saw the concern in Brian's puppy-brown eyes. Wouldn't it be the perfect ploy for a serial killer to pose as the person trying to stop himself?

Don't be a ninny.

"I can't see anything with the exception that there are several people on that list I loved very much."

"I'm sorry. I know how hard that must be."

"I don't see how. Your father's still alive." Remembering brought a very fresh pain of responsibility for Jeremy's accident. *Accident.* Not murder. She was the one who had taken off instead of snorkeling with him. "I'm sorry, Brian, that was rude."

"It's all right. This information is out of the blue from a complete stranger."

"You aren't the first to come to me with this type of conspiracy story. One of Jeremy's friends spread it across

FriendshipConnect. But just like all the others, you can't offer a reason why anyone would want us dead. Nor do you have proof. So...I'm leaving now and I'd appreciate it if you didn't contact me again."

Lindsey threw her bag over her shoulder and left before the sympathetic cowboy could talk her into staying. Her hand found the pepper spray—just in case. Good-looking or not, he had a look in his eyes that promised he wouldn't let this story go. What he'd gain from it...what any of them gained from it, she had no idea and would never understand.

She used her shoulder to push through the door. The afternoon heat wasn't too bad for mid-October. But she was used to much cooler temperatures. Nothing even close to the record-breaking heat wave they'd experienced through the summer in the Dallas–Fort Worth area.

She searched her bottomless pit of a purse until she felt the familiar shape of thick-rimmed sunglasses and pushed them onto her face to block the UV rays. At the next doorway, she ducked under the awning, close to the window, to get out of sight in case Mr. Sloane followed her again.

Someone wanted to murder her? *Ridiculous. Right?*

It didn't make sense. Jeremy had drowned. There were forty other people snorkeling on that reef from his boat. Another twenty-seven from a second tour. They'd all been interviewed and no one had seen anything unusual. Nothing except people snorkeling.

They assumed Jeremy went too deep. From the scratches around his ankle, it looked as though he'd gotten caught on the coral. Nothing foul or sinister. Just tragic.

If I'd been there...I could have prevented his death.

The stinging sensation that preluded tears was just

behind her eyelids. They were seconds away from shedding, just like most days. She watched a couple walk by, shopping bags looped over their shoulders, hands clasped together, no determination in their stride. Perhaps a fun day off?

Maybe she needed a manicure or a sweater since it was beginning to cool down in the evenings?

No. That was the old Lindsey. The one who would take off, not caring if her supervisor got upset, not caring about the job. There was always another job. Not this time. Now she worked regular hours, at a regular job, with the possibility of advancement. There would always be a demand for cell phones, and she was due to start her shift in an hour.

What was here that didn't require spending money? Nothing. It was an outdoor strip mall next to the only real shopping for miles. In fact, her store was just around the corner. She'd have to avoid that section or just be early. She could do that—be early for once. Turn over a new leaf. Take that new start Jeremy wanted for her.

"Okay, then." She left her car parked by Craig's sandwich shop and walked to her boring job.

Seven boring hours later, she rounded the building to empty storefront parking. The lone exception—her car. Jeremy's car, really. The other employees had parked closer and all these shops had closed about an hour before. It was a busy street corner. Lots of traffic, well lit, and she still got a creepy feeling crawling up her spine. She couldn't see anyone. No tall paramedic-psycho-cowboy nearby. She jumped out of her skin when her cell buzzed in her pocket.

Beth.

"Just wanted to make sure you were all right, Lindsey. It seemed like you had a rough day. We all miss him, you know."

"I know. I'm sorry I'm on the verge of crying all the time. There's no mystery why. I live in his apartment. I drive his car. I'm working in the store he managed. I don't just have survivor's guilt because I didn't drown, I'm living his life." She stopped and dug the keys from her purse. "Oh, gosh, I'm sorry to dump on you like that."

"I wouldn't have asked if it wasn't okay. You at your car now?"

Keys in hand, she was close enough to click a button to unlock, she answered, "Yes, I'll see you in a couple of days."

She'd become very used to the little luxuries that had filled her cousin's life. Having a dependable car with hands-free capability was a must from this point forward.

Relaxation would be hers soon. In twenty minutes, she'd be soaking in a hot bath, bubbles up to her chin and lots of candles on the windowsill. There was little traffic on her route home, but a flashing light and detour sign had her turning on an unfamiliar street. Then again. Where was the button for GPS?

The route between apartment and store was easy, but if she got turned around, she could easily get lost on the south side of Arlington. She hadn't been in the area very long and she'd never had a good sense of direction. Another mile and she was so turned around it was silly to try to get back without directions.

No signs at the intersection. She stopped on the right shoulder far enough from the corner to let traffic pass by, then put the car in Park and tapped the screen. The GPS switched on and she looked up in time to see a car approaching behind her. The road was narrow, but with no other cars around, she powered the window down and waved the car to pass her.

The car didn't slow. Was it swerving? Still on a collision course with her. She jammed her foot on the gas. The lights blinded her in the mirror as she sped through the red light.

The impact at the rear of the car was an ear-piercing sound. The jolting crash hurt almost as much as the abrupt stop at the fence post across the street. She closed her eyes and choked when the air bag exploded in her face, feeling the burns shoot across her skin like skidding hard on cement.

By the time she could look up, the only lights around her were from the dashboard. She heard the engine rattling and cut off the ignition. Then nothing. She half expected an evil car to be sitting on the road, racing its engine. But nothing.

All alone.

Sore with every move, she searched for her purse and cell phone, then dialed 911 and explained what had happened.

"Rescue assistance is on the way. Do you want me to stay on the line with you?"

"I'm shook up but I think I'm okay." She reached to disconnect with shaking hands, and that creepy sensation returned. It had sure seemed as if that driver had meant to hit her car. "On second thought, do you mind talking? There aren't any cars around and I…"

"I'd be glad to stay on the line until the police arrive. The squad car is only a couple of minutes out."

Her narrow escape had been close.

Too close?

"Did you see the vehicle that hit you?"

"Not really. No." But it had deliberately swerved onto

the shoulder. She was sure of that. "I think there was a black car following me earlier."

What were the odds of a hit-and-run accident on the very day someone claimed she would be a murder victim?

Should she tell the police about her meeting? What if he actually was the crazy psycho who'd followed? Would they laugh at her like they had Brian? Or was it time to find her own answers? Would anyone believe her except Brian?

"Ma'am? Do you see the police?"

"Yes. Thank you."

She should take charge of her destiny. Take charge. That sounded a lot better than becoming another "accident."

Chapter Three

"Who wants him?" Brian gave the vitals as they came through the emergency room doors. They pushed the gurney to a room where the victim was quickly assessed as stable and blood drawn for an alcohol level. He was the only victim after running a stop sign and causing a multicar pileup in downtown Fort Worth.

"Don't go anywhere, Sloane," his favorite nurse, Meeks, instructed. "After you hand him off, wait for a doctor to stitch up that forehead."

"You know that's not going to happen." He touched the cut and looked at a bloody finger. "Thirty years without stitches and I'm not starting now."

Cam, his rig partner, had laughed when their patient had lashed out, taken him by surprise and knocked him to the floor. Distracted by a pair of sky-blue eyes and convincing himself there was no way to see them again, the drunk John Doe's flaying had sent Brian's forehead into the defibrillator. He hadn't shared the real reason he'd been caught off guard—just complained about the bumps in the road.

He swiped at a drop of blood, keeping it from falling into his eyes.

Meeks ripped open a package and handed him a sterile dressing. "Sit."

"I'm fine."

"You have to wait for the doctor anyway." Meeks pointed to the chair in the corner and Brian sat, applying the dressing to his gash. "You're staying. Wow, he reeks of liquor. It's one of those nights. Someone said it was quiet around here and now we don't have enough doctors."

"Meeks! He's coding," a voice shouted from across the hall.

He could use the E.R. staff owing him a favor. So he waited with his patient while they were called away. Drunk Driver Doe was still out cold and snoring.

"I'm going to clean some of your blood out of the rig. Back in a few."

"I really don't need stitches." He jumped up and spoke to an empty room. At least empty of anyone who could get him out of here.

The gauze quickly soaked with blood. He hadn't taken a good look at it and there weren't any mirrors in the room. So he mentally agreed to wait with Drunk Doe. He looked at the man's vitals again and leaned on the counter. The chair looked more inviting with every throb in his skull. So he sat again.

Closing his eyes, he was immediately immersed in memories of the night of the fire. He hadn't thought about it for twelve years and now that was all he could see. Or hear. Or smell. He and his brother, John, had gone over their movements of the night that had changed their lives so often in the past four months that it played in his head like a movie.

"Sorry I took so long, took me a while to get some coffee. Hey, partner, you okay?" Cam asked, his arms full of their gear. "You're um…dripping."

"You've got to be kidding." Brian was on his feet. The

bloody gauze was on the floor next to him instead of in his hand. "I must have slept a couple of minutes in spite of all the noise around here."

"Passed out's more likely," Meeks added behind Cam.

"Yeah, man. I was gone close to twenty-five minutes. Dispatch is calling, I have to take this." Cam left, answering his cell, his voice fading so fast Brian couldn't hear what he was asked or reporting.

"Sit back down." Meeks donned gloves and assessed his wound, took his BP and asked him standard memory-loss questions. "I'm finding a doctor for those sutures. You're most likely concussed and need a scan."

There was nothing wrong with him except a growing headache—more from all the fuss than injury. But he took it all in stride. If it had been Cam sitting here, he'd have done the same thing. His best efforts to think of another subject led him straight back to his gorgeous bundle of trouble and how to convince her that her life was in danger.

After their first meet, Lindsey Cook thought he was a stalker. He needed to move forward and put the past behind him. Without her. Hadn't he done everything he could do?

So why did he have a bad feeling in the pit of his gut? Why was he trying so hard to convince himself he'd done everything possible? Memories of the town uproar after he'd claimed the fire had been his fault came pressing back to weigh him down. He'd thought he'd done all he could do then, too.

Claiming responsibility for an accident so his brother could continue in the Navy had been the optimal option at the time. But if they'd just talked about that night instead of being so hardheaded, they wouldn't have lost twelve years. Hard years neither of them would get back. Years that had set a chain of events into motion. Not only for him and his twin, but for his family, the ranch, the town and all of Lindsey's family.

If they'd stopped this maniac by forcing the police to discover the truth twelve years ago, how many deaths could have been avoided?

Now he was grateful he'd waited on a doctor. He never wanted to fight with Nurse Meeks. An ironic name for Cindy's demanding personality. Old enough to be his mom, ornery enough to be a prison guard and still loved by everyone who came through her E.R.

A new intern entered pushing a tray. "Are you Sloane?"

"About time. The patient's been unconscious since transport—"

"Wait. I'm not here for him. Meeks said you needed some, um, sutures."

I trust a shaky EMT rookie more than a green first-year med student. "Does Meeks hate me?" If this kid did a terrible job of it, he'd walk out. "Why'd they send you?"

"Everyone else is tied up and they said it would be good practice." He filled a syringe and got the needle ready to deaden Brian's skin.

"Dispatch is ordering you home, buddy," Cam said.

"Ow. Take it easy."

Cam laughed. "Call when you're ready to leave and I'll see if we can swing by and take you back to your truck."

"Come on, Cam. Get one of the real doctors." He kept still while his partner shook his head and covered his laughing hyena mouth. "On second thought, get out. I'll get my own ride back and convince the old man to let me finish my tour."

"Paid leave, man. Take it." Cam patted him on the shoulder and started to leave. "You need to be cleared by a…" He looked the intern over and snickered again. "A real doctor before showing up tomorrow."

Brian was stuck in more ways than one. The strong odor of booze mixed with antiseptic as the intern irrigated the wound, and kind of made him woozy. The kid spun on the little stool and picked up the needle and suture. Then he spun back with shaking hands, seemingly eager to jab the thing into Brian's forehead.

"Hoover Dam, kid!" Brian swatted the intern's fingers away from his head. "Wait for me to deaden up or hand that needle over to me."

"Sorry. We're sort of busy, so I was in a hurry. I forgot."

"Well, go check on a patient or something and come back in a few."

As soon as the kid left, Brian grabbed the needle and planted himself in front of the counter. *Cell phone, flip the camera, instant mirror.* He took a look at the deep gash, couldn't feel anything above his brow and put a couple of clean stitches in the middle.

"Not half-bad," he said to Drunk Doe. He added some tape and was washing his hands when the door opened. "You can tend to your other patients, Doc. I took care of it. You ready to take this patient off my hands?"

He spun around, expecting the intern, but found those sad blue eyes that had haunted him for weeks.

"Hi. I bet this seems strange to track you down in the middle of the night," Lindsey Cook said, as if she hadn't threatened a restraining order that afternoon.

"A little. I didn't think I'd see you again after this afternoon." The abrasions on her face screamed for him to ask, but she'd sought him out for some reason. Maybe he should wait to ask, but her face was ashen. If he wasn't mistaken, she was in a great deal of pain.

"They said you'd been injured and might need a ride home." She sounded less confident. Almost afraid.

"Don't take this the wrong way, but you don't look so hot yourself."

"I'm fine." She sat on the rolling stool he'd just vacated. "So you really are an EMT."

He didn't want to correct her on the difference between an EMT and paramedic. "Yeah, I am. How'd you find me?" *More important, why did you want to?*

"I called a Fort Worth fire station and asked for you. One fireman was kind enough to explain that the ambulance service is a different company. I found the number and they assumed I was your sister-in-law for some odd reason. I didn't bother to correct them."

The shy smile she shot his direction didn't hide that she'd lied to find him. She reached to push her hair behind her ear and winced. Even an untrained person could figure out she was hurt.

"I guess it didn't dawn on my colleagues that my sister-in-law would just call my cell." He tapped his phone still on the counter.

"Not if she had a surprise. But they assumed you were getting a CT scan or something and couldn't answer your phone."

He pointed to his head. "No scan for me. So why didn't you just call me? You had the number."

"Well, I wanted to have this conversation face-to-face."

So she'd done her own amateur detective work, found him and had something to say. The room was a little small, throwing them within touching distance. Something he'd wanted more of since shaking her hand that afternoon.

"I'm sorry for frightening you today. I just thought

you'd want to know," he said to start the conversation again. The intern would be returning soon and it would be even more awkward.

She seized his hand, clinging to it with a sense of desperation he knew all too well. The desperate need for someone to care and make you feel like you weren't alone. He'd been there four months ago when his father had suffered a major stroke.

"I think someone tried to kill me tonight," she whispered, her eyes darting to the drunk on the bed.

"What happened?" He moved to lean on the counter. Nothing jerky, but it shifted her arm.

She released a sharp hiss between her teeth. "I got lost on the way to Jeremy's house and—"

"Hey, first things first. Did you see a doctor? Where are you injured?"

"My shoulder's hurting. It's just bruised from the seat belt."

"Mind if I have a look?" His fingers were already heading toward her.

"Do you really know what you're doing?"

He had to laugh. "Yeah, I've been doing this over eight years now. More if you count all the horses on the ranch I've nursed back to health." When she turned those baby blues on him he had trouble focusing. "You didn't answer me. Did anyone look at your shoulder, and how long ago did it happen?"

"The EMT checked it around ten. And another doctor at the E.R. I'll be fine."

Seat belt injury equaled car wreck. He gently probed her left shoulder through her shirt where the strap would have bruised. "So you got lost and had an accident?"

"I don't think it was an accident," she whispered again.

She didn't jerk away, just looked at Drunk Doe. "Is it safe to talk here?"

"He's unconscious. We have plenty of time to go over what happened while I get one of the doctors to examine you."

"No. Please. I've already been to the emergency room. It's okay, really." She caught his hand again. "Does that mean you'll help me? You're the only one who might believe me."

"What can I do? I'm a paramedic, not a bodyguard."

Brian wanted the truth, but attempted murder was out of his league. He had other problems to think about anyway. His twin brother was home for good and married with a kid. His family's ranch was getting closer to foreclosure. And he wanted to say yes so badly to this woman his mouth was forming the word.

"If someone tried to kill you, then the police are working your case. I should probably stay out of it."

The relief rushed his body like a warm shower. He could focus on finding the money to take over the ranch payments. Maybe stop working as a paramedic and focus on breeding champion quarter horses again. Maybe see a little more of the world. Maybe watch some Sunday football. Buy a boat and get some fishing in. Lots of boring choices instead of working every minute.

Nothing like his brother's life as a Navy SEAL. And none of which involved spending time with a beautiful blonde.

"I hate saying this, Brian, but I'm afraid to go home alone. I need your help. You're my only hope."

"I'm not a hero in some movie. I'm a nobody." He pushed on her shoulder to make sure it was in place. "I think it's just bruised. Did they get an X-ray? I'll call a nurse."

"Wait." She latched on to his biceps. "You're the only reason my car didn't shoot into a telephone poll. Your warning made me extracautious and I kept watching the car behind me. If you hadn't spoken to me this afternoon, I wouldn't need your help now. I'd be dead."

He was dang tired of being anyone's *only hope*. His brother twelve years ago. The ranch. His dad. He'd warned her. That was all he could do. "This is a job for the police, not an amateur with some friends who did some digging for him."

"But they won't. The police officer called it an accident and blamed me for not pulling farther off the road." Those picture-perfect eyes filled to their full mark and one tear escaped down her tanned, freckled cheek. She swiped at it with the back of her free hand.

"God-d...bless America." He couldn't say yes. "This is such a bad idea. I'm not the guy you need to help you."

"But you're the one who told me—"

"I'm going to have a doctor look at your shoulder." Brian gently cupped her injury, gave it a soft you'll-be-all-right pat and grabbed the door with every intention to march into the hall, shout for Meeks and continue his life. But that nagging gut feeling wouldn't let him. "What is it you want me to do?"

"Tell me how to convince the authorities someone's after me."

"I haven't had much luck with that."

Was this the same woman he'd met earlier, so full of confidence protecting herself at the sandwich shop? Injured, sitting with her shoulders slumped, waiting on answers he didn't have. If he hadn't put the idea of murder into her life, she wouldn't be afraid to go home. It would have been just another car accident.

Another accident.

"How do you know it was deliberate? You're certain the car swerved off the road? Were there any witnesses?"

"I can tell when a car swerves directly toward me." She sat straight with confidence. "How did you get that cut on your forehead?"

Leave. Forget Miss Blue Eyes and your curiosity. You can't do anything to help.

"I fell." His hand was still on the door handle. "Why?"

"Any witnesses?" She rubbed her shoulder. "I'm sure the police will believe you. It shouldn't be a problem, but you could have been in a fight. Or drunk. Lord knows you smell like you bathed in alcohol."

"Got me. You didn't mention to the cop at the scene about your family history? Or that I think the family accidents might actually be murders?"

She pressed her lips together, shook her head and nervously raised a finger to twist her hair. "I sort of told them, but they wouldn't believe me when I said I didn't know who you were."

"You had my number and I could have confirmed your details. Why wouldn't you? Oh, I get it. You think if you tell the cops that I'll be in trouble?"

"Hey," she said, standing and putting a hand on a hip. "I don't know what to believe. Right now, I'm exhausted but there's no way I can go home alone. No, no, no, you get that look out of your eyes, mister. I'm not asking you to come home with me. Shoot. I sort of thought you might have been the guy who hit me. I don't think you are, since the other firemen confirmed your shift began at seven. But honestly, I don't know you."

"Did you hit your head?"

"No. At least, I don't think I did. The air bag scraped me."

He watched the realization of his words wash over her in an embarrassing shade of pink.

"Oh, no. I'm sorry. When I get nervous, I tend to babble. I think you misunderstood what I meant earlier."

"What part? When you asked for help? Or when you thought I might have tried to murder you?"

"All I want is a cup of coffee and some pancakes." She cradled her arm closer to her side.

Pancakes? He could go for some pancakes. "Cafeteria's closed. Will Pan-Hop do?" Maybe she could fill in some blanks in his research?

She nodded. "Great. I love their double-stack special. What about him?"

"I almost forgot about Drunk Driver Doe." He pressed the nurse call button. "Meeks. I've gotta leave."

"I'll be right there, Sloane."

"For the record," Lindsey said with the confidence he'd seen when they'd first met, "I don't know why I started looking for you, but this seemed like my only option. I don't intend to have any more *accidents*."

"The folder's in my truck back at the lot. My captain's already told me to head home." He pointed to his bandage. "Get me pancakes and I'll tell you everything."

"My moment of feeling sorry for myself is over. I want all the details. Everything you've learned about my family."

He could pass along what he'd discovered. Maybe not everything. He couldn't admit that he'd been admiring her gorgeous body since seeing her picture on her website four months ago. Probably better to keep that information to himself. At least for a while.

And why today? If this guy waits years, planning his murders to disguise them as accidents, then why attempt a hit and run? Had he brought Lindsey to the murderer's attention? Or worse, sped up his timetable?

How could he walk away if he was responsible?

Chapter Four

Lindsey restrained herself through the short drive, asking only how Brian had received the cut. He'd laughed as he'd said to avoid an inexperienced intern with over-eager fingers, he'd stitched it himself. But the story had left her queasy after dropping him off at the ambulance company's home base. The Pan-Hop was right around the corner.

While she waited, the memory of the car lights blinded her again. The awful thought that her life had been about to end replayed over and over. Because of Brian's visit earlier that day, she was still alive. She'd only been alone waiting for him to arrive about five minutes before a tap on the window made her jump out of her skin.

"You ready to go inside?" Brian asked.

She grabbed her purse and locked the car. He'd changed into the street clothes he'd worn when they'd met that afternoon. A lifetime ago. She hadn't noticed his scuffed boots until he'd held the door and she'd looked to the ground. The only boots she'd noticed before were on men shopping for a new phone. She hadn't been in Texas too long and hadn't made an effort to get to know anyone or discover any real cowboys.

Now one had found her.

He waited, holding the restaurant door open while

she looked past him through the windows. Any of those people could have been driving the car that rammed her off the road. It could be anyone…anywhere.

A creepy feeling crawled up her spine. He was out there. She could feel him staring from his hiding place. Pure panic drove her. She spun and searched the dark.

"We going to eat?"

"I can't." Darting under his arm, she began clicking the rental's key, trying to unlock the door. The car alarm set the horn blaring and she looked closer to see which button was which, but her eyes were full of embarrassing tears.

Tears? Now? She'd remained calm throughout the accident and police. But couldn't handle pancakes in a public place.

Brian clasped his hands over hers, tilted her chin toward him and took the keys. The alarm stopped, then she heard the horn beep that it was reset. He hadn't looked away. His dark eyes reassured something deep inside. More than basic attraction, sort of as though he shared part of her no one else could—or would—ever understand.

Even with his eyes comforting her, the panic bubbled. She looked into the dark corners of the building, right at the edge of the light. He was there, watching.

"What's wrong?"

"I can't go in there, it's…it's too crowded." Her mind acknowledged that the restaurant was more than half-empty, but it just didn't matter. She couldn't force her feet to move through the entrance.

Brian seemed to understand. He led her by the elbow to his truck, opened the door and removed a bag from the floor. "Want me to help you inside?"

It was an older model and it took a little doing one-handed, but she managed to climb in on her own.

"Mind if I hook you up? This thing can be sort of stubborn." He pulled and held the seat belt forward.

She nodded and he leaned across the seat. She would never have been able to lift her arm to lock herself in and he'd helped without her asking. He smelled of a mixture of hay and man. Attractive. Musky. Like a guy who did honest work or who'd driven with the top down on a bright sunny day.

His hair was short, but didn't look like his normal style since he kept tossing his head as though there were longer locks there. She recognized that toss of his head and the nervous running of his fingers across his scalp. She did it herself to get short wisps away from her face. It looked as if it was growing out from a military cut close to his head, curling at the base of his neck.

He hadn't been exaggerating when he'd said the seat belt was stubborn. It wasn't just a play to get closer. His hands touched her hip more than once and as hard as he tried not to, his arm grazed her stomach and thigh.

The urge to twist those curls around her finger was a little heady. She'd acted on impulse before. It would be so easy to reach out and use her nail to trace the lean tendon leading down to his shoulder.

She watched her hand sort of float down, getting closer to that musky skin.

"There." He stood straight, brushing her hand to the side with his shoulder, smiling from ear to ear as though he'd accomplished something much harder than snapping a seat belt. "Dang thing had an animal cracker stuck in it."

"Great." She didn't feel great. Maybe she had hit her head because she was definitely a little dizzy. He seemed perfectly fine and totally unaffected by all the touching.

"Your shoulder okay?" he asked, adjusting the strap to make it a little looser while holding an animal cracker tight in his palm. He was thinking of his niece, not her. He just wanted her to be safe while in his truck.

Shoot, he was a paramedic. He probably got hit on all the time. Girls probably fell at his feet. Well, that was the old Lindsey. The new Lindsey didn't fall at anyone's feet. She used her own. The tenseness she felt had nothing to do with the physical and everything to do with the potential threat on her life.

Anyone would feel like this.

"Great, thanks. Your mother must be very proud of raising such a gentleman."

The smile faded from his eyes and his lips twisted tightly into a thin line. He quickly shut the door. "Mom died of cancer a long time ago," he said softly through the open window.

He walked around the back of the truck, pausing to drop the bag in the back and again at the door. His face was out of sight, but she heard the deep inhale and slow release.

Trying to pay him a compliment, she'd brought up a terrible pain. She knew all about the death of a parent and felt two inches tall for the remark she'd made about him still having his father when they'd first met.

He got in and pulled from the parking lot. "Don't feel bad, Lindsey. You didn't know."

"I meant it as a compliment."

"And that's how I took it. She's been gone a long time."

"My parents' accident was six years ago. When I remember that day...all the horrible feelings make me hurt all over. I can't imagine it ever gets easier."

"It does and it doesn't. Hang on to the good stuff." He shifted gears and stopped at a red light.

The streets were practically empty. She looked around for a black car, trying not to but paranoid. Each time they stopped, she searched.

"I doubt he's going to do anything when you're with me. This guy makes it look like an accident. That's why no one's caught on. So where do you live?"

"You must already know, since you're headed there. It's really okay. I looked up a couple of things about you, too. The fire did more than kill my cousin. It destroyed all your plans and your family's. I think it's cool that you're an identical twin. You might have told me what happened this summer. Your story made the news. And your poor little niece."

"You didn't seem too receptive to more talking this afternoon. Were the articles and pictures helpful?"

"Yes. You can't blame me for checking out your story. You could have been driving the car that ran me off the road for all I knew."

"And yet, you didn't tell the cops my name."

"How did you know?"

"I don't seem to be in police custody on suspicion of murder."

"Right. The police already thought I was drunk or high or just crazy. Then there was the mess when they thought I'd stolen Jeremy's car. *That* took forever to clear up. So I let them take me home and used the internet."

"Wait, go back. They thought you stole a car?"

"That's beside the point, but if you must know, Jeremy left me his car. I've been making the payments. The bank wouldn't put it in my name. When I told the cop at the accident that the owner was dead…" She rubbed the scratches she'd gotten from the handcuffs they used while escorting her to the police station to sort things out. "Part of the reason it was so late when I found you was that it took a long time to find Jeremy's lawyer and verify everything."

"Is this your place?"

"Jeremy's, really."

"If it's got a lock on the door, you'll be fine. Want me to walk you to the door?"

"Yes. I mean, aren't we going to talk? You can tell me what your plans are. How do you plan to catch this guy? Oh, wait, we should talk inside. But what if it's bugged or something?"

"Lindsey." He lifted a hand as a universal stop sign. "Lindsey, slow down. I'm not that guy."

He reached forward and gently popped her seat belt loose. At some point he'd already undone his and twisted on the old vinyl. Draping his arm over the back of the seat, he rested his head in his hand.

He arched his brows, waiting, but she didn't know how to respond. She didn't completely understand the question, so what did he want?

"Look, kid—"

"Stop right there. I'm not a kid. You can't be more than three or four years older than me. Remember, I did research on you, too. So I'm not your kid, sweetheart, baby, doll or whatever nickname you can create. My name's Lindsey."

"Yes ma'am. Like I was saying, I'm not the guy you want defending you. I have no resources, no knowledge, no experience or desire to protect you. You need someone who knows what they're doing."

"But who else is going to believe me, Brian?"

"You've got me there. I had a helluva time just getting myself to believe me. Then Mabel did some research and all those accidents didn't seem so accidental."

"You'll help?" She focused on his eyes, the slight tilt

of his mouth that was much more comforting than those tight, strained lips.

"I don't know what I can do, *Lindsey,* but I'll tell you what I know. Stay there and I'll help you out before you hurt that shoulder again. The muscles are probably stiffening up about now."

He scooped the folder from the seat and she waited while he walked around the truck. If he wanted to be gallant, she'd let him. Allowing him to open the door for her wasn't being a pushover—especially if he wasn't doing any pushing.

She creaked to the edge and stepped down. Brian was right. She ached all over.

"Aw, I told you."

The wince had probably given her away. She would have stumbled to the ground if he hadn't been there helping. "I can't believe how sore I am all of a sudden."

"The adrenaline's wearing off and I bet you'll be out as soon as your head hits the pillow."

"No way. We have things to discuss. I want to know everything you know."

"And I'll be here in the morning. Does that perplexed look indicate you don't know if it's a good idea or not?"

"I just… I mean, just because I tracked you down doesn't mean I invited you to spend the night." *Remember, someone's trying to kill you.* A little voice in her head, sounding so much like Jeremy, kept reminding her to look around. The paranoia had her doubting Brian's motives.

"I thought we were past all that. I didn't try to kill you. You can trust me."

Fear made her anxious. She could feel it trying to take over again. Then Jeremy's voice prodded her, *You need his help. What about your mother and father's accident?*

You may have been murdered. You need to find the truth and this guy's already found a great deal. Don't stop until you get the psycho who's been destroying our family.

She scraped her scalp with the metal key ring still in her palm as she shoved her hand through her hair. She'd been doing so well on her own. She shook her head, wanting the answer to be different than what was obvious. She couldn't do this on her own. Good or bad, she needed him.

"I'm sorry. This situation is just a little overwhelming." She stretched her neck back to get a look at the most comforting eyes she'd ever fallen into. They made her next words much easier to say, "Would you mind staying awhile? I'd feel safer."

He held out his hand for her keys. She'd promised herself never to ask for help again. Did this count?

THE KEYS DROPPED into Brian's palm and they moved inside with no more debate. Lindsey was obviously on her last ounce of energy, stumbling out of her shoes and falling onto the leather couch.

"Why don't you head to bed?" He flipped on lights, set the file on the coffee table and wanted to remove his boots. If he could just close his eyes for a few... The exhaustion from his shift was intensifying the pounding behind his eyes from the slight concussion.

"I'm so wound up, I really don't think I can go to sle..." She stopped, staring at the goldfish tank on the corner of the desk.

"What's the matter?"

She moved next to him, no longer wilting. "Someone's been here," she whispered. "Could they still be in the house?"

"How can you tell?" He pulled her close under his arm, as if that would actually protect her if someone attacked.

"The fish-food container was on top of Jeremy's papers. Not next to the bowl. Feeding them was one of the last things I did before I left this morning." Her whispering voice shook with fright as much as her body shook under his hand.

"You're certain?"

"Yes."

"We're leaving."

"But—"

"Now, Lindsey. Out."

She turned and ran. He didn't linger. He wanted to check things out. Might have if he'd been alone. But he wasn't. For whatever it was worth, Lindsey had chosen him as her protector and he'd do his best. That did not include a fool idea that he should seek out trouble.

Trouble had a way of finding him all on its own.

When he pulled away from her home, Lindsey explored her purse until she removed her cell. "Shoot, my battery's nearly dead. Can I use your phone?"

"I don't think calling anyone is a good idea. Let's talk first and come up with a game plan. Sound good?"

"But what about prints or stuff like that?"

"I don't think this guy left any sign he's been in your house. He's been pretty darn good about covering his tracks."

"Okay, we'll play it your way right now. Just know that this is my life and if *I* decide to make a call, I will." She hugged her sore shoulder close to her chest.

"Absolutely." He pulled to a stop and snapped her belt. "It's over an hour to my place. You can use my jacket for a pillow. One of us should get some sleep."

He drove the truck, trying not to be distracted as she

shifted and got comfortable without another word. Hell, he'd shut down for months when he'd thought John had accidentally started a fire that had killed Mrs. Cook. He couldn't really fathom what it would be like to have someone try to kill him.

"Thank you, Brian."

"You're welcome. Now try to get some shut-eye."

He should force her to go back to the police or hire someone who could help. Taking her to the ranch seemed the easiest choice he'd made recently. Since he and John had cleared the air and actually talked about the night that had changed their lives forever, decisions he'd made on his own for years about the ranch were suddenly up for a group discussion.

For four months he'd craved catching the murdering son of a bitch who had destroyed his future. Now it was more important than ever. He couldn't leave Lindsey to handle this on her own.

The hour zoomed by—even in the old Ford his grandfather had bought and used for fifteen years. Brian tinkered with the engine, keeping it running smoothly. It might not have AC, but it was his. The bank couldn't repossess it like they were trying to foreclose on the ranch.

One trouble at a time.

Keeping Lindsey alive was more important than finding a way to buy the ranch. He turned down the drive, cut the lights and parked next to the barn. Lindsey was still out. She mumbled a little when he shifted her to open the door.

The wind had blown her hair across her face. He leaned close, gently blowing the small strands to the side. He couldn't resist. His lips grazed her forehead so softly he wasn't certain he'd connected with her flesh until his lips cooled again. He scooped her up in his arms, cradling her head in the crook of his shoulder.

He was behaving like a sentimental and romantic idiot. He knew all there was about Lindsey Cook. More than he wanted or needed to know. No way would she go for a cowboy like him. He wasn't anywhere near her league of resort-hopping rich and didn't know how to get there. Didn't want to get there.

Dawn was just around the corner. Time for the morning chores, and no extra hands to do any part of them. What would this beach bunny think of his family's ranch?

The old house needed a coat of paint. The barn needed a new roof. The stock tank needed to be dredged. And there were hardly enough horses left to be considered a farm anymore. It wasn't anything to show off, but it was his.

Or could be. He'd done a lot of thinking since John had come home. Since he turned fifteen, the one thing he'd been talking about doing was leaving this small piece of real estate. Now he couldn't figure out a way to keep from being kicked off the place.

Brian got through the door without the screen slamming shut, a sleeping beauty still in his arms.

"I thought your shifts were for three days?" His brother yawned and scratched his head coming into the kitchen. "Want coffee?"

John finally looked up from the pot that had automatically kicked on and brewed. He pointed and raised an eyebrow, recognition at Lindsey's identity twisting his face into shock, then anger.

Brian was tired and didn't want to wake his new responsibility with loud voices or explanations.

"Don't ask, bro. Just don't ask."

Chapter Five

Serendipity at its best. He could do nothing except admire how the universe worked to bring him back to the only man to have received acclaim for one of his masterpieces.

The Sloane brothers had been the perfect pawns. He'd switched on the voice-activated microphone he'd installed years ago to record his work. There would come a day when someone would transcribe his dictation and print his book, *Details of a Successful Serial Killer*.

"Will Brian Sloane's primitive investigation cause problems for your last plan?" He asked himself the question as if a reporter sat in the room. "The paramedic is a growing pain in the ass and will be eliminated as soon as the opportunity arises."

After he was gone, someone should know what he'd accomplished. There shouldn't be any supposition regarding each case. When the world discovered his lifelong achievements, it should be in his own words.

The idea came to him after the second successful death. Each plan was chronicled and stored in a fireproof safe once completed, but there was nothing like hearing about the conceptualization or nuances that made each one different to execute.

"But that wasn't the question, sir." The reporter in his mind continued to dig. "Will he present a problem?"

For several years, he'd been using the recording device like an audible journal. At first, it had been to document his work. Basically, he was so good at creating *accidents* that no one knew he'd done anything.

"Keeping track of the Sloane brothers for twelve years hasn't been difficult. They lead uneventful lives with the exception of John's return home. He set off a chain of very unfortunate events. That has only forced me to accelerate my plans for the last Cook family member. With Lindsey's death, there are no claims on what's been mine for many years now."

He pushed away from his desk, preferring the supple leather of his couch for what amounted to a debate with himself to logically reason his way through a new challenge.

"If those laughable amateurs who kidnapped Lauren Adams hadn't gotten greedy, the Sloanes would never have discovered my craftsmanship with the Cook deaths. Hiding Gillian's murder within the barn fire was convenient, but also brilliant. I was so close to perfection."

He opened and poured a shot of his favorite vodka. He needlessly swirled it in the cut glass, waiting for the right moment to consume.

"To recap, Gillian checked on the fire pit each time those high school children left her property. One swing of a board and she was unconscious as the barn burned around her. Convenient, yet brilliant. No one has ever discovered the truth of her murder."

There was a right moment for everything. People had forgotten the art of patience. Waiting made the win worth savoring.

"I'll need to get rid of them both. Soon, and without a lot of fuss." He downed the clear shot. One was his limit.

He enjoyed the burning sensation as it traveled through his body, immediately craving more of the fiery liquid.

"No, there isn't a problem. But I am conflicted. Arranging a major accident would get the entire ranch out of my way for good, yet forcing an accident on their ranch is irrational. There would be too many witnesses. The pertinent question is, how do I get Brian and Lindsey to leave the ranch?"

He brushed the back of his finger under his mustache, verifying no drops of liquid moistened his upper lip. Reaching for the bottle, he realized the cool glass was in his hand and shouldn't be. He slammed it on the table, shooting drops in the air that landed on the polished wood.

"How can I overcome this setback? Strike that. I consider this puzzle a welcome challenge. I haven't had any in many years." He leaned into the leather, resting his head, focusing on the microphone in the ceiling tiles. Closing his eyes, he pictured the horse ranch where Sloane had taken Lindsey. It was the only logical place he could go. He envisioned the buildings and the distances, places to hide, the horses and where they wandered.

"I have to admit, this challenge is the first time I've desired to meet my opponent face-to-face. If the opportunity presents itself, I might consider doing so. But that's part of the beauty of this operation. No one knows. Not even my victims knew I controlled whether they lived or died."

He'd given his word to himself and anyone listening to these tapes that they'd always be completely truthful. The last murder had been slightly different than the rest.

"Addendum. Pathetic Jeremy Cook most likely saw a distorted image through his snorkeling face mask. That was the closest I've ever gotten to any of my victims.

When I was within striking distance, he was still completely at ease. My sheer strength kept him underwater. Fear never showed in his eyes until the last bubble of air escaped from his lungs. Then he knew. He knew there was no escape."

Reliving the experience made his heart race and made him need more of the same exhilarating excitement. He wouldn't put that on the tapes. Doctors or the media would twist the pleasure he took from a well-executed plan. They'd distort it and turn his excellence into something sick that needed analysis.

"Back to the problem at hand. How to eliminate the Cook line and take care of the Sloanes with the same deed." The map of the property was firmly in his mind even after twelve years. As were the images of each building, the road, the fields, the pond...all there, creating a secret thrill he couldn't share. He ran the idea from start to finish.

Excitement. Anticipation. Reward.

"Brilliant. Yes, a tip to the press connecting Brian to a possible hit-and-run accident will work nicely. A photographer should spook them sufficiently to where they are alone and vulnerable. I'll record the details upon completion. There's no need to repeat myself in dictation."

Some men were thrilled by the hunt. Some by the kill. He poured another shot. It was time to celebrate. He held the glass in the air.

"A toast. To twenty years of excellence in murder."

The vodka did its job, and he rose to switch off the recorder. There was one part of himself that he refused to share with the world. They'd label him perverted if they discovered his need to hear the moans of torture. He hid his tendency, only allowing himself to indulge as a reward for his greatness.

Fate had stepped in and brought him an opponent for his last plan. His own intelligence would be Lindsey's downfall, and deserved to be fed and stroked. Seeing the report of another assumed overdosed prostitute in the news would meet his growing need for acknowledgment. It would also satisfy him in other pleasurable areas while she or he died.

The perfect subject for his reward had already been chosen and would fit into his plans nicely. But not a random death on the street. He had the perfect place to carry out his deed.

The celebration after his Cozumel success had been near Jeremy's home. With Lindsey secure with the Sloanes, it might be risky to return there. But Jeremy's bed would make the satisfaction all the sweeter.

Chapter Six

Brian's head throbbed. He was tired. Not just from hitting his temple earlier. He needed sleep and a couple of days off. It seemed like years since he'd sat down and wasn't on the clock, looking at ranch records or researching murders. Recently, the spare hours he'd had between shifts were spent following Lindsey's every move. His bed looked very inviting. His father's bed even more so with Miss Blue Eyes curled under the sheets now.

If he was lucky, he'd be under some sheets with her fairly soon. She had to be feeling the chemical reaction every time they were in the same room. Right? Hitting the hay with her could happen once they knew each other better, but not here. Not with a houseful of his family around.

The rooster crowed at the first peek of dawn. He might as well help with the morning feeding for once since he was up. It beat balancing the ranch books. Changed and gulping down a cup of coffee, he caught up with John halfway through feeding the stabled horses.

"Ready to tell me what's going on?" his brother asked.

"There was an accident."

"You didn't do anything stupid, did you? We talked about this." John sounded like an older brother or more like a former Naval officer used to getting answers.

"I didn't do a damn thing, John. Lay off." He pushed his hat to the back of his head. "And stop lecturing me every time we have a conversation. I've been taking care of this place for twelve years."

"What the hell happened to your head?" John's hands framed Brian's face, turning it so he could get a closer look. His thumbs stretched the laceration, tugging at the bandage. "You're bleeding."

"Blast it, John. Stop treating me like I'm ten." Brian shook free and swiped at his forehead. "I've got a father and don't need you to baby me."

Sometime during the past four months they'd switched their traditional roles. Identical in every visible way, Brian had always been the responsible one, older by minutes but by light-years in responsibility. The complete opposite of John's jokester personality. His little brother had finally grown up while in the Navy. Or maybe it was coming home, making amends with his high school sweetheart and planning to adopt her daughter.

"Whoever stitched you up did a crappy job, bro. That's going to leave a scar. And don't think *I'm* slicing my forehead so we can switch places again."

"Seems as though every time we've switched it was your idea and I was getting *you* out of trouble."

"Don't change the subject. What happened?" John stepped back, stiffening, as if he was at attention, commanding his men. It was obvious he wasn't continuing with scooping oats until he got an answer. "After you went to the cops and they laughed in your face, I thought we agreed that it was over."

"Stand down. This ain't the Navy, man. Nothing major happened to me. This is from a drunk in my rig." He straightened his hat. "Lindsey's the one who had an accident. She's a little freaked to be alone, that's all. I brought her here. That's it. No big deal. Now, I'm awful tired, so why don't we get through the chores and I'll explain after breakfast. Once. To everyone. Alicia will be home and Dad can pretend that he's been home all night. Right, Dad?"

His father popped his head around the open double doors leading to the paddock. "I didn't want to interrupt."

"You're not interrupting. Maybe Blue Eyes will be awake for your interrogation. That work for everybody?"

"Blue Eyes?" John and his dad questioned together, sounding so much alike it was creepy.

"Yeah, Lindsey."

"You agreed to leave this alone. What happened twelve years ago doesn't matter." John picked up the scoop and measured oats for the horses.

"It matters to me. And I never agreed. You ordered and I reminded you that I don't take orders from you."

Brian left each bucket in a different stall, feeding the trained quarter horses he'd been trying to sell for months. He was ready to move to the next chore when John began laughing. "What's so dang funny?"

"It just occurred to me, you put those stitches in yourself. Right?" He slapped his thighs, stumbling back a couple of steps, laughing hard at his own joke. "I knew it."

"What stitches?" his dad asked, leaning on his cane. Not bad for a man recovering from a major stroke four months ago. He walked a good two miles every day just coming home from Mabel's across the street.

"John's losing his mind. Glad you're here to take care of him if he starts convulsing." Brian lengthened his stride to leave faster. "I'm going to make breakfast."

"We need to talk about the ranch, boy-o," his father said loudly. "The bank called again."

"Can't right now, Dad. I have a date with the griddle."

Brian left as John expounded on the crooked sutures. If his brother noticed, it was probably a good idea to let his sister-in-law, the professional nurse in the family, redo his sutures.

Right now, he was starved and needed to get his mind off some sky-blue eyes and corn-silk hair spread over a pillow in the front bedroom.

"Yum. Pancakes."

The distinct smell of a hot griddle and syrup wafted into Lindsey's nose, encouraging her to breathe deeply and enjoy. She stretched her arms above her head. No surfing today, her shoulder was a little sore. She rubbed it as she sank back into the pillows, surrounded by the comforting feeling of her favorite place in Florida. The sun streamed through the windows every morning and she'd breathe in the soft, fresh smell of sun-dried sheets. There was a plus side to not owning a dryer.

Snuggling the quilt closer to her chest, she wanted to spend the rest of the morning asleep. But there was work or something she was supposed to do. And pancakes. Her eyes fluttered open to an unfamiliar room.

Wide-awake in an instant. Panic. Aches.

Where am I?

Then her memory kicked in with Brian's words that he was taking her to his home. Darn. She was on a ranch, not back at the beach. She'd be inside the storefront cage where she worked by three that afternoon. Stuck inside. It couldn't compare to working in the sun, walking in the sand or having the surf as part of every conversation.

She missed the sun. But she was responsible now, with a real job and possible advancement. A permanent roof over her head instead of crashing with relatives during the winter season when she was broke. Responsibility was a good thing.

The room didn't look like Brian at all. Pictures in old frames were placed on a dresser around a handmade doily and jewelry box. Grandparents, baby photos of two identical boys and a stunning woman in a wedding dress from the 70s. Either the loner she'd met wasn't much of a loner or it wasn't Brian's room after all.

She was still completely dressed except for her shoes—a good thing, no awkward moments. She made the bed like a good guest—she'd been one often enough. Hit the bathroom, then not wanting to disturb anyone, she tiptoed through the hallway leading to the living area. She followed the heavenly smell of pancakes, hoping to find her cowboy rescuer.

A man was crashed on the couch. His face was pressed into the back cushions, but she knew it was Brian. His boots were at one end with his hat resting on top. She wasn't surprised he was still asleep. He'd worked all night, then stayed up with her. What she couldn't believe was that he'd carried her to bed and she hadn't woken up.

"Shh. You'll get in trouble if you wake up Uncle Brian," a little girl tried to whisper from the kitchen entrance, placing her first finger across her lips but speaking loud enough to be heard across the room.

Lindsey followed the little girl into the kitchen, hesitating before interrupting the woman cleaning up, uncertain how to explain why she was in her home. These two had to be the new additions to the family. She recognized their pictures from the articles she'd found involving Brian and the little girl's kidnapping last summer.

"Mommy," Brian's niece said, sending her pigtails bouncing over her shoulders.

"Lauren, you know you have to eat before you can

go outside. Get back in your seat and leave Uncle Brian alone." She didn't look away from the dishes in the sink.

"Brian's lady is up," she announced, and her mom turned. Lauren laced her fingers through Lindsey's and tugged her across the kitchen. Mother and daughter looked alike; both had rich, dark brown hair and the same arch to their brows.

"Hi, I'm Alicia. Brian said y'all got here at dawn. I didn't expect you up this soon." Alicia wiped her hands on a dish towel. There had been a moment of hesitation with her smile, but it looked genuine now that it was in place. Then she knelt by her daughter. "Lauren, you didn't go and wake Miss Lindsey up, did you?"

Another surprise, Alicia Sloane knew her name. "Oh, no, I had a great sleep," Lindsey rushed to explain. "I met Lauren in the living room. Oh, and I'm not Brian's lady. We just met yesterday and he brought me here because I had no place to go. Great, that sort of sounds horrible. I mean, the story's a little complicated. A lot complicated, actually."

Alicia smiled bigger, stood and tapped Lauren on the bottom, scooting her toward her booster seat at the table. "Thank you for minding me, sweetie. Now get up there and finish eating. Don't worry, Lindsey. Brian explained everything over breakfast. Are you hungry? I was instructed to give you hotcakes as soon as you were ready."

"They smell delicious. Can I help?"

"Guests don't cook, silly." One of the cutest giggles she'd ever heard came from tiny lips and a mouth full of pancakes.

"Lauren, that was rude. You don't call grown-ups silly." Brian's sister-in-law retrieved the batter from the refrigerator and slid it onto the mixer stand. "And you don't talk with your mouth full."

"But you do. You said Uncle Brian bringing a guest to Pawpaw's very full house was silly." She folded another half of a small pancake and stuffed it in her mouth, smiling with a drip of syrup on her chin as she chewed.

"Oh, gosh." Alicia's hand covered her cheeks. "I'm so sorry."

"It's okay. You're right, me being here is quite silly. Um…" Lindsey understood. Staying here wasn't only awkward for the Sloanes. She had a bit of background, but what did she really know about Brian? "I guess I should go. If you know where my purse is, I'll call a cab to take me home."

"Don't be silly," Alicia said. "Oh, my, there I go again. What I meant to say is you're more than welcome to stay here as long as you want. This is Brian's house more than mine, and I shouldn't have spouted off about a lack of space. Lauren, we'll talk about this later, young lady."

"I really think I should go." She backed up, trying to leave gracefully. Maybe she'd missed her purse in Brian's room. Two strong hands cupped her shoulders, steadying her as she tripped into a rock-solid body.

"You've got nowhere to go. Remember?" Brian's voice said just above her head.

"Are you in trouble, Mommy? Uncle Brian looks mad."

"I'm tired, baby girl. Just tired." His warm breath tickled her spine. "I get ornery when I only get a half hour of shut-eye."

"I told you to sleep in our room," Alicia said.

"That will never happen." He laughed. "Don't worry about it. I function on naps all the time. Besides, the smell of that griddle made me hungry again." He patted Lindsey's shoulders and guided her to a chair at the old-fashioned table. "How's the shoulder?"

"A little sore, but fine."

The strange part of the scene around her was that she didn't feel unwanted or a burden or even more than slightly awkward. When Brian was in the room, she felt at home. Her hand skimmed the table top as he pushed her chair closer to the table.

Metal legs, green Formica, scuffs, a few crayon marks—old and newish—made her feel as if the table had been there a very long time. The extension was in the middle and six quaint matching chairs were in place.

"How long is your lady friend going to be here, Uncle Brian?"

"I have to be at work this afternoon, so I should be heading home," she explained to Lauren, but looked at Brian, who raised an eyebrow and rested his head on his hand.

"After some pancakes, right?" Alicia set a stack in front of her. Big and fluffy with a dab of butter melting over the top.

"Go ahead. This is second breakfast for me," Brian said, or encouraged, or ordered. It was hard to tell. The man spoke with such authority, she was compelled to listen and wanted to follow his instructions. He was like a lifeguard even without water around.

"She likes 'em, Uncle Brian."

"I think you're right, baby girl. Her eyes just rolled back in her head for a second."

Lindsey completely understood why Lauren had spoken with her mouth full. The pancakes were wonderful and she wanted to let Alicia know as soon as they touched her taste buds. And the coffee was simple and excellent. She'd thought she was spoiled with Jeremy's one-cup flavored machine or the corner coffee shop at work. But there was something about the rustic flavor of black coffee that went with the pancakes and pure maple syrup.

"These really are great, Alicia. Thanks for going to the trouble." Lindsey stuffed another big bite between her lips. Totally in heaven.

"All I did was flip 'em. That paramedic sitting beside you learned some secret ingredient and won't give it up." Alicia pointed the spatula toward Brian. "He mixed up the batter and cooked breakfast before he caught some shut-eye."

If the screen door hadn't shut behind two men and startled her into silence, Lindsey probably would have blurted her astonishment at how kind this man had been to her. The men were close in size to Brian, but one was on a cane.

The other, once he removed his hat and wasn't backlit, she could tell was John, Brian's duplicate. "Woman of the house, two starving men need some lunch."

Alicia set the pancakes on the table in front of Brian. "As if one of them in the room wasn't enough."

"I was thinking that exact same thing." Lindsey watched John kiss and twirl his bride right back to the sink. The older man joined them at the table and a cup of coffee appeared at his fingertips. He had to be their father—they looked just like him. All three men took turns adding the same dollop of milk to their cups.

"Lindsey Cook, that jerk pawing my sister-in-law is my younger brother and this old man is my dad." Brian patted his dad's shoulder.

"Younger by twenty-three minutes but older by necessity, Scarface," John said.

"Let me see these stitches." His dad pulled Brian's face closer. "Alicia, I think you need to take a look at this mess."

"I'm done, Mommy," Lauren informed everyone, dropping her fork on an empty plate.

Alicia and John whispered softly behind her.

You're the only one left. You're the only one left.

The family voices teasing each other in playful exchanges swirled in her head. As everyone grew closer to the table the walls began closing in behind them. *Someone tried to kill me last night.* The pancakes turned to cardboard. She couldn't untangle what happened around her; it all mixed together just like when they brought Jeremy's body to shore. She could hear them, but she couldn't actually hear anything except a buzz in her ears.

"Lindsey, you okay?"

She whipped around and had to think twice about who had a hand on her shoulder. *Brian...murder you.* "I need out of here."

She shook off the help, the questioning concerns and just ran. The screen slammed behind her as she got her bearings and headed down the gravel drive. The second slam of the door let her know that someone was following her, but she didn't stop. She had to get free of everything.

Jeremy, his life, his dreams... If she disappeared, whoever was after her couldn't kill her. She could go back to her life on the beach, not worrying about responsibility.

"Lindsey! Where are you going?" Brian shouted.

"I can't stay here." She turned to face him but kept walking backward. Her shoes would be ruined from the gravel but she didn't care. She wouldn't need them on the Gulf beaches. Or maybe she'd try her hand up the East Coast. Get a job on a yacht or something. She had experience and knew some people.

"You can't walk back to Fort Worth, especially in those things."

"I'll call a cab."

He laughed. "Sweetheart, Aubrey doesn't have any cabs. Let's go back to the house."

"I can take care of myself. I don't know why I tracked you down last night." She must have been out of her mind. "And how do those people know who I am? Not one of them was curious about a strange woman in your bed. Do you pull this *danger* routine regularly?"

"For the record, the only female who's ever slept in my room happens to be five years old. Lauren took it over and I sleep on the couch when I'm home. That was Dad's room and I didn't know you'd get so upset—"

"I'm not upset. Why would I be upset? You claim someone's trying to kill me. What's to get upset about?"

"You're right. It's more like you're hysterical. I know a lot's happened to you since yesterday—"

He dashed forward and grabbed her arm before she could turn and run.

"Let me go." She twisted, flaying her arms.

"Ow, damn, that was my ear." His arms wrapped tighter, bringing her closer to his chest. "I'll let you go when you calm down."

Upset or desperate, she didn't know which, she just knew she needed to get free. She kept twisting. His arms tightened their hold. Soon her cheek was flattened against his cotton T-shirt. Grass and sunshine. His scent from working that morning should have put her off, but instead it attracted her like crazy. She tipped her head back, taking a long look.

He seemed relaxed. His jaw wasn't clenched, just sprinkled with a five-o'clock shadow. His chest expanded with normal breaths, as though the effort of chasing her hadn't been an effort at all. And he had the kindest brown eyes. Eyes that were easy to get lost in and forget exactly why she wanted him to release her. Eyes that cut through to her soul.

This man wouldn't have brought her to his family if he'd intended to harm her. Brian Sloane wasn't responsible for Jeremy's death or the car accident. He was helping her find the man trying to kill her. It was just that simple. Her overactive imagination screamed to a halt. Even if her racing attraction didn't.

Chapter Seven

If Brian didn't watch himself, he would be kissing the blonde in his arms and damn the consequences. Once he did, there'd be no turning back. He'd fall. Fast and hard and completely. Alicia waved from the kitchen door, verifying everything was all right. Last thing he needed was another lecture about getting involved with Lindsey Cook.

"Let. Me. Go."

"God…bless America. I'm too dang tired for this." He released his grip and the woman he'd like to devour fell into the tall Johnson grass between the fence and gravel.

Sitting on her backside, she drew her knees to the breasts that had so recently pressed against him. The urge to swing her back into his arms, jump in the truck and drive away from the pressures of job, ranch and family was right there. Obtainable, just a few steps away.

He couldn't leave. He was stuck here. His hands were hot resting on his thighs, itching to soothe Lindsey's back. It was the weirdest feeling ever, knowing so much about a person you didn't know at all.

"We're just trying to help." He finally forced words out. They weren't the words he wanted to say to her. Nothing close.

"I know. I'm…" she said with her forehead resting

on her kneecaps. "I'm sorry about the meltdown. I don't know what's happening to me."

"I'd normally say it doesn't matter, but I think it does." His ear was still ringing from the accidental slap he'd received on the side of his head. "What happened back there? Are you afraid of us?"

"No," she emphatically replied. "You wouldn't have brought me to your family if you intended to hurt me. And you aren't responsible for the accident last night or Jeremy's death. But the talking...the closeness of the kitchen...so many people. It just sort of all caved in on me and didn't make sense. I couldn't think or catch my breath."

He knelt beside her. "Are you thinking now? Breathing now?"

She looked at him, defiance and determination turning her eyes a deep, rich blue. The leaves from the oak trees lining their drive created a soft pattern of light and dark across her blond hair.

The sutures itched from the sweat popping out on his forehead. Desire pounded through his blood. The swiftness knocked the air from his lungs. He felt sucker-punched crazy. "What the hell's the matter with me?"

"What? I don't understand." The confusion brought her delicate eyebrows together.

"Nothing." He stood and extended a hand to help her to her feet, this time dreading the touch of her silky skin against his rough palms. He'd never given a second thought about blue eyes or corn-silk hair. Never. Thirty years old and he'd never had a notion to take a woman on a third date, let alone home to his family.

He could answer his own question, knowing what was the matter, even if he never admitted it to himself or to John. Especially John. The infatuated fool would be in hog heaven knowing he was riding the same love-sick bronco.

He released her hand as soon as she was on her feet. "You okay now? I don't have to worry about you trying to walk home, do I?"

"No. Not in these shoes. But for the record, you'll never catch me in a pair of those." She pointed to his scuffed-up, broken-in boots.

"Great. Let's go to the barn for some privacy." He shoved his hands into his pockets to keep from guiding her with a touch. He couldn't risk it, not until he got himself under control. "We're going to sit and talk like we should have last night at the Pan-Hop."

She walked next to him, silent, watching the ground.

"Do you have panic attacks often?"

Her head snapped around, her face full of question. "Never."

"You've had two in twelve hours." He propped the door open for ventilation. He was already hotter than blazes.

"How do you know they're panic attacks?"

"First off, I've seen a few professionally. And you have plenty of logical reasons to be upset."

"Is there any way to make them go away?" She sat on a bale of hay, legs and arms crossed.

He shook his head. "But you'll be okay. Promise." Stupid promise that he had no way of knowing how to keep.

"Why are you doing this, Brian?"

"You know why. I need to find out who framed my brother and me for murder."

"I get that part. I meant, why bring me here and involve your family? Why were none of them surprised I was here? And why do I get the feeling they aren't too happy about me showing up?"

He picked up and straightened tack someone had left on the rail. Delaying, but knowing he had to admit everything. She needed to know what was driving him and he needed to tell her.

"Finding information about your family has been a Sloane project for a couple of months now. I tried to tell you yesterday how we pieced everything together. And I guess they aren't too happy about more trouble on their doorstep."

"Because of Lauren's kidnapping and the court case deciding the future of her trust fund?" Lindsey scooted back and leaned on the post behind her, smiling. "I have a smartphone, too."

"Yeah, things are kind of up in the air about that. Any calls to the police or trouble around here, well, it might cause a judge to look unfavorably on my brother. He's trying to adopt Lauren."

"They want you on your best behavior and yet you contacted me anyway." Her lips tilted upward. "So you *have* been following me."

"Yes."

Lindsey's reaction wasn't what he expected. She tilted her head back, looked into the rafters and let out a long breath. The action eased his guilty conscience, but did nothing to ease his attraction. With her body arched backward, her breasts thrust upward. She did a little kick thingy with her feet slightly off the ground, and then she laughed.

Hoover Dam! He searched the barn entrance for work. Tack, salt, saddle, something heavy to lift and force his body into submission. Fifty-pound feed bags were ready to put in the storeroom. He hefted one on his shoulder and dragged another with his free hand.

There was something between him and Lindsey Cook.

Somehow, he knew it would be very good if he just gave it some time. That possible relationship—if he understood the use of that word—would go nowhere fast if he gave in to desire and crushed her body to his. What he wanted versus what he needed were fighting a battle, and he really didn't know which would win.

"Can I help?" Their hands collided on the edge of a feed bag.

"No." He hefted the bag to his shoulder and forced another under his arm. Work. Good, honest sweat would keep him on track. Head down, one foot in front of the other. Nothing to watch except his boots. "You should head back to the house."

"Not so fast, mister. I want some answers."

"I have work to do before I take you back to your rental." He stacked the feed and turned for the last bags.

"You agreed to tell me everything." She placed a searing hand on his chest.

"That's not a good idea right now." He looked at her hand, but it didn't move. Such a small thing that had him stuck in his tracks.

"We aren't leaving until you start spilling what you know."

"Drop it." He meant her hand. He'd tell her what he'd discovered. He just needed sleep and some space between them. Preferably an entire room, maybe filled with his family.

"I will not."

She pushed at his chest a little, nothing he couldn't have withstood, just enough to get closer and make him need to back up. But soon there was nothing behind him other than a stack of horse feed. She kept pushing and he sat, the bag he was carrying falling to his side. He went from looking at the part in her silky hair to staring up at her heaving breasts in a blouse that had no business in a barn.

Especially *his* barn.

"Okay, okay. You win." He threw his hands in the air, closing his eyes to block the view. Praying she'd back away with his surrender.

Silence blasted through him. The point of entry was her hand. No longer just a finger forcing his retreat. Her palm had weight behind it. He could hear her breathing hard, smell the maple-coffee scent of her warm puffs across his cheek. If he opened his eyes, he'd see her closer than she'd been since he'd carried her to bed this morning.... *If* he did that, there'd be no stopping his body from doing exactly what it wanted.

"Open your eyes," she whispered.

"Not a good idea." His body was about to betray his resolve and if she took a closer look...

"But you need to see this thing." Her breathy whisper was having an irrational affect on his senses.

"I don't think so."

No way they were talking about the same *thing*. But when she shook his shoulder, he opened one lid and then the other. Her look of iceberg fright was the complete opposite of his volcanic heat. He tilted his head, but his hat got in the way.

"Don't move. It'll get you."

By the look on her face it had to be a barn critter. "Is it a snake or a mouse?"

"Just be still and maybe it will slither away."

"Sometimes those things hang in the rafters until a mouse creeps by. You don't have to be afraid of—"

Lindsey's hand cut him off. Her stare moved behind his right shoulder and her body slowly inched on top of his. Within seconds she'd shifted and pulled herself onto his lap, and the simple rat snake disappeared under something in the corner.

"You can stand up now." And she should hurry up before he forgot what he wasn't doing in this small space with a gorgeous woman on his lap.

"But it's…"

"Hell's bells." He scooped her into his arms and marched into the sun before setting her on the ground.

When he let go, her arms were still locked around his neck and his arms steadied her at a tiny waist. Satiny red shirt to sweaty T-shirt. Slacks to jeans. Designer belt to rodeo buckle. City high heels stood on top of his country Western boots.

LINDSEY WAS COMPLETELY aware of standing on Brian's toes and pressing against every part of him. She didn't want to move. Safe from the snake and other horrible four-legged crawly things, she kept her arms where they were for a much simpler reason.

She liked Brian's hands where they were. Maybe it was the whole knight-in-shining-armor thing—even though she hadn't seen him near a white horse. But if her lips began moving, she'd babble nonsense and he'd never kiss her.

And, man alive, she wanted to know how he kissed. Bad, bad, bad idea.

Either way, she couldn't get higher or closer to him. He'd have to bring his chiseled chin down on his own. The smolder in his eyes she'd seen earlier when she'd run down the driveway returned and she knew what was next. His head tilted to his right ever so slightly, he bent his neck and then…

Tsunami tidal wave.

Brian Sloane was a skilled kisser. He had controlling

firm lips, just the right amount of curiosity mixed with pure desire. He applied the right amount of pressure on her back to tow her tighter against him without trapping her. She parted her lips and encouraged more exploration, doing a bit on her own.

He wrapped his arms tighter and raised her to his height. Her fingers had been itching to play with that hair growing at the back of his neck. His cowboy hat toppled to the ground.

Go for it. Encouraged by her body, she shifted and wrapped her legs securely around Brian's waist. He did some shifting of his own, including a move with his hands cupping her bottom.

"Uncle Brian?"

Lindsey's feet hit the hard dirt faster than she could blink her eyes open. Lauren stood holding Brian's hat, smiling and looking as though she knew something they didn't.

"Whatcha need, baby girl?"

Even though her heart was surfing faster than she'd ever surfed before, the little girl's cute giggle brought another type of smile to Lindsey's lips.

"Pawpaw said to give you back your hat 'cause…'cause your head was getting too hot."

"Thanks." He kissed his niece's cheek, shoved his hat on his head. "Now skedaddle back to your pawpaw."

Brian grabbed Lindsey's hand, forcing the rest of her to follow him back into the darkness of the barn, shutting the door behind them.

Desire skirted her like champagne bubbles popping up the side of a glass. More kisses? No. They couldn't. Brian dropped her hand and headed straight to the pile of leather, turned his back and untangled more rope.

"I think it was a very wise decision for your dad to

send Lauren outside. Don't you? I mean, your family's here and I've got a nut job trying to kill me."

"You're right. We're too different for this to work out."

"Oh, I wouldn't say that. My old self would be all over you for a beach romance." But they weren't at the beach. They were on a ranch. And someone wanted her dead.

"Old self? Beach romance?" He quirked one of those wing-tipped eyebrows.

He didn't need any more information about her. She was the one in the dark when it came to him and his reasons for helping her. She shimmied onto the bale of hay, just so no little creatures would crawl across her shoes. "Forget about me. Spill it. Where do we start looking for this monster who's been killing my family?"

"I've explained before that I'm a paramedic, not a bodyguard. Do I really have to tell you how I am not trained or skilled enough to investigate twenty-year-old murders?"

"You keep denying you're capable of looking for this guy. Yet you've discovered more than anyone else. I knew about my immediate family, but twenty years…? I don't understand how he hasn't been caught." She brushed aside a piece of hay that poked her backside and pulled her legs back tightly against her chest, keeping them far from the barn floor. "And by the way, I can hold my own."

"Right. That's why your feet have barely touched the ground since we've been inside." He waved toward her sitting position.

"Don't deviate from the question."

"Deviate? Son of a biscuit eater." He yanked a bridle or something to the dirt and the rest tumbled after. The tall man shifted his hat, blocking his eyes from her view.

He wasn't pleased. He mumbled a couple more disguised expletives, scooped up the tangled mess and started over.

"I can explain something I bet you don't even know."

"Is that right?" He looped a rope, finally free from the rest, into a coil and hung it on a post.

"I know all those 'sons of biscuit eaters' and 'Hoover Dams' are your attempt at not cursing in front of a five-year-old."

He acknowledged her with a *hmph* and a finger pushing the brim of his hat a little higher on his forehead.

"And I know why you brought me here."

"Why's that?" He looped a second rope over one palm, making it all nice and tidy.

"You hoped that if I met your family, I'd trust you and your information."

"Or it could have been I was tired, my head hurt and you were asleep in my truck."

"I don't think so. You wanted me to trust you and I think it worked." She could see the truth of her words reflected in his eyes. He had a hard glare when he was hiding emotion, but it was very easy to spot if you knew the signs. And she did.

"Got me all figured out?"

"You think you know me because you've done all that research and followed me around." She searched the shadows along the wall to verify they weren't moving, then she stood and leaped to the door. "There are so many things in my life that can't possibly appear on paper, Mr. Sloane. Aren't you just a wee bit curious?"

She backed out of the barn door, almost tripping on the way. She turned and squinted into the bright sunshine, raised her hand to shade her eyes and found herself face-to-chest with duplicate Brian.

"Back inside before they see you out here." John spun

her around and through the door. "We've got a visitor taking a close look at the property from the south."

"Why were you watching the road? Did you think we were followed?" Brian asked, moving quickly. He pulled keys from his pocket and went to a newish-looking locked cabinet. "How many and where?"

"Old habits are hard to break." John shrugged. "Same van parked across from Mabel's place now was in town three hours ago when I went to get the buttermilk. Binoculars or a camera lens reflected in the sun while I was trying to get a better look from the stock tank."

"Someone want to fill me in?" she asked. "I'm completely lost even though I hear English being spoken."

Brian and John removed weapons from the cabinet. They were a wonder to watch as they moved as one, without instructions, each anticipating where the other was reaching. They handed each other ammo and they both pocketed it, but left the guns empty.

"Whoever's after you found you." Brian connected a scope to a rifle on the edge of a stall.

"That's plain enough. What do I do?" Surprisingly, her voice hadn't quivered like her insides currently were.

"Sit tight," John and Brian answered together.

She swallowed the panic. Now that Brian had put a name to the overwhelming apprehension, it made it a little easier to handle.

"Just wait. Let us take a look," John continued as Brian slung the rifle across his back and climbed the ladder to the loft.

The horses, silent before except for a few shakes and tail flicks, whinnied or neighed—whatever the noise was that sounded so nervous. She could feel it, too. The tension from the two brothers radiated off them like sun reflecting on the white sand.

"I was hoping to avoid this for a while when I mustered out," John said, pushing the gun in the waistband of his jeans. "But someone insisted on sticking their nose into places—"

"Give it a rest, bro."

"See anything?" It wasn't the time for a sibling squabble. She didn't have a brother or sister, but she recognized the signs of an *I told you so* starting a fight. She'd had them often enough with Jeremy.

Now that her eyes had adjusted, she could see the tension in John's face and body movements. He was worried. His wife and daughter, along with his and Brian's father, were inside the house. All at risk because of her.

"I didn't mean to put your family in danger." She hoped she spoke softly enough that Brian couldn't hear her from the rafters.

John had been watching his brother but looked at her, quirking that identical brow in the same way that she adored on her cowboy knight. It didn't work. No magic tingling shot up her spine.

"But Brian did put them in danger, whether he meant to or not," he answered in a strong voice. Brian apparently overheard and responded with another *hmph.*

"Was that the reason you were upset this morning? I get it. Brian went against you guys and you think he chose me over his family."

"Are you through summarizing things you know nothing about?" He shook his head and looked away like she was entirely off base. Gone was the feeling of playfulness she'd had with Brian. With John, his intimidating looks made her feel inferior.

"Sorry."

For all the ways these two men were exactly the same on the outside, they couldn't be more different at their cores. Where John came across as commanding, Brian seemed helpful. Navy versus paramedic? Had their careers changed their basic personalities so much?

"You're part right, part wrong. It's more complicated than a two-minute conversation." John clapped a strong hand on her shoulder. "I'd feel better if you were in the tack room."

He'd pointed to the tiny closet with the snake. "There? No way."

He mumbled real curse words and stomped to the bottom of the ladder. "Got anything?"

"Plate's blocked. One guy. Camera. Don't see a gun." Brian stuck his head over the edge. "Lindsey confused me with a reporter yesterday. Any chance this could be one?"

"Give me your shirt and hat. Then you can find out." John loaded his handgun while Brian practically jumped from the loft.

Both men tugged their T-shirts over their heads. John's sunglasses slipped to the ground, Brian picked them up. Identical muscles rippled as they pulled the borrowed shirt over their heads, changing identities. Brian tucked his in like John had looked before undressing. His brother left his out, hiding the weapon at his waist.

An untrained man shouldn't confront a potential killer. "You can't send him out there. Aren't you the Navy SEAL?"

"Was. Now I'm a rancher, just like him." He jerked his thumb toward Brian.

"I can handle myself."

"You keep saying you're just a paramedic," she argued. Brian handed his brother his hat and she saw the teasing smile. "What's so funny?"

"Nothing. I'm just glad you finally believe me. Don't worry. I'll be fine."

"I don't believe you're doing this. Why not call the police?" Lindsey wanted to kick off her shoes in spite of the creepy crawlies and run with him.

"John." Brian ripped the white bandage off his forehead and stuck out his hand. "Keys?"

The twin now dressed like Brian dangled his car keys above his brother's palm. "Don't do anything stupid like follow him and wreck my car."

"Alicia's car."

"Community property state." John flipped the handgun, handle to Brian. "Be careful."

Brian checked the weapon, nodded and stuck it in his waistband.

"Will someone tell me why we don't call the police and report a trespasser?" If something happened to Brian, it would be her fault for convincing him to help her. "I get the feeling this is more complicated than Lauren's adoption."

"That's a long story, Lindsey. John can explain while I'm gone. Don't forget…he may look like me, but John's a married man." He kissed her lips in a brief flyby and headed out the door.

She stared after him in a stupor, not really knowing how to feel. She'd been so confident she was breaking through that tough exterior just a few moments ago. And their kiss—whew. The heat of it still had her insides all gooey.

Chapter Eight

"Come on, Lindsey." John spoke in a calm voice, but those tense lines were still straining his good looks. "Let's take a look out in the paddock and give our paparazzi a show. Remember to stay between me and the house. If he does have a gun, he'll never get a clean shot."

"What? Do you think he's going to shoot at us?"

"I don't think that's his M.O. From what I've seen, he seems like a guy who likes to plan things with a little more control of the outcome."

The roar of a muscle car coming to life and driving too fast up the gravel made John cringe and shake his head. He seemed so much older than his brother. Older and more experienced.

The duplicate of the hand she loved curved around her waist, touched her back and guided her around the metal fence. John was just as handsome as his brother but strangely, she felt nothing. No pings or tingles of excitement. Only frightened worry about Brian.

The Sloane house was far enough off the road, you could barely hear a car drive by. Even a muscle car with a muffler as load as Manhattan.

Screeching tires. Then a shove to her knees kept her from turning to see the cars on the road.

"Damn it, Brian. I told you not to go after him," John shouted, slapping his thigh as he stood straight.

"I take it he didn't listen to you?"

"Never does." He stepped a little farther away from her now that he wasn't playing Brian for the man in the van. "Let's head inside."

"Aren't you going after him?"

"In what? Brian's truck? That thing belonged to our granddad. There's no way I'd ever catch them."

"Then you should call the police."

"Yeah, about that. The police won't be stopping Brian Slone, they'll be stopping John Sloane, who will probably say I'm running off more reporters."

"You'll explain that in a slightly less cryptic way once we're inside?" She was totally lost. They had a problem with reporters, too? The questions about why the police wouldn't help spun her around harder than a wipeout in Malibu.

"Sure."

They sat at the table again and Alicia joined them. The plastic wrap was removed from Lindsey's pancakes and they were popped in the old microwave, which took up a third of the kitchen counter.

"Mrs. Cook was the coolest teacher in school," John began. "She let our class hang out on her property. We had plenty of fires there in a pit her husband had used at one time. Nothing ever happened until the night she died."

Alicia laced her fingers through her husband's. "My guy here," she patted his hand, "was about to leave for the Navy and we were arguing about what would happen. He was upset, fought with Brian and they both stormed off. They didn't speak for twelve years."

"Back then we shared the truck and always left the

keys in it. I needed some time so I spent the night alone. Brian came back to the Cooks' place in the morning. But witnesses saw our truck leaving the actual fire."

"It wasn't stolen?" she asked. "And neither of you left in it?"

"That's right. For twelve years I thought Brian drove it home and he thought it was me. You see, it was our responsibility to put the fire out that night. It spread to the barn where they found Mrs. Cook—"

"My second cousin."

"Everyone thought she tried to put the fire out and the barn collapsed on her. She had massive head injuries." Alicia continued the story. "Brian took the blame for the accident. He didn't want anything to stop John from getting into the Navy."

"He said he did it, even though he thought you were responsible for it spreading?" This morning, the brothers had moved together as though they'd never been apart. What must it have been like back then when they hadn't been separated for twelve years? "Wait, that still doesn't explain why the police won't help him."

"This town blamed Brian for Mrs. Cook's death and treated him like a convicted felon even though it was ruled an accident," Alicia explained, while John's knuckles turned white in a death grip. "He lost a full scholarship to college and each time something goes wrong in town, the cops blame him."

"Like for Lauren's kidnapping? I did some research of my own."

"They arrested him, then tried to beat a confession out of him before he made it to the jail." John's look turned to steel. He might say he was a rancher, but the man in that chair was every inch a Navy SEAL. "He still hasn't told me how many times it happened over the years."

"Too many," Alicia whispered.

"But he's a paramedic, he helps save lives."

"No one knew that except Alicia and Dad. Everyone else thought he was a drug dealer."

"You aren't serious?" She couldn't believe it. That shy cowboy/paramedic? "How could anyone get that impression from that teasing smile of his? I've known one or two— Sorry, but he's definitely not into drugs."

"We know that, but he never cared what the town thought and wouldn't let us set them straight," Alicia said.

"Why does he want to find the murderer so badly?" A shiver shot up her spine. "It's still hard for me to believe someone really wants me to die."

"He's been obsessed with clearing our name since we cleared the air."

Alicia jabbed his shoulder. "Since I threatened you both if you didn't speak to each other."

"I was wondering why he'd go to all the trouble to help me, especially after the police didn't give his theory any merit." She toed off her shoes, dreading having to walk on gravel in them again. "So what now? Will he come back soon?"

"Those shoes are a disaster waiting to happen," Brian said behind her, then pulled the door open. "I go chasing bad guys and you can't keep a sharp eye on things? I've been standing out there for five minutes. Some Navy SEAL."

"Give me some credit. I heard the car pull in. Maybe you needed to hear how ridiculous it is for you to continue this investigation."

"I caught up with the photographer in the van. He said he got a tip there might be a story. He snapped a few pictures." He looked at his brother. "You know what that means."

"What does it mean?" Lindsey asked, looking around the room.

"We should go." Brian latched on to her upper arm.

"Don't be silly," Alicia said. "The way the sheriff watches the ranch, this is probably the safest place for you both."

"Yeah, it's better if you take off before more show up. Or someone we don't spot gets too close." John was really talking about the murderer.

"I can't believe you're agreeing with him, John." Alicia was clearly upset.

"It's okay, everybody. I need to head to work at three." She gently removed her arm from Brian's grip.

"You aren't going to work. Too much exposure. My family's at risk now and I'm sticking to you until we figure this thing out."

"But I—"

It was useless to defend her point of view. He'd made up his mind, and left the room.

"John, you can't let him just take off," Alicia pleaded with her husband.

Lindsey could see that they needed privacy. There wasn't much space to give them in the tiny house, but she went into the living room.

An older man raised a finger to his lips. Lauren was asleep on his lap.

"I'm JW and you must be Lindsey. You'll be safe with him," he said in a low voice. "He's got reason to be broody, but don't let him be. I think you'll be good for him."

"I beg your pardon?"

He grinned. It was a window to the future on how his two sons would look at his age. Still handsome and charming. "I'm the one who sent Lauren out earlier."

The heat of embarrassment spread up the back of her neck. First, Brian's father had seen that hot kiss, and second, he already had them as a couple. "It was just the intensity of the moment."

"You might call me a dirty old man for spying on you. But I'm not and wasn't. I just happened to look. And you two were kissing where anyone could see. Including the man in the van." He lifted his chin toward the hall bedrooms. "He knows that. The man who's after you. He'll assume you're with Brian now."

"So I really have put everyone in danger. I'm so sorry."

"Not your fault, Lindsey. That madman started the feud with my family twelve years ago. I just wish I was strong enough to come with you."

Brian filled one doorway with a bag over his shoulder. John filled the other with Alicia ducking under his arm and snuggling against his side.

"We'll keep looking into the records, trying to make sense of the deaths," JW said.

"Ready?" Brian asked.

"You should get a cheap phone. Same as during the kidnapping, we talk through Mabel. Don't underestimate this guy. He's got a lot of practice and he's patient."

JW moved Lauren to the couch and stood. The little girl was in a deep sleep. Brian hugged his dad with one arm, very manly, then bent to kiss his niece, very sweetly. Alicia hugged him and opened her arms, hugging Lindsey before she could react. John just tapped her shoulder, pressed his lips into a straight line and nodded.

"Got plenty of ammo? Any idea where you're headed?" John asked. "Never mind, we don't need to know."

"You take care of each other. And don't forget to eat. I think we forgot to eat for three days. Hiding out isn't easy, but sometimes it's necessary." Alicia looked up at her husband, who winked.

"You'd better take the car," John mumbled, but his reluctance was evident.

If she wasn't mistaken, there was a story behind that car. She envied the family dynamic between these people. Their courage through Lauren's kidnapping was unmistakable. There might be strain between the brothers, but they were trying to make it work.

"It'll be at the airport when we pick up a rental," Brian said, making an executive decision.

"I should call Beth and let her know I won't be at work." Alicia handed her a cell and she dialed.

"Keep your head down, boy-o."

"You don't have to tell me twice, sir."

Brian gathered a few things while she lied and left Beth a message that she wasn't feeling well.

No one followed them out. She slipped her feet into the heels, following Brian to the trunk of the cherry-red Camaro. He threw his bag inside along with the rifle she'd seen him with earlier. She watched him retrieve her purse from his truck. He gallantly opened the muscle car door to let her in.

"You okay?" he asked, tossing his hat in the back.

She wasn't sure she could answer him clearly.

"Are you certain about leaving with me? I'm far from certain you're doing the right thing. In fact, I'm not sure I understand what it is we're actually doing."

He kissed her over the window. Crisp, clean, on the lips as if he'd been doing it for years. And she kissed him back the same way. Wanting more, knowing there would be more.

"Are you going to tell me what we're doing?"

"We're going to catch this son of a bitch."

Chapter Nine

Entering his office, he turned on the recorder before he talked himself out of documenting his mistake the night before with the car and again when Lindsey had run to Brian for help. He'd already gone through the pros and cons of admitting he'd underestimated his opponent. And now he had a new one—Brian. It seemed the twin cowboys were slightly more complex than he'd given them credit for.

"What made you expose yourself to— Strike that. Expose is the wrong word. I became too inquisitive and forgot the key to my success—patience. The real question is how Brian Sloane could make me forget my protocol."

That answer needed pondering. The leather of the couch creaked under him as he stretched out.

"Side note. Brian Sloane is certainly good-looking. Many would say he's handsome, especially in his work jeans and T-shirt, but he would never succumb to my… indulgences. He'd never beg for his life. Perhaps that's why he's higher on my radar than Lindsey."

He sat straight, realizing he'd recorded the wild, uncontrolled side of his personality. The half he rewarded, not the disciplined planner he wanted the world to have firsthand knowledge about. He could rerecord that particular segment—just run it backward and tape over it again. It was almost cheating.

"And I hate cheaters."

The selected words he left here were for history. He didn't need to *cheat* by deleting the tape. Just clarify.

"That's what's so frustratingly brilliant about the Sloane brothers. Facing two of them is almost like they're cheating. I watched Brian while he was with my next victim. He's very attached to her. Even through the camera I could see his attachment growing."

He smiled at his play on words. Then eyed his decanter, longing for the sharp sting of the liquor washing down his throat.

"Brian's feelings for the Cook girl will eventually work against him." The vodka decanter caught his eye again and he swung his legs off the couch, sitting closer to the clear ambrosia.

"When John turned from their drive, I knew he would pursue me. Very predictable, since I would have done the same thing. And that's what I'll enjoy most about this last campaign. Those brothers will force me to be more creative in my thinking. I must also be careful and not misjudge them again. This game is different. They think they know something about me."

He picked up the vodka decanter and tipped two fingers' worth into his glass.

"They think I'm patient and predictable, waiting for an opportunity to strike. No one understands me, nor will they. The best time for me to strike is soon and unexpectedly. Catch her off guard and blame the Sloanes, just like I did twelve years ago."

He turned the recorder off, then swirled his drink and

saluted the hidden microphone in the ceiling. Knowing he had to finish his reward sooner than he'd wanted.

"They'll never see me coming."

Chapter Ten

Brian drove the speed limit, not taking any chances about being pulled over. This wasn't the time to push his luck with law enforcement. His one saving grace through the past eight years had been his boss at the ambulance company. He'd looked at him as a person and given him a chance when no one else would after a background check.

Playing the part of a supposed criminal had been rebellious for a while, but when he needed money to supplement the ranch, there'd been nowhere to go. An EMT course at a junior college and the trust of one man willing to hire him showed him a different path. He'd advanced as a paramedic in Fort Worth but had never cleared up that bad-boy image his hometown had accepted.

"I really hope you know what you're doing," Lindsey mumbled again. She'd been doubting him from the moment he'd pulled out of his drive and stated they were headed to her house.

It was clear as a hot summer's day that he didn't know what he was doing. When would she catch on? How was he supposed to find a man who had orchestrated fatal accidents for fourteen people and never been caught?

"You know, Lindsey, I'm a rancher or a paramedic, depending on what day you choose. I can track a bobcat or keep you alive with a rig full of equipment. But keeping you safe from a murdering madman? I think that needs some special training."

"As in police?"

"You got it."

"Then why are we headed to Jeremy's?" she asked, maybe picking up on his hesitation to pull into the driveway. "What are you looking for?"

"We'll take a quick look at your cousin's papers and hopefully find a place for the police to begin an investigation. If the cops have evidence, they'll have to get involved and offer you protection."

"Are you certain you want to go back there?"

He shook his head. "We need your cousin's papers and you need clothes. And sensible shoes."

"I have hiking boots and running shoes."

"Get them." He backed into the driveway. "Can I park in the garage?"

"Sure, the opener's in my purse. Give me just a sec."

What was he doing? Was she in danger here? Was he so desperate to find a clue that he hadn't thought about her safety? He was out of his depth and needed to convince her. He couldn't protect her. He shouldn't be trying to. He'd been forced to get Lindsey away from his family and that was as far as he'd thought about it.

What if the rat bastard chasing her took his vengeance out on Lauren? That couldn't happen. They'd been through enough with the little girl's kidnapping and Alicia's crazy stepfamily.

"Here it is." She pointed and clicked before he could say wait.

Garage was empty, not even a lawnmower. And there probably wasn't anyone in the house, but he needed to make certain.

"Why don't you get behind the wheel and I'll go inside

to check things out. Alone. Just in case, be ready to get out of here in a hurry."

"Sorry to disappoint, but I'm not staying anywhere by myself. That'll be my scared-to-death hand hanging on to your back belt loop as you search the creepy dark rooms." She got out of the car. "My door is staying open for a fast getaway. You should leave yours open, too."

He began to shut the Camaro's door, but left it open after a cute, manicured finger pointed directions to do so. He'd laugh if she weren't so serious. Then again, being cautious couldn't hurt. He unlocked the trunk and retrieved his SIG. Gun in one hand and keys in the other, he unlocked the dead bolt.

A gentle tug on his pants assured him Lindsey was just behind, hanging on tight. He cracked the door open, listened, slid through the opening and flipped on the lights. Total silence in the house with the exception of the gurgling fish tank. They made a thorough search, room by room. They flattened curtains to the wall, opened closets filled with her cousin's things.

It was midafternoon. The curtains and blinds were closed in the main bedroom, making the room darker, but nothing was blacked out. But even if it had been, he recognized the smell of death. In his line of work he experienced it often. The distinct smell of blood hit his nose as soon as he cracked open the door.

"Go wait in the kitchen."

"Why?" she whispered, death grip still on his jeans.

"I don't think you should see this."

"I stay with you. Period."

"Shut your eyes and cover your mouth. Whatever's in there…don't scream and have the whole neighborhood calling 911."

She did as he instructed. One glance at the body on the

bed and he knew the person was dead. Between the smell and the amount of blood on the white sheets, there wasn't any doubt. It was recent; most of the blood hadn't dried.

Lindsey moved to his side, released his jeans, and he knew what was next. He wanted to scream along with her. Or shout and curse the animal who had done this. The sound began behind him, but he was able to shut it down by blocking her view and placing his hand over her open mouth.

The light from the master bath was a beacon in the dimness. He shoved Lindsey through the door and she immediately knelt by the toilet, heaving. He left her there.

There was even less afternoon light with the door pulled closed. He used the back of his hand to flip the light switch. Eight years as a paramedic and he'd never seen anything that turned his stomach. This did. He hadn't noticed it in the dim light, but now that his eyes were adjusting, the blood was everywhere.

Some of the blood spatters on the wall were dry. Could the murderer have done part of this after they'd left? Had he been here waiting for Lindsey to come home after the accident?

If he had dropped her off at the curb last night, that would have been Lindsey.

The woman was bound to the headboard, her blistered hands limp. It looked as if she'd been forced to hold a searing iron. Brutally tortured. There were dozens of slashes and burns on her body. She'd been in a lot of pain for hours.

Checking for a pulse would be useless, but the paramedic in him had to be certain. There was no way to get near the body without stepping in her blood. He reached the head of the bed and raised the blood-soaked throw pillow by its corner.

The fright in the woman's eyes—he'd never seen any-thing like it. Patches of her face had been skinned. He couldn't imagine what type of psycho would do some-thing like this. He touched her carotid artery.

Dead, but not yet cold.

The victim had pale blond hair, sky-blue eyes—she could easily have been mistaken for Lindsey. But the man chasing the last of the Cook family knew her. Had studied her. Wouldn't make the mistake of killing some-one in error.

No, he'd done this deliberately to make it look like Lindsey was dead.

"Oh. My. God. Oh, my God." Lindsey stood in the bath doorway. "Brian, how could anyone do this? She doesn't have— There's nothing left— Didn't anyone hear her scream? Didn't she scream? There's so much blood. How could someone do this to another human being?"

Dropping the pillow, he leaped away from the bed, spinning Lindsey away from the horrific scene and slam-ming the thin door behind him. Lindsey's breathing be-came erratic. She shook, her hands flailing and hitting his shoulders.

"Look at *me*, Lindsey. You are not having an attack. Not now. Do you hear me? We don't have time for you to fall apart. Get control. You're hyperventilating and we need to slow your breathing."

Her panicked eyes locked with his as he slipped his hand over her mouth, allowing her to draw air through his fingers. He slowly laced his fingers of his free hand with hers while her breathing slowed. He needed her to hold it together.

"You okay?" he whispered, swallowing down the bile gathering in his throat and wanting to forget everything he'd seen in the bedroom. "Do you know her?"

She shook her head, eyes still wide with disbelief.

"You said you had a pair of hiking boots?"

She nodded.

"Grab 'em, along with some jeans, T-shirts, a coat. Anything you might need. You aren't coming back here."

She drew a deep breath. "We should— What about the police? We can't just leave without—"

"Yes, we can. I've been picked up too many times over the past twelve years. They're going to lock me up *now* and clear me *later.*" He looked at the blood he'd tracked onto the tile. "If I'm lucky."

"That's ridiculous. We can prove you had nothing to do with her death. The...the photographer. He knows you were at the ranch this morning."

"I didn't get the guy's name. There's a bunch of circumstantial evidence pointing toward me." He'd researched her family, tailed her, confronted her at the sandwich shop. Then the accident and witnesses who saw them leaving the hospital together. "Damn, how could I be so stupid? The man trying to kill you is smart. He's been following you, yet you haven't seen him. Hell, *I* followed you and didn't see him."

"What are you talking about?"

"The van. Seeing the van parked so obviously on the road directly in front of the barn. He wanted us to see him, to feel threatened and leave the ranch. That was his plan. This girl hasn't been dead long. It's a setup to get me out of his hair. While I'm in jail, he'll eliminate the last Cook."

Lindsey's face went pale under her golden tan. "That's despicable. I can't imagine anyone going to that much trouble to kill someone. You can't know that for certain."

"Right or wrong, we don't have much time." He gently walked her back a couple of steps to crack the door open behind him. "I have a feeling the killer will phone in an anonymous tip, bringing the police here shortly."

"That's ridiculous. I've been with you the whole time. Or your family was right there."

"And during the time you're proving all that, who's going to be protecting you?"

"The police, for one."

"They won't. You'll be alone. Vulnerable to attack."

"What if I'm with someone? You can take me to Beth's house or Craig's. I can hide there with his wife." She shoved her hair back from her face. "No, that would put his family at risk and Beth lives alone. They'd all be in danger."

"That's why we leave. Together."

"All right. But I'm not going back into that room to get my stuff."

"I'll take care of it. Did Jeremy have a laptop?"

"It's in his study, mine's in the living room."

"I'll get you a couple of days of clothes. Where's a suitcase?"

"In the hall closet. Brian…" Her soft touch down his bare arm stopped him. "I'm sorry for getting you involved."

He pulled her to his chest, speaking into her hair. "You aren't to blame. The psychopath targeting your family is the only person responsible."

"But what about your job, your family? I can disappear and not worry about this guy again." She tilted her head back. Her soft blue eyes were filled with fright and questions. "You don't have to do this."

The idea of her walking out of his life forever made his brain scream no. If she really wanted to leave, he'd go with her. But would this guy walk away, too?

"Whoever's trying to kill you has been at this for almost twenty years. Do you think he'll give up? Ever? After seeing what he did in that room, I don't think he's going to stop with you. He likes it." Saying the words left a disgusting taste in his mouth, but he knew they were true. "We have to stop this guy."

"You're right." She dropped her forehead against his chest again.

Keeping his arm around her, he placed a towel across the counter, very aware of every minute they delayed. "Put what you need on the towel. And grab stuff for a first-aid kit."

She slipped from his arm and was done in seconds.

"Trust me, Lindsey." She nodded and he placed a second towel loosely around her face to block the view and smell, then walked her back to the living room. "Did your cousin have any legal papers? Anything that might help us figure out what this guy is after?"

"I'll find them."

"We're out of here in five. If—"

"No ifs. I'll get everything from his office and be ready."

He left her and went back to the murdered woman, hating to disturb the scene even more, but he had to. He couldn't wipe this place clean just in case the killer had left evidence. But the police would find out who Brian was fast enough. His prints were in the system, not only because of his job. The police in Aubrey had booked him when he'd confessed the night of Gillian Cook's death.

He typed a detailed text to his brother and took a minute waiting for the reply, deleting the phone history afterward. Then he composed a message to an officer he knew in Fort Worth and left it on the screen, leaving his phone on the dresser in plain sight. He hoped the cops would find the man in the message and he'd give a word in Brian's favor.

The phone was useless since the GPS could ping their location as soon as he turned it on. His brother knew where to meet him. That message would be retrieved, but the police would be delayed ordering the phone records. He didn't need much time at the apartment. A couple of hours of rest and a plan. That was all.

They wouldn't be able to show their faces in public, so he grabbed the things on top of the towel and shoved clothes from her dresser inside the carry-on and turned off the lights.

Lindsey was scrubbing her hands at the kitchen sink, a laptop bag next to her feet. There was something wrong with her actions. The rubbing got faster, almost frantic. She was in shock.

LINDSEY WAS CERTAIN blood was on her hands. How it got there, she didn't know. She hadn't touched the dead woman, but it was there. The afternoon sun was bright coming through the kitchen window, and her hands were covered in soap as she used the scrubber to claw at her fingers. But she could feel the cold blood sticking to her skin.

Brian's warm exhale skimmed her neck, and his fingers wrapped around hers under the scalding water before he reached around her and cut the faucet off. "It's okay, Lindsey. We should leave now."

He put the strap of the bag over his shoulder and nudged her toward the garage door.

"Wait. We'll need food." She pulled cans and frozen dinners and health bars and dropped them into grocery sacks.

"We should go—"

"Stop. We need this." She dropped everything that wouldn't spoil into a sack.

Brian backed away and carried the bags to the back of the car without another word of protest. There was a small ice chest in the bottom of the pantry and she dumped ice inside for the milk and orange juice along with the six-pack of beer and bottle of wine that had sat in the back of the fridge since Jeremy's death. The freezer door shut and she was eye to eye with a picture of her and her cousin. She jerked it from under the magnet and shoved it in her bra.

Brian lifted the cooler and guided her to the car.

"Wait! There's bottled water still here from Jeremy's funeral. It's behind the door."

"I'll get it."

Lindsey buckled up and looked at the picture of her cousin. The weight of the water being added to the trunk shifted the car a little, but all she could do was stare at Jeremy's image. *Now what?*

"One more thing." Brian sat in the driver's seat. "Take the battery out of your phone and put it in the glove box."

She did as he asked. "How are we supposed to run from a man capable of the butchery inside the house?"

"First thing we're going to do is head to my place and get some sleep."

"Sleep? There's no way. How can we go back to the ranch?"

"I share an apartment in Fort Worth with several of the other paramedics. They switched us to twelve hours on and twelve off, so my partner, me and four others from the firehouse went in on a place to sleep—and only sleep. It's cheap and my name's not on the lease. My partner's taking the day off since I'm on mandatory leave and it's the beginning of the others' shifts. We'll have the place to ourselves."

"You've got this all figured out, then."

"Hardly."

"Wait!" She stopped his hand before turning the ignition. "Jeremy had a fire safe for important papers in his bedroom."

"Stay put and I'll get it."

Lindsey tried to wait once Brian was back inside the house. She hadn't told him the safe was on the shelf and hadn't given him the combination.

He could find it. She could handle five minutes by herself.

Five minutes crept by. Then six. She entered the kitchen, expecting him to laugh at her silliness.

The house was empty. Still…it felt as if the walls were shaking. Impossible. It must be her insides.

Brian had been right. Now that she knew about the panic attacks, she could recognize the signs and try to prevent them. She peeked around the door. A creepy feeling hit her, like watching a scary movie where you knew someone was about to die. Creepier still…the shaking couldn't be her imagination. Impossible. It must be her insides. She took a deep, deep breath and let it out slowly.

No shaking. No panic.

Entering the hallway, she ran her fingers along the wall to guide her. Something hit the other side…in her bedroom. "Brian?"

"Lindsey! Run!"

Chapter Eleven

The body slams, crashes and sounds of a fight grew louder as Lindsey ran straight to Brian's voice. The dresser overturned, the mirror smashed in front of her at the door. She flipped the lights on. Glass and small objects had been knocked from the dresser and mixed with the blood on the bed.

Worrying about the dead woman's body struck her as a bit bizarre. She watched a man dressed in a black jumpsuit wait for Brian's attack near the closet. Brian swung, connected with the man's ribs, spinning him sideways. But the man in black countered by slamming the back of Brian's thigh, forcing his knee to the carpet.

Then the man in black lifted something shiny from the floor.

"He has a knife!"

"Get out of here, Lindsey!" Brian shouted between defensive grunts. "Now!"

Trying to help Brian didn't make a lot of sense. She should run, but couldn't. If no one heard the woman scream, they wouldn't hear her either. He needed professional help—the police. Her phone was in the car. Frightened for them both, she released her grip on the door frame and turned. The bedsprings creaked and time slowed.

It was as though each second was recorded in her mind with an exclamation point. The creak made her look behind her.

The man leaped across the bed, stepping on the poor woman's legs. His arm stretched toward her.

Two more steps and her body lurched in reverse, back into the bedroom. He jerked her hair, yanking while she screamed. She lost her footing, slamming to the floor. He was over her, the knife raised.

Even his eyes were distorted with thick, shaded glasses. The knife descended, she threw her hand up to deflect. Pain. Her own hiss and scream blocked out all the other sound. Where was Brian?

A deep shout, more of rage than warning, and the man in black disappeared from her view.

She rolled to her stomach and blinked away the automatic wetness in her eyes. The knife shot against the door, bouncing past her into the hall. The man kicked the side of Brian's knee sending him to the floor. He jumped over her, scooped up his knife and ran.

"You okay?" Brian asked, pursuing him through the door.

"Catch him," she gritted through her teeth.

Brian's running steps vibrated the wood floor where she rested her cheek and sucked a few painful breaths through her teeth. She crawled to her feet, staggered to the hall bath, got a hand towel for her arm and locked the door.

If Brian didn't return… *He will*.

The door shook with the pounding. "Lindsey!"

She trembled so badly it was hard to turn the knob to let him inside. Should she? Was he alone? Was there a knife to his throat forcing him to call out to her?

"He's gone, honey. I saw him drive away. You all right?"

"I'm...I'm fine." She twisted the knob and lurched backward as Brian stumbled into her. She tried to get past him. "Let's get out of here."

"That bastard cut you?"

"Let's look at it later." She turned her injured arm away from him, trying to shove the rock in front of her aside. "Did he hurt you?"

Brian used his calming gaze and gently prodded her to the sink. Looking into his face and feeling his soothing touch made her think everything would be okay.

"You're going to need sutures. I'll get the wound cleaned a bit, then get you to an E.R." He turned the water on, ready to clean her cut. "This is going to hurt."

"Later." She jerked her arm to her side, blood oozing from the gash. He reached for her arm again and she turned from him, reapplying the towel. She moved away from his comforting arms. "No doctors. Please, just get me out of here."

"We do this now, Lindsey, or I drive you straight to the hospital."

Didn't he know he was covered in blood? Was it his or the dead woman's? She was beginning to gag at the thought.

"Please take that shirt off. Jeremy's clothes are still in his room. I'll rinse my arm while you get rid of it."

From the corner of her eye she watched him in the mirror as he shoved away from the counter and jerked the T-shirt over his head. "I need to take care of this now."

She closed her eyes. "Please change."

She heard the running stride of his boots, then they disappeared on carpet.

Before she lost her courage, she quickly forced her arm under the running water, gritting her teeth in agony as the sink turned red below her. Queasy and surprised she hadn't pulled out all her hair, she got a clean towel and put it on her arm.

Brian reappeared in a tight-fitting T-shirt Jeremy had worn all the time. "Got first-aid tape?"

"Maybe in the cabinet behind me."

He looked at the wound, pulled the sides together and replaced the towel. "The closest hospital is on I-20. I can get us there in eight or nine minutes. They'll take good care of you."

"I'm staying with you."

"That gash is deep enough to need sutures," he said as he dropped the tape on the counter.

"You did your own."

"But—"

"You said this killer won't stop until I'm dead. All the reasons we weren't going to the police still apply." She tapped her finger against his chest. She knew he agreed with her when his brows drew into as straight a line as his lips. "I'm sticking with you until we catch this son of a bitch."

Chapter Twelve

"Choose a bed, Goldilocks." Brian set her suitcase down next to the bathroom and tugged her cousin's shirt over his head.

Wicked-tight jeans drew her attention to his bare lower back and then up to his sculpted shoulder blades. He put water on to boil. She was either completely woozy from the cut and car ride or the attraction was growing so strong she couldn't stop thinking of running her fingers over his strong shoulders again.

Then he faced her and she noticed the tint of his skin was pink from the blood-soaked shirt he'd left at Jeremy's.

"I'll get my sewing kit." His long stride took him into the bedroom faster than she had time to react.

She knew what the water and kit were for. Cleaning her arm and his scrapes. There would be no complaints from her. Complaints would land her dropped off at an emergency room. The last thing she wanted was to be separated from this man she'd come to trust so quickly.

Convincing the authorities she was in danger would be very difficult without evidence. This murderer couldn't be infallible. Somewhere, at some time, he had to have made a mistake. And she was going to find it.

"You weren't kidding about beds and nothing else," she said, loud enough he could hear her in the bedroom. With a stiff upper lip, she peeled off the packing tape Brian had used to hold the towel in place. She tried not to dislodge the towel, afraid it would start bleeding. If it hadn't stopped, Brian swore they'd be on their way to the hospital.

"Kick your high heels off and get comfy," he said from behind the closed door.

The place was tiny but open. There was a futon on one wall folded as a couch, with the sheets folded on the end. She sat facing the television, leaning back to get rid of the wooziness in her stomach.

"This place is surprisingly clean. Are you sure it's six men sharing? I expected a lot worse."

"Yeah. Six males, but I'll admit that one of the guys pays Debbi—she lives down the hall—to pick up, do the dishes and the laundry."

"Now the cleanliness makes sense." She had the tape off by the time Brian returned without the pink-stained chest.

"I pick up after myself," he said, swiping his chest dry. "I do let her wash my towels and sheets since we all share them."

She closed her eyes, unable to watch as he peeled back the makeshift bandage. He wore gloves, and had gauze pads ready to replace the dish towel on her forearm.

"You ready?" he asked with a steady voice.

She nodded, her mouth suddenly dry, silently praying it wasn't as deep as he'd thought. But behind her closed lids, she fell onto a carpeted hallway, a man with bottle glasses and a large knife headed for her. She jumped when Brian touched her arm.

"You drifted a minute. I'm ready to give this a shot. Are you certain?"

"It was just the gloves. They reminded me of the attack."

Brian's finger touched her chin, coaxing her to look into his rich brown eyes. "This is really going to hurt, Lindsey."

"Is this normal practice for paramedics? To scare their patients before beginning?" His eyes soothed her as much as the gentle touch he had through his gloved fingers. "Did you learn how to stitch people up in paramedic school?"

"Taught myself for the horses. Cheaper than a vet coming out when one of 'em got sliced." He went into the kitchen.

"You mean—"

"Drink this." He set a tea glass full of her favorite deep, dark merlot onto the side table.

"If I consume all that on an empty, woozy stomach, I'll be drunk. I may even throw up."

"Something important for me to remember—the lady can't hold her liquor." He sat on a chair he'd brought from the card table in the kitchen. "I'm serious. I need you relaxed. I can't deaden it and it'll hurt worse if you're jerking your arm."

When he picked up the needle and wet thread, she picked up the wine, squeezed her eyes shut and guzzled. She concentrated on a picture of his jeans and tapered waist. The muscles in his back. The picture of him was so vibrant there was actually a catch in her breathing.

"Don't worry. I know what I'm doing," he soothed.

Her imagination didn't prepare her for the level of pain that a tiny needle created when punched under her skin. But his voice assured her through everything he did, every step of the way, no surprises. Once he was done, she saw six neat stitches before he covered her entire upper arm with a bandage."

"Think you have enough tape?" she asked remembering some of the images she'd concentrated on of him in those tight-fitting jeans. She'd drunk the wine much too fast and was definitely tipsy.

"If you won't let me take you to the hospital for antibiotics or... Yeah, you're keeping the bandage. First sign of infection and there won't be any talking me out of a real doctor. Got it?"

"I agree. No arguing." She carefully formed her words so they wouldn't slur. "Thanks for doing...well, for everything, Brian."

She'd been a flirt since the second grade and Ronnie Willhite had told her she was pretty and wanted to kiss her. She wanted to crawl onto Brian's lap, wrap her arms around his neck and kiss him until his vision was as blurred as hers. But she slumped back against the cushion instead.

One short nod and he put away his equipment. "Showers and then some shut-eye, unless you feel like eating."

The thought of food made her head swim. "I don't know how you expect to sleep while that murdering serial killer is still out there."

"I plan on relaxing and closing my eyes."

"But—" He handed her a second glass of wine.

"I can't drink that. The room's already spinning."

"Good. You need some shut-eye." He set the glass on the table next to her.

When he smiled, she wanted to forget everything except the kiss they'd shared that morning. She wanted to be back in front of the barn with her legs wrapped tight around his waist. Or maybe sitting on his lap again, even with a snake slithering in the corner. It beat having a serial killer slither free outside their door.

"We can't stay here. It can't possibly be safe."

"We weren't followed, and a former Navy SEAL and former Marine will be outside watching the place very shortly."

"You forgot to explain."

"I sent a message to my brother. He got in touch with one of his buddies. We'll get some rest, and as soon as the cops show up at the ranch, he'll take the Camaro home, leaving us Mabel's sedan. For the moment, we're safe enough for you to get some rest. You're going to need it."

She lifted the glass and he clanked it, following a salute with his beer bottle. He walked to the window covered in thick black curtains, lifting the edge to take a look at the street below.

"A Marine and a SEAL?"

"That's right. John's calling a buddy. One'll be out front and the other 'round back. That should make you feel safer than a police squad car. Mac's already here." He disappeared into the bedroom, continuing his explanation. "He'll have a phone for us. If you want on the Net, codes are taped to the side of the TV. Bolt this thing behind me. Or you could fall asleep. I've got a key."

He ran out the door, pulling a T-shirt on, hiding the handgun stuffed in his pants, and she was alone. She should be upset that he'd made the arrangements without telling her. Or maybe she wasn't because she was relaxed enough not to care. Either way, she would not be falling asleep anytime soon.

Not even with guards to protect her and being slightly drunk. But she could begin searching Jeremy's laptop and powered it up. Most everything she did on the internet for the past four months had been on her phone. She'd lost most of her web clients after her cousin's death because she'd been dealing with his affairs and getting into the habit of working somewhere every day again.

Now she was glad she hadn't given away any of her cousin's things. Even his clothes hung in his closet. It was time to give it all to charity. The idea of being so alone no one else would want anything you left behind made her so sad. But there wasn't anyone left.

She was alone.

All because of a horrible man targeting their entire family. "Why? Why us?" The laptop didn't power up correctly. It was trying to open nonexistent files on a memory stick Jeremy had left plugged in. She removed it and dropped it back in the bag. When everything was booted and signed on, she skimmed one file, then another. Brian walked in, moved the merlot closer to her fingertips and she sipped.

"Should I tell someone I won't be coming into work tomorrow?" She sipped again, the merlot warming her shakes away. "Beth will probably stop by Jeremy's after work tonight to see if I'm okay."

"They might get a call before they close. Homicide arrived at your house shortly after we left."

"How would they know where I work?"

"Paystubs? Did you ever sell a phone to a neighbor? Anybody around there know where you work?" He walked to the window again.

"Oh, I guess they do. It's more likely that they remember Jeremy managed that store."

"That's good." Then back to the kitchen, where he put some of the food she'd taken from the house into the refrigerator.

"Oh, my gosh. You want the police to think that dead woman is me?"

"For a couple of days. Long enough to find out why this guy wants you dead. He's obsessed with your family. There has to be a reason."

She set the laptop on the futon and quickly stood. She probably would have fallen straight off her high heels she'd been wearing all day. She was shaky even on bare feet. "Brian, did that woman look a lot like me?"

He encircled her within his arms and she knew the answer before he said, "Yes."

"That's the reason he did those things to her face?"

He nodded, holding her tighter. "He also burned her fingerprints away."

"That's horrible. She died because of me. How can I live with that? No one else can die, Brian." Her fingers curled into a ball around his shirt. "Who's to say my life was worth more than hers?"

"Me, for one. Not more, but just as important. And I think your cousin would want you to live." He kissed her forehead, keeping her safe in his embrace.

"You don't know me." She tilted her face to look at him.

"Then that's something we'll have to change."

Brian delivered a trail of hot kisses down the side of her face. His short, practical fingernails gently gathered her hair as his lips continued a path back up to her forehead. Lindsey turned her mouth into his path, and the fireworks were as explosive as the kiss earlier that morning.

Their tongues danced and explored. His fingers barely grazed her waist and then she felt a tug on both sides of her shirt. Brian backed away, leaving her lips cold and desperate for more of him.

"As much as I'd like to keep on with this—" he dropped another kiss on her cheek "—I'm dead on my feet and heading to bed." He stood and stretched his arms high, raising his shirt to expose an inch of his flat belly. "And no, that's not an invitation, unless you want to curl up in my arms. Our first time is not going to be when we could be interrupted at any moment by my brother."

She stood there with her mouth open at the audacity of his words. *Our first time?* If she hadn't agreed with him, she'd be insulted at his assumption. But she was super attracted to him and wanted to explore more of those abs she'd caught a glimpse of.

There was something about the way he took everything in stride. She'd seen the horror on his face at finding the dead woman. He couldn't hide it as much as he tried. But he didn't allow it to override his ability to think on his feet and come up with a safe place for them to go.

"A Marine and a SEAL. Sounds like the title of a book."

Books!

Jeremy had been reading a book in Cozumel. She opened the link to his electronic library. There were lots of mysteries, thrillers and action books. Then she found the one that had stuck out—*Texas Real Estate and Land Titles*. Why would her cousin be reading this heavy material on vacation? It had to be connected.

But how? She reached for another sip of merlot and realized the glass was empty. She should get some water before she was seriously tipsy. The apartment spun as she stood to fill her glass. She barely made it back to the futon and definitely couldn't do anything with the clean sheets. She'd laugh and giggle but was too busy yawning.

Laptop closed, sheets used as a pillow, she curled on the mattress with her back secure against the cushion.

She drifted off thinking of how well Brian's hands fit around her bottom.

If they'd only met before all this...

SOMEBODY HAD TIED one on before coming to the apartment to sleep. Brian banged on the wall between his bed and the front room. "Come on, guys. I'll remember this the next time I come in and you're getting some shut-eye."

A few seconds was all it took to remember he was here only with Lindsey. The thrashing continued. SIG palmed, he was barefoot and shirtless at the door to the other room. He stuck his head around the frame, staying low like his brother had reminded him.

A nightmare. Lindsey was alone and fighting only someone in her dream. The loose sheets were in knots at her feet. Her red silk shirt was tangled high under her breasts, showing him a flat, tanned stomach. He returned his weapon under his mattress and noted that he'd been asleep a couple of hours.

Lifting his blue-eyed dream into his arms, he cradled her, shushing her nightmare like he would have Lauren. He placed her in his bed, then gathered her stuff, bringing it all to his room and locking the door. If any of his roommates did venture past Mac in the hallway, they wouldn't barge into his room.

The vent blew right on his bed. That was the way he liked it. But Lindsey was already shivering. He pulled the covers around her and had every intention of being a gentleman. He'd stay on his side of the bed, not touching or exploring or...anything.

He did manage to lie on his back and not move. Completely prepared to hit the hay again. Yep, that was his intention. He could do it.

Right until Lindsey curled tighter, sidling up to him.

He lifted his arm and she molded herself to his chest. Shifting to his side was more comfortable, then they were spooning. He couldn't very well keep his arm above his head and get any sleep. Was it his fault if it wrapped around her middle?

Sleeping—really sleeping—with a woman wasn't something he was used to, because he never did it. There was no reason to. He didn't bring women here and certainly didn't bring them home to the room next to his father's.

Sleeping at the moment wasn't happening either. He was too aware of the soft breasts pressing on his arm. Enjoying the rise and fall of her chest, the silkiness of her hair against his chest. Everything about her made him want her and yet made him want to wait until the time was perfect.

Finding a murder victim in your house—not to mention in your bed—was repulsive enough. Running from the murderer probably didn't make you very amorous either.

Yet, he was wide-awake and only thinking of making love to the woman in his arms. He should be thinking about a plan. Since he wasn't sleeping, he should go down and talk with his brother.

That was the last thing he wanted to do, but he eased away. By the time he sat on the second bed to pull on his boots, Lindsey was tossing as though she was in another bad dream.

Making sure Lindsey got some rest was as important as figuring out a plan of action. He didn't want her to fall apart or have more panic attacks. His boots were soundless falling back onto the carpet. He slipped in beside Lindsey before he could change his mind.

Resting on his elbow, he traced her troubled brows,

smoothing them like his mother had after his nightmares. A rhythmic motion that he'd always thought hypnotic. Her jerking slowed, then stopped, and she relaxed into his side.

John had already outlined a plan and could tell him details later. Differences aside, he'd be the good, inexperienced brother and salute when told what to do in order to save Lindsey and his family.

It would be the only time John would get that level of cooperation from him. To keep the woman in his arms sleeping soundly, he slipped an arm under her head and the other around her tiny waist. Even with his eyes closed, he could see her sky-blue eyes sparkling like diamonds in the sunlight.

Diamonds in the sunlight? What the heck? He wasn't a poet and had never thought like this about any woman. Hell, he'd never thought like that before, period.

Chapter Thirteen

"I'm in blessed shape and health for a man of my age. I will, however, admit that fighting a younger paramedic proved tiring."

The wall panel hiding his souvenirs and recording equipment slid open. He placed the bag with the clothes he'd worn during the fight with Brian Sloane along with the rest. All neatly labeled and vacuum sealed to preserve the DNA.

"I should remind curious minds that I have no desire to be blamed for crimes I did not commit, nor will I be denied the accomplishment of one either. It will be hard for authorities to believe my flawless record. I have kept the necessary proof of each and it is properly organized." He pushed the button, closing the panel behind his wall safe, then shut the doors to the actual safe and replaced the heavy books on the shelf, hiding the catch.

"What an exhilarating day. The police believe Lindsey has been killed, and now Sloane is wanted for her murder. Yes, quite an accomplishment. I will have to work late into the night making up for what landed on my desk today, but it is well worth the time I spent."

Time for his vodka. Then the work that paid his bills.

"Sloane acted exactly as predicted. Until the time that the police place him in jail, it will give me the necessary interval to plan the next stage of my Cook finale. I daresay I hate to postpone the preparations for the hunt." He toasted himself, letting the vodka heat his throat. "And the kill."

Chapter Fourteen

"She doesn't deserve nightmares." Brian had tried to explain to his brother several times about his fascination with Lindsey. He barely understood it himself, so the words he'd stubbornly uttered over the past month sounded like a lovesick cow speaking a foreign language. Today was no different.

"I'm sure there are other people who can handle that problem." John pushed a piece of notebook paper across the card table. "My plan is the only way to be safe. I've written everything down for you. I'd like your word that you'll follow my instructions."

John, the man with all the answers, casually tipped his chair back against the wall and linked his fingers behind his head, waiting. Brian knew that look. He'd had one himself years ago when he was confident and certain his way was the only way. Before life got complicated with possibilities.

Walking away from the ranch or from years of paramedic training. Losing his heritage or starting a new life. His dad and John thought they knew his answer. Hell, he didn't even know his answer, so how could they? He reread the list.

Number one in big red caps: Brian surrenders to police. Two: Lindsey secretly travels to a friend's house—

alone. He glanced through the ways to avoid getting noticed. And the last thing on his brother's instructions: let the police find the murderer.

"You want me to sit around and do nothing? Did that work for you?" With a flip of his wrist, Brian sent the list back across the table. "I've already given my word and I won't go back on it. You might as well understand that I'm not going to salute you like one of your soldiers. You can't order me to retreat into a jail cell and wait for this all to blow over."

The Naval Lieutenant inside his brother didn't get it. Brian wasn't leaving Lindsey's side. Not voluntarily. Not until she was safe and had choices for her safety.

John ignored the paper as it floated to the floor. "You can't be serious."

"As serious as you when you were wanted for murder a couple of months ago and kidnapped Lauren to keep her safe."

"That was different, Brian. You don't know the first thing about this woman."

"You didn't know Alicia after being gone for twelve years, yet you jumped in when she was in trouble." He scrubbed his face with his hands, trying to think, and ended up irritating the sutures on his forehead. His brother's look hadn't changed. If anything, he was more irritated with the mention of his wife. "Come on, John. I need you to back me up here."

"I've trained for rescue missions. We had a plan and were lucky it worked."

"You know your instructions are a death sentence for Lindsey. We have to find this guy. If we run now, he'll disappear again and kill her later."

"There's no choice here, bro. We can't do anything

with your name and our mug shot on every television screen in the state."

"That didn't stop you from helping Alicia."

John stood, knocking his folding chair to the floor. "Damn it, why won't you listen to me? Every cop in Dallas–Fort Worth is out for your blood. The P.D.'s catching all sorts of flak for not taking her reported threat seriously."

"Good."

"Not good. They don't want explanations, they want your head on a media-frenzied platter. And she's not even dead."

Brian tapped the table, trying to think. He wanted to understand and accept his brother's advice. But shouldn't his brother understand why he wanted to help Lindsey? John hadn't ever been supportive of him finding the truth behind Mrs. Cook's death. Saying things like "what good would come of it" and that "they all knew the truth so why did finding whoever was responsible matter?"

Well, it mattered to Brian. He was the one who had been blamed for her death. Not John. Not his father. And not the murderer.

"Even if I did follow your suggestion, Lindsey won't leave town. Not without me."

"You don't know that. You haven't asked her." John stood at parade rest.

The way he thought he knew everything they should do now, and how they should act, ticked Brian off. It was his breaking point. He slapped the table, prepared to brawl to win this argument. "This dictator role you've taken on needs to stop. Just accept the fact that we're not running. It's done. Now, explain what you would be looking for on the laptop and we'll do it. Lindsey used to run a website company. I bet she could—"

"Finding hidden files has nothing to do with design. You're over your head trying to rescue your new girl-friend and can't see that you're both drowning." John kicked at the cheap chair. "I told Alicia you'd be an idiot about this."

He put a lid on the feeling of self-pity and screwed the lid on tight. He was the one who chose to take the blame for the accidental fire. Not John. Not anybody. If he'd trusted his brother back then, twelve silent years could have been avoided. He wasn't going to cause a rift be-tween them again.

"Hey, stop shouting. I hear fine and Lindsey's still in there sleeping. I know we'll need to find a safe place to lay low until the police eliminate me as a suspect. What I don't know is why you're so reluctant to help."

"The news is reporting her murder and you're the pri-mary suspect. Unless the police talk to her, know that she's alive, how are they going to eliminate you other than with a bullet between your eyes? They will find you, Brian. Then what?" John asked. Genuine concern or au-thority oozed out his military straightness. He hadn't an-swered Brian's question of what was holding him back.

"It'll be okay. I have a solid alibi."

"That's right, he does," Lindsey said from the bed-room door behind him. "Don't you need to be at home talking with the cops, John? I mean, you're part of his alibi, too. Can't you tell them that poor woman isn't me?"

"Right. Like they'll believe me."

"You doing okay, Lindsey?" Brian watched his broth-er's spine straighten even more with Lindsey's presence. She looked as if she'd been dragged through the wringer. Her hair was prettily tangled from the tossing and turning she'd done even while she'd been safe in his arms. Her eyes were slightly puffy with smudges of mascara. He wondered if she'd taken a look in the mirror or avoided it, afraid of what she'd see.

"Just peachy." She grimaced as she folded her arms across her chest. "I found a memory stick last night. It might mean something."

Brian remained at the table, willing his brother to leave. He didn't want to argue any longer, just wrap his arms around Lindsey and maybe take off to hide in the mountains.

"What happened to your arm?" John asked. His brother was calm enough on the surface, but Brian could see his tolerance chipping away.

Right then, he didn't feel like the older, responsible twin at all. He tried to catch Lindsey's eye before she filled John in on the details he'd left out about their encounter with the murderer. Luck wasn't on his side.

"A maniac sliced it with a knife after he murdered an innocent woman in Jeremy's house. A woman who looked just like me, apparently."

Apparently she didn't like him holding back information either. It was Brian's turn to stand suddenly and let his chair collapse with a clang to the floor. The noise didn't slow John or Lindsey's discussion.

"You heard the authorities think you're dead?" She nodded and John's eyes narrowed. "My brother neglected to mention you'd been wounded. Did you see a doctor?"

"It was a minor altercation." Brian tried to play it down. An identical set of jaws clenched, and fingers formed fists. Maybe they'd get that brawl in after all.

"Brian stitched it up last night." Lindsey lightly stroked the overkill bandage he'd wrapped over the sutures. "I will never doubt the power of a deadener again."

"Are you nuts, man? She needs a real doctor, a hospital, antibiotics."

Lindsey shook her head and compressed her gorgeous lips into a straight line. "Let's get past this, John. You've argued too long and need to admit that you've lost this battle. I'm following Brian's lead regarding this matter. If you can't help, then you should go."

As tall as his blonde beauty was, she still had to tilt her chin to meet his eyes. But there was nothing weak or confused about her glare at his brother. She wasn't bluffing. She'd made a decision and that was the end of the discussion.

John placed his chair back at the table and mumbled about stubborn women and idiot brothers as he sat. There was a new energy and assuredness to Lindsey's step as she crossed the room, scooped up John's list and opened her cousin's laptop. Brian watched, leaning on the kitchen wall, completely confused as to why he suddenly felt proud.

"How long before we need to leave?" Lindsey's nails gently clicked keys while she raised one blond brow in question.

"Soon," he said, along with his brother.

"Did either of you hear me when I said there was a memory stick with Jeremy's laptop? I should show you what I found last night before Brian got me drunk."

"Drunk?"

Brian pointed to his upper arm and mouthed *stitches* to his brother.

"I remembered something strange from my last trip with Jeremy." Lindsey ignored his brother. "I teased him because he was reading a Texas real estate manual, even highlighting passages. Who reads that sort of book *after* you buy a house? Anyway, it's still on here."

"It's a start. Is there any other file that might be un-usual?" he asked, not needing his twin's challenging glare. He knew nothing about computers. He rode horses or in an ambulance. Neither allowed a lot of time for gaining computer skills.

"I'm not sure, but the drive indicates there's a lot of data there. I can't find a file list. It looks as though Jeremy just used a hidden file program. You can get them off the internet. The trick will be thinking of his password."

"I have friends who can take care of that." John had a shoulder against the wall, listening, a hand rubbing the stubble on his chin.

"I can figure it out. Jeremy was like my brother. I knew him pretty well."

Brian looked up to see the same "yeah, right" look on his brother's face. Lindsey harrumphed.

"The concept might be foreign to the two of you, but I did know Jeremy. Thanks for the offer, but these are my files now and I'm keeping them." She shook her head looking back at her keyboard. "The protection program he used was just a GUI."

"Did you say gooey?" John asked.

"Yes, a Graphical User Interface that's easy to install and use."

"I think Lindsey speaks your lingo, bro." Brian crossed his arms and leaned back in his chair, striking the same pose his brother had earlier.

"Can I see you for a moment?" John asked.

He stood, and the first thought that raced through his head was what would break when they came to blows in the bedroom. Nothing important or nothing at all. He'd successfully controlled his temper for twelve years. He even avoided the teens around Aubrey who didn't know why their parents were angry at him. They just liked to pit their fighting ability against the town's bad boy. John was the only person who got under his skin far enough to get a rise.

His brother turned, and they were face-to-face. Once again, it was like looking in a mirror. Gritted jaws. Clenched fists. Narrowed eyes. John moved and instinctively Brian brought up his hands to defend himself.

"Damn it, Brian. I don't want to fight you." John clapped a hand on his shoulder. "After I leave, I can't help you. You won't be able to come home. It'll be more than the local police camped out on our doorstep and it won't be safe."

Brian jerked away from his brother, feeling more alone than he had in the twelve years they were apart. "Don't worry. I wouldn't put you guys in danger. I'll keep my distance and keep you out of this mess."

"You're taking this all wrong. I didn't mean it like that." John scrubbed his face, then his head, the worry apparent in his eyes. "I was thinking it might be easier if we switched. You stay at the ranch and I'll protect Lindsey."

"I thought that wasn't possible with my new scar?"

"Don't be too hasty and hear me out. I have special skills and training that might come in handy."

"I think I can hold my own. We're not much different."

"With most things, sure." Both of John's hands went to the top of Brian's shoulders. It was the closest they'd gotten to a brotherly hug since they'd graduated from high school. "You know this guy's not going to stop. What are you going to do when you find him?"

Be more prepared than the last time. His hand went to the gun at his waist.

"Are you prepared to pull that trigger and kill someone?"

"If it comes to that." He didn't have to debate it. The

answer was clear in his head and heart. He'd defend Lindsey without question.

"You could both die." His brother sounded more like his father for a minute.

He understood wanting to protect his twin. It was exactly the reason he'd stepped forward and taken the blame all those years ago. "It means a lot that you want to take my place, but this is something I have to do."

His brother clapped him on the shoulder, squeezed his fingers. "I figured. I've seen the way you look at her. I didn't think you'd do anything different, so I got Mac to let you use his place for a few days so you could lie low."

AFTER THE SLOANE men headed to the bedroom, Lindsey had been tempted to follow them and eavesdrop at the door. But only for a second. If the thin walls didn't allow her to overhear an argument, just like it had earlier, she'd ask Brian what John had to say later.

The brothers were identical in so many ways, and yet different in so many, too. John acted so confident, but she had a sneaky suspicion he was just worried about losing his brother. Brian had appeared so withdrawn at first. It was much easier to like him when he was around his family. Whether he realized it or not, he smiled more on the ranch. Maybe it was the youthful playfulness even when he argued with his brother about serious subjects. Or maybe he was just cute. Period.

Right now she needed to find a lead. Some tiny bit of information to begin a search. There had to be something.

The slash on her arm ached. If she rubbed it or complained, Brian would insist she go to the hospital. He'd be arrested and she'd have no one to help her find this madman or a connection to her family. If the police hadn't found a reason to investigate any of their deaths before, why would they now?

"Lindsey have you seen my folder with your family information?" Brian began thumbing through Jeremy's papers.

"Hmm?"

"I had the folder last night at your place when you noticed the fish food had moved," he said, looking at her. "Then I— Son of a biscuit eater, I left it on the coffee table."

She went through the picture of her living room in her head. "It wasn't there this afternoon when we went through the house."

"He knows exactly what we know." John walked to the window, taking a quick look through the blinds.

"How can he use that against us?" she asked. "Isn't it more important to concentrate on why he's killing my family?"

"What if he doesn't need a reason and he's just a nut job? How are you going to stop him then?" John asked.

John was right. The murderer was patient and had outsmarted them twice already. All he had to do was wait until the police stopped investigating him. Then one day when she was alone, he'd resurface and finish the job, crossing her off whatever insane death list he had stuffed somewhere.

"You okay? You look woozy and didn't answer."

"Maybe she needs the hospital after all. Mac will take her."

"I'm fine, and I'll decide if I need to see a doctor." The nausea she felt had nothing to do with her arm. It was from being scared down to her bone marrow at the idea of being hunted for the rest of her life. Hunted and never knowing why.

"You sure you're okay?" Brian asked. "The police wanted a motive. If we find the reason why the murderer has a feud with your family, we'll find him."

John looked at his watch. "I need to hit the road and would feel better if you got going."

"He's right, Lindsey. We need to head out. Mac gave us the keys to his place for a couple of days while we come up with a plan."

"There's got to be something to this book and memory stick. It's just going to take me time to piece it together." She shut the laptop, then held her hand out to John. "I'm so sorry I've brought more chaos into your family, but I'm so grateful I'm not facing it alone."

"It's more as though we brought a killer to your doorstep." John pulled her into a bear hug. "Don't let him do anything foolish," he whispered.

"I'll try not to."

John nodded toward his brother. They both paused, and he left.

"Are you absolutely certain that we're doing the right thing? Your brother seems very upset at the idea of us trying to catch the killer." She shoved the laptop in its case and slung the strap over her shoulder. "Shoot, I'm upset about finding a murderer."

"Sometimes he forgets who's saved his hide more than once. But if you have any doubts about my abilities—"

"No. It's nothing like that." Maybe she trusted too easily, but she did trust him. He'd put everything on the line for her, a virtual stranger.

With her bag of clothes over his shoulder, his hands warmed her inside and out when he slid them along her back to draw her closer. He smoothed her hair behind her ear and trailed his fingers across her now-flushed cheek.

"I'll do my best to keep this guy away from you, Lindsey. I promise."

"I believe you." She thought she spoke, maybe a broken, breathy sentence. But it didn't matter.

Brian tilted his head and leaned close. Her hand felt the wild cadence of his heart under the thin cotton of his T-shirt, along with the strong muscle tone. He oozed protection and sexiness. As his lips claimed hers, she remembered the feel of her legs wrapping around him, how he'd lifted her with ease and how she wanted to repeat the wild forgetfulness from earlier that morning.

Gentle, firm, in control. He was all those things. She wanted more, wanted to drop their bags, kick off their shoes and head back to his room. Who was she kidding? She wanted his arms tight around her and didn't care if they moved another inch.

His lips gently pulled away, replaced by his finger smoothing the fire-parched surface.

"It's a good thing my brother was in here for the past hour. Otherwise—" he touched his lips to her ear "—I might have kissed you when you woke up and taken you straight back to bed."

She gulped, wishing they'd met last week when she'd first noticed him in the coffee shop. She dragged her nail across his lips, avoiding his teeth when he tried to snag it. "That's pretty presumptuous, considering we just met yesterday and you haven't even bought me dinner yet."

"We'll get that taken care of as soon as the police aren't trying to arrest me for your murder."

"Absolutely, cowboy. It's a date."

Chapter Fifteen

They were in another unremarkable four-door car that belonged to the woman across the street from Brian's family. The car couldn't be traced back to them, but she still turned her face away from drivers pulling alongside. Lindsey had picked up enough at the ranch to understand that JW Sloane was spending his nights at Mabel's and she was practically family.

It had been a long while since her family had consisted of more than Jeremy. And she was ashamed to admit that she'd put him off several times before begging him to come to Cozumel with her. He'd gotten his life together and she'd kept "bumming around," as he'd put it.

"You sounded pretty knowledgeable with all that computer lingo back there. I guess I should hire you to get a website together for the ranch."

"I let all that go when I moved here."

"Aren't you good at it?"

Brian's question seemed like ordinary conversation and probably was. She was half mad at herself for walking away from that dream. She'd been getting new sites and had loyal customers. It was hard to explain to an outsider that one of the last conversations she'd had with Jeremy was about keeping her word and responsibility.

"I hold my own."

"Then why'd you give it up to sell mobile phones?"

She'd promised Jeremy that Cozumel would be her last "fling." She hadn't meant it at the time, knowing full well that she'd talk him into another spur-of-the-moment vacation later. But when he'd died, it all rushed her as though she'd been hit by the lip of a wave and totally wiped out. She hadn't surfed since.

"Why are you riding around in an ambulance instead of on a horse?"

"Touché. So you know how to surf?"

"I practically lived on the water. I surfed every day I could." The rush and power of doing something well hit her as strong as the desire to run back to the ocean. Leave searching for the serial killer to someone else trained to find a sicko like that. Leave and disappear on the beaches with some waves and a good board.

"Wow. Not sure I'd like it out there with sharks under my toes."

"I loved it at the time."

"Is there any money in web design?" Brian drove, seeming as though nothing was wrong. Not as if they'd seen the killer or were running from the cops. He was so laid-back she could easily imagine him as a surfer. No bumps in a wave for him.

The conversation was such that two people might have on their first date. She knew so little about him other than he was a rancher who supplemented his income by working as a paramedic.

"I suppose there's money in it for those who try. I mainly did it for friends. I couldn't spend much time on it while at work. There wasn't good internet access at the beach huts."

He rubbed his forehead, scratching the stitches on his wrinkled, confused brow.

"Most of my jobs revolved around renting boogie boards to tourists. I'd follow the coast, working in different cities, crashing with different friends—or a friend of a friend. Sunup to sundown. Barefoot with sand between my toes. Spring break until it was too cold to open the rental huts. I made enough helping with websites to pay my share of the rent when the beaches were closed. That's all I cared about."

"You sound like you miss it."

"I shouldn't. There was no stability in that line of work. And I'd never get ahead, as Jeremy constantly reminded me. Wouldn't you know that as soon as I have my act together, a serial killer smashes my car trying to murder me." A cracked laugh escaped from high in her throat, making her sound a bit frazzled. Or a little loony.

Brian cleared his throat, creating a nervous silence that she didn't know how to get herself out of. There was nothing to comment on except the darkness. In the middle of nowhere, on the edge of civilization, but far enough away to remind her just how much light streetlamps provided. Brian slowed for a stop sign and her heart jumped into her throat.

It had only been twenty-four hours since her car had been hit. There weren't any other headlights, but her hands gripped the edge of her seat, bracing herself. A warm hand covered hers. His strength shot a different type of adrenaline through her system.

"It's okay."

His deep baritone voice whispered a complex comfort in its simplicity. Something her body understood more than her mind. His calloused fingertips rubbed her cold hand back to life. She no longer concentrated on the crash. The excitement of his kiss washed over her and she wanted to recapture all the exhilaration she'd felt moments before leaving his apartment.

The dashboard lights softened the sharp angles of his face and smile. He waggled his eyebrows before he looked both ways along the deserted road and stepped on the gas again. Bringing her hand to the side of his thigh, he laced his fingers through hers and held tight. So did she.

"Mac's place should be around one or two more curves," he said after a couple of minutes.

"Have you been there before?"

"I never heard of the guy until my brother texted me. I am, however, great with directions. I never got lost when I drove the ambulance."

It was on the tip of her tongue to ask if they should trust a man they didn't know, but it wasn't necessary. Mac had already proved his friendship to them both by guarding the door while they slept. She also wanted to avoid speaking of the reason they needed to hide. She was enjoying the silence and holding Brian's hand.

Two days ago, if Beth had told her those two things would be appealing, she would have fallen over laughing. Now having this man's thumb tenderly caress her hand was sweet and sexy at the same time.

The stress of the past day had kept her adrenaline at extreme levels. There was a strong desire to forget all of it for the rest of the night. Just being on an even, relaxed keel was appealing. But not as appealing as being safe enough to explore every inch of the man beside her.

The thought of how they could fill some downtime had her blood bubbling with excitement and tingling so much, her body shivered.

"I know you want to plan out our next move. So do

I. Let's find Mac's place and then we can work our way through Jeremy's paperwork."

"Sure." She didn't want to think about papers or trails or clues. But most of all, she didn't want Brian to let go. And she didn't want to think about why.

How could she consider an interlude—to put it nicely—with a guy she just met yesterday?

Impossible. No way. That was the old Lindsey. The Lindsey who tossed her sleeping bag on a beach chair half the summer. She was responsible now and couldn't do things like that. She wouldn't sleep with Brian Sloane, no matter how much she wanted to. No matter how tempting or how safe she felt with the man trying to save her life. She would not break her promise to Jeremy.

"Here we go." Brian used both hands to turn the big car onto a dirt road overgrown with tree limbs in spite of the drought they'd seen all summer. "Mabel's going to have a cow if these sticks scratch her paint job."

"Uh-huh." She stuck her hands under her legs to keep them from wandering back to Brian's.

Less than a minute of driving and the tree limbs stopped creeping near the car and then were gone. Camouflage for the Marine's home that was at the end of the short road. What had seemed like a dark trail actually opened onto a large open field surrounding the small house.

"You okay?"

"I'm fine, and you can stop asking me that."

He parked the car in back, off the driveway and close to the back door. He twisted in his seat, no longer looking casual, but very calculated as if he was thinking about how each word would sound before they crossed his lips. "If you're upset about what I said earlier, I can apologize."

"I don't need an apology." And hated that he thought

she did. "I need something to let me know that I'll eventually wake up from this nightmare."

JUST HIS LUCK. Hold a girl's hand and she calls it a nightmare.

Brian knew it wasn't him and could admit he had no business telling her earlier he'd rather take her to bed. Crass. Rude. Ungentlemanly. And a couple of other things if his daddy found out. Being nearly thirty years old wouldn't stop the old man from giving him a good earful on how to treat a lady.

"One day the nightmare will be over." He hoped. "Remember, we're going to catch—"

"This creep." She laughed, finishing his sentence. She dropped the partial braid she'd been nervously plaiting and slapped her jean-covered thighs. "I think that must be our mantra for this adventure."

"And a damn good one to remember until we do." Brian laughed. Easy, pleasant and infectious. "Adventure, huh? Ready to find out if Mac has running water and electricity?"

"Where are we?" she asked as they unloaded and unlocked the door.

"A little north of Fort Worth. Not too far out in the boonies."

"It feels like the boonies. I'm horrible at directions, but it doesn't seem possible that we're still near Fort Worth."

"We're not far. Straight highway and we can be back at your place in half an hour. Good, he has lights."

"You were just joking about the running water, right? I never did get that shower."

"Try that door." He pointed to one next to the small kitchen.

She cracked the door enough for him to see a sink,

gave him a thumbs-up and disappeared behind the closed—and locked—door.

Mac's house was totally off anyone's radar if they were looking for someplace Lindsey would be hiding. She'd be safe here, which was Brian's primary objective. He heard the shower and a long, relieved sigh through the thin wall. He finished unloading the food from Mabel's car, breaking a sweat and making the skin under his bandage itch.

But that wasn't all that was itching. His skin was irritated by the T-shirt as he put away the last of the beer and wine. He was irritated at himself when he realized he was looking for an excuse to take it off. The idea of meeting Lindsey bare chested prompted him to open the new stainless-steel fridge and pop the top on a beer.

He took care of the basics, securing the doors and windows, getting the bed ready, putting a pillow and blanket on the leather couch. All the while having no trouble picturing Lindsey's sun-kissed skin lathered in soap. And no problem imagining the small bubbles being rinsed away. Or how he wished he was in that shower with her.

"Damn it. Get a grip."

The water stopped and he reached for another beer.

"You look as if you've gone for a run," she said, stepping from the bathroom in a short, skimpy T-shirt and shorts cut up to her hips. Her hair was wrapped inside a stark-white towel that made her skin all the more appealing.

He gulped down the cool liquid, swallowing the desire building low in his belly. Any sweat on his upper lip was purely from his heavy breathing, not any labor he'd done while she was cooling off.

She crossed the small area rug in her bare feet, making him glad he was still in his boots. Maybe checking the perimeter one more time was a good idea. It would get him out of the house and out of arm's reach.

"How do we start looking for someone we know nothing about?"

"We know something about him." He tipped the end of his second beer between his lips and crushed the empty can before setting it on the table. "He can't fight worth a Hoover Dam."

"Well, neither can I." Lindsey unwrapped the towel and shook her hair down her back, finger combing and fluffing the damp wheat-colored strands. She dropped the towel over the chair next to him. "Seriously, where do we start?"

He had himself under control. Right up to when she batted those long lashes in his direction and those baby blues taunted him with their brilliance.

She took a step back and he caught her hand. With a little tug and footwork he remembered from the couple of times he'd danced in public, he had Lindsey securely wrapped in his arms. It might be very ungentlemanly, but he had every intention of kissing her until she admitted she wanted to see if the bed was as new as the kitchen appliances.

"How 'bout where we left off?" he whispered, almost afraid to ask. He had to ask, of course. Because as much as he wanted to show her she couldn't resist him, the decision had to be hers.

She didn't move, but she was far from frozen. With his free hand, he traced the outline of her mouth. She sighed as her lips parted and her eyes closed. Her head tilted to the perfect angle for him to enjoy his prize.

He expected something to happen. An interruption. Someone handing him his hat or waving from the porch.

But no one was there. They were alone. Far from his family or danger. No one would be stopping them but them.

He hesitated too long and she opened her soft, sexually charged eyes. Then she followed the path his finger had taken and moistened her lips. He was a goner. Had been the moment he'd sat at that table and finally spoken to her at the sandwich shop. His dad had told him more than once that when he fell, it would be hard, and there'd be no coming back.

He leaned closer, breathing the same breath she didn't seem able to catch. His hand skimmed her silky skin and continued down her back. Her curves met his chest with little resistance, just as her lips crushed into his. She might not realize that he'd fallen and couldn't come back. It might not be the time to tell her, but it was definitely the time to show her.

If he did it well enough, maybe she'd fall just as hard.

Chapter Sixteen

Staring at Brian's lips made Lindsey want to devour him
like fresh water after hours in the surf. Tasting him?
Wow. Just wow.

He sipped her like hot chocolate on the beach in front
of a bonfire. She could hear the surf pounding between
her ears, building. The crescendo had never felt so welcome or right.

Making love to Brian here, in a strange house owned
by a man she'd never met, was a little more than crazy.
But she kissed him back. Long and hard and enthusias-
tically.

They only made it a few steps away from the table.
Her arms risked a journey to his back, pulling his work-
hardened body closer. Anticipation pulsed through her
with every gulping breath. She wanted to get the feel
of cotton from under her fingers and leave nothing between them.

Kissing Brian took her to the top of the highest wave
she'd ever ridden. She should rethink, slow them down.
But just like being at the top of that magical crest, it was
too late to turn back. The hard ridge against his zipper
left no doubt where he thought they were headed.

He ran his tongue down her throat, nipping sensitive
places along the way—places she had no idea existed.

It was as if they'd never been discovered before. She clamped her eyes shut as all the blood rushed from her brain and her knees.

Lindsey hadn't thought about the way she'd dressed until Brian's hands slipped higher under her shirt, brushing skin and nothing else. Her hands rose and slowed his advancing fingers. When she'd left the shower, she hadn't allowed herself to imagine being this close to Brian. She'd been ready to get started on their manhunt, not curl up next to him. When she lifted the pressure from his hands he'd find out just how ready she'd become. But he knew that. She could see it in the smoldering embers of his eyes.

Lindsey tugged the soft, worn shirt over her head and her damp hair swished against her blistering skin. Her arms came down on top of his shoulders. Before she could discover the sinewy lines of his muscles, his mouth captured one nipple while his fingers circled the other.

The instant his calloused palm brushed her, she wanted to scream for more. There was no way to stop the reaction building inside. She wanted to torture him by running her nails across his tanned muscles and teasing him into mindless oblivion.

Somewhere in her brain, some neurons fired a warning. Where they were exploring was dangerous waters. She'd never been the type to venture too deep without her surfboard. Even though she knew it could only end in disaster, she wanted him beyond reason.

A relationship with Brian would be like a tourist on a bodyboard preventing real surfers from enjoying the waves. Or worse, pearl diving off the front of her board on takeoff. Why would she set herself up for failure? She knew nothing about family, roots, ranches or animals. Her life had been waves, sand and sunsets.

Unfamiliar thoughts floated through her mind, mixing with the sexy essence of who Brian was. Someone she'd been attracted to from the first time she'd noticed him. It was one of the reasons she'd remembered him so clearly from the coffee shop. There was something familiar, something comfortable and something so sexy she couldn't think straight half the time she looked at him.

Her fingers reached for his belt buckle, big and all cowboyish. His mouth nipped her breast, causing a hitch in her breathing. She was used to drawstring swim trunks and baggy jeans, but she'd noticed Brian's tight jeans once or twice. Maybe three or four times if she was forced to admit the truth.

The way they hugged his thighs and backside. Just thinking about him made a shiver travel the length of her body. She had her fingers on his zipper when he twirled her around and wrapped his arms tight—one covered her breasts, the other kept her waist close to his rigid body.

"Are you sure you want to go there?" he whispered in her ear. His breath shot all sorts of tingles down her spine. "Once we reach the bedroom, I'm not sure I can turn back."

"Yes and yes again." The words were spoken without a thought to any of the concerns she'd had seconds ago. Her body was already humming for release. "Don't you want—"

"Definitely." His voice was deep, husky, sexy. He nipped on her neck to the soft flesh of her shoulder. The evidence of just how much he wanted to continue pressed against her as she squirmed in delight. His hands wandered over her aching flesh. "Walk."

"How can I when you're... Oh, my."

His fingertips dipped under the elastic of her shorts. Teasing her before pulling back. He swung her into his arms and carried her to the bedroom, dropping her on the bed.

"If we don't get naked fast, I'm going to make love to you with my boots on."

They laughed together, kissing and tugging at his clothes. He ripped his shirt off over his head, baring his strong shoulders, revealing a smattering of chest hair that made him even more sexy.

As much as she adored her cowboy/paramedic, she wanted to see all of him. She tugged at his jeans, lifting one leg into the air, reaching for his boot. He lost his balance and toppled next to her on the bed.

Brian smiled the most genuine grin she'd seen, lying nose to nose next to her. One of those moments she'd dreamed about imitating from a book or movie. A moment where grins and laughter turn into a monumental life-changing instant. Maybe the thought changed her expression, but in an instant, Brian's changed.

He reached out and cupped her cheek, turning to his side, close enough and suddenly so serious she wanted to remember every detail. This time was different. She felt it. Knew it.

At this exact moment in time…this was exactly where she was supposed to be. With this man who looked at her as though she was the only woman who could ever make him smile like that.

Later, she may get mad at herself for being irresponsible. But she had such a strong desire to be the only woman who would be in this position with him again. And that scared the daylights out of her.

Brian watched the laughter leave Lindsey's beautiful face. He almost jumped off the bed to save her the embarrassing trouble of talking her way out of his arms and back into her clothes. Then her lips parted, waiting for his kiss.

There was no mistaking the longing. He felt it in the depths of his soul.

Playfulness was replaced with frenzied touching and heavy caresses. They rolled, scooted, shifted to the middle of the king-size bed. Overkill for the room, but he didn't care and wasn't analyzing why Mac didn't want more than a bed in the bedroom.

He cupped a set of perfect breasts, dragging his thumbs across each, causing the perfect rose-colored peaks to tease him more. Lindsey tugged at his belt, not realizing the tip of her tongue was squeezed between her lips and driving him insane. She unbuttoned the top of his fly and he couldn't resist. He devoured every inch of her skin, shoving the short shorts down her hips as he discovered all her contours and secrets. He still couldn't believe she was his.

For one night or a single moment.

"You still have your boots on." She sighed, arching her back as his hand continued exploring.

Fortunately, he could toe his boots off and did so without much difficulty. His jeans were a different story. He might get them off if he stood, but there was no way he'd stop the passion that was building inside of Lindsey. And then there was the problem of preparedness. He hadn't exactly been thinking of casual sex, since he'd spent all his free time following Lindsey during the past two months.

So his pants would stay zipped and they'd be safe. But there was no reason Lindsey couldn't have some fun. He could see her getting closer and closer to fulfillment. She tipped her head back, surrounded by a halo of hair. Her body arched into his hand and relaxed, finally opening the eyes he loved to look into.

"I don't think this is at all fair." She paused, gesturing to his jeans. "You still have clothes on."

"And they're staying there." No condom. No sex.

"What?" Realization washed over her face. "Oh. I saw…" She shivered under his hand again and drew in a deep breath. "He has them on his…in his bathroom."

"Lindsey, we can't do—"

She sprung from the bed. "Get out of those jeans. No socks either." She ran from the room.

He didn't waste any time. He stood, stripped his jeans, boxers and socks and by the time he'd stopped dancing on one foot, she was waltzing back into the room, tearing a small package.

One look at him and she stopped in her tracks, taking a long stare at his splendid physique. A lesser man might have been intimidated. Hell, he might have been if she'd stayed in the doorway too much longer. When she leaped on him, he fell backward onto a soft mattress and he stopped wondering about everything.

With a hand on either side of his shoulders, Lindsey lifted herself open for a fun attack. He dropped light kisses across her clavicle, finding her pulse strong and rapid at the base of her throat. He skimmed his chin stubble across her smooth flesh, causing her to sit up.

She lightly raked her nails from his shoulder to his hip. He sucked air through his teeth as she shifted on his lap and rolled the condom into place. Brian ran his hands around her thighs to her bottom. He pulled her hips closer, using himself to excite her until she dropped her chest to his, catching her breath.

Panting, she took his face in her hands and kissed him deep and long. Her hair dropped around them and he splayed his fingers through the golden mass. It fell around their kiss, forming a small cocoon.

Shutting out the world.

He searched her sky-blue eyes, close enough to see the darker flecks and count the freckles adorning the tip of her nose. He wanted to believe he had an emotional handle on this ride.

If he was honest, he was barely hanging on to the words he wanted to say. He knew what type of person Lindsey was on paper. He knew what he thought she was like from what he'd seen in the past twenty-four hours. He just needed time.

Time to discover if she could feel the same way. Even if she couldn't, he'd fallen long and hard. He really hoped Lindsey wouldn't mind keeping a piece of his heart tucked somewhere safe.

Stopping his teasing, he flipped her onto her back and slid inside. They moved together, their bodies hitting a rhythm age-old but unique only to them. Sweet, tender, hard and sexy until she cried out and it echoed through the house. He followed with a sweet release he wanted to repeat. They kissed, sated and smiling. He rolled to lie by Lindsey's side, the breeze from the ceiling fan cooling the fine sheen of sweat making love to her had created.

Simply dragging her nails lightly back and forth across his abs created another burn that wouldn't be doused easily.

No more debate why Mac had gone with the large bed.

Chapter Seventeen

Lindsey was totally and completely exhausted. Brian was a marathon champion lover. Their schedule was completely off. She hadn't had four hours of straight sleep since leaving his ranch. They'd drift off, touch in the middle of the ginormous bed and wouldn't be able to stop the nuclear blast until they were both on their backs breathing hard to recover.

Exhausting, but wonderful. She'd never imagined spending every waking—and sleeping—moment with a man would be this rewarding.

"You know, we're going to have to trek back into the real world sometime soon." She pointed to the empty box of condoms that needed to be replaced. "The last two are on the nightstand."

"We've spent two days in bed. Searching, talking and—" he kissed her shoulder "—other things. It's time to make some decisions, Lindsey. We're even out of frozen food."

"I could always make a run to the store. I doubt anyone would recognize me and I hardly think you want to give delivery boys directions, as if anyone would deliver out here in the middle of nowhere to begin with." She popped the laptop open and read Jeremy's notes on the real estate book. It was what she'd been doing when

Brian had awakened and a simple kiss had led to a delectable round of lovemaking. But she was determined to find the reason Jeremy had been looking into the sale of mineral rights. It had to be a clue.

"You've been at that memory stick for two days. Making any headway?" He quirked his brows together, causing his crooked stiches to wrinkle. He was propped against the headboard, finishing off the orange juice they'd mixed up from frozen concentrate. "Mac's going to need his place back soon. We should probably think about our next move."

"I think we're close." She focused on the screen, hiding Brian's rippling muscles behind the lid. His simple movements made her want to close the laptop and continue hiding with him here in the cabin. No. They had to finish at least one conversation and make progress.

"You said that yesterday," Brian said from his side of the bed, swinging his legs over the edge and sitting.

"Well, it's true." She closed the lid and set the laptop aside, trying not to let her frustration show. "If we don't come up with something, then where do we stand? What do we do then?"

"Leave?" He stretched as he stood.

"The murderer is still out there and determined to kill me, Brian. Or kill the both of us now. You're the one who convinced me that running wasn't an option." She tossed the large pillows against the wall, then flipped the silky sheet aside. "Who'll run the ranch if you leave?"

This particular conversation would chase him from the room and she was going to follow him this time.

"Same people Dad sells it to next month."

They'd talked every minute they weren't making love or sleeping. She knew all about the ranch's financial problems and a little about how the town had treated him over the past twelve years. "Stop being a jerk. You told me you don't want him to sell."

She admired him for sticking it out, continuing to live there and help his dad. She even knew how Alicia had finally made him fight his twin so they'd start talking again. What he wouldn't admit was how much he loved working with horses. But she could tell. It was his life, his passion.

When he spoke about training a spirited animal, his face lit up. And she'd learned quickly if she wanted him excited to ask about how he'd improve or how to get a stronger breed. Then she'd watch the disappointment drain his energy when he remembered it was just a pipe dream.

"The bank will never give me a loan."

She rounded the bed and wrapped her arms around him, burying her face in his shoulder. "You don't know that, Brian. You haven't applied."

"I asked you to drop this subject the last time you brought it up, Lindsey." With the tip of his finger he drew a design on her skin, down her back, then back up, getting closer to her breast with each pass.

"Don't change the subject this time. This is important to you. Running away isn't a possibility."

"It may be necessary for you to stay alive. Are you saying you'd rather do it alone?"

"I'm not admitting defeat yet. I still want to find this guy." She lifted her face toward his, seeking a kiss.

He kissed her into silence and she let him. She was still tingling in all the right places from waking up in his arms. The desire to change his plan of attack and avoid this conversation just wasn't strong enough.

Making love to Brian Sloane was a pleasure she didn't want to give up.

BRIAN STOOD NAKED, drinking directly out of the carton of milk. The only light slicing through the darkness was from the open fridge door. It was a small pleasure, but one he'd enjoyed many times over the past two days.

"Tell me again why standing there like that makes you happy?" Lindsey had slipped into one of his T-shirts. The shirttail hit her low enough to make his wandering eye curious to see more—even when he'd seen more many times.

"It's simple. Because I can." He tipped the remainder of milk into his mouth, then wiped his mouth with the back of his hand. "I never get to do this. I live with too many people to walk around 'nekid as a jaybird.'"

Her arm circled his waist as she leaned past him for a bottle of water. Her soft breasts molded to him before she eased back to stand next to the counter. She crossed her arms and could barely drink through her smile.

"What's going on?"

"I think I've found it."

"A connection? Are you kidding?" He wanted to grab her around the waist and twirl her in celebration before she said anything else. Before they could discuss it further and realize there wasn't a connection at all.

But if he touched her, they'd end up back in bed. Two days of making love to her hadn't quieted the need even a little. So he stood here with a hand on his hip and an empty milk jug in the other.

"I wanted to know when Jeremy got curious about real estate, so I checked the actual downloads on his laptop. And that stupid memory stick that didn't have anything listed, but said it was full? I finally thought of the password to open the hidden files, and there are a ton of them. Copies of research and references to emails. An email that occurred after a string of conversations regarding mineral rights that weren't transferred with the sale of property about twenty years ago. The current property owner wanted to know if Jeremy would be interested in selling."

"Was he?"

"Jeremy didn't own them. They thought he was part of the corporation that does."

"How does this connect to a man trying to kill your family?" Brian searched the fridge for something to take his mind off the long and very sexy legs in front of him. If he attacked her right now in the middle of her discovery, he might not hear the end of it.

"The rights are worth a lot of money now. Jeremy was trying to determine which family member sold them to the corporation. He couldn't find any records."

"So you think the guy he was emailing decided to kill him?" He leaned an elbow on the top of the door.

"We could go see."

"Right. Just ring the doorbell and ask if this guy is trying to exterminate the Cook family?"

"Of course not. I haven't thought of everything." She smiled, taunting him by crossing her arms under her braless breasts and showing him the bottom half of her derriere as she spun around. "But I did think of something to pass the time until we have to leave."

It hit him. Just like that, he didn't want to leave. Didn't want her in danger. He tried to hold his finger off the panic button, but it wasn't working. He wanted her safe, wanted to turn the evidence over to the police and keep her hidden somewhere. He wanted to tell her he loved her.

Just like that. In an instant, he knew.

"Lindsey?" He took a step, spun her into his arms and let the fridge door shut. His eyes adjusted as he stared into hers, wanting to tell her. He couldn't wrap his mind around saying the three little words aloud. He'd never done it. Never expected that he ever would.

"What's the matter? You said we needed a game plan. The lady lives straight up Interstate 35."

"I wanted to…" After. He should tell her later. Somewhere romantic. Not naked as the day he was born in a kitchen. "Never mind. You said a woman?"

"I searched the map for her address. One of her emails said she divorced a second cousin of ours years ago. But his name is on your list of accidents."

"We should probably talk to her."

"You don't sound very excited."

Should he be? "I guess I didn't expect you to find anything."

"I would have found it sooner if I hadn't been so distracted by other things." She smiled, hiding a glance at his body.

"So there wasn't anything wrong with the…um… memory stick."

"Nothing that I found. Oh." The double entendre hit her and she blushed from head to toe.

"You surprised me, Lindsey." He reached out, trying to bring her into his arms.

"Wait. I thought you believed I could do this all along. If you didn't, then why did you take up for me in front of your brother? Was it just to score points or to get him out of the way?" She jerked her injured arm free from his hand. "Why did you bring me here?"

"There's a guy trying to kill you and—"

"And I was your alibi in case you couldn't avoid the police."

"No. I've been trying to help you."

"Right. And now that I have a real lead you don't want to." Lindsey tiptoed backward, facing him like a cornered she-cat, claws extended and ready to pounce to protect herself.

"A lead to what? Jeremy might have been helping a friend. Have you read all his emails?"

"I think you're wrong." She shook her head back and forth. "You have to be wrong. Doris Davis was married to one of our cousins and had nothing to do with Jeremy."

"Then why isn't she dead, too?"

Lindsey ran into the bathroom, slammed the door and turned the lock. He leaned against the door, wondering if he needed to coax his way inside. He heard a few words he assumed were surfer slang. Words like *feeling maytagged* and *launched from the nose of her board.* Stuff from a different world that he didn't understand. The shower started and then he heard tears. What did he know about those?

How could he apologize for making her cry? He didn't know what to apologize for, let alone understand half of the conversation that had just taken place in the kitchen.

He could be a jerk and ignore it. Pretend he didn't hear her crying. Repeating the conversation in his head, he could see that Lindsey might have been excited about her clue. It had just taken him by surprise. *So tell her!*

He knocked.

"Lindsey?"

"Go away. I don't need your help."

"Come on, now. Whatever you think you heard, I didn't mean it."

"Think I heard?"

The door flew open. His blue-eyed beauty was covered in soap bubbles—not far from what he'd imagined the first night here. The fire in her blood turned her eyes a deep sea blue. He hadn't seen them close to that color before.

One hand was on her perfect hip and the other on the door until she started wagging a finger at him. "What do you mean, think I heard? Because I know what tone I heard in your voice and I know what we've done for the past two days."

"I didn't bring you here to stay in bed."

"But we did. You didn't do anything to try to find the family connection to the murderer." She pushed his chest with her finger, slipping a little on the tiled floor.

He reached to steady her. She was as slippery as a newborn colt that didn't want to be handled. "You took me by surprise. That's all."

He'd been prepared for another round in bed, not a revelation that she'd found a connection that would put her in the murderer's path again.

"I think you wanted me to fail so you wouldn't have to help me. We could wait it out here until your brother's friends figured everything out and the police caught the guy."

"What's wrong with laying low and allowing someone with experience to help? It's better than spending the time in jail."

"You want to know what else I think? I think you *want* to run away from home. Away from all the problems you've been facing. Maybe someplace where you can be *nekid as a jaybird*." She impersonated his heavy Southern accent perfectly.

"If I'm such a jerk, maybe you shouldn't have anything to do with me." He released her and she skidded across the floor, catching herself before she fell.

"I don't think—"

"Wait. You got your turn to talk. Now it's mine." He didn't really want to say anything at all. But he didn't want to hear an explanation from her either. He'd claimed it was his turn and she was waiting on him. "I knocked on this door to apologize. For what, I didn't know, but I was going to do it. We just met and I get that. I understand where you might get the impression I wasn't enthusiastic about tracking a murderer. Go figure. I'm not thrilled about being a murder suspect—in your murder, no less. But you should probably rein it in a little before assuming you know what makes me tick. You don't have a damn clue."

He left her near the side of the tub, her eyebrows drawn together in confusion, but he didn't care. He didn't really know Lindsey Cook. He knew the woman he'd created in his head.

He was used to people assuming they knew what type of person he was. Used to people assuming the worst. Used to— He swallowed hard, pulling on his jeans. He was used to being alone.

Chapter Eighteen

"Where is she? Where can that little bitch be hiding?"

Pacing the length of his couch, he chided himself to hold his chatter to a minimum. And promptly reminded himself he hadn't switched on the recorder this evening. He'd decided against rambling and would record a summary of this segment of the chase after he was done.

Talking to himself had become a habit. Especially in his office. Frustration would make him look bad and he was never going to let anyone see him in this panicky state.

He'd been checking various places for two days. After the police had finished with an apartment in Fort Worth, he'd taken a visit to see if any clue as to their destination had been overlooked. But to his consternation, nothing. No one had returned to the apartment. Even the paramedics hadn't returned. Neither Brian Sloane nor Lindsey Cook had called or been to the ranch since he'd encountered them at Jeremy's home.

One delight, which shouldn't have surprised him, was the amount of information Brian had collected on the demise of the Cook family. Sloane had managed to discover all the victims, putting together cities and timelines. There were a lot of question marks in the margins of the murder articles. And someone had put together a family tree, including carefully printed death dates.

He'd placed the rendering safely with his other keepsakes.

He poured himself yet another vodka. He'd lost count how many he'd had since sending his secretary home for the night. The decanter was nearly empty. Frustration did that to him. It made him break his rules.

If the couple would run, there would be hours of searching and traveling. He had looked forward to this segment being over. It would take him a while to devise a new plan, find new victims, new rewards.

If they had run...

"*If* they had run. But that's just it, I don't believe they have."

The police, however, no longer thought Brian had murdered the prostitute. After assurances from John Sloane and his Marine Corps friend that Lindsey was very much alive, Brian was only wanted for questioning.

"That's it! How could I have forgotten the Marine? He provided them a place to stay hidden. A home or piece of property the police don't know about."

Staying in the area meant they'd be surfacing soon. He didn't have to look for their hiding place; they'd reveal themselves soon enough. Did they really think they could match wits with someone of his intellect?

"The thing about those who hide...they always come out to see if someone's still after them."

There was nothing pressing on his desk, just a bit of paperwork that he didn't need to file until the end of the month. Other than the day he'd closed for his trip to Cozumel, he hadn't taken a vacation in years. Closing again wouldn't draw special attention. Perhaps it was time to finish this game.

He filled his glass with the last of the fiery liquid from the decanter. "A toast. May the best hunter win."

Chapter Nineteen

Brian unfolded his tall frame, grabbed his hat and shut the door. He stood at the corner of the car, waiting on Lindsey to follow. The car would be hot and she already had a layer of itchy sweat accumulating on her skin. She opened the door and swung her legs to the gravel.

"You coming?" Brian asked, not hiding the impatience in his voice. He looked at his watch as if he had an appointment to keep.

Behind the wheel, he hadn't been relaxed. He'd rarely smiled. Shoot, he'd been more relaxed after being in a knife fight with a murderer. And as many times as they'd ridden in a car together, this was the first time he'd rudely listened to the radio instead of talking with her. Going so far as to turn it up when she tried to mention the emails.

Mrs. Doris Davis lived about an hour north of Mac's secluded house. A house that hadn't been as far out in the middle of nowhere as Lindsey had originally thought. The drive seemed to take five times longer since Brian wasn't communicating with her. He was polite enough, speaking when necessary. But things had changed between them.

It was as if he had no vested interest in her situation any longer. More like he was treating it as an obligation. It had only been two days with an amateur—her—

searching, but this was their only lead. Maybe not even that. Jeremy might have been curious about something he found while researching his family heritage. There was no way to be certain other than actually talking to this woman.

As excited as Lindsey was to be at Mrs. Davis's home, she was more devastated that things might be over with Brian. If she could just explain… Maybe tell him how much she was scared the connection wouldn't pan out. How frightened she was of facing a lifetime of running.

She'd messed up. He was right. She shouldn't have assumed anything about Brian's motives. With her limited people skills, it was easier to move to the next beach instead of working through problems with people she liked. And she really liked this man. In fact, she could just be falling in love for the first time in her life.

"Lindsey?" Brian stood in front of her, hand outstretched to help. His fingers clasped around hers and, simply put, she felt safe.

Two hours without him on her side and she wanted to cry. How could she figure all this mess out alone? *Stop!* She couldn't assume anything else. Right now, she was about to verify what type of clue she'd uncovered— useful or useless.

"I feel stupid because I never realized someone was killing off my family," she blurted, staring at the ground. "If you hadn't done the research and tried to warn me… What if we never find out who he is?"

Brian pulled her into his arms, burying her face in his shirt. "There's nothing you could have done to prevent any of it. No one caught on, Lindsey. People with a lot more experience than us labeled the deaths as accidents. Hell, I hardly believed it myself until we found that poor girl."

"If I had paid more attention, Jeremy might still be alive."

"Or you could be dead, too." He tipped her chin so she'd look at him. "You were right about me wanting to stay at Mac's. But you got the reason wrong. I don't want you to risk getting hurt or worse."

"We can go back. Let your brother's friends take care of the investigating."

The front door opened. "You two coming in or what?"

DORIS WAS THRILLED to receive guests. They arrived for morning tea, just as scheduled, and she had the service all set. A full English tea along with a variety of cookies. It seemed very out of place, but so did the frilly yellow house surrounded by prairie grass and cattle.

Tea wasn't really Lindsey's thing. It was something you ordered cold, with lots of ice at dinner. Hot, flavored with lemon or milk? She didn't know which would be better with the vanilla macaroons she'd fallen in love with.

Brian sat next to her on a tiny settee, leaning forward across his knees, sipping out of a delicate china cup. His tight jeans hugged the thigh muscles she'd run her hands along such a short time ago. And honestly, he looked very uncomfortable. As if he were sitting in on a tea party for a child.

Doris, a petite woman less than five feet tall, refused to talk about her ex-husband during tea. Brian sipped away, and with every question popped another cookie into his mouth, then gestured back to Lindsey.

"So how long have you two been a couple?" Doris asked from her window seat.

"Us?" Brian shook his head and waved in Lindsey's direction.

Leaning forward like he was, she couldn't give him a

stern look to stop evading conversation. If she was going to do all the talking, he could just live with her version of the story. "Brian followed me around like a puppy for months before he gathered the courage to ask me out."

The cowboy almost spit out his latest bite of cookie. He stuttered over the word *no* for several seconds before giving up. Good. He could choke a little more.

"Yes, the poor thing is so shy," Lindsey continued, gently patting him on the back. "You'll have to forgive him. Even now, you can see he's barely talking to you."

The man finally turned his head, wrinkled the new scar on his forehead and growled a little at her. Doris didn't catch it. The silver-haired matron seemed to be a little hard of hearing.

Doris put her cup on the rolling service tray. "That's okay, dear, my third husband was just like that. I love the strong, silent type. At least for a while."

Lindsey laughed along with her hostess. Brian choked a little more, quickly swallowing more of his tea.

"Now, you wanted to know about your distant cousin, which would have been my second husband, Joel. Quiet man and terribly boring. I was so surprised to hear about his sudden death. When was it? Almost twenty years ago?"

"Yes ma'am," Brian answered, then shot Lindsey another look.

"Horrid little man, really. He didn't leave me a thing in his will. Now, if you wanted to know about my side of the family, if they were related to me, they were wonderful people."

"Can you tell me—us—why Jeremy was so interested in Joel's will?" Lindsey asked.

"We only got into that a little. I had no idea your cousin had died, Lindsey. The emails and phone calls stopped and I thought he must have been one of those scammer people out fishing for information. That's why I insisted on meeting you in person. You just can't be too careful nowadays."

"Right," Lindsey agreed. "You never know if someone's going to lead a serial killer to your door or not."

On that-below-the-belt jab, Brian set his delicate teacup aside and stood. She knew he hadn't meant to speed up the killer's timetable. And she also knew that Brian was the reason she was alive. But she was a bit miffed at him and he deserved to feel a little uncomfortable.

"Do you need the facilities, dear?"

"No ma'am. I just…have a cramp." He halfheartedly rubbed at his thigh. "So what did Jeremy ask about?"

"Joel sold his family home when we married and moved in here. The house wasn't worth much, just an old building that the next owner was going to tear down. Thank goodness his mother wasn't alive to see that happen. Anyway, your cousin Jeremy wanted to know if I might have a copy of the deed. He mentioned something about a trust that was looking for heirs. He was particularly interested in the mineral rights."

Lindsey was ecstatic that she'd been right. So happy that she had a hard time concentrating on what Doris actually said next.

"I don't think your cousin could obtain copies of the sales if they were available. It gets a little confusing."

"That's a shame. Sorry we bothered you," Brian said quickly.

"Hold on, Mr. Sloane." Doris motioned for Brian to sit back down, which he did. "That's what started our conversations, but it's not what really caught Jeremy's interest."

Lindsey sat forward, almost even with Brian. She

wanted to jump up and down. Detective work was fun if you could forget about the murder portion. She wanted to hold Brian's hand again. Good news or bad, it would be better with him along for the ride.

"You might have noticed all the cattle wandering around here when I am far—" she waved at all her frills in the room "—from being a rancher. I lease my land. Lots of people do."

Lindsey was trying to be patient, but she didn't want a lesson about ranching. Brian's hand reached out to cover hers. Maybe she was showing a little more angst than she had thought. She laced her fingers through the strength he shared and stopped her toes from the rapid, nervous *tap tap tap.*

"I not only lease my grazing land, I lease my mineral rights. Did you know you can sell your mineral rights?"

Brian nodded yes but Lindsey was trying to string the information together. Joel. Property sales. Murders. Mineral rights. "This doesn't make sense. Why would anyone want to kill Jeremy over his house?"

"Jeremy was killed? The internet said he drowned in Cozumel."

"We should go." Brian stood and drew her to her feet. His eyes told her not to say anything else. She pushed him to the side; he hit the tea cart, scooting it inches but rattling the china.

"Doris, why is it interesting? I don't understand."

"Remember I told you Joel sold his mother's house? Well, there's no record of the mineral rights being sold prior. So who owns them now?"

"Let me guess, the house is right in the middle of the Barnett Shale."

"You'd be guessing correctly," Doris confirmed.

"I don't understand."

"Natural gas that's being extracted by fracking, dear."

"There's our motive," Brian cursed.

Something significant had just been revealed, and Lindsey was still confused.

"Thanks for your time. It was nice meeting you."

"You'll need the address." Doris handed him an envelope.

Brian ushered her outside and hustled her into the car.

"Why are we leaving? I had a ton of questions."

"We don't need to involve Doris. She's been safe so far. She needs to stay that way."

"Why wouldn't she be? And where are we going?"

"We need some answers."

"You're confusing me, because I thought we were getting answers back there with Doris."

"We need more information than Doris can provide."

"So we should have let Mac search Jeremy's computer to begin with."

He slowed at a four-way stop and instead of moving forward, he draped his arm over the backseat and got two bottles of water from the cooler, handing one to her.

"We don't need a hacker, at least not yet. Property owners are listed at the county tax office. We just need to fill out some forms. I went through that looking for the owner of Mrs. Cook's property. That's how I found the rest of your family."

"Won't the police arrest you if you show up at the county clerk's office?"

"Maybe. That's a risk I need to take. But just in case, I still have John's military ID." His smile was back.

Her confidence was returning by the minute. Brian would help her put an end to this madman's killing spree. Maybe somewhere along the way she'd find the courage to tell him how much she appreciated him saving her life.

Chapter Twenty

"Is this still a risk you're willing to take? Should we tell that to the judge?"

Lindsey laughed, smiled, seemed relieved and sort of drooped in her chair. She was handcuffed to the desk across the aisle from him and acting as if she was as carefree as a wild mustang. If Brian was jealous—there was no way he actually was—he might get the impression she was flirting with the officer assigned to wait with her.

It was almost an unnatural kind of fun drunk. Unnatural because he knew she hadn't been drinking. Yet her flushed cheeks and behavior suggested that she had been.

They were waiting to see if his fingerprints were in the system as John or Brian Sloane. They didn't believe he was John. They shouldn't believe he was John, but he wished they had.

Three hours had passed while they took their statements and waited for confirmation he wasn't John. He'd been very stupid about taking her to the county clerk's office, thinking no one would recognize him. The first person at the counter was very helpful and said she'd start looking for their request. Half an hour later he was under arrest.

What would happen to Lindsey when they put him in a cell? All he had was a working theory of why this serial killer wanted Lindsey dead. They had no hard proof. Who would believe them? Especially with Lindsey acting almost drunk.

"I can't believe they're arresting you for abducting me—a completely bogus charge," she directed at the officer sitting next to her. "Don't *I* have to press charges or something?"

She turned back to face him. He could tell her eyes were dilated and her speech was slurring a little. "I mean, I insisted on coming with you. And you weren't obstructing justice or fleeing a crime scene. You were protecting me. So how can they, you know, claim that you had anything to do with that girl's murder?"

Brian shot a stern look at Lindsey, attempting to communicate that she needed to be quiet. It didn't work.

"I can promise you—" she switched her attention back to the officer, but dropped her head toward Brian "—*he* didn't do it. He was with me the entire time. I mean, Brian was, 'cause that's John over there that you're trying to arrest."

She giggled and grabbed the officer's sleeve.

"Keep your hands to yourself, ma'am," the officer stated and pried her fingers free, allowing her hand to drop to the top of his desk. "Did this man give you anything? Have you been drinking?"

"Me? Just tea. Awful tea. Who puts milk in tea?" She tipped a water bottle upside down. "Empty."

Brian had heard that silly laughter before. When he'd gotten her half drunk before suturing her arm. He caught the officer's eye. "I think she needs more water or maybe coffee."

The officer shook his head, gave a disapproving look and walked into the hallway.

"What the hell happened?" he asked Lindsey, whose

head was sort of wobbling. She stared, her eyelids looking heavy and staying closed longer with each blink. He kicked the desk with his boot, causing a loud noise and drawing the attention of the officers in the hallway. "Come on, man. Can't you see something's wrong with her? Somebody slipped her something."

"Not here they didn't. Now shut up," the officer shouted as he left. "Your lawyer's here to pick her up."

Lindsey cradled her head in her arm, resting on the cop's desk. "I'm okay, Brian—I mean, J-John. Jus' really tire…"

"She's out. And you're headed to holding, Brian Sloane," a different officer said as he came over and began unlocking his cuffs from the desk."

"Seriously, man. There's something wrong with her. She has a cut on her arm. I haven't checked her today, but maybe she needs a doctor. Can you get her to a doctor?"

"There's something wrong, all right. You. Maybe when she sobers up she'll be pressing charges, too."

"You've got to believe me that she hasn't been drinking. There's something wrong and she needs your help." Brian got to his feet and had the overwhelming urge to use his elbow to knock the officer away from him. He'd been angry, but never over a woman.

"Nothing's going to happen to her in the middle of the squad room. I guarantee that."

Brian wanted to jerk away, wanted to run back to Lindsey. He watched her as far as he could strain his neck to see her. Once in the hall, he turned straight, catching the eye of a man who quickly looked down at his expensive shoes.

"You'll get your turn in a minute, counselor," the officer said as they passed him.

They rounded a corner. "Counselor?"

"Right. Your attorney saw the report that you'd been arrested and he's been hanging around waiting his turn."

It was on the tip of his tongue to state he hadn't asked for an attorney, but there was something about the guy. He couldn't remember ever seeing him before, but he'd helped a lot of people as a paramedic. Yeah, there was something about the way he'd avoided eye contact that set Brian's teeth on edge.

Brian was led to another small room. No one-way mirrors. Just a camera in the corner near the ceiling. He tugged at the cuffs out of frustration. It wasn't his first time in a police station. He'd fought hard to keep his job with as many times as he'd been hauled needlessly into jail.

There wasn't a way to shrug this arrest off. He'd be booked for dang certain. If that guy was a real lawyer, he had to make the cops understand just how much Lindsey was in danger.

He rested his head in his chained hands. The sense of utter failure hadn't hit him like this since the first time he'd been in jail for another crime he hadn't committed.

They'd been so close to finding this bastard. Twelve years of wondering why Mrs. Cook had tried to put out the fire and died. Twelve years of being isolated, never allowing anyone close because he didn't want to explain why his life was a mess. The first time he cared about a woman and he might lose her because of his stupid pride.

The door opened and the man from the hallway entered, carrying a briefcase that he set on the edge of the metal table. He took a step back into the corner. And if Brian hadn't already seen the camera pointed directly toward him, he might not have noticed that the man kept the top of his head available for the recording and nothing else.

The man shoved his hands into his pockets instead of introducing himself. Odd, but each thing built on the next and that fuzzy memory gnawed at him. Something about his body language. The way he stood, ready to pounce. And his eyes had a gleam as if daring him to...

It's the son of a bitch responsible for everything!

"Why are you here?" He knew he was right. Everything about the man told him he was.

The stranger's brows raised, inventorying Brian's position like a hunter ready to raise his bow. "So you've connected the dots. You are my most worthy opponent. I say that in all honesty."

"You don't have the right to say the word *honest*. You're a serial killer. A butcher. You slaughtered that woman for no other reason than she looked like Lindsey."

"You're slightly wrong there. I might have selected her because of your girlfriend, but I had such delightful fun. So there was definitely more than one reason."

Brian swallowed the rage building in him. Nothing good would come of him losing his ability to think. This murderer was baiting him. That was all. He had to see this through, get the man to reveal himself to the police.

"Guard?" Brian looked at the camera. Was anyone watching? Did anyone realize a serial killer was here impersonating a lawyer?

"Ah, yes. I realize you want me gone. I soon will be, I'm afraid. But not as soon as you'd hope. This isn't recorded." He pointed to the camera. "Privileged information and all that."

"What do you want?" he asked between gritted teeth. The muscles were tensing in his arms. He wanted his hands around this man's neck. It was the first time in his life he had considered seriously harming another human being.

"Why, Brian, I'm here to drop my gauntlet for a private battle."

"If I agreed, you'd have me at a disadvantage." Brian shook the metal, letting it make noise against the table. "Why the hell would I *battle* you anyway? You ran from our last fight."

"You did take me by surprise at Jeremy's. That won't happen again."

"Quit talking riddles and just say what you came to say." Brian laced his fingers. The small room was much hotter than where he'd left Lindsey. His skin seemed almost sunburned, a red haze almost. He was hot and mad at himself.

"I can see the wheels turning in your head, Brian Sloane. Don't be stupid. You can't cry out. No one will believe you anyway. I'm a respected lawyer who felt sorry for the way you've been treated throughout this terrible ordeal."

"It may take time, but the police can discover the truth. I know about your mineral rights trust."

He finally pulled a hand from his pocket, swiping at the corner of his eye as if he was laughing so hard he cried. "Oh, Brian. That's so funny. You've been accused of murder. Your DNA is at the scene and will match their samples. And of course, they'll find the knife you used on the prostitute in your barn."

Brian's hands were fisted; the metal rings pinched and scratched his wrists as he tugged and then tugged again. He knew he couldn't break them, but the gesture kept him from losing it completely.

"Not to mention the testimony of your lawyer when I attempted to get you to surrender after being interrupted at your prisoner's home." He laughed in a tenor old lady voice. "You're making this too easy. I thought you seemed the sort to fight. Are you, Brian? Are you willing to fight me and save the damsel in distress?"

Brian swallowed hard, keeping it together because of Lindsey. Wanting to tear this guy apart with every word from his mouth. "You know an awful lot about me. Aren't you going to introduce yourself?"

"In due time." He slipped his thumbnail in the small space between his two front teeth. "In due time."

"What's your definition of battle?" *You raving lunatic!* "And if you want to fight me again, you're going to have to get these charges dropped. Hey, you could do that, couldn't you? Confess to the murders and they'll let me go."

He nodded. "Right. And on a more realistic note, you know that the only leverage I have over your behavior is Lindsey? She's resting, by the way. I slipped a little mickey into her soda. So easy, no challenge at all. But you'd already guessed that, hadn't you?"

"Why are you telling me all this?" Brian could feel his chest rising and falling rapidly. His hands shook from the adrenaline. His eyes were slits because of the anger. He deliberately took a deep breath, trying to calm down. It wasn't working.

Nothing riled him and made him lose control, especially when he was aware of the situation and was debating with himself. He'd taken too many hits over the years and never swung back.

Teenagers, cops, drunks. They'd all hit him and he'd never taken a swing at anyone except his brother. It couldn't be the thought of Lindsey. In fact, his thoughts were different than the physical reaction his body was having.

"You drugged me."

"Yes, as a matter of fact. I gave you a natural something or other. Of course, I gave you much more than the vitamin store suggested. Are you feeling a little anxious? Is your chest getting tight?"

"You really are a freaking…madman." Hyperventilating. He closed his mouth, breathing through his nose, attempting to slow down the racing in his body. "Why are you…you trying to…"

"Trying to kill you? Why would you think that? You're the most fun I've had in two decades." He leaned forward to pop his briefcase open and pulled out a card. "You might go into cardiac arrest and these oafs might not be able to revive you. I would hate that. Such a disappointment since I'm looking forward to the climax of our story."

Even telling himself not to, Brian strained at his handcuffs without getting any closer to his target. At this rate he might break his wrists. His pulse pounded in his head, the veins in his arms popped to the surface, he felt his head rocking and couldn't stop.

The lawyer, murderer, serial killer leaned forward and slid the card down his shirt. The four corners made his skin itch on the way down.

"Don't disappoint me. You might have been clumsy enough to get caught, but I'm smart enough to get you free." He shut the briefcase. "That is, if you really want to end this venture and you're willing to do whatever it takes to save your little Lindsey."

Brian tried to call for help. It was a weak attempt. He swallowed air, not spit. Mouth too dry. Whatever this maniac had given him, it was fast and hitting all his senses. He finally croaked out, "Guard."

"We're finished for now. We should be able to tidy up loose ends soon. I'm ready to be done with this cat-and-mouse game and move on to something new."

The tightness this brute mentioned felt like a stampede on his torso. His jaw clenched tighter with each breath. The amount of restraint it took to keep from reaching up, grasping this killer's neck and snapping it…was only surpassed by the pain growing across his chest.

"You need to remember this, Brian. Do you think you can? Your car's waiting for you at the E.R. Clever of you to drive Mabel's. I'm going to collect Lindsey. I just happen to have a document assuring the court I'm her lawyer. I'll convince them I should take her to her doctor. I can be very persuasive. We'll be waiting. The card shows you where. Can you remember?" He tapped on the door. "Guard!"

Brian used his last bit of remaining strength to push forward, his hands jerking him to a stop inches above the table, he threw his shoulders from side to side, feeling as though he was about to explode. "You son of a… If you touch her…"

"Oh, I plan to, Brian. Many, many times."

Chapter Twenty-One

Every inch of him hurt. Brian had been thrown from plenty of horses. Had the breath knocked from his lungs more times than he could remember. Broken his collarbone and his tailbone, but he'd never hurt like this before. He ached all the way through and his fingers were crossed it wouldn't last long.

"Lindsey." He had work to do.

He was in the Denton Regional Medical Center emergency room. He recognized the sounds and the room even through his blurred vision. He'd dropped off his sister-in-law plenty of times. Why was he—? He lifted his arm…handcuffed and in a hospital gown. His foggy memory mixed bits and pieces of scenes flashing between shards of pain.

Lindsey. Jail. Drugged. Serial killer. Pain. Nothing.

Either all those jumbled memories had actually happened or he'd been kicked in the head by one of his horses and was having a very realistic dream. Yeah, it had all happened. He could remember the taste of Lindsey's skin, the face she'd made at the bitterness of Doris's tea. His days and nights with her were very vivid.

Alicia walked into the room, her finger across her lips to caution him from speaking. He caught a glimpse of a uniform at his door. "We came as soon as your story broke on the news. They said you began having seizures while at the jail. And we're both very lucky they haven't changed my ID yet. I doubt the police would let your sister-in-law check on you."

"God, please tell me you haven't seen me naked. And if you have, lie."

"Get a grip, brother-in-law. I see that exact body every day on John. But no, I just came on shift so I didn't see anything. John's in the parking lot." She pumped up the pressure cuff already on his arm, looking over her shoulder toward the door.

"Have you heard from Lindsey? That bastard's got her. I've got to get out of here. Fast." He tried to sit up, but his head swam, turning the rest of the room to a blur. The metal handcuffs banged. His sister-in-law shushed him.

"Hold on, buster, you aren't going anywhere. You're a very sick puppy."

"He drugged me."

"Are you stating or asking?" She flipped his chart to where he should have been able to read it. "They pumped your stomach. Juanita was on duty and called us when you were brought in. She said it was a little touch and go. Your heart nearly stopped, Brian."

The writing was blurry. He couldn't make out why they'd pumped him, but it explained why his voice sounded scratchy. "Alicia, get John in here. He's going to kill Lindsey."

"Are you still feverish? John's not killing anyone," she whispered, stuck a thermometer into his mouth and then wrote down his vitals.

"I'm dead serious, Alicia," he mumbled around the stick under his tongue. "I need John. The freak didn't tell me his name. He's a lawyer or faking at being a lawyer. But we found out he's working some kind of scam stealing mineral rights when properties are sold. He drugged our drinks in the middle of the freakin' squad room."

She removed the thermometer and disposed of the covering. "Calm down. You aren't making sense."

"Just call John. I need him to wait this one out for me."

"What are you suggesting? You know he's better trained to find this lawyer. Did you consider just telling him? You want him to go to jail for you?"

He tried not to be angry. He wanted to say the words that hung between them. *How many times had he gone to jail because John left and their small town blamed him for Mrs. Cook's death?* He didn't. They hung there until she pulled her cell, talked, hung up and then took his IV out.

"You're going to have a horrible headache. Can you even see straight?"

"Straight enough." He'd be lucky to see a hundred feet in front of the car, but he had no choice.

"I suppose you'll need my keys."

"Mabel's car is out there."

"How do you know? Oh, gosh, I don't want to know that answer, do I? How are you even going to find this killer if you don't know his name?"

Remember this, Brian. Can you remember? He'd put something scratchy down his shirt.

"Where's my stuff? I think he dropped a business card in my clothes." She shook his clothes. The T-shirt was ripped in half, his jeans looked just as bad. His Ropers were fine. He would take John's clothes, but he preferred his boots that molded to his feet instead of John's Justins.

Alicia tipped the second boot upside down and out fell a card.

"Victor D. Simmons, attorney at law. You didn't imagine him, but it doesn't mean he's a lunatic who poisoned you. It could have been that woman with the tea." She must have seen his confusion. "You called after leaving her house. John and I both tried to talk you out of going to the county clerk, but no, you had to rush in. You're as bad as your brother."

She straightened the room, putting his clothes back in a bag, stowing them, swiping at a tear and trying to hide a sniff from the tears.

"Hey." He bent his finger, gesturing for her to come back. "Sorry."

"Lauren misses you and your dad sends his love even though he's a stubborn Sloane man and just squeezed my shoulder." She smiled and her phone buzzed. "That's John. Pretend to be asleep when I leave. I'll get the officer to help me and John can get in here while he's away from the door."

She waved nervously and backed up, wheeling a crash cart behind her. She deliberately hit both sides of the cart on the frame. Brian closed his eyes when the uniform moved to hold the door open. "Thank you, Officer. Could I borrow you just a sec? The wheels on this thing… Don't worry about him. He's sound asleep, will be for hours. We had to sedate him."

The door swung gently shut. Behind his closed eyes, Brian saw his world spinning out of control. Alicia had been friends with him and John for a long time. She'd married his brother. He could forgive her for thinking he was crazy. The thing was, the jumbles in his brain had *him* thinking he was nuts.

"You were waiting outside?"

"You have to ask? Alicia filled me in. Why would a murderer risk walking into a police station and drug two people?" John asked, already working on picking the lock on the second handcuff. "It doesn't make sense, man. Then hand you his card? It has to be a fake card."

"Look him up. The cops seemed to think he was legit. He said he was my lawyer and waited until they verified who I was. I don't know how he convinced them to talk to me. Or how he could just walk out of there with Lindsey. It was as if he was waiting on us at the courthouse. He even told me Mabel's car had been moved here for my getaway."

"He drugged you so you'd be delivered to the E.R. instead of transferred to Arlington for questioning. Pretty smart."

"Smart or not, he's got Lindsey and I need out of here so I can find her."

"You going to be able to handle this? You were so out of it you didn't know I'd come into the room or hear Alicia fill me in." He finished and pulled his shirt over his head. "Are you even certain he has Lindsey?"

"If she's not at the ranch, then yes, I'm sure."

"Then find him before they lock me up, will ya?" John handed him his service weapon.

They switched clothes and John got on the gurney. "I hate to say this, but you're going to have to put a needle in my arm."

Brian found a clean IV needle in the drawer and stuck his brother's vein on the first try. He adjusted the IV to the slowest drip possible.

"You're pretty good at that. Ever think about becoming a doctor?" his brother asked.

"Not ever. I want to raise quarter horses." The response was instinctive, not thought about, not debated. He wanted the ranch.

"We have a lot to talk about when this is all over."

"Right. Now I need to concentrate on finding my girl."

"You know I'd go for you," he said, clapping a hand around his shoulder, smiling.

"I have to do this."

"That's what I thought. Do you know where to start?"

With a bandage over his forehead to cover the missing scar, the IV tape in exactly the same spot and handcuffed to the rail on either side of the bed, John looked exactly like Brian, with one exception—

"We forgot about the blasted hair. You cut yours."

"You should have cut yours. Hell, Brian, they won't notice with me just lying here. Alicia's going to check on me. The shift changed from when you were admitted. She'll cover. Just don't leave me hanging, bro. So again, do you have a clue where to find this guy?"

"The bastard said to remember. I can start with his flippin' business card." He looked on the reverse side. "Or follow the map he conveniently left with me."

LINDSEY HAD BEEN groggy for a long while. Sort of aware that she was moving and unable to react. Her eyes hadn't opened fully since giving her statement to the police in Denton. She remembered that. Remembered Brian and... confusion.

She'd lost control, feeling more like a lump of flesh being directed, molded and fixed in place. She couldn't see, barely could feel, but the fog was lifting.

How she'd gotten out of police custody wasn't clear. Neither was what happened to Brian. She didn't think he was with her. It didn't seem as if he was with her.

Blindfolded. That was why she couldn't see.

Someone was there; she'd heard the unidentified person breathing. The madman snickered a few feet in front of her. It had to be the man wanting to kill her. She didn't know how she'd ended up in the paws of the monster. But she was there.

A flapping noise—maybe startled birds flying away.

Wrists tied with plastic rings, she could feel the edges biting into her skin. Her arms were stretched forward, bent but not high above her head. Her feet seemed to be free. A smooth surface was at her left hip, something like a wall.

No one was coming to her rescue except her.

She slid her hands a little and a rope rubbed against her fingers. That was how her hands were extended in the air. A rope tied around the plastic. She took a small step. Could she shift enough to remove the blindfold? Maybe there was enough slack if she moved forward.

She screamed as her right foot stepped into nothingness and she fell. The rope jerked the plastic into the flesh of her wrists, halting her descent a split second later. Dangling like a fish on a line, she stopped kicking her legs and lifted her feet back to the beam where she'd stood before. At least she wasn't flaying around in midair.

A man's laughter. The monster was watching.

"What do you want? My hands are cut and tied. You can't possibly think this is going to look like an accident."

Was he having fun?

When he didn't answer, she strained, lifting her body weight until she could get both feet back on whatever she'd stood on before. Then she pulled on the taut rope, tugging until she was back where she started.

If there were birds... A beam, perhaps. An image of a high-rise under construction, workers walking on beams and steadying themselves on the beam above.

Was that where she was? High in the sky with no safety net? She didn't hear traffic. She heard nothing except her blood rushing, frightened, through her veins. Then the snickering of the murderer laughing at her.

She couldn't hang like this indefinitely.

With both her feet on the support—whatever it was—she held on for dear life and stretched her left toes until they pointed down. She had about six inches to stand on. What was at her hip? She gently kicked out, hitting something metal, a hollow sound like a chute of some sort.

"What do you want from me? Or from my family all these years?"

Even if she knew where she was or how to leave or any other small detail that may save her life, how could she get free? No, she was staying put, hands tied and already aching from pulling on the rope to keep her balance.

"Your Prince Charming will be here soon enough. That is, if he survived at all. Shame if he didn't, I was looking forward to our battle."

What was he talking about? Brian was in jail. She didn't remember leaving the police station. Didn't remember much after the initial interview at all. But they'd been in custody, she remembered that.

She also remembered the fright she'd felt at Jeremy's house. Face-to-face with the creature who had carved that woman's face off her. Then when she'd seen the knife coming toward her neck but slicing her arm.

The knowledge that she was on her own shot the same panic up her spine. She couldn't depend on anyone but herself. No one else knew she was here or knew she was even missing. She wasn't ready to die. She'd just found Brian and wasn't about to give up on him. Or her own abilities.

Her arms and legs shook, partly from the stress but also from the drugs. She was already weak, but had to get herself free. But how could she, with that maniac watching and laughing at her efforts?

She turned her head toward the creaking of old wood on metal. She hadn't heard him in a while, but she knew she wasn't alone.

Sunshine reflected off something. She could see it around the edges of the cloth tied over her eyes. She held tighter, scooted forward until she could lift her shoulders one at a time and inch the blindfold to hang around her neck.

Her first look made her dizzy, and not just because her eyes had been closed for so long. She was a heck of a long way up in the rafters of an abandoned building. Three long flights of stairs. Rusted beams, ducts and pipes crisscrossed around her. If she fell, she'd die from blunt-force trauma from everything she'd hit on the way down.

Heights normally didn't bother her. She'd been on waves taller than this. It must be the drugs still in her system, slowing her down and messing with her equilibrium.

With her arms in this position, it tugged at the stitches Brian had put in her arm. The strain from balancing and easing the pressure on her shoulders had started a definite trickle of sweat down her back. It felt like bugs crawling on her, which started her imagining all of the creatures that holed up in barns.

Including snakes. Hadn't Brian talked about barn snakes in the rafters? *Please, please, please...no snakes in these rafters.*

"It's very entertaining watching you discover your surroundings and trying to compensate. Good job, Lindsey."

"Is this some kind of test?"

"Oh, no. We're just having a little fun until Brian arrives." He returned to a post just above her where the stairs turned.

Logically, if this man killed her, he'd finish an objective and get away with it. No one knew who he was and wouldn't know as long as he kept his mouth shut.

"Brian was arrested. So unless you mixed up his fingerprints, you're wrong."

"My dear, I've gone to great lengths to assure he'd be here. So he'll be here. If he lives up to half my expectations, it'll be a worthy fight."

Had the other people he'd killed felt this way? Had he ignored them as insignificant? He'd been targeting her family members for at least twenty years. Why was Brian so important now?

"Did you kill Jeremy? Or my parents? Why? Why do you want the Cook family dead?"

"You want to alleviate your conscience? Make yourself feel better? Tell yourself that your cousin's death wasn't your fault?" He paced along a short wooden platform—it was the creaking she'd heard earlier. "That information isn't ready for public knowledge yet. Unfortunately, you won't be alive when it is."

"Can't you at least tell me why you want my family dead? Or even who you are? What did we ever do to you? And what does Brian have to do with it?" The sun was sinking, the shadows were getting longer. But she saw bright light from a porch or window. Someone was nearby, if only she could scream....

"Don't think about it, Lindsey." He leaned over the rail with a finger over his lips. "If—and I mean that in the slimmest way possible—*if* you manage to get their attention and they venture here to see why we're on the premises, I will be delighted to kill them, too. No thought or debate needed."

Dear God, what if a child wandered in here?

For all she knew, they were in a populated area and this man didn't look worried about being caught. Maybe he wasn't the one responsible for all the deaths after all? Maybe he worked with someone else and couldn't make the decisions on his own.

There had to be someone else involved. Someone had been following her. She couldn't recall ever having seen this man. Was he the butcher in black clothes who had tortured that poor girl? This well-spoken egomaniac was the same man who had nearly sliced her throat?

"Since I'm not the public and you assume I'll be dead when your statement's ready, it won't matter if I hear the imperfect version. Would it? I don't think you're the beast responsible for killing my family. You lack…authority."

He didn't like that at all. He ran down a flight of stairs until he was even with her, until he could look her in the eye and point his finger at her face.

"I am Victor D. Simmons. How did your arm heal after our encounter at your home? Or should I refer to it as Jeremy's home, since that's how you refer to it?"

"That proves nothing. The real murderer could have told you lots of details."

"You aren't going to goad me into admitting I'm the mastermind. I have nothing to prove to you."

"So you did kill him. You're the monster. A horrible little man who never fights face-to-face."

That got his attention. "What makes you assume that?"

"You cut me loose and I'll show you what happens when you give one of us a fighting chance."

He threw his head back in laughter, slowly clapping his hands. "Brava, Lindsey Cook. It's going to be thrilling to describe how you die."

Chapter Twenty-Two

There was only one place in Aubrey Victor D. Simmons could be referring to on his map. Brian knew the small town like the back of his hand. He'd avoided the main roads for several years when he'd been the focus of every questionable action that happened. Many years ago he'd learned the habits of the police and the sheriff—when they liked to eat, what streets they liked to drive looking for troublemakers and especially the speed traps on 377 where weekenders heading for the lake would forget to slow down.

That was exactly where he hoped both cops were tonight. Those heading up to the bigger lake, Texoma, would be heading home now. He took a slightly longer route, Sherman Drive from the hospital instead of the more traveled road. Speeding with blurred vision and taking risks he didn't ever consider while driving the ambulance, he actually made fairly good time.

Lindsey had to be in the abandoned peanut-drying plant that still sat on either side of the railroad. Rusty from top to bottom, it had been officially off-limits but just sitting there for a couple of decades. But every kid in town had played there sometime in their life. It was one of the few places he still remembered with fondness.

It was in the middle of town, across a gravel parking

lot from the fire department, which was next door to the police station. Brian couldn't just drive up to the front door and ask him to hand Lindsey over.

He also knew he couldn't involve the police if he wanted to keep the woman he'd fallen in love with alive. As his head cleared, he deciphered more of the jumbled visit with Victor D. Simmons.

The beautiful body he'd explored extensively meshed with the image of the woman slain in Jeremy's home. The words in that small room just before he'd passed out— *If you touch her... Oh, I plan to, Brian. Many, many times.*

She was alive.

She had to be alive. He wouldn't think of her vibrant personality any other way. Rage coursed through him with any thought of the lawyer's hands on her. Leftover effects from the drug that had been pumped from his stomach. He had to get himself under control and think clearly.

Running would clear his head. He parked the car two blocks from the building and ran, pushing through the aches and clearing the throbbing in his head. He avoided the police station, noting that no squad cars were there so that meant both were out on patrol, but Polly's car was in the lot so someone was manning the dispatch. He stopped at the corner where the city kept the fire truck, catching his breath.

Two peanut buildings—both were on his map. If he held someone captive, where would he do it? Hell, he didn't know and there was no way he could think the same way as this guy. He'd never have broken his opponent out of jail or been as bold as to face him in a police station.

Trying to understand a murder was not solving the problem. The only thing different about *this* Cook murder was him. It wasn't because he'd tried to think like a killer for the past couple of months. It was because he'd thought like himself. He was the difference.

He pulled the magazine from John's gun. Full, but that was it.

An all-volunteer squad meant the fire station was empty. He twisted the knob. Locked. He pushed up on a window and hit the jackpot. It was unlocked and he could get inside. He needed another weapon. A plan.

The way the adrenaline was still pumping through his system, it was hard not to rush in shooting and ask questions later. That was what John would do. He and his brother hadn't ever had the twin connection that people talk about. He'd accepted responsibility when he screwed up and John had sweet-talked his way out of more than one problem. Neither would work this time.

What he really needed was his brother and some of those SEALs he worked with. They'd have a lot of gadgets to locate Lindsey and extract her from a hostile environment. He should have swallowed his pride and just told John to take care of the rescue. But he hadn't, and he wasn't his brother.

Then why was he deliberating what his brother would do? The knowledge to save lives worked both ways. It was his grit that would find the way to get both him and Lindsey out of this alive.

And stop Victor D. Simmons forever.

LINDSEY WAS TIRED and drained. If she weren't perched on a six-inch beam three stories above the ground, she'd make fun of herself for being totally out of shape. It had been hours and several attempts to get herself untied, always resulting with a slip and jerking her arms from their sockets when she fell.

At the moment, exhaustion was her most immediate enemy. If she fell again, she wouldn't be able to lift herself back to the beam. She'd be useless if help arrived. *If help arrived.* At the moment she had her doubts.

Without any explanations or reason why he thought Brian would be arriving to honor him by "doing battle," her captor had stopped talking and disappeared. As if there was any honor in murder or abductions. Almost dozing, she wobbled on her perch.

Catching her balance, she looked again for a way to reach the knot. Her fingers were numb and raw from gripping the rope to stop the plastic from cutting her skin. She startled herself awake again, her hip hitting the chute next to her.

This time when she'd almost fallen, there hadn't been a snicker from some odd location in the building. Could she hope that he'd left her alone? Maybe she could get someone's attention if they passed by. But for as long as she'd been trapped in the rafters, she'd only heard a couple of children's voices, and that had been before night had fallen.

Groggy as she'd been, she had no idea how he'd gotten her onto this beam. And as weak as she was, she had no idea how she'd hold on to anything to get down if she could get free. The stitches pulled, her arms shook, everything ached, especially her neck.

A train whistle sounded in the distance. She heard the birds rustle. Then the familiar creak of wood. Her captor was on the platform. Somewhere to her right. Moving up or down or across, she didn't know.

"How long are you going to keep me here?"

"Long enough."

"Why haven't you just killed me?" her parched throat

hoarsely whispered, and didn't expect an answer. She'd asked before. "This is senseless."

"Nothing I do is without purpose."

Now she could see his outline in the dim light. The sound of the train grew louder.

"Ha. It's very easy for you to claim whatever you want since you refuse to explain."

"You're trying to taunt me, Lindsey? How very predictable."

"Oh, I'm not taunting. I think you're an idiot. There's no way that Brian Sloane is coming anywhere near this place. He's in jail by now. I'm just wondering how long I have to endure your threats."

"I think you understand that I don't threaten. I succeed."

"But at what?" She pushed the words out through her parched throat, loud enough to be heard over the train passing next to the building. A bit of dust falling from the ceiling caused her to shut her eyes.

Her captor appeared close to her at the rail, just to her left. Close, and yet not close enough to kick out and do damage.

"I set things in motion to make it impossible to say no. As predictable as human nature is, I'm confident he cares too much for you not to handle it himself."

"Flaw number one. Brian's smarter than that. His brother has kick-ass Marine and Navy SEAL buds. Why in the world wouldn't he let them tear this place apart and you along with it?"

The train passed the building, doing weird things with the light coming through the side panels that had broken free over the years. She tilted her head up. The monster looked even more frightening. Dressed in black again, his eyes loomed large in his shadowed face.

His fist pounded the metal pipe used as a rail. "He has to come."

"Flaw number two. I barely know this guy and our relationship hasn't been a piece of cake. Assuming he wants anything to do with me any longer is a huge assumption."

She didn't have to see his fist hit the panel of the chute that hung over his head. It shook next to her. Perhaps it was stable with birds resting on it, but along with the slam of his fist came loud creaking and a trail of dust from overhead.

"Flaw three. If—and that's a big if—someone decided to rescue me, why in the world would they meet you face-to-face for this 'battle,' as you put it? Even if you're honorable—" she tried not to choke using that word "—why do you think they are?"

"Shut up! I've planned this. My plans always work."

She'd finally gotten to him. Or maybe the wait had. Maybe he had his own doubts about whether anyone was coming. Whatever the reason, he raced up the stairs. Loose particles rained from the ceiling. She closed her eyes and dropped her chin to her chest.

When the train had passed and was somewhere in the distance, she could hear every creak and moan from the building. Including every wing flutter and scurry of small animals' nails clicking on the metal beams and pipes. The metal staircase and wooden platform creaked as they had every time the savage had approached.

She didn't want to look up, petrified she'd goaded him into action. Action might mean he finished her off. She ignored him, tired beyond reason and with no thought left other than keeping her balance.

More debris fell on her neck, sticking to the sweat, begging to be brushed aside. *Concentrate on your grip. One thing. Keep your head down and don't fall.*

A larger sting. More creaking. She didn't listen to herself, she opened her eyes, letting them adjust to the low light. In seconds she could see someone…

"Br—" *Brian,* she finished in her head, immediately stopping when she saw his finger across his lips.

How had he gotten free from the police? Why had he come for her? What difference did it make? He was there. She was free.

He held up a finger, then a palm. *One stop?* She shrugged, not understanding.

He moved two fingers pointing to the ground. *Walking?*

Pointed to his chest. *Him.*

Patted his back. *No!* She shook her head, silently screaming no. He couldn't leave her here. He just couldn't.

He held up four fingers and then pointed at her. He was coming back for her? She lost her footing with all the movement, one foot sliding off the side, and she wobbled. Brian was half over the pipe rail. She locked eyes with him, hoping that her fierce glare told him she was okay.

Her arms ached from the strain, but she managed to nod her head in the direction of the stairs. He stopped, one leg over the rail, ready to come to her rescue. She shook her head, this time agreeing he needed to take care of their tormentor first.

There was only one quick way down, and that wouldn't happen as long as the rope held. Freeing her was much more complicated than it looked. She was stabilized, and yet Brian wasn't moving away. She pulled herself upright, wanting to cry out, biting her lip so she wouldn't. Hoping beyond all reason the madman wasn't watching and ready to push her rescuer over the side.

She'd tapped into a strength she'd never realized she had and got her feet under her again. Brian waved, used his broken sign language to indicate he was coming for her now. She shook her head, mouthed "no," then, "I'm okay."

Tears of pain washed her eyes clean, but she was able to see the last sign he made for her. He stood with the rail between them again, put both hands together in the shape of a heart.

It was enough to make her lose it as she watched him climb the stairs. A heart. His? Hers? She waited, knowing this time she'd torn a muscle in her shoulder. The raw pain wasn't easing like it had before. She clung with her left hand to the rope and balanced on her right foot—her left ankle now caught between the beam and the metal chute.

She couldn't move and was completely helpless if the monster returned victorious.

Chapter Twenty-Three

Brian turned his back and climbed the stairs. He left her, obviously needing to be cut down and gotten to safety, one of the hardest things he'd ever done.

The noise of the train had covered his entry through the door. Overhearing the exchange between Simmons and Lindsey caused him to take the bottom three steps to intervene when the murderer lost it. But the knife had disappeared and Lindsey was no longer threatened, allowing Brian to press against the wall and hide. Simmons had returned to the roof where Brian had seen him keeping watch.

Leaving Lindsey now, dangerously hanging there, was tearing his guts out. It put another burr under his saddle as he took the steps two at a time.

It had been a long time since he'd climbed to the eagle's nest—what they'd called the east peanut elevator as kids. He rushed through to the outside, remembering that the stairs turned back over the roof. He could see Simmons ahead of him, dressed in black, but showing up against the rusted tin roof as plain as day.

Hang on, Lindsey.

Since Simmons was running, he probably knew Brian was chasing him. They both pulled on the handrail, taking the stairs. The place had been structurally sound sixteen years ago when he'd gotten caught exploring. Now he could feel the joints giving way, wondering if the rusted bolts would pop with the weight of two grown men.

He took the last step to the metal grating, did a one-eighty, grabbed the ladder rungs to the top. Just as he raised his eyes, his opponent stopped, and Victor's work boot caught him in the chin. He lost his grip, falling a couple of feet until he hooked his arm in the circular safety cage on the outside of the ladder.

Simmons couldn't come down the ladder with Brian blocking it. It was the only way down. If he descended on the outside, Brian could still grab him. He heard Simmons scrambling around the far side of the catwalk.

The blurred vision from knocking his head cleared a bit. Once he knew Simmons was headed across the chute to the roof, Brian bent and twisted to get upright again. He grabbed a rung, then a second until he pulled himself free to follow.

As Simmons jumped the rail to descend to the roof, Brian twisted through the safety rail and slid to the warm tin in time to grab the man's foot. Simmons kicked out. Brian avoided being hit by rolling to his side. He stopped and began racing up the steep slick metal. Brian caught the older man just as he straddled the building's ridge to head down the other side.

Simmons lifted his leg to strike out again, but Brian kept hold. Victor D. Simmons may have been older, but he gave as good as a weakened Brian. They rolled, and Simmons threw himself to the west side of the roof. Brian didn't let go and couldn't stop the headfirst slide.

Brian couldn't slow the three-story downward tumble on his own, but the hackberry branches helped.

"Grab hold!" He released Simmons and the man did

as directed. Brian grabbed a second branch before plummeting over the edge.

Why had he told the man what to do to save his hide? Simmons was able to sit, and began kicking at Brian's grip. Then he rolled to the roof joint, crawling over the edge before dropping to the lower side.

Brian caught his breath before following the maniac to the west-side ladder. Simmons was three or four seconds ahead of Brian, dropping to another peanut chute and running along the metal grate. Going up was the only way to get down. Brian didn't trust his swimming head or shaky hands to climb the pipe on the side of the ladder.

As he took the first step onto the grate, Brian remembered the gun tucked inside his waistband. He pulled and released the safety, but Simmons made it over the edge before he could fire. He dropped to the grate, looking for a shot, pulled the trigger, nothing. Pulled again, but he still couldn't hit Simmons mixed in with the crisscrossed metal supports.

Again, Brian was just slightly behind. He followed Simmons to the ground and ran as if he was racing from an explosion. Across the uneven dirt, back into the old building, swinging around the bottom of the stairs and each zigzag landing back up to Lindsey. He was within five feet of Simmons.

But seconds behind was all the bastard needed to lean over the rail, tug and then slice the rope.

"Lindsey!"

LINDSEY HAD PREPARED herself. If she fell, it meant her death. When the monster cut the rope, there was a moment of unadulterated panic. It was going to hurt. Her foot was caught and she'd be lucky if her ankle didn't snap.

There had been moments like that on a wave. She'd

known she was about to wipe out and the eternity clock began ticking. It only took thirty seconds to fall, but you can't scream underwater. Maybe that was why she was coherent enough to fall and stretch for something to grab with her good arm.

Her fingers grabbed the bottom of the platform where the monster now rolled in a struggle with Brian. She shifted, latching her hand in place where a board was missing. Then she became conscious of the pain in her ankle and screamed.

Hanging and watching the fight as if the men were defying gravity, Lindsey saw them roll and exchange punches. She clung tightly with one hand as the arm of her injured shoulder was useless. Still zip tied together, she couldn't get a better grip or reposition her good hand.

The psychopath scurried up the stairs, kicking at Brian, who followed. Then Brian fell hard onto the platform. The jolt caused Lindsey's grip to shake.

"Brian, the gun," she tried to warn. The weapon that had been tucked at the small of his back fell through the wooden slats. It clanged again and again as it hit metal on its journey to the floor she'd been staring at all afternoon.

Lindsey tried her best not to scream and distract her rescuer. But her foot was working free from her shoe. Once it was, all her weight would be hanging thanks to the loose grip she had on the edge of wood that was already cutting into her hand.

"Brian, I'm slipping."

The monster laughed as he stood on a step out of Brian's reach. Attached to his leg was a handgun. He unstrapped it and pointed it at Brian.

"Don't move, Brian," the lunatic commanded.

Her heel slid farther from her shoe. "Oh, God, please."

Brian turned on his side, his hand on hers. "Go ahead and shoot me, Simmons. I'm not going to let her fall."

"Uh, uh, uh. Not until I say go."

"If you wanted her dead, you would have killed her when you got here," Brian spat at him, but his fingers moved closer to her wrists and to the plastic tie.

"All right, hold on to her and pull her up."

Brian locked his hand on her wrist, her foot moved and she swung side to side in the air. Maybe the pain shooting throughout her body had short-circuited the neurons that needed to fire to scream. Or maybe it was the simple confidence that Brian wouldn't let her fall.

"You wanted to save her, so save her," Simmons demanded. "I'll watch you from here. I would like to inform you that I can officially declare myself the winner of our battle. It's time to finish this project."

"He's a monster."

"Forget him, Lindsey. Focus on me. Are you okay?"

"Just...peachy," she said through gritted teeth. "But I might...pass out."

"Come on, Lindsey. Stay with me."

Brute strength saved her. She could do nothing other than keep her eyes from completely shutting and passing out. She hung there as Brian lifted her like a free weight and saved her.

Maybe she did pass out for part of it as he pulled and tugged to get her through the rail. Lying on their backs, Brian clasped both her hands in his, bringing them to his chest. She didn't care how awkward or how much it tugged at the torn shoulder muscles, she needed his touch. Needed to know he was really next to her and she wasn't facing the rest of this night alone.

"Time to get up, lovebirds."

"I need a minute," Brian said, still breathing hard.

"It took you much longer to get here from the hospital, Brian. I'm afraid you got us off schedule."

"Schedule? You have a schedule to kill us?" she asked. She was too injured to stand and walk anywhere. Brian squeezed her hand.

"I didn't give you the impression that I'm a planner? Get up." His voice changed with the last command.

Brian stood, using the rail to help himself, then he helped her sit up.

"I said we're leaving. Get up, Lindsey." He kicked her thigh.

Brian turned on the monster, who acted more as though he welcomed another fight. He looked disappointed when Brian backed down.

"She can't walk on that ankle." He pulled his T-shirt off. "She has a dislocated shoulder that I'm going to stabilize. Unless you want her screaming in pain walking across Aubrey."

She'd had no idea they were back in Brian's hometown. All of the fighting and noise the two men had made and no one had called the police. They were still at the mercy of this madman.

"Cut her cuffs. I can't stabilize the shoulder with her wrists pressed together."

"Back up and hook your leg through the rail. I want to make certain you don't come at me."

Brian did what he said. The man pulled his knife and cut the plastic between her wrists. He put the knife away and Brian returned to her side.

Brian worked quickly. He didn't try to put her shoulder back in place. He angled her arm around her waist, ripped his shirt and tied her arm to her torso. He lifted her and took off down the stairs before Simmons realized he needed to keep up.

"Where are we going?" she asked, trying to use her good arm to hold around his neck and not doing a very good job. She rested her head on his shoulder. She was past any level of exhaustion she'd ever faced.

"Trust me, Lindsey," he whispered, then brushed her lips with his. He turned his head to speak to the monster. "Good question. Simmons, what now?"

"We need your car. Your story needs to come full circle for this town. Their hatred with you began during another *accident*. This one will validate all their fears."

She wanted to sleep, rest, not move. Every step jostled a part of her that ached.

"My ride's inside the firehouse."

"Convenient."

Brian had already been heading straight across the parking lot to the fire station. *Trust me, Lindsey.* He had a plan and he knew who this murderer was. Simmons. There were so many questions she wanted to ask. Brian's jaw muscles tightened along with all the muscles in his neck. He was either angry or very determined. Probably both.

Whatever Brian had planned, he didn't seem to like it.

"You're setting me up to take the fall for the Cook family killings?" Brian asked.

Where was everyone? It was just after dark and they were in the middle of town. She could see shadows of people from the lights behind the drawn curtains. Cars in the driveways. Flowers on the porch.

If she could see all that, what was stopping these neighbors from noticing a fight on a roof or the noise from the shouting? She raised her head, looking at the man Brian called Simmons.

Just a man. Not a monster or devil. A man who could

be defeated. She did trust Brian. They would find a way to escape.

"You really are an egotistical psychopath, holding me in a building down the street from the police station and a playground."

"And if you had called out to any of them, they'd all be dead. Keep that in mind, Lindsey. Just like now." He pointed the gun at Brian's head. "You call out. Someone gets curious. Someone else dies."

"Trust me," Brian whispered so softly she wondered if she actually heard him speak or if the words were echoing in her head. "Why come here, to town? Why risk being seen instead of going directly to where you're going to stage this last accident? Why the fight?"

"After our fight in Jeremy's home, you piqued my curious nature."

Brian spun to face the madman. "Curious about what?"

"Well, who was the better man, of course."

"I'm curious. Who are you?" she asked, looking over Brian's shoulder. She watched his eyes. Wild. Dark. Insane. There was no other explanation for his rash, odd behavior. Then again, was there ever a rational explanation for someone planning multiple murders?

"He didn't introduce himself? This is Victor D. Simmons, attorney at law."

"A lawyer who I bet works with people selling property and steals their mineral rights."

"I was right to assume that the two of you together would be my toughest challenge."

"My car's inside the fire station bay."

"Then we should get inside before we're seen."

"You'll have to open it, my hands are full." Brian stepped to the side, revealing the door.

Lindsey paid close attention to his brown eyes, wondering if he'd set some sort of trap inside. Simmons must have wondered the same thing. He tipped the gun back and forth like a wagging finger.

"Why don't you empty your hands and go through first, Brian."

"Okay." Brian kept one hand around her waist, letting her slide down his side a little, keeping her high enough that her feet didn't thump to the ground. He turned the knob and let the door swing open. "Nothing there... except maybe some field mice."

"Get inside." Simmons pulled the door shut behind him. "Where's your vehicle? I thought you said it was here."

Brian walked across the open floor toward the office, set her on her feet close to the wall and flipped a switch that turned on a row of lights with a high-pitched whine. "I lied."

"Stop," Simmons cried out, losing his composure. "We've already fought and I proved myself the better man."

The portion of the man who had screamed at her from the stairwell came into full focus. The man who totally lost it when someone said he was wrong. Brian was using it against him. But that man still had a gun and Brian had nothing but his hands.

Hands that saved lives.

"You see, I don't agree. You're not the better man at all, Victor 'D is for dumbass' Simmons. I think you're a coward. You can't call the peanut-dryer chase a real fight. I've had better fights with one of my horses."

Even in the dim light, she could see Simmons turning red. He was about to explode. Brian kept inching forward. His thumbs were hooked in his jeans and he didn't look as if he was about to fight with anyone. That casual, withdrawn voice was calming—no matter what antagonizing words were coming from his mouth.

Lindsey held her tongue, but while Simmons's focus was on Brian, she searched for a weapon. She quickly found the source of the whine.

They weren't weaponless after all. Brian had turned on the defibrillator.

Chapter Twenty-Four

When John had asked Brian if he could pull the trigger, he'd said yes. In his head and heart he knew if it came down to it, he could. But he'd had a crazy, wild thought while sitting in the police station—he didn't particularly like explaining himself over and over to the cops.

The empty firehouse reminded him it would be a lot easier to take Simmons alive and let him explain himself. So he'd gone into the abandoned peanut-dryer warehouse thinking he could capture a serial killer who had been at it for half of Brian's life.

Stupid. He'd stepped right in the middle of it. At least he'd had a backup plan.

Brian might not know a lot about how to extract a target, which was his brother's world. He did know a lot about what would take a man down without a weapon. And a defibrillator was perfect.

Now all he had to do was get Simmons near the paddles that had begun charging when he'd flipped the lights on. And he had to do it before he realized what the beeping noise behind them indicated.

"Are you a coward, Simmons?" He needed the gun put away, not fired.

"How dare you talk to me that way." Simmons looked

as if he was going to pop a gasket. He was agitated and his gun hand shook. "I have nothing else to prove."

"Don't you?" Lindsey asked. "You don't think I need to know why you were killing my family, but I'm the only one who can judge the real victor of the fight on the staircase. If you hadn't cut the rope, Brian would have won. So I think you cheated."

Victor Simmons laughed. His gun wrist went limp when he crossed his arms and relaxed. Brian hadn't expected that. A different man stood before them.

"Such a valiant effort deserves my appreciation, not my rage. I heard the defibrillator charging next to Lindsey. Did you really think you could manipulate me and shock me?"

Brian saw his chances of disarming Simmons waning. He began to charge when Simmons came to attention, pointing the gun at his chest.

"Far enough, boy. Don't you think I'm accomplished at the art of killing yet? It's been twenty years." He faced Lindsey. "You don't deserve to know anything. You're barely a footnote in my manuscript."

"Manuscript? You've written down how you killed my family? You really are a monster." Lindsey shuddered.

"Nothing personal, my dear. It must have been fate that brought your relative to my office. It began with a mistake. You see, mineral rights automatically sell with a property unless excluded in the contract. I made sure of that, but I didn't assign them to anyone. Joel Cook thought I was trying to cheat him and wanted my head. We exchanged words. Then blows. Unfortunately, he died. Purely an accident."

"There was nothing accidental in the other thirteen family members you killed."

"Oh, there have been more than thirteen."

One side of his mouth tilted in such a smirk, Brian itched to knock it from his face.

"I can see your anger building. You want to kill me for all the harm I've done."

Brian stretched his hands open, not allowing himself to keep his fingers balled into fists. He opened his palms, as if he was calling a stubborn horse. "That's not my decision, man."

"Where's your car?"

Keeping his back to Simmons, he walked to Lindsey's side. He didn't want to lose Lindsey before their relationship really began. This man would kill them both. He stood just in front of the defibrillator. It was charged and ready to go. All it needed was a patient.

In front of his chest, he motioned for Lindsey to grab the paddles and shock him. Simple. His heart would either go into AFib or stop. Either way, it would give her a chance to run. A chance to live.

She shook her head. He gave her a thumbs-up.

"Don't be stubborn, Brian. It's time to go," Simmons said.

Brian ignored him, counting down with his fingers: three, two, one.

He turned, screamed like a Highland warrior and leaped the last six feet before Simmons could pull the trigger. The gun flew from his hand. They both fell to the cement floor and rolled, only stopping because of the engine wheel.

Brian landed on top and got in the first punch. Simmons no longer had a smirk on his face to wipe off. He shoved hard with both hands, and Brian's shoulder and hand hit the engine. Hard. He thrust the pain aside and threw himself at the murderer.

Lindsey stood ready with the defibrillator paddles. Simmons was scrambling for the gun.

"Not so fast." Brian jerked on the man's pants cuffs, skidding him across the cement. He kicked out, keeping Brian a leg length away, then rolled and twisted to his feet.

Brian quickly followed. The man's eyes were narrow slits; he used the back of his hand to remove the blood dripping from the smirky tilt to his mouth.

"You want a rematch? Come on, boy. I'll teach you a thing or two." Simmons gestured for Brian to come at him. Taunting.

Brian normally didn't respond to taunts. He normally turned the other cheek and walked away because he was the one who always got thrown into lockup. He looked around the dimly lit firehouse. A place where he should have been able to volunteer and save lives.

But he couldn't volunteer in his hometown, helping the people who should have been his friends.

Because of this man. This man's plan to systematically kill off Lindsey's family had destroyed too many things...too many people.

His fingers curled into fists, but his center was ready to do serious battle. Just because he didn't seek fights didn't mean he was a pacifist or didn't know how to fight. He did. He and his twin had fought so much, his mother had enrolled them in tae kwon do.

His fists relaxed, he steadied his breathing, found his calm and waited for Simmons to advance.

"You think you can beat me?" Simmons danced from side to side in his work boots.

Brian watched for the first kick and deflected it with one of his own. He turned and kicked backward, connecting with the center of Simmons's chest. He absorbed some of the momentum when he took a few steps back.

Brian followed with two punches to the abdomen and then received a right cross that he had not seen coming. They both used trained punches and blocks, sending each of them into walls and the truck. Each time Brian thought he was getting Simmons close enough to Lindsey to jump stop his heart, the older man would kick or roll or throw a punch that could loosen teeth.

LINDSEY STOOD READY to blast Victor Simmons with a shock, hoping that she understood how to use the darn things. Braced against the wall, she'd loosened Brian's T-shirt so she could hold the paddles in her hands. She had to wait for the men to get close to her, unable to drag the machine away from the counter.

Brian was an excellent fighter. He could take a punch, but the way his body rippled was something to admire. If it weren't a life-and-death situation, she'd let him know how impressed she was. And she'd allow herself to be more excited about seeing his shirt off.

Each time the monster in black kicked or shoved or swung, Brian countered with a beautiful kick or punch of his own. She was so caught up in the actual fight, wanting Brian to knock this horrible person out for the count, that she almost forgot what she was holding.

Simmons crawled on his belly, trying to get to something. The gun. Should she drop the paddles and run to the other side of the garage for it? She couldn't run. Just balancing on her foot was too painful for words. Gripping the paddle with the hand of her torn shoulder was excruciating. She had to stay where she was and hope for the best.

The fight was slowing a bit, both men drawing longer breaths, both a little slower to get up. Brian threw a punch, pounding Simmons's inside thigh, and he gave a scream. Brian hit him time and time again. The psycho couldn't get his arms up to deflect or defend. Brian kept at him, backing him toward her. One last hard kick and Simmons went flying into the office door next to her.

"Are you okay?"

Brian winked at her. It was over.

Simmons lay on his back, crumpled and passed out.

"Get the gun. It's at the front of the engine by the door," she told him.

Brian turned to pick up the weapon. She turned to set hers down just as a bloodied hand grabbed her from behind. Simmons wrapped one paw around her chest. And held the knife to her throat, ready to slice her from ear to ear with one stroke. He used her body as a shield from the gun that Brian pointed in their direction.

"Put the gun down or you can say goodbye to her forever."

"Won't that mess up your accident plans, Victor?"

"I have contingencies." Simmons tugged on her neck a little. "I can still make this look as if you decided to kill her. That you abducted her and me and held us captive. Drop the gun."

Her eyes locked with Brian's. He looked as though he was apologizing. He couldn't do it. This devil couldn't win.

"He's not going to win." She didn't want Brian to surrender. He was the only hero in her life and she trusted him. She knew what she had to do.

"No!" Brian shouted.

Trusted that whatever happened, he'd save her.

Brian ran, the gun falling to his side.

"I trust you," she said, raising the paddles to Simmons' arms. She pushed the buttons that sent the electric shock jolting through both of their bodies.

Chapter Twenty-Five

Lindsey jerked and the paddles fell from her hands. Brian wished everything happened in slow motion, but it didn't.

He erupted forward as soon as he saw the look in her eyes. She'd placed both paddles directly on Simmons, but didn't she know the electric charge would travel through her, too? She had. *I trust you.* Dear God, to bring Simmons down, she'd shocked them both.

Lindsey trusted that Brian would bring her back from having her heart stopped. She crumpled to the floor, the murderer falling on top of her. Brian ran to the paramedic case and half dragged, half kicked it near the defibrillator.

Not so gently, he rolled Simmons off the bravest woman he'd ever known. The only woman he'd ever loved or wanted to love. The murderer had no pulse. Lindsey was facedown; there was a flutter, a chance. He'd told her he could keep her alive with a rig full of equipment. It was time to keep his promise.

The backboard was in place. He'd left it there, ready for Simmons. He skidded it next to Lindsey and gently turned her over to rest on it.

Training took over. He went through the steps that eight long years of practice had turned to muscle memory. Pulse. Breathing. Airway. Air bag. Monitor. AFib. Charge. Paddles. Jolt. Stop. Pray.

Pray harder, it's Lindsey.

Listen.

Give it a second. No more.

He was about to shock her heart another time when he detected a regular rhythm. Where was the phone? He searched the room perimeter. Nothing. He broke the window on the office door, grabbed the phone on the wall and dialed 911.

"Send emergency vehicles to Aubrey Fire Station. Police and ambulance."

"Please stay on the line, sir."

"Brian?" Lindsey called, her head twisting from side to side.

Brian dropped the phone, leaving the line open. He knelt between Lindsey and Simmons, attempting to block her view of the dead man. Taking her hand between his, he brought it to his lips, more grateful than he'd been since his dad's stroke that she was alive.

"I'm so…tired. Is he…?"

"Dead? Yes. You shouldn't talk. Just rest."

"Will they think we… That…I killed him?"

"He was a serial killer. We did what we had to do."

"You saved me." Her hand curved around his chin.

He caught it and kept it there, wanting to kiss her and tell her everything would be all right and she was perfect. But he didn't know if it would. Simmons was dead from the shock. Lindsey was still in danger.

"Shh, sweetie. I called for help. If I had the keys to this engine, I'd take you to the hospital myself."

"Selling Jeremy's house. Never step foot again. I want my beach. Don't you love beach?"

"I don't think there are too many horse ranches on the beach, hon."

"Nope. Not many boots…in sand. So sleepy."

"Lindsey, wake up, sweetheart. Stay with me." Brian patted her cheek and her blue, blue eyes opened, acknowledging him with a soft smile. "I hear the police, darlin'. Stay awake now, okay? Concentrate and promise me."

"I prom— Kiss me bye."

"Not bye."

He bent down and dropped his lips against her cool cheek. She turned her head, sealing their lips together. He wanted to devour her; the need hadn't gone away. If anything, it got stronger the more they went through. He straightened onto his knees again, hearing the squeal of tires on the pavement outside.

"Get away from her," Ronnie Dean shouted, pulling his handgun. "Cindy, I have two down," he spoke into his radio. "Confirm ambulance needed. Where the hell's the volunteer EMT?"

"Holy smokes, it's the fugitive, Brian Sloane," a second officer said, charging through the door. "What's he doing, trying to kill her?"

"Step back, Sloane."

The dialogue continued between the two officers who had pulled the Sunday night speed trap duty. He ignored them. The most inexperienced. The youngest.

Lindsey's eyes closed. Her head fell slack.

"Lindsey? Come on, hon." He shook her chest. "Wake up." He grabbed her wrist, her pulse was erratic. "No. No. No! I am not going to lose you."

The monitor showed her heart was AFib again.

"I told you to get away from her," the guy he didn't know shouted.

"Ronnie, you guys can shoot me and let her die. Or you can let me do my job and try to save her life."

Ronnie nodded and stuck his hand out to stop the other officer.

"She's in AFib. I need to get a regular beat back. Clear." Brian shocked Lindsey's heart a third time.

"But you're not a doctor. Should we let him do that?"

"Do you know how to work that machine?" Ronnie asked the younger man. "Go outside and call Cindy. Check on the ETA of the ambulance."

Lindsey had a regular heartbeat. Brian dropped his head to his knee, more than a little emotional and not wanting to lose it in front of these guys.

Once the younger cop was gone, he knelt to feel for a pulse on Simmons. "He's dead."

"Yeah, I know."

"How long until your rescue unit shows up?"

Ronnie shrugged, "Who is she?"

"Lindsey Cook."

"She's wanted for questioning. You kidnapped her?"

"No. He did." Brian nodded to Simmons's body.

"How do I know you didn't kill him, too?"

His beautiful, brave woman did.

"You don't. But you'll be the next one lying here if you try to move me before help arrives for this woman."

The younger cop came back inside. "About five minutes on the ambulance. What should we do?"

Brian listened to Lindsey's heart, now beating in a normal rhythm. Her chest rose with normal breaths.

"We're going to watch. If anything looks wrong, we'll take him down," Ronnie ordered.

They stared at him and he stared at Lindsey, willing her to beat the odds and survive. She had to live. They were a good team. She thought so, right? He stroked her hand and saw where the plastic cuffs had bit into her wrists. He dressed the gouges, biting back the emotion. Using the back side of his hand to indiscreetly wipe his eyes.

Then he secured her shoulder and strapped her to the

board for transport. He didn't want there to be any delay. It was a long way to Denton Regional.

The ambulance arrived, he gave them Lindsey's vitals and history, they loaded her and they were gone.

Brian didn't care what happened next. He was handcuffed and stuck inside a squad car while Ronnie argued with the Denton P.D. that had been patched through and wanted him transported ASAP.

Lindsey's care was out of his hands. If she forgave him for getting her captured by that monster, as she called him, he'd go anywhere and do anything she wanted.

Terror that she might die hit him. He couldn't hold back any longer. He dropped his head as low in the car as possible and let go. He kept the noise to some sniffs and a couple of deep breaths. If anyone had been watching him closely, they would have seen the tears of fright mixed in with the prayers.

Lindsey Cook wanted to go to the beach.

Brian Sloane would make sure it happened.

Just let her live.

Chapter Twenty-Six

Brian was asleep—or should have been—on the couch in his home. Or what would be his home for about six more weeks. Until the bank took possession of his family's ranch.

He'd showered and was glad to be clean, ready to smell like horses again. Even if it was only for a couple more days. He scratched his morning stubble and scrubbed his face, ending up on the new scar on his forehead. He hadn't received it fighting one of the worst serial killers in Texas history, but it would always remind him of finding one.

Brought home by a patrol car, he'd been released from jail in the middle of the night with the apologies of the P.D. No media frenzy. No reporter to tell the world he was innocent. No longer newsworthy. No longer employed as a Fort Worth paramedic. And no longer with a reason to follow Lindsey around night and day.

Except one.

He smelled toast, bacon and coffee. Time to get the day started. Time to face the family and tell them his decision. He heard the discussion and stayed quietly on the couch so he could listen. While in jail, no one had bothered to tell him why Simmons had killed the Cooks.

"The news said he wrote everything down," his sister-in-law explained. "In the beginning, he wanted the Cook family mineral rights. He faked their sale, was discovered and began killing. When he got away with it, he killed again. It became an obsession. The authorities said he enjoyed it and considered it a challenge to outsmart the police, so he began killing prostitutes. They aren't releasing how many died until they notify all the families."

"That was one sick SOB," his dad said. "If he confessed and they had a blasted book about it, we should sue someone for keeping Brian in jail almost a week."

"There wasn't a paper manuscript, JW. Simmons dictated tapes and hid them in a safe. So it took the police longer to sort through it all," Alicia explained patiently. "We're not going to sue anybody. We're darn lucky they didn't press charges against John for helping his brother escape from the hospital."

"Come on, Dad," John said. "We're burning daylight. Gotta get this place in shape for the appraiser if that financing is going to come through in time."

Financing?

"John, Dad, wait a sec," he called from the couch, looking long and hard at his boots. He'd miss them. His family and the boots, but he'd made a decision.

Alicia was drying her hands on a dish towel, John had just put his Navy SEAL ball cap on his head and his dad leaned lightly on the cane that was more for Mabel's peace of mind now than for real stability.

"What's up?" his brother asked, standing at his normal parade rest.

Brian leaned forward on his knees, tired when he shouldn't be after "resting" in jail for four days. "I need to say something, so don't interrupt. Got it?"

They all nodded their heads.

"First off, I'm sorry that I dragged you kicking and screaming into finding Lindsey and ultimately Simmons."

"Right, like we're going to be mad that you single-handedly stopped one of the worst if not *the* worst serial killer in history," Alicia said, putting the towel around her neck and leaning into John's side. "Right?"

"He said not to interrupt." John wasn't smiling, but he did drop his arm around his wife.

"We should apologize." His dad sat on the arm of his reading chair. "We could have been more supportive."

"That's not what this is about." He looked at his dad. "We've avoided talking about the ranch long enough. You're moving in with Mabel. Don't deny it, Dad. You practically have already. John and Alicia will have her properties to run. And I'm leaving. Well, there's no reason to refinance the ranch. I won't be here. I'm giving it up, heading to Florida with Lindsey. If she'll have me."

All three of them spoke at once. Irate, indignant, mad and just plain hurt. Then he realized there weren't just three people yelling at him, there were four.

Lindsey's sweet voice rose above the rest and asked from the kitchen, "What's he saying? I promise he told me he wanted the ranch."

"He told me the same thing the night in the hospital," John threw out.

"What are you doing here, Lindsey?" He stood, pulled her to him from behind his brother and kissed her as though he hadn't touched her in a year. "You still feeling okay?"

"I'm great. Are you? Okay, I mean?" His family had gotten strangely quiet. "I think we're all a little stunned by your announcement. I thought you wanted to be a rancher?"

"It's not that I don't. I—" He looked at his father and brother. "Any way we could get some privacy?"

"We all live here, bro."

He grabbed his boots and Lindsey's hand and pulled her through his family, straight out the back door with no explanation. His brother's laughter didn't slow him down.

"Hey, cowboy. Take it easy, my ankle's still swollen."

Taking the gravel in his stocking feet wouldn't have put a hiccup in his pace, but Lindsey reminding him she'd been severely injured recently changed his mind. He swung the best thing in his life into his arms and proceeded straight to the barn, where he set her on some feed bags. Once inside, he shut and bolted the door.

"Wow, it's dark in here."

He sat and pulled his boots on, letting his eyes adjust, watching her shy away from the horse stall. She watched for critters that might be near her feet. What was he thinking? She hated this place. She wanted to live at the beach, not in an old house falling down around his ears. But he had to explain, had to tell her.

"Don't get comfortable. Follow me." He led the way to the hayloft and opened the east doors, sitting down and dropping his legs over the side. The sun was just peeking over the treetops of the oaks that lined the drive to their house.

"It sure is pretty here."

"I love watching the sunrise from up here. Some mornings, especially the first week Dad was home after his stroke, it was pretty much the only pleasure I got during the day. I love the smell of hay, working with my hands, the feeling of success when one of the mares foals."

"I'm not sure I know one end of a horse from another. And I'm hopeless where cats are concerned. They don't like me and hiss all the time."

"It means something to me that this place has been in my family for over a hundred years. I was looking forward to setting things right, getting it back on its feet."

"What's stopping you? Money? Because I think we have someone willing to refinance the place." She paced behind him while he tried to understand.

Did that mean she planned on staying here? He craned his neck to watch her as she told him her plans.

"You see, once my financial stuff is settled—like selling Jeremy's house—we can get a loan in our names. What's that look for? If it's not money, then what's making you leave?"

"You."

"Me?" She sat next to him, dangling her boots over the edge next to his.

"Those are Justins. And they're extremely pink."

"Aren't they great? If you'd told me they came in this color, we would have bought some the first day. I needed some stuff and couldn't go back to…you know…" She pressed her lips together and shrugged. "So Alicia and I went shopping."

"You bought boots?"

"Of course I did. If I'm going to live on a ranch, I need boots to walk around in the mud and other stuff. Don't I?"

"I don't think those are mud boots." He shook his head at her expression, thinking he was crazy. "Lindsey, you love the ocean. You said you wanted sand between your toes. I planned to move because you wanted to live on the beach."

"Brian Sloane, it's you that I've been looking for. I was looking for someone to fall in love with. Not a wave. Not a job. Not a lifestyle. Even though I'm scared to death of snakes and I don't think I'll ever learn which ones won't eat me. Don't laugh at me."

"Come here." He was laughing and smiling so much it hurt. He maneuvered them back into the loft and onto the hay. "Did you just propose to me?"

"I don't recall the words *will you marry me* coming from my lips."

Their greeting kiss had been in front of his family. Not this one. It was a reunion. He tugged her to mold their bodies together. There was no doubt how much he'd missed her. She gave as good as he did and after five minutes there was no doubt how much she'd missed him.

He sat her on an old apple crate that had been there since the time of his grandfather—but maintained by him as a thinking stool. His answer didn't take much pondering. He'd probably made up his mind about Lindsey before he'd ever met her.

"I think I will."

"Will what?" she asked, the sunshine creating a halo of light behind her.

"Now that you've asked politely, I'll marry you."

"Oh, you. Stop fooling around." She threw a handful of hay at him. "I love you, but I refuse to say yes before we have an official date."

"What did you say?"

"That I want a date first?"

"No, ma'am. You said you love me, and that's a real good thing, 'cause you're the only woman I've ever wanted to say this to."

He pulled her into his arms. Sunbeams were flooding the old hayloft, and her eyes were the perfect color of blue that matched the sky behind her.

"Uncle Brian," came a young singsong voice from the yard below.

"Yeah?"

"Pawpaw wants to know if you asked her yet. And said to tell you to hurry up 'cause we want pancakes."

"Skedaddle, baby girl." He plucked some straw from Lindsey's golden hair as his niece left the barn. "Living here's going to be an adventure every day."

"I believe it."

"I love your boots." He kissed one of the bruises on her cheek from their previous *adventure*.

"They say with the right pair of shoes, a girl can do anything." Lindsey dragged a finger across the pulse point in his throat. "If she's lucky, she might even catch a handsome cowboy/paramedic turned detective/bodyguard."

"I'm done with all those jobs. I only have one now. Loving you. That's it."

"I'll take it and love you right back."

* * * * *

A sneaky peek at next month...

INTRIGUE...

A SEDUCTIVE COMBINATION OF DANGER AND DESIRE

My wish list for next month's titles...

In stores from 20th June 2014:

❑ Wedding at Cardwell Ranch – BJ Daniels

& Stranded – Alice Sharpe

❑ Explosive Engagement – Lisa Childs

& Undercover Warrior – Aimée Thurlo

❑ Hard Ride to Dry Gulch – Joanna Wayne

& Sanctuary in Chef Voleur – Mallory Kane

Romantic Suspense

❑ Lone Wolf Standing – Carla Cassidy

Available at WHSmith, Tesco, Asda, Eason, Amazon and Apple

Just can't wait?

Visit us Online

You can buy our books online a month before they hit the shops! **www.millsandboon.co.uk**

0614/46

0614/MB476

THE
CHATSFIELD®

Enter the intriguing online world of
The Chatsfield and discover secret
stories behind closed doors…

www.thechatsfield.com

Check in online now for your exclusive
welcome pack!

Join the Mills & Boon Book Club

Want to read more **Intrigue** books?
We're offering you **2 more** absolutely **FREE!**

We'll also treat you to these fabulous extras:

-  **Exclusive offers and much more!**

- **FREE home delivery**

- **FREE books and gifts with our special rewards scheme**

Get your free books now!

**visit www.millsandboon.co.uk/bookclub
or call Customer Relations on 020 8288 2888**

The World of Mills & Boon

There's a Mills & Boon® series that's perfect for you. There are ten different series to choose from and new titles every month, so whether you're looking for glamorous seduction, Regency rakes, homespun heroes or sizzling erotica, we'll give you plenty of inspiration for your next read.

By Request
Back by popular demand!
12 stories every month

Cherish™
Experience the ultimate rush of falling in love.
12 new stories every month

INTRIGUE...
A seductive combination of danger and desire...
7 new stories every month

Desire™
Passionate and dramatic love stories
6 new stories every month

n o c t u r n e™
An exhilarating underworld of dark desires
3 new stories every month

For exclusive member offers go to
millsandboon.co.uk/subscribe

WORLD_ M&Ba

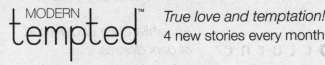